SUPERNATURAL™

RITE OF PASSAGE

ALSO AVAILABLE FROM TITAN BOOKS

Supernatural: The Unholy Cause
by Joe Schreiber

Supernatural: One Year Gone
by Rebecca Dessertine

Supernatural: War of the Sons
by Rebecca Dessertine & David Reed

Supernatural: Heart of the Dragon
by Keith R.A. DeCandido

Supernatural: Coyote's Kiss
by Christa Faust

Supernatural: Night Terror
by John Passarella

Supernatural: Fresh Meat
by Alice Henderson

Supernatural: Carved in Flesh
by Tim Waggoner

Supernatural: Cold Fire
by John Passarella

Supernatural: Mythmaker
by Tim Waggoner

SUPERNATURAL™
RITE OF PASSAGE

JOHN PASSARELLA

SUPERNATURAL created by Eric Kripke

TITAN BOOKS

Supernatural: Rite of Passage
Print edition ISBN: 9781781161111
E-book edition ISBN: 9781781161142

Published by Titan Books
A division of Titan Publishing Group Ltd
144 Southwark Street, London SE1 0UP

First edition: August 2012
10 9 8 7 6 5 4

Visit our website: www.titanbooks.com

Did you enjoy this book? We love to hear from our readers. Please
email us at readerfeedback@titanemail.com or write to us at Reader
Feedback at the above address.

To receive advance information, news, competitions, and exclusive offers
online, please sign up for the Titan newsletter on our website:
www.titanbooks.com

A CIP catalogue record for this title is available from the British Library.

Printed and bound in the United States.

For Andrea, who quietly took care of everything I neglected or forgot while I wrote this one.

HISTORIAN'S NOTE

This novel takes place during season seven, between
"Season 7, Time for a Wedding!" and
"How to Win Friends and Influence Monsters."

PROLOGUE

With the dying gusts of a damaging series of thunderstorms, Tora entered Laurel Hill, New Jersey—not as a consequence of the meteorological destruction; rather, the storms served to herald his arrival and the devastation that would follow. Yet nothing about his appearance would alarm the citizens of the bustling suburban town. That was by design. Contrary to his nature, he had purposefully chosen a civilized appearance and calm demeanor for what amounted to a brief period of reconnaissance. A study in black, he wore a bowler hat low over his deeply furrowed brow, a double-breasted suit and black shoes. The exposed narrow wedge of a white dress shirt provided the only relief from this cloak of darkness, his ruddy complexion the only touch of color.

Though he walked with a stout wooden cane, its handle and pointed tip bound in iron, nothing in his gait suggested the cane's purpose was supportive in nature, so that a casual observer might conclude the cane and bowler were sartorial affectations. For now, it served his purpose to foster these misconceptions. Only later would they realize that affectation had been disguise; as Biblical idiom would have it, he was a wolf in sheep's clothing. He needed some uncontested time to take his measure of Laurel Hill, so he would endure an uncharacteristic bout of patience.

Ahead, on Bedford Drive, something intriguing caught his eye. The perfect opportunity to indulge his natural tendencies. As a sadistic smile spread across his face, he acknowledged to himself that patience was easier in small doses.

Joe Sedenko finished securing the last ridge cap on the Sloney roof and stood with the nail gun held loosely in his right hand, trailing the air hose which snaked across the roof, over the edge and down to the rumbling compressor two stories below. On one knee next to a vent pipe, Greg Beechum applied sealant to the nail heads around the flashing for extra leak protection. Near the edge of the roof, tossing the last bits of trash over the side in the general direction of the roll-off Dumpster in the driveway below, stood Mike Mackiewicz.

After two full days, they were nearly done on the roofing job. They'd spent the first day removing the old, damaged asphalt composite shingles, removing and replacing sections of rotted sheeting, and then laying down new tarpaper before calling it a day. That was the messy and dangerous part of the process, with all the debris and tripping hazards. The second day was more methodical and cosmetic, shooting all the new shingles, staggering the seams, cutting a few around vent pipes. So, naturally, Joe frowned when he spotted the gleaming titanium flat bar on the eave of the roof beside Mike. The tool was invaluable for extracting nails on day one, but not so much on day two, which involved the roofing coiler firing nail after nail through the new shingles and tarpaper into the sheeting. Joe assumed Mike had taken it out of his tool belt during clean up, but he should have known better than to leave a hefty metal object so close to the edge of the roof. That was all Sedenko Roofing needed, for the flat bar to fall off the roof and crack open Mrs. Sloney's skull when she came out to check on their progress or brought a pitcher of iced tea to the base of the ladder.

At that moment, Mike took a sideways step toward the flat bar, seemingly oblivious to its presence.

"Yo, Mike!" Joe called. "Watch out."

"What?" Mike glanced down, left and right, then located the flat bar. "How'd that get there?"

He took another step, bending over from the waist to pick up the tool. Joe nodded and started to look away, but froze when one of the starter shingles slid out from under Mike's planted foot. Mike fell sideways, hit the roof hard and rolled off the edge, his hand haplessly flailing at the gutter before he vanished from sight. At the sound of the heavy thud below, Joe stood frozen in shock. The nail gun slipped from his numb fingers, struck the shingles below the ridge cap line with a much softer impact, and skittered down the sloped roof as if pulled by the air hose.

"What the hell, Joe?" Greg said, looking from Joe to the retreating nail gun. "Where's Mike?"

"He…"

Greg placed the blue metal caulking gun, loaded with a tube of black tar, above the vent pipe and scrambled down the roof to catch the roofing coiler before it fell over the edge. The air hose whipped back and forth, flicking the roofing gun away from Greg's grasping hand time after time, leading him all the way down to the eave.

While Joe had been helpless to stop his longtime friend from plummeting to the driveway below, something about the wriggling air hose galvanized his legs. He scampered down the roof, intent on catching up to Greg before he suffered Mike's fate. Out of the corner of his eye, he glimpsed a blue object jarred into motion, but his mind failed to register what was happening as the object slid away from the silver flashing at the base of the vent pipe. He was too intent on catching Greg, already dangerously close to the edge of the roof.

With one last swipe, Greg snatched the roofing gun as it flipped over the gutter.

"That was close!"

The air hose pulled taut, overbalancing him.

Greg pitched forward as Joe lunged to catch the back of his belt.

Joe missed by a hair's breadth, then fought for balance—swaying forward far enough to witness Greg's head slam against the edge of the roll-off with a sickening crunch, before he reared back to avert his own fall. The "easy day" had turned doubly fatal in a heartbeat. Trembling, he took a careful step away from the brink.

His foot came down on something hard and mobile, his weight shifting as the blue caulking gun shot out from beneath the rubber sole of his work boot. Falling forward, his legs swept out behind him over the eave of the roof and his momentum carried him the rest of the way. He caught the gutter in one hand and swung wildly toward the side of the house. But his momentary relief transformed into a fresh spike of fear as the flimsy metal creaked and rusted screws popped loose. An instant later he was spinning backward, his view flashing from sky to tree to lawn to cracked sidewalk before everything went dark.

Washing dishes after her stop-at-home lunch, Michelle Sloney glimpsed something dark sail past the kitchen window and wondered absently if it was a large bird, maybe one of those god-awful turkey vultures that perched atop homes near the woods as if lamenting the infrequency of road kill. But when it landed in the yard, she saw it was one of the new roofing shingles. Probably damaged, meant for the long construction Dumpster occupying her driveway, maybe it had glided away, across the lawn.

Though the quick movement in front of the window had startled her, pulling her attention from the task at hand, she could have sworn she had heard a thud near the Dumpster and couldn't imagine what Sedenko's crew might have tossed off the nearly restored roof. She stood there for a few moments, soapy water dripping from her hands, as a grim possibility dawned on her. But, no, she would have heard yelling, sounds of alarm, when all she heard was—

Another impact made her flinch.

The second impact seemed impossibly loud, perhaps because she had been listening for a reaction from the roofers after the first. She wiped her sopping hands with a dishtowel as she hurried to the front door. Stepping outside, she called, "Mr. Sedenko, I thought I heard…"

She froze under the small portico, not believing her eyes.

Sedenko appeared to be performing an awkward backflip off the roof.

His face swept beneath his body and slammed into the sidewalk that ran along the side of the house to the driveway. Under the full weight of his falling body, his neck snapped and Michelle knew without a moment's doubt that he'd died instantly. The damaged gutter creaked in the slight breeze and a section of the downspout clanked to the ground.

"Oh, my God!" she whispered.

Hands to her mouth, Michelle stumbled forward as if trapped in a horrible dream, her gaze traveling past Sedenko's body, to a second broken body beside the long Dumpster— Greg something—with blood pooling around a disfigured skull, and a third body a few feet from Greg's. Mike. She remembered his name was Mike. It looked like another broken neck. She looked to her new roof, almost expecting a murderous fourth workman to return her gaze. What else could cause three experienced roofers to fall to their deaths, one after the other? Somebody must have shoved them from the roof. But nobody was there, and she had only ever seen three of them working together on the roof.

She backed away from the bodies, retreating to her door, her breathing shallow, on the verge of panic. She glanced distractedly toward the curb where the Sedenko Roofing van was parked. Beyond the red maple that overhung her driveway was a tall, broad-chested man in a bowler hat and black suit walking as if he hadn't a care in the world, practically twirling his cane. He must have seen something.

"Call 911!" Michelle shouted. "These men are dead!"

He glanced at her with an inquisitive smile and cupped a hand behind his ear, as if he couldn't hear her.

She looked from him to the three dead men sprawled across her property in plain sight.

"Oh, never mind!"

Hurrying, she grabbed her front door and flung it open. The edge of the door struck her in the face, below her right eye. Only when she pressed her hand to her face did she realize she had been crying, probably since the moment Sedenko fell. She glanced at her palm, wondering if she would find blood there, and experienced a measure of relief that she hadn't lacerated her face, immediately followed by guilt for fretting over a possible flesh wound when three men had just died.

She ran across the kitchen to grab the wall phone—quicker than locating her cell phone in her voluminous pocketbook—but the heel of her shoe skidded across a patch of wet tile and she fell hard on her rear, belatedly cursing her clumsiness. As she grabbed the counter to pull herself upright, her hand closed over the knife she had used to slice carrots for her salad but had neglected to wash afterward.

The sharp blade bit into her fingers, drawing blood.

After another string of muttered curses, Michelle took several deep breaths to calm herself before climbing gingerly to her feet and carefully lifting the cordless receiver off the base with her uninjured hand. She dialed 911 with exaggerated care, wrapping the damp towel around her bleeding fingers to slow the flow of blood as she waited for the emergency operator to pick up

She looked out of the kitchen window, scanning right to left and back again, but saw no sign of the tall man in the black suit.

Tora hadn't intended for the homeowner to notice him. When not actively engaged in wielding his destructive power, he could fade from human perception—a shadow at the periphery of their vision, a sound too muffled to identify— but this cloaking ability required conscious effort on his part and he hadn't bothered. Nevertheless, he was surprised she called to him for assistance as, clearly, all three men were beyond the need for medical intervention. But he knew shock and fear made people irrational, which often worked to his advantage.

Feigning ignorance or incompetence or some combination thereof, he continued on his way, assuming he would be forgotten by the middle-aged woman as she suffered an inevitable series of painful accidents—though none as devastating as the trifecta experienced by the roofers. Subtlety was not in his nature and while the roofers' deaths were not a grand gesture, they were a definitive statement declaring his arrival.

Less than two blocks away, he noticed a man standing on a ladder propped against a thick tree branch wielding a chainsaw to cut away a damaged fork of the branch that overhung the roof of his garage. Spinning the ironbound handle of his cane in his palm, he smiled and watched as the man leaned away from the ladder, shifting his center of gravity. Another possibility.

With an efficient slicing motion, the man on the ladder severed the damaged section. As it fell, the healthy part of the branch sprang upward, depriving the top of the ladder of its support. The ladder pitched forward and the man's engaged arms swept down, driving the saw's chain through his jeans and grinding into the meat of his thigh before he could release it.

Roaring in pain, he fell across the aluminum ladder, splitting his nose against one of the rungs. He rolled onto his back, both hands clutching at the raw wound in his leg. Blood gushed out, squirting between the man's fingers, dying his jeans and his lawn crimson. The chainsaw had sliced into the femoral artery. If the blow to his head hadn't already made him woozy, the rapid loss of blood would have done the job.

In his final moments, the dying man saw a dark figure through the mask of blood from his mashed nose and reached out with a trembling hand, his mouth working but his voice no more than a fading whisper. Then, without so much as a last gasp, his arm fell back, his unblinking eyes staring at nothing.

Tapping the handle of his cane against his palm, Tora

looked across the lawn at the blood-spattered and idle chainsaw, silent now thanks to the safety feature known as a dead man's switch.

Sometimes, he thought, *they make it too easy.*

Dark energy had begun to buzz inside him, like a fire he would stoke as his plans developed.

He strode toward the heart of the town.

ONE

Dean Winchester parked their latest beater—a rust speckled blue and white Plymouth Duster from the mid-seventies that shimmied whenever the speedometer topped sixty miles per hour—a hundred yards downwind from the isolated Victorian house in upstate New York, then he and his younger brother, Sam, climbed out of the old car and eased the doors shut. Side by side, they strode up the deserted two-lane country road toward the dilapidated home. Dean cast anxious glances in all directions, careful to check the late-afternoon sky directly overhead. Sam looked from the scrap of paper in his hand to the sprawling home, pausing by a battered green mailbox atop a leaning wooden post with the three-digit house number painted in black on its side.

"Is this the place?" Dean asked.

"636 High Hill Road." Sam nodded toward the paper in

his hand. "That's what the mailman gave us."

"It looks abandoned," Dean commented. A gross understatement.

Twenty years ago, maybe ten, the beige Victorian, with bold green trim on the posts and railings of the wraparound first- and second-story porches, backed by a three-story octagonal tower topped by a widow's walk, had probably been an impressive residence. But the intervening years had not been kind. Paint had faded and cracked, and wooden posts were split or missing, as if carted off by giant termites from a lost Roger Corman film. Gaps between wispy, moth-eaten curtains behind fly-specked windows revealed uninviting darkness within.

"I guess they don't entertain much," Sam said quietly as they approached the front door.

Before Dean climbed the porch steps, Sam caught his arm and pointed downward.

A greasy gray feather lay on one warped step.

"Right place," Dean whispered.

As they crossed the porch, the wooden planks creaked under their weight. *So much for the element of surprise,* Dean thought. He knocked, waited in vain for an answer, and knocked again, louder. He shot a glance at his brother. Sam shrugged. For a silent moment, Dean debated picking the lock versus kicking in the door or putting an elbow through a window, but was spared the decision when an irritated voice shouted, "Go away!"

"Animal control," Dean yelled. "We're investigating reports of illegally imported birds."

Sam and Dean had spent a week investigating multiple disappearances in the Adirondacks. The victims had been young and old; several solitary joggers, a night shift worker on a smoking break, a woman walking her Pomeranian, a camper who wandered off to answer a call of nature, an insomniac who stepped out on his balcony for some fresh air, and a hiker who had left his group for a more challenging ascent. All the victims had been out alone after dark. Otherwise, no similarities, no pattern an FBI profiler would ever unravel. Families received no ransom calls or notes. No bodies were found. There were no witnesses. No fresh tire tracks or suspicious vehicles lurking in the area of the disappearances. It was as if the victims had vanished off the face of the earth.

That had the Winchesters—who often found answers outside the box—wondering if someone or, more likely, some*thing* had, literally, lifted them off the earth. Sam had made the suggestion first. Dean wondered if they were dealing with dragon abductions again, but fellow hunter Bobby Singer noticed a dark, grimy feather on the side of the road near where the police had found the cowering Pomeranian. Return trips to several of the crime scenes turned up a few more feathers.

After reviewing the timeline, they determined that the first disappearance—a jogger—occurred shortly after the arrival in town of three odd women, the Yerakidis sisters. Their behavior bordered on reclusive, but on rare occasions they would appear in town for supplies, always together, wearing bulky, hooded cloaks, no matter the weather.

They talked to one another, heads bobbing together in brief intimate exchanges, but rarely spoke to anyone else. According to clerks in stores they patronized, they seemed to lack social skills, resisting attempts by anyone to engage them in casual conversation.

"Go! Away!" the shrill voice repeated.

Sam shrugged, unsurprised by the hostile reception.

Dean raised his fist to knock on the door, but paused when it was yanked open.

The hooded head of a woman with a pinched face darted forward through the foot-wide gap in the doorway, as if she meant to bite Dean. She had black marble eyes over a hooked nose and a wide, almost lipless mouth.

"Last warning," she squawked, her words punctuated with a blast of foul breath.

Before Dean could utter a reply, she slammed the door in his face.

They heard the deadbolt click, followed by an eerie silence.

Dean nodded and took a step back. "On my count," he said to Sam, who moved beside him. "One, two… *three!*"

The combined force of their kicks smashed the deadbolt free of the weathered doorjamb and the door burst open, rattling on rusty hinges. Pulling their automatics, they entered the house, backs to each other as they sighted along the muzzles of their pistols.

A mixed bag of threadbare and damaged furniture cluttered the first floor. Boxes lined the walls, stacked high enough in places to block several windows and cast the rooms into unnatural gloom. Everything looked as if it had been abandoned by the prior tenants.

A sudden movement caught Dean's attention.

A cloaked figure pitched toward him.

He held his fire at the last moment, recognizing an empty cloak draped over a coat rack. *But who had—*

Behind him, Sam's gun roared.

There was another blur of movement as something swooped toward him from the stairwell landing. His own shot missed as it crashed into him, knocking him over the back of a grimy sofa onto an oval coffee table that collapsed under his weight, taking Dean's breath away.

In the fall, Dean had lost his gun. Expecting an immediate follow-up attack, he rolled to the side and grabbed a detached table leg to wield as a makeshift club. Instead, the wooden leg became a crude shield as one of the sisters hurled a crumbling cardboard box filled with hardbound books at him.

Across the room, Sam ducked and leaned away from a flurry of claw swipes by a second sister. He got off another wild shot before she caught him off balance and hurled him against an empty hutch. As he staggered away, she dumped the hutch on top of him, then whirled on her heel and bolted up the stairs

From above, the first one shouted, "Hurry, Te!"

"Coming!" shrilled the second.

Before Te turned the corner of the first landing, Dean caught a glimpse of long wings, folded behind her back, extending from her shoulders to her calves. He hurled the table leg at her—but a moment too late. It gouged a divot out of the drywall and rebounded down the stairs while Dean recovered his gun.

"Sam?"

"Go!"

Dean bounded up the stairs, two at a time. Behind him, he heard the hutch crash as Sam climbed out from under it. Though the second floor was darker than the first, Dean's eyes had adjusted to the interior gloom. He dodged a padded bench in a hallway, following a rush of clicking footfalls on hardwood. As Sam thundered up the staircase behind him, Dean ducked through a doorway into the tower section of the house, and glimpsed a flutter of movement as one of the sisters rushed up a wrought-iron spiral staircase.

By the time he burst through a trapdoor onto the widow's walk, enclosed by a chest-high wrought-iron railing, he stood alone. He checked the sky, turning in a slow circle, gun raised, as Sam joined him. A moment later, they heard the unmistakable sound of a car engine starting. A green Chevy Suburban pulled away from the back of the house, spewing gravel until it fishtailed onto the country road and roared back the way the Winchesters had come.

Dean stared down at the three-story drop and rattled the wrought-iron railing in frustration.

"Friggin' harpies!"

By the time they descended two flights of stairs and sprinted the hundred yards to the Plymouth, the harpies were long gone. To add insult to injury, one of the car's worn tires was flat. Sam volunteered to replace it while Dean checked the house for any clues to the sisters' destination. Other than the abandoned cloaks they had worn to hide their wings and scattered feathers littering the premises, he found nothing of interest. Until he opened the refrigerator. On the top shelf sat several translucent plastic containers dappled with dried blood and carefully labeled with strips of masking tape to identify the contents: liver, kidneys, lungs, brains. Off to the side, a mason jar held a selection of human eyeballs, shriveled optic nerves still attached. With a pained expression, Dean shoved the door closed. He would never look at pickled eggs the same way again.

As he hurried back to the Plymouth, he called Bobby on his burner cell. "It was them, Bobby," Dean said. "The Yerakidis sisters are harpies."

"Noticing the present tense," Bobby said.

"Yeah," Dean said, frowning. "They flew the coop."

"You see them fly?"

"Not exactly," Dean said. "They lit out of here in their green Suburban."

"All three?"

"Two," Dean replied. "No sign of the third."

"Aw hell," Bobby said. "Another jogger's gone missing."

They guessed the third harpy would join the other two, but had no idea where they might meet. To cover more ground, they searched separately, with Dean and Sam in the Plymouth and Bobby on the other side of the small town searching for the Suburban in his Chevelle.

Shortly after nightfall, Bobby spotted the SUV and tailed it to a foreclosed house, waiting at a discreet distance until the Winchesters could provide backup. They joined him by a sign planted in the corner of the front lawn that read "Foreclosure. Price Reduced."

"Any sign of the third one?" Dean asked.

"Or the jogger?" Sam wondered.

"Not a damn peep," Bobby said, nodding toward the house. "Waiting in the dark."

"Like maybe they know we're here?" Sam asked.

"To hell with bumbling in the dark again," Dean said. "Let's torch the place."

"What if the third one brought the jogger here before the other two arrived?"

Dean recalled the plastic containers in the fridge. "The poor bastard might thank us," he muttered.

"Look," Sam whispered urgently.

Dean followed his gaze to the peak of the gable roof. At first he saw nothing in the darkness. Then two hunched shapes resolved, silhouettes darting with eerie grace toward the edge of the roof. First one, then the other launched from the roof, broad wings spread and pounding against the air. In seconds they soared over the road and higher, over the treetops of the forest on the other side, and vanished.

"Come on!" Bobby said. "We'll need rifles."

Dean braced the deer rifle across his chest as he stumbled through the underbrush of the unnaturally quiet forest. Sam followed behind him, sweeping the dark ground ahead with a powerful Maglite, his other hand on the hilt of a hunting knife. Bringing up the rear, Bobby—the best shot of the three of them—like Dean, carried a Browning A-Bolt 30-

06. Sam had wanted a rifle for this hunt too, but Dean had vetoed the idea.

"Dude, no," he'd said, before they followed a deer trail across the tree line. "It'll be bad enough with two of us bumbling around in the dark with rifles. We're in the middle of this, what happens if Lucifer decides to put on a puppet show in your head? I get a bull's-eye on my back? Or Bobby?"

"I'm fine, Dean. I was fine in the house."

"Yeah, you're fine until you're not fine. A pistol in daylight, okay. But a rifle in the dark? Baby steps, Sammy."

Sam wanted Dean to believe he was okay, but he had admitted that he sometimes had trouble separating reality from his visions of Lucifer. They weren't memories of the pit either, released when the wall inside Sam's head collapsed, but actual psychotic breaks. That freaked the hell out of Dean, he wasn't afraid to admit. And though Dean had helped Sam distinguish between reality and his Lucifer-vision, Sam was far from acing that test on a regular basis. Sam tried to hide it, but now and then Dean caught his brother squeezing the scar on his left hand, prompting real-world pain to push reality back to the surface of his mind.

Sam turned to Bobby, looking for support. "Bobby? Back me up here?"

The older man, the Winchester brothers' honorary uncle, averted his gaze momentarily. "I'm with Dean on this one, Sam."

Bobby reached into the trunk of the Chevelle. "Near as I can tell, bullets won't kill 'em, just slow 'em down long enough to use this." He handed Sam a sheathed hunting knife.

"Got two more of those?" Dean asked.

"That I do."

Fifteen minutes later, they were wandering through the forest in the general direction the two sisters had flown.

The toe of Dean's boot caught on an exposed tree root, causing him to trip. He released the stock of his rifle and caught himself against a tree trunk. For the third time in fifteen minutes, he patted the hilt of the knife in the sheath looped around his belt. Right then, he would gladly trade the rifle for a pair of night-vision goggles.

"You okay, Dean?" Sam asked.

"Yeah," Dean said. "I tripped over a tree root."

Bobby flicked on his rifle-mounted flashlight and focused the beam on the ground near Dean's feet.

"That ain't no tree root." Bobby nodded toward the spot. "Had to guess, I'd say that's a human femur."

Sam used his flashlight to scan the area in question. He kicked aside some dead leaves and dirt, exposing more bones. "One victim."

"Picked clean," Bobby observed.

"We're on their turf now," Dean said.

"Thought crossed my mind," Bobby said. "Maybe that's what they intended from the jump."

"So we're walking into a trap," Sam said.

"Awesome," Dean replied.

"Gonna pretend that's not in the job description?" Bobby asked. "Maybe toast a few marshmallows? Or do something useful?"

"Right." Dean sighed.

He flicked on his rifle light and they moved deeper into the forest.

They found a fire pit and Bobby spotted a charred fragment of red sweater and what looked like the corner of a brown leather wallet. The harpies had burned their victims' possessions, leaving nothing behind but bones buried in shallow graves.

Now that they knew what to look for, they discovered more graves, at irregular intervals and then with more frequency.

"Aw, hell…" Bobby said.

Dean followed the beam of his rifle light to a low branch and the partially eaten body hanging over it with a broken back. A man in his twenties, eyes plucked out, half his face and throat eaten, glistening loops of intestine hanging low enough to touch the forest floor. They stood in silence.

Plop! Plop…

Blood dripped from the man's throat wound to the dead leaves below.

"Fresh meat," Bobby said. "The missing jogger. Means we inter—"

Dean glanced up as a shadow momentarily blotted out the waning crescent moon. There was a rustle of leaves behind them, a gliding shape swooping down.

"Bobby, look out!"

Dean swung the barrel of his rifle up to take a shot, but the harpy was behind Bobby, coming in fast. Bobby ducked, but not fast enough. Hooked claws on her feet dug into the shoulders of his vest, took hold and lifted him off the ground. The sudden impact dislodged the rifle from Bobby's hands. His legs cycled back and forth in a pantomime of running as he rose several feet in the air.

As Dean jumped back to avoid a collision between Bobby's knee and his face, Sam grabbed Bobby's rifle from the ground, tracked the creature with the mounted light, aimed and fired. The harpy cried out and flinched, losing a couple of feathers before pounding her wings furiously to lift her prey out of reach.

Dean looked up at Bobby, almost directly overhead. The angle was too narrow for him to risk a shot. He could try for the arms, but they were a blur of movement. Instead, he decided to change the physics and hoped Sam would keep his head about him.

Slinging the rifle over his shoulder, Dean jumped and wrapped his arms around Bobby's calves. His toes skittered along the forest floor for a few seconds before he felt himself being lifted up. Trying to keep their combined weight airborne was definitely putting a strain on the harpy. Dean looked at Sam.

"Do it! Take the shot!"

Sam had worked the bolt after his first shot, expelling the spent cartridge, and took aim for a second shot. Since the rushed first round may have caused a flesh wound, he took an extra moment to target the torso—and fired.

The dark wings faltered once, twice, and stopped beating. She plummeted to the ground, causing an explosion of dead leaves and twigs, and dropped Bobby and Dean in her wake.

Dean scrambled to his feet, brushed himself off and looked back at Sam.

"Good shot."

Sam shrugged. "I had a one in three chance of hitting the right target."

"You're hilarious."

Before Bobby flipped the creature over, Dean spotted the entry wound, central-mass. If they were lucky, Sam had hit the heart. That would keep her docile long enough to finish the kill.

"Hold her down," Bobby instructed.

Dean pinned the harpy's shoulders to the ground as Bobby pulled out his knife.

Her unclothed flesh was covered with a soft down, medium to dark gray, but she was a messy eater. Human blood and bits of gore streaked her wild, stringy hair, face, torso, arms, and fingers—remnants of her interrupted meal. Black marble eyes stared sightlessly toward the clear night sky.

With his knife held in a double-handed grip, Bobby drove the tip down through the exposed chest, into the harpy's heart. For a brief moment, her body arched and a mournful shriek burst through her pointed teeth and cracked lips. Then her body sagged.

"Should keep her down and out," Bobby said. "Least till we burn her."

"How are your shoulders?"

Bobby rolled them, winced slightly. "They'll keep."

An answering screech sounded from high in the treetops.

"Incoming!" Dean said.

In a blur of motion, a second harpy zipped through the clearing, caught Sam's wrist and dragged him past Dean and

Bobby, before hurling him bodily into the base of a tree trunk. Sam grunted with the impact and rolled away dazed, but still clutched the stock of Bobby's rifle.

"You killed Podarge!" she shrieked. "They killed Po!" The second comment was directed skyward.

As she beat her wings and rose away from them, Dean took aim and fired. The bullet breezed through a wing, dislodging a dozen feathers, but failed to slow her down, let alone wound her. She dropped onto a sturdy branch and glared at him with glassy black eyes.

"Hold that thought," Dean whispered, and worked the bolt as he sighted along the rifle.

From behind him came a whistling sound, rising in volume.

"Oh, crap!"

The third harpy drilled him like a middle linebacker.

Dean rolled with the impact, executing an awkward somersault and losing his grip on the rifle, but snagging the shoulder strap as he sprawled across a bed of broken twigs and what looked and smelled like harpy droppings.

"That's just nasty!"

After knocking Dean over, the third harpy lost momentum and dropped to the ground, stumbling forward a few steps as she spread her wings to brake.

"Rip his throat out, Lo!" the second harpy shouted from her perch.

Lo strode forward, clawed fingers raised before Dean. "I'll carve out his liver, Te. Eat it while he watches!"

"What? No Chianti?"

Dean glanced at Sam and saw his brother was still groggy,

shaking off the cobwebs.

Dean returned his attention to the approaching harpy, curling his fingers around the rifle's shoulder strap. He still had a round in the chamber, ready to fire, but he would need a second or two to bring the rifle to bear, aim and shoot.

Lo saw the rifle near his right knee and wagged a taloned finger at him. "Naughty boy," she chided, flashing a horrific smile filled with rows of pointed teeth. "I'll pluck your eyes out before you pick it up."

Okay, Dean thought. *Forget about aiming. Just grab and shoot.*

He was about to chance it when Bobby said, "Like hell!"

Three shots rang out in quick succession.

The first shot caught Lo in the ribs, the second in her sinewy left arm, and the third ricocheted off her jaw line, taking a chunk of flesh with it. Fright-wig hair whipped around her face. Dean wasted no time. He had the bolt-action rifle in his hands, sighted and drilled a round through her chest. Lo staggered backward, spraying blood from her mouth as she shrieked in fury. With a practiced motion, Dean worked the bolt and fired a second shot into her chest, close to the first.

Alternately gurgling and gasping, the harpy toppled over backward.

"Don't just stand there, ya idjit," Bobby called, waving the automatic he'd had holstered in the back of his belt. "Put a fork in her ticker."

"Aello!" Te shrieked and launched herself from her perch.

She dropped toward Dean like a hawk with a rabbit in its sights.

Bobby followed her trajectory with his arm extended, firing until his magazine ran out. A few of his shots burst through feathers, one or two scored the creature's flesh. Nothing slowed it down.

Dean whirled away from the supine Aello to face Te, raised his rifle and tried to aim, but she came in too fast and he only managed one wild shot, which gouged a furrow across her cheek. She extended her legs, clawed feet reaching for him.

Dean threw himself sideways. The harpy's left foot struck his upper arm, spinning him. As he struggled to rise, he did a quick damage assessment. Fortunately, she hadn't broken his arm. A little higher and he would have dislocated his shoulder. But he had lost the rifle.

She rushed him with long strides, wings beating to increase her momentum, her clawed fingers raking toward his face. He raised his forearm defensively and felt claws slice through the denim sleeve of his jacket. Te's other arm slashed downward and he blocked with his other forearm.

This time she clamped onto his right arm and yanked him skyward—five, ten, fifteen feet.

Fumbling at his belt with his left hand, Dean pulled out his hunting knife. In flight, the harpy's body was almost parallel to the ground and he was dangling from her extended arm. She was out of reach of the knife, except for the hand that clutched his forearm. Stretching, he reached up and, in a backhanded right to left motion, swept the blade across her wrist. The knife sliced through flesh and ground into bone.

With a pained shriek, the harpy released her grip and Dean plummeted toward the ground. Flailing, he managed to hook his elbow momentarily over a branch on his way down, breaking his fall, but he landed awkwardly and had the wind knocked out of him.

He struggled to suck air into his lungs. Feeling helpless as a kitten, he watched the night sky as the bird-like silhouette looped around and descended toward him. He reached out with splayed arms, brushing aside dried leaves, brittle twigs, small pebbles and clumps of soil.

The knife was gone.

Sam hadn't broken any ribs when the harpy hurled him into the tree trunk, but it was a near thing. The impact stunned him and briefly doubled the number of visible stars. A nasty lump was forming on his scalp and a killer headache had already begun to percolate in his skull.

As he struggled to rise, he saw Bobby and Dean take down Lo, the second harpy. Then the third, and biggest, harpy attacked Dean before he could stab Lo in the heart. Dean lost his rifle in the initial attack, but managed to slash Te's arm before she could carry him off and make a meal out of him.

Te rose above the treetops and began to circle, coming around for another diving attack.

A bit woozy, Sam took a step forward, lifting Bobby's rifle by the strap, trying to get a proper grip on it.

Lucifer stood beside him. He gave Sam a disappointed shake of his head.

"In a spot of trouble, Bunk Buddy? Bet you wish you were back in the cage with me. Oh, wait, you never left."

Sam grimaced. "Shut up."

"Where's the fun in that?"

Sam *knew* Lucifer wasn't really with him in the woods. It was just a side effect of having his head metaphorically shoved in a blender after Castiel removed the wall. But Lucifer looked and sounded as real as, well, reality. No drop off on the believability scale. Sam's only defense was to remind himself that Lucifer was a delusion, a bizarre construct of his damaged mind, and then ignore him. Not always a simple task. In addition to appearing as himself, the Lucifer conjured up by Sam's mind sometimes took the magic lantern show to the next level, appearing as Dean or Bobby or any damn thing from Sam's head. Knowing you have a disease doesn't give you the ability to cure yourself of it. But you do learn to recognize the symptoms.

"You have a rifle," Lucifer observed gleefully, moving forward with Sam. "Hearing the siren song of a clock tower?"

"Go away!" Sam whispered fiercely.

"Careful where you aim that thing, Sam," Lucifer said. "Sometimes up is down, down is up."

Te circled and swooped low, dropping next to Dean, who was sprawled on his back, dazed and weaponless.

Sam jabbed his thumbnail into the scar on his left hand. Real pain helped keep the delusions at bay. At least long enough to do what he had to. He staggered toward his brother's position, willing his cobwebs away.

The harpy lifted one of her feet over Dean's midsection,

flashing a nasty set of claws, clearly intent on eviscerating him.

In his peripheral vision, Sam could see Bobby reloading his automatic, but knew he was too far away for much accuracy with a handgun. Sam had a clear shot with the rifle, though. Lucifer was gone, and he had to believe the harpy was standing over Dean and not the other way around.

As Sam's finger closed on the trigger, Bobby fired his automatic. The bullet ripped through a row of feathers. Sam smiled and fired.

The rifle bullet struck the third harpy in the upper back, just left of the spine.

Dean rolled out from under the hovering talons.

The harpy staggered, fell to one knee, wings spread wide, and coughed up blood.

Working the bolt, Sam fired again.

Te collapsed face down, her right leg twitching for a second or two.

"Knife!" Dean called.

Sam pulled out his knife and executed an underhand throw, hilt out.

Dean snatched the knife out of the air, rolled the harpy over with one hand, and drove the tip of the blade into her chest with the other.

"We're a knife short," Bobby yelled. "And Lu here is getting fidgety."

Dean cast about then reached down. "Found it."

He looked at Sam and nodded appreciatively. "Again, nice shot."

Sam flashed a brief smile.

Dean spread his arms as he backed away. "Okay, I was wrong."

"No arguments here."

Sam followed Dean, feeling his smile fade away. He knew it would be hard to win back Dean's trust if he couldn't trust himself. On that front, he was a work in progress. But he was relieved Lucifer didn't reappear to rub it in.

With the harpies' hearts skewered, they remained catatonic. The hunters grabbed them by the ankles and dragged them to a nearby fire pit, lined up the trio side by side, sprayed them head to toe with lighter fluid, and torched them.

They stood upwind, in silence, watching as the sisters burned.

Dean glanced at Bobby. "Are we done here?"

"Kind of jackass leaves a fire burning unattended?"

"Right," Dean said, and pulled his flask from a jacket pocket, "I wouldn't want to miss out on the merit badge." He took a swig from the flask and walked a few steps away from the funeral pyre.

Lucifer had taken Dean's place beside Sam, and was warming his hands over the fire.

"Feels like home!"

Sam closed his eyes, pressed the scar hard, counted to three, and opened his eyes again. Lucifer was gone, but Dean was back.

"These birds look extra crispy, colonel," he said.

Bobby ignored the jibe and nodded, satisfied. They kicked dirt over the dying flames. The harpies' remains crumbled, with no more substance than burnt leaves.

Once they were on the road and miles away from the harpies' feeding grounds, they would place an anonymous call to the police to expedite the recovery and identification of the victims' remains. For now, Sam hurried along the deer trail leading back to the roadside to catch up to Dean, who seemed in an unusual hurry. Mindful of the uncertain footing, Bobby brought up the rear at a measured pace.

Drawing level with his brother, Sam asked, "You okay?"

"Yeah. Fine."

Sam sniffed twice and wrinkled his nose. "What's that smell?"

"You really don't wanna know," Dean grumbled.

TWO

Tora sat at the back of the South Jersey Transit bus with the bowler tilted low over his deeply creased brow, his cane upright between his knees, both hands gripping the ironbound handle. Had he planned to crash the bus, he would not have boarded it. His interest lay in its route. For the same reason, he ignored opportunities to tamper with the lives of the passengers—early shift workers, probably food service or manual laborers by the look of them. Most wore casual shirts and jeans or shapeless polyester uniforms. A handful sported business attire. With his bowler, black suit and cane, he looked the most out of place on the bus, hence his decision to sit behind the other passengers, where he could observe without attracting undue attention. Of course, he could use his power to fade from their awareness, but saw no reason to expend the effort.

Of all the humans present, the obese bus driver, with his florid face and labored breathing, his girth straining the seams of his black vest and white dress shirt, offered the easiest possibility. But a medical emergency would probably prevent the completion of the bus's route. Better to forego a small reward in favor of a bigger prize. Another test of his patience.

When the bus approached the intersection of Route 38 and Kressen Boulevard, he sat up straighter, attentively glancing left and right to observe the volume of rapid rush-hour traffic. A broad smile spread across his ruddy face. As the bus slowed, several passengers stood to disembark. After a mischievous look in the bus driver's direction, he followed the other passengers to the back door, ducking his head and turning sideways to step out. When the door hissed closed behind him, he tapped it with the pointed tip of his cane, an action unnoticed by the passengers who remained behind or those who left the bus before him. While they crossed the intersection or turned down Route 38 with clear purpose, he stood next to the traffic light as if undecided about which way to proceed.

Someone had taped multiple copies of a colorful flyer to the traffic light pole, as if worried they would succumb to attrition and at least one must last until the upcoming Sunday at 10 a.m. The chamber of commerce was sponsoring the Laurel Hill 50th Anniversary Parade to commence at Broad and Main in something designated the Classic Business District. That the town had planned a celebration he found amusing. He chuckled, a deep, rumbling sound.

The heavy flow of traffic along Kressen Boulevard and Route 38 dutifully obeyed the mechanical commands of the traffic lights dangling overhead. Predictably, the drivers pushed their luck, running yellow lights, jamming their brakes at the last second, and yielding reluctantly. Conditions were ripe. But he would need a few moments to expand his awareness.

First things first. He stared down Kressen Boulevard until he spotted, several intersections distant, the receding form of the bus he had recently vacated. With the index and middle finger of his right hand pressed to his temple, he recalled the image of the bus driver. After a moment or two, the recalled image transformed and became the present. He saw inside the bus, heard the driver's labored breathing and watched as his heavy foot pressed the accelerator pedal. Ahead of the bus, a T-intersection loomed. The driver would have to turn left or right or—

The third option held the most promise.

Tora rubbed his thumb over the head of the cane in concentration.

The bus driver gasped, clutching his right palm against his chest. Sweating profusely, he tried to speak but merely moaned in excruciating pain. His foot floored the accelerator and the bus shot through the T-intersection and jumped the far curb. Realizing the bus was out of control, several passengers screamed.

Directly in front of the runaway bus, on the far side of a narrow parking lot, the floor-to-ceiling plate glass windows of an athletic club revealed an impressive row of treadmills, stationary bicycles, elliptical machines and stair climbers—all facing away from the parking lot. The club members toiled away with no forward progress, either staring at the mounted row of flat-screen television sets provided for their entertainment or listening to private music through their earbuds.

The bus shot across the parking lot unimpeded, still gathering speed as it raced between two narrow bollards in front of recently vacated parking spaces, jumped the sidewalk and crashed through the plate glass windows. Two club members died instantly as the bus bowled over their cardio machines. Flying debris and smashed flat-screen TVs injured several others. Several bus passengers broke limbs or suffered concussions. One died from a broken neck. Fractured, the Laurel Hill Fitness Zone sign above the plate glass windows fell on either side of the bus. Within three minutes, the bus driver would die.

Tora frowned, slightly disappointed now that it was over. Aside from the delightful shock value, the accident had produced negligible results. No matter. He would accept it as an extemporaneous warm-up act and proceed to the main event.

Again, he focused on the alternating flow of traffic, the give and take of racing and braking vehicles on Route 38 and Kressen Boulevard. Those on time wanted to arrive early; those running late needed to make up time. Either way, the commute became a daily ritual of gamesmanship, fueled by equal parts anger, resentment, distraction and carelessness. A perfect storm... with a little help.

Facing the intersection at a forty-five degree angle, he stood with both hands clasped over the iron handle of his cane and focused his attention on the flow of traffic, in one direction after another. With each passing second, his awareness spread farther from the intersection along each traffic artery. He filtered out the cars, SUVs and trucks as they exited the intersection, removing them from the organic equation of coincidence forming in his head. And yet that was insufficient for what he planned. He needed to see more.

The bowler hat rose slightly on his brow as he stretched his deeply creased forehead, revealing a rounded lump in the center, and the closed lid of a third eye. Finally, the dark eyelid fluttered open, exposing a milky white orb with several odd pupils—or at least what passed for pupils. The black oblong shapes drifted randomly across the nacreous surface of the eye, sometimes submerging and reappearing in a different location before sliding along the surface again. Humans who observed Tora's third eye for more than a few seconds often became violently ill. Few lived long enough to tell the tale.

With his third eye exposed and active, he could complete his assessment. Now he saw farther than was possible with his other eyes. He saw the interconnectedness of every action and reaction, like a vast clockwork mechanism. One by one, the necessary gears resolved before the examination of the eye—

A man distracted by an angry cell phone conversation.

The woman driving beside him texting her husband.

A middle-aged man shaving in the car behind her.

A harried mother yelling at two children fighting in the back seat.

While nearby, a man adds artificial sweetener to an uncapped cup of hot coffee propped on his dashboard.

A driver of a battered pickup with a missing gate, the truck bed loaded with loosely tied propane tanks.

The teenage boy in a nearby car repeatedly changing radio stations, seeking the perfect song.

And racing along Route 38, approaching the intersection, a long-haul tractor-trailer driver who has spent too many consecutive hours behind the wheel.

As if cuing an orchestra to begin playing, Tora tapped the tip of his cane against the traffic light pole. Instantly, the red light facing Route 38 flickered from red to green.

With his traffic light green, the exhausted truck driver never touched his brake pedal, failing to notice traffic along Kressen Boulevard continued to flow, and well above the posted speed limit.

Closing his nacreous third eye with its drifting and submerging pupil, Tora relaxed the creases in his forehead, adjusted the bowler, and smiled.

First, the semi smashed into the angry cell phone talker's car with a sound like an explosion, spinning the car almost three hundred and sixty degrees and blocking two lanes of traffic. Then, one after another, the distracted drivers reacted too late and slammed into the car in front of them a millisecond before getting rammed from behind.

Realizing he lacked sufficient braking distance to avoid the growing pile-up dead ahead, the teenager fiddling with his radio presets swerved violently to the right. A front tire blew out and his car rolled over three times before reaching the far shoulder. In the process, his fuel line tore amid a shower of sparks. Flames raced across the highway in all directions, followed by the thunderous explosion of the battered sports car.

At the same time, the foam coffee cup on the dashboard of the sweet-toothed caffeine addict tipped over, spilling the piping hot beverage on the man's lap. Yelping in pain, he involuntarily jerked the steering wheel and cut off the pickup truck loaded with propane tanks. The truck driver swerved and slammed broadside into a blue Mini Cooper. Several propane tanks became airborne, bouncing around the highway like metal beach balls. One was sandwiched between two colliding cars, resulting in another explosion near the intersection.

Some drivers climbed out of crushed and damaged cars, while others screamed in pain, trapped in what became metal coffins. Most of those who did escape their cars suffered death by shrapnel from the explosions or were squashed between tons of flying and skidding metal. Few escaped the carnage, none without significant injuries.

A truly satisfying symphony of death and destruction.

None of the out-of-control cars, roaring flames, concussive explosions or flying shrapnel touched Tora where he stood next to the traffic light pole. With a broad smile, he enjoyed the sounds of agony and grief, the smell of fresh blood and burning flesh. Unmoving, he stood by the pole as if in a trance, joyfully soaking in every moment. Until the arrival of emergency vehicles. They brought order and succor, diminishing pain, delaying or preventing death and, therefore, sapping his pleasure in what he had wrought. But even as the rush of euphoria waned, he sensed the power building within him. He would need all that power and more to reach across the town to finish what he had started.

The morning's exercise was only the beginning.

Soon, they would hear his call and come to him.

THREE

Dean thought he might have to twist Sam's arm to get him into the Greasy Griddle diner on I-87, but it was the first eatery they passed after their night in Harpy Valley, and coffee had risen from a priority to a necessity. Fortunately, in addition to high-octane java, the busy truck stop offered a selection of bran muffins and a fruit cup, so Sam was set. Bobby had a poached egg and grapefruit. Dean ordered the Double Triple, which featured three eggs any style and three breakfast meats. Not wishing to complicate things, Dean requested everything fried.

From the stiff way Sam and Bobby had walked across the parking lot of the diner and then eased themselves into the booth, Dean assumed they were as sore as he was from the harpy battle. Bobby seemed crankier than normal, Sam quieter. Dean's sleep, what little he managed during the short night, had been fitful. Chugging aspirin and whiskey hadn't helped as much as he'd hoped. Coffee throughout breakfast, however, smoothed out the kinks.

Lately, relaxation came in small doses, especially in public. Ever since the Leviathan created dark-side doppelgangers of the Winchesters for a cross-country killing spree, Sam and Dean had to continually look over their shoulders in case somebody made them as the infamous serial killers. Because the doppelgangers purposely drove a black '67 Chevy Impala during their crime spree, the Winchesters had to abandon Dean's baby for a series of stolen beaters, none of which would be missed before they switched to the next. As the Leviathan now hunted the hunters, the Winchesters also had to abandon their old fake IDs and credit cards, switch to burner cell phones and avoid leaving behind an electronic trail. In addition, the brothers had to develop a strong aversion to security cameras. Hell of a way to live. But sound advice, nevertheless, from Bobby's bipolar and extremely paranoid acquaintance—friend was too strong a word—Frank Devereaux.

The Greasy Griddle was just what the paranoiac ordered: a high-traffic truck stop frequented by a series of anonymous faces and not a security camera in sight. They would pay for their meal in cash and have no need to give a name or flash a fake ID.

After their waitress, a middle-aged bottle blonde with a plastic smile who looked like she'd seen it all more than once and stopped registering the details long ago, cleared their plates, Bobby left the booth to settle their check at the register. With his stomach full and his cup topped off, Dean felt about as content as he ever did between hunting jobs these days. Sam, on the other hand, had already turned his attention to his shiny new laptop—courtesy of Frank Devereaux's Paranoia Emporium—and flipped through some paper printouts he'd assembled earlier, a clear threat to Dean's admittedly brief "between jobs" contentment.

"Dude, did you sleepwalk to a Kinko's?"

"Might be onto something…"

At that moment, Bobby returned from the cashier's counter with a late edition of the county paper and dropped it on the table in front of them. "Above the fold," he said. "'Cannibal Woodsman?'"

Dean reached for the paper and spun it around, skimming the text for details. "'Anonymous call leads police to grisly killing grounds… half-eaten… stripped bones… shallow graves… no suspects.'" He pushed the paper back to Bobby and spoke softly. "Got the 'grisly' right. But they'll waste months looking for Jeremiah Johnson with a dog-eared copy of *To Serve Man*."

"You want 'em to find super-sized bird nests?" Bobby asked after checking for any potential eavesdroppers. "Hell, the victims' families will get closure. Least as much as they'll ever get."

"You're right. Nobody needs to know Uncle Ed or Cousin Jimmy was a Harpy Happy Meal."

"Guys," Sam said. "I think I have something here."

"No rest for the wicked," Bobby commented.

"Laurel Hill, New Jersey," Sam said, looking at the

printouts. "Three roofers fell off the second story of a house yesterday, one after the other. Two broken necks. The third split his skull open. Also broke his neck. The homeowner says they all fell within minutes of one another."

"Weird," Bobby said, frowning, "but not outside the neighborhood of weird coincidence. Laurel Hill?"

"Why?" Dean asked. "You got something?"

"It'll keep," Bobby said. Then to Sam, "Go on, son."

"Few blocks away, couple minutes later, guy on a ladder trimming a tree with a chainsaw falls, slices open his femoral artery and dies on his lawn."

"Weird enough for you?" Dean asked Bobby.

"It gets weirder," Sam continued, turning his attention from the printouts to the screen. "This morning a mass transit bus driver has a heart attack and drives his bus right through the front window of a fitness center. Guy on a treadmill and a woman on the elliptical machine next to him were killed instantly—"

Dean leveled an index finger at his brother. "Sammy, don't ever mock my health choices again."

On a roll, Sam let that pass. "Few minutes later, less than a mile away, seventeen car pile-up. Multiple explosions and fatalities."

Bobby shook his head. "Sounds like the bad luck fairy ripped Laurel Hill a new one."

"I'm game," Dean said. "Bobby, you in? Or you wanna head back?"

Bobby scratched his beard at the jaw line, his gaze thoughtful under his trucker's cap.

"Something about Laurel Hill?" Sam prompted.

"Know somebody there might help," Bobby said. "Emphasis on the 'might.'"

"A hunter?" Dean asked.

"Yes and no."

"I'm not even sure I know what that means," Dean said.

"Problem in a nutshell," Bobby said. "I'll call. He agrees not to slam the door in our faces, we'll have a basecamp."

"If not?"

Bobby shrugged. "Fleabag or abandoned rat-trap. Pick your poison."

Sam drove the Plymouth south on I-87. Bobby followed in his Chevelle, on the phone again with his Laurel Hill contact. The first call, in the diner's parking lot, had been short, ending with an emphatic hang-up on the other end. But Bobby wasn't giving up… yet.

After about fifty miles of silence, Sam glanced at Dean sprawled in the passenger seat, ostensibly relaxed but definitely scowling. He had taken one pull from his flask before settling in for the long ride.

Finally, Sam asked, "Wanna talk about it?"

"No."

"About last night. The harpies."

"Still no."

"If something's bothering you…"

"It's a job, alright," Dean said. "Do the job. Get out. Don't need to sit around toasting marshmallows and singing 'Kumbaya.'"

"No. I get it, Dean."

Dean was right. It wasn't like they celebrated a monster kill. Mostly it was a relief. Do the job, because it's what they did as hunters. No glory, no after-parties. But Sam couldn't shake the sense that something deeper was troubling his brother. He decided to let it rest.

Then Dean surprised him.

"I'm not like you," he said. "Not anymore."

Sam considered that statement before responding. "How so?"

"Even with a bat in your belfry, you're okay with everything," Dean said. "Wrap up one job, turn the page, move on to the next."

"Look, Dean," Sam said, "I know there's a cost. I give a damn, okay? It's just… This is what I have. Here. Now. This keeps me… focused."

"Right."

Sam glanced at his brother again. "Dean, we're hiding from the Leviathan. We have no idea what their game plan is, no clue how to kill them, but we know they want us off the board. They killed all those people while wearing our faces to neutralize us."

"You think maybe I forgot?"

"So, what? You want to quit?"

Dean heaved a sigh. "No," he said softly. "That's not what I'm saying."

"Then what?"

"That guy on the tree branch," Dean said. "Broken back, guts ripped out, bleeding." He shook his head bitterly. "The poor son of a bitch never had a chance, Sam."

"No."

"If we'd got there an hour sooner," Dean said, slapping his palm down on his knee angrily, "half hour, maybe…"

They'd had this discussion before. The cruel facts of hunter life: you couldn't save everyone, you didn't always arrive in the nick of time, but you took solace in the lives you had saved.

"We stopped them, Dean," Sam said. "There won't be another vic."

"Wrong, Sam," Dean said grimly. "There's always another one. No matter what we do…"

FOUR

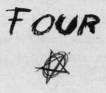

On foot again, miles from the multi-car pile-up, Tora strolled along Parry Lane, a suburban street in Laurel Hill. As he walked along the tree-shaded lane, his iron-tipped cane tapped a steady rhythm on the sidewalk, interrupted only when he sensed a human presence inside a house. By opening his third eye, he could see into those homes, like peering through a floating keyhole. Extending his awareness and influence, he sought any opportunity to wield his power. For in exercising his ability, he honed it, made it more responsive to his whims.

Pausing in front of a two-story Tudor-style home, he stretched his brow, opened his third eyelid the merest slit, and peeked inside.

The images came to him in short bursts, like excited breaths.

A harried housewife filled a canvas hamper with clothes for laundering. Instead of making two sensible trips to the washing machine, she piled up soiled clothing from several bedrooms until the hamper overflowed. She carried her burden along the upstairs hallway, her view obstructed by the mound of clothes. Her sneakered foot missed the action figures stacked near the doorway of a child's bedroom. A sock fell from the pile, unnoticed, and her feet fell on either side of it. Then she turned to the stairwell and failed to notice the cat lying on the second step from the top. The domesticated beast assumed its owner saw him and continued to sprawl on the step.

The woman's foot came down on the cat's tail.

The cat yowled in pain and bolted.

Startled, the woman cursed and jerked her foot away. She missed the step and pitched forward. The burden in her arms prevented her from reflexively grabbing the nearest railing. By the time the hamper flew from her hands, her head struck a riser, her face smashed into a baluster and her neck, twisted at an awkward angle by the jarring impact, snapped before she came to a stop at the bottom of the stairs, a soft landing atop the scattered mound of soiled clothing.

Moments later, the cat crept out of his refuge under an end table and sat beside the woman, licking her outstretched hand several times, no doubt expecting a show of contrition or affection on her part.

All things considered, the cat was fortunate to have survived, though Tora had no direct influence over animals. Large disasters, such as the multi-car pile-up, could easily doom them, but that was a matter of happenstance. He put the cat out of his mind and contented himself with the arranged death of the woman.

With a sigh, he continued along Parry Lane.

Three doors down, he sensed another lone presence in a house and eased open the folds in his forehead to peer inside.

An older man was finishing a shower, a ring of white hair plastered to his scalp as he rinsed out shampoo suds. Warm water splashed off his bowed head and bent elbows, striking the shower door and passing through the narrow gap to gather in small puddles on the tile floor of the bathroom.

Outside the house, Tora raised one hand from the cane's iron handle to massage his temple with his index and middle fingers, reaching out further, extending his awareness into the man's life.

Hal Norville… a medical professional, put others to sleep. An anesthesiologist. He had taken the day off… for a round of golf with colleagues.

He opened the shower door and reached for a towel to pat water from his head and face. As he stepped out of the shower, the ball of his bare foot came down on one of the soapy puddles and shot out from under him. His free arm darted out to catch the towel rack, and missed by half an inch. The back of his head slammed into the shower door track, which cut deep. His blood flowed freely down the drain, tinting the last of the shampoo bubbles crimson.

At the end of the block, a retired woman had already put a load of wet laundry in her clothes dryer. Tora stopped in front of her house as she slipped into her afternoon nap. For a while, she remained safe from any physical mishap. But a bit of probing revealed that her dryer's lint trap hadn't been cleaned in a while and its exhaust vent was clogged. Assuming the dryer was failing, and without the means to replace it, the woman ran every load on the hottest setting. One convenient spark ignited an impressive fire. Unfortunately for the woman, she hadn't replaced the batteries in her smoke detectors in a long time. Humans were so forgetful at that age.

Soon flames were engulfing the first floor of the house, the woman had died from smoke inhalation, and he was several blocks away, seeking other opportunities. But he continued walking without bothering to peer into any other homes until the fire engine sirens had faded into the distance.

With his cane tapping as regularly as a metronome, his long strides consumed two miles before he slowed again, intrigued by something in the sky.

Two broad, colorful rectangles slowly descended.

Parachute canopies.

Looking up, Tora pushed the brim of his bowler out of the way to watch the skydivers. Above the parachutes, a red and white plane looped around. Excited, he walked faster, holding his cane parallel to the ground.

Soon the cluster of houses thinned and he saw the small airfield, its perimeter secured by a ten-foot tall chain-link fence topped with concertina coils. By this time, the two skydivers had landed and gathered their parachutes, before returning to a hangar with Skydive Launchers painted in broad letters on its side.

As he hurried along the border of the airfield, following the line of the fence, the red and white airplane dropped to the runway with a slight shudder and proceeded to taxi toward the hangar. By the time he was close enough to distinguish individual voices, another plane was preparing to leave with more skydivers.

He paused, hoping he appeared to be nothing more than a curious onlooker, and massaged his temple, probing. The three new skydivers had already packed their chutes and walked to the second plane, otherwise he could have interfered with the chutes in packing, but that opportunity had passed. With his third eye, he peered into the backpack container, the pilot chute, main parachute, reserve chute, lines and risers and, finally, the AAD or automatic activation device, a sliver of metal with an onboard computer chip that deployed the reserve chute at 750 feet if the skydiver could not or became distracted during freefall. Switched on in preflight, the AAD measured air pressure to determine altitude and recalibrated every thirty seconds to account for changes in atmospheric pressure. But if all proceeded according to plan and preparation, the AADs wouldn't need to perform their lifesaving function. It would be a simple matter for him to cause a malfunction in the device. Now that he knew what to look for, he disabled all three AADs.

Anticipating an exciting challenge, he stood with both hands resting on the handle of his cane and watched as the red and white plane, a Cessna 182, with the pilot and three jumpers aboard, taxied onto the runway.

While the plane climbed steadily to 13,000 feet, which

would give the skydivers about sixty seconds of freefall, he extended his awareness to follow them up into the thin air and buffeting winds. Briefly, the link became tenuous, but he concentrated and kept his third eye on them. Even at two and a half miles elevation, they could not escape his attention and manipulation.

He skimmed the surface of their minds, touching on each of the three jumpers, plucking their names out. Dave Jackson, Art Polan and Robert… McGlaughlin, although the others thought of him as "Mac." Since a plane crash was less of a challenge, he ignored the woman pilot and the condition of the plane itself. Crashing the plane would kill the skydivers, but the accident wouldn't test him, wouldn't improve his abilities the same way tackling three targets individually at that distance would. Plus, he had a ticking clock challenge. Once the skydivers jumped, he would have to work fast.

As they waited excitedly for the pilot to give them the signal that they were over the jump zone, the three skydivers compared notes about their jump count. They had jumped together since their senior year at Rowan University, for Mac's twenty-first birthday. Since then, Dave had missed a jump due to a family emergency—a child's burst appendix— and Art had missed a jump while attending his grandparents' fiftieth wedding anniversary. That made Mac senior man.

"I'll jump after you clowns," he shouted over the noise of the plane.

Moments later, the pilot gave them the thumbs up.

Dave stepped through the doorway first, falling away

from the plane, closely followed by Art. With those two out of the way, Mac placed one booted foot down on the footrest outside the plane. As he was about to push off, the plane was jostled by a bit of turbulence and Mac's foot slipped sideways off the rest and, instead of falling forward, he fell back. His helmeted head bounced off the footrest, dazing him, and he flipped end over end all the way down.

Normally, at 750 feet, the AAD would release the reserve chute and the unresponsive skydiver would owe his life to the failsafe device. Tora thought it appropriate that Mac, the senior man, hit the ground first.

Initially, Dave and Art failed to notice Mac's plight. They enjoyed almost a full minute of freefall before they attempted to open their chutes. Dave, who jumped first, looked around and finally noticed Mac spinning out of control. He pointed toward the tumbling figure behind Art, to direct his attention. Art mistook the gesture as a sign to throw out his pilot chute.

On the ground, gazing up at the three men, Tora smiled.

Though pulled out as expected by the pilot chute, Art's main canopy failed to deploy properly. With the canopy partially open, he spun out of control and quickly became disoriented. Tugging on the toggles, he attempted to help the ram-air canopy open, but soon gave up and pulled the handle on the three-ring release. That freed the lines on both risers and the main parachute. Art was in freefall again. When he pulled the reserve chute handle, nothing happened. Stunned, he waited for the AAD to fire and automatically deploy the reserve chute at 750 feet.

He waited for the rest of his life.

Dave threw out his pilot chute a few seconds after Art. But something went wrong. The canopy opened instantly, pulling Dave up so hard he grimaced in pain. Glancing up, he saw the nylon slider that held the lines together had ripped apart as if rotten. The force of the opening tore several cells of the ram-air canopy. He watched in horror as the tears spread, crippling the canopy's integrity, which offered less wind resistance with each passing second. Worse, the lines began to snap, one after the other. The chute was a lost cause.

On the ground, Tora looked up intently, squeezing the ironbound handle of his cane. Precision work demanded his full concentration, but it was progressing smoothly. One dazed and helpless, while a second waited in vain for a reserve chute to open, and now the third man had more than he could handle.

Dave released his main canopy, too preoccupied at this point to notice that Art had already attempted the same strategy. With a silent prayer, he pulled the handle to deploy his reserve chute and sighed with relief as it popped open above him. But his relief was momentary. He felt rather than heard the rugged straps around his shoulders and thighs begin to tear. Once snug, now they pulled away from him. He clapped a hand over a shoulder strap, felt it separating at the seam. As precious moments ticked by, the nylon crumbled in his hand. The whole harness tore away from his body, dangling from the deployed reserve chute while he plummeted toward the ground, quickly approaching terminal velocity.

Fifty feet from the perimeter fence, Mac slammed into the ground, dying instantly. Less than ten seconds later, Art and Dave followed, like echoes. All three broke most of the bones in their bodies, rupturing internal organs and crushing their skulls. Dave struck the ground a hundred yards away from Mac, while Art's remains splattered across an asphalt runway and would delay flights for the rest of the day.

Tilting the brim of his bowler down to block the bright sunlight, Tora chuckled in delight and turned away from the airfield's imposing perimeter fence. Though he had enjoyed the unique challenge of the skydivers—and the prospect of another three-for-one had almost seemed poetic—he had larger plans to set in motion.

Returning to the rows of suburban homes, he heard the laughter of a group of small children. Curious, he followed the sound to a long, one-story stucco building with a rainbow painted on one wall near a wooden sign that read First Step Forward Preschool. A chain-link fence surrounded the property, which included a busy playground. Unlike the airfield fence, this one was not topped by razor wire. Of course, the airfield fence was designed to keep intruders out, while the daycare fence kept children, none more than six years old, within its borders.

Some boys tossed beanbags at a plastic game on the ground, while a row of girls monopolized the swings. A group of boys played a game of tag, running in circles around annoyed girls who were chatting with dolls while others attempted to jump rope.

A ring of boys tossed a big purple ball back and forth, the

type of ball found in the bargain bin of a toy store. It was a game in which the object was to keep the ball away from one of their number.

Tora lifted one hand off his cane and surreptitiously made a quick come-here motion with his index finger. The next time one of the boys facing him threw the ball, it sailed over the head of its intended target and struck the side of a sliding board, bouncing high toward the fence. The ball one-hopped over the chain-link fence and settled at the curb by his feet.

"Jimmy, you missed it," yelled the boy who had made the errant throw to the one who hadn't jumped high enough. "You gotta get it back."

Jimmy looked askance, unconvinced by his playmate's logic, then sighed and jogged across the playground area, pulling up short when he came to the fence. Jimmy looked up and up, startled by the tall man standing before him. Squinting into the sun, he raised a hand to shield his eyes. The back of his hand exhibited several shallow scratches, stippled with blood.

"Hey, mister, can you get the ball? We can't go out."

"Certainly."

Bending over, Tora palmed the ball in one hand and stepped up to the fence.

One of the children's guardians had noticed the stranger by the fence, apparently talking to one of her charges. The young woman hurried across the playground, her brunette ponytail swishing from side to side. "Jimmy! Stay back from the fence."

"Huh?"

By this time, she had closed the distance between them. She placed one hand protectively on the child's shoulder, as if physical contact would prevent the child from suffering any harm at the stranger's hands. "The children aren't allowed near the fence," she stated flatly.

In his most pleasant voice, Tora said, "I was simply retrieving the child's ball."

"Of course." The woman forced a smile.

The few seconds of interaction had allowed him time to accelerate the spread of an aggressive MRSA virus he had placed on the surface of the ball. With exaggerated formality, he extended his arm over the fence and lowered the ball into the child's raised hands. "There you go—Jimmy, right?"

He glanced at the woman for confirmation. She nodded uncomfortably. She hadn't revealed any personal information about the child in her care, but obviously the minor detail of his given name was no longer secret.

"Enjoy your game, Jimmy," he added.

"Thanks," Jimmy said, and hurried back to his playmates.

Later, the town would refer to the boy as Patient Zero.

"Good day," he said to the woman, tapping the brim of his hat with the handle of his cane in an old-fashioned salutation.

Without waiting for a response, he returned to the sidewalk and continued on his way. He felt her gaze on his back, but resisted the urge to look over his shoulder. Despite her suspicious mind, she hadn't witnessed anything to stoke her fears of child endangerment.

In the distance, the sirens of emergency vehicles wailed, heading toward the airfield to restore unpleasant order to the delicious chaos he had generated. For now, Tora contented himself with a productive outing and moved on. The more he stretched and stressed the town's resources, the better.

FIVE

One hundred miles north of Laurel Hill, the hunters stopped for lunch at another anonymous diner. Afterward, Dean acquired a medium-blue 1976 Monte Carlo with a few dings on the chassis and a small square of the grille missing. Judging by its layers of caked mud and the profusion of bird droppings, nobody would miss the car any time soon. Before they hit the road again, Dean inflated the sagging tires and ran the car through a self-serve carwash. Clean, the Monte Carlo was barely recognizable as the same vehicle. And while it passed the roadworthy test, as a source of driver envy it was pure fail, not worth a second glance. Sadly, in their post-Leviathan existence, that made it the perfect car for the Winchesters.

"Bobby," Dean called as the older man opened the door of his Chevelle. "This maybe-hunter you know. Does he have a name?"

"Roy Dempsey."

Dean looked at Sam. "Any bells ringing?"

Sam shook his head.

Dean turned back to Bobby. "Is he onboard?"

"A firm tentative."

"What does that mean?" Sam asked.

"Yes," Bobby said, "with conditions."

"What conditions?" Dean asked.

"Wouldn't say," Bobby replied with a shrug. "Better'n his first answer."

"Which was?"

"'Go to hell, Singer.'"

Dean nodded. "So the ice is thawing."

"Cracked, more like."

The last leg of the trip consumed two hours. Roy Dempsey lived in a log cabin home in Lynnewood, a small rural town north of the larger, bustling Laurel Hill. Dempsey's house was set back from the road, accessed by a long gravel driveway. Hulking trees a few rows deep shielded the backyard from view, and the nearest house on either side was a couple of hundred feet distant. The house itself was all dark wood with a gable roof and, at night, would probably blend into the tall trees behind it.

Bobby drove down the long driveway ahead of the Winchesters in the Monte Carlo. The loose gravel crunching under their tires functioned as a proximity alarm. Dean half expected the maybe-hunter curmudgeon to come out on the covered porch waving a shotgun and giving them until the count of three to get off his property.

Bobby parked behind a dark green El Camino about as old as the Monte Carlo, but in better shape. About a decade past its model year, a silver Dodge Ram was parked beside the older car. Rather than block both vehicles, Dean steered the Monte Carlo behind Bobby's Chevelle. He and Sam stepped out of their car and approached Bobby.

"I'll do the talking," Bobby said. "Least until I take his temperature."

Dean made an "after you" gesture and they followed Bobby to the porch, but waited at the bottom of the three steps. Bobby rapped his knuckles against the door and waited. No answer.

"Get off your ass, Roy! It's Bobby Singer."

Dean looked at Sam. "Tough love?"

The door swung open to reveal a tall man wearing a green T-shirt under a black leather vest, faded jeans and scuffed boots. He had a grizzled jaw and long, graying hair bound in a ponytail. It took Dean a stunned moment to process that the man had lost half his left arm, the stump ending above where his elbow would have been.

Frowning, Roy said, "Not deaf, you old bastard."

"Old?" Bobby said. "Ever hear about pots and kettles?"

"Told you I was out of the life, Singer. Not looking to jump back in."

"Not asking, Roy. We need a roof. That's all. Won't cramp your style."

Continuing to frown, Roy scratched his jaw. "Don't know about this."

"Thought we had this squared."

"Nothing etched in stone, Singer."

"Couple days. All we're asking."

"And these two," Roy said. "Winchesters, huh?"

"Sam and Dean," Bobby said, nodding at them in turn.

"All over the news a while back, those two."

"Impostors," Bobby said. "Told you three times on the phone."

"Yeah, yeah," Roy said, conceding the point. "You'll leave me out of it?"

"Word of honor."

"Don't want no trouble."

"Would say we ain't looking for any, but you know that ain't true."

Sam, who had been watching the terse exchange with increasing concern, took a step forward. "Bobby, we'll find something else…"

Imagining a drafty shack with rats underfoot and no indoor plumbing, Dean shot his brother a look: *Are you kidding me?*

Roy sighed. "Couple days," he agreed. "But whatever you're hunting, don't bring it here. And don't ask for my help. In fact, I don't even want to hear about it." He waved his stump in the air for emphasis. "This here is my retirement card. No fight left in me. I'm out. Understood?"

"Crystal," Bobby said.

Roy stepped back and held the door open for them.

While Dean retrieved a cooler stocked with beer and hard

liquor from the Monte Carlo's trunk, Sam glanced around the interior of Dempsey's house, hoping his snooping wasn't too obvious. Roy's unexplained pain sat beneath the surface, under a thin film of emotional ice, and Sam doubted the man wanted to answer any questions that would force him to revisit traumatic events in his past.

The dark wooden walls absorbed all the light in the house, creating a gloom that complemented Roy's mood. Or maybe it was the other way around. The great room faced the kitchen with its counter and stools and the staircase to the upper floor. To the left was a bay dining area, to the right a fireplace. The house had the look of a bachelor pad—there were no flowers in vases or other feminine touches, but it was clean and orderly. A mahogany coat rack stood by the door, a couple of Navajo throw rugs spread on the floor, a big analog clock over the stove. It was efficient but almost impersonal, like a rental unit, with Roy as the caretaker rather than homeowner.

The one small personal touch was a row of framed family photos on the wall beside the kitchen. In one, a much younger Roy with shoulder length hair had his arm wrapped around the shoulders of an attractive brunette. Another photo showed the same woman holding a baby boy. A third showed the same boy, now a young man in his late teens or early twenties, standing in front of the green El Camino, smiling as he dangled a set of car keys from a raised index finger. In a fourth photo, the young man stood at attention wearing a police uniform and a serious expression on his face.

Dean walked past Sam, carrying the cooler on his way to the kitchen, and noticed the photo that had caught Sam's attention. "A cop?" he whispered, glancing sidelong to where Bobby was talking softly with Roy, probably trying to smooth some ruffled feathers.

Dean shook his head slightly and took his liquid stash into the kitchen, setting the cooler on the counter.

Recalling the El Camino outside, Sam asked Roy, "Do you live alone?"

"What of it?" Roy asked irritably.

"Nothing," Sam said. "I saw the photo of the El Camino."

"My son's car," Roy said. His tone softened as he walked over to stand beside Sam. "Killed four years back."

"I'm sorry," Sam said, caught off guard.

"Top of his class," Roy said proudly. "Cop right here in Laurel Hill. Less than a year on the job. One night, he pulls over a speeder." He cleared his throat, jaw muscles working to suppress his emotions. "Standing there, examines the man's license, registration, insurance card. Same old drill, right? Gone through it dozens of times before. Except that night, another driver comes along. Man in his late seventies. Wilfred Banks. Confused by the lights. Too damn old to be behind the wheel, basically. Hits my boy, drags him under his car for two hundred yards before he figures out which one's the brake pedal."

"I'm sorry," Sam repeated.

"Some people don't know when to quit," Roy said, more to himself than Sam. "Old bastard lived two more years after killing my boy." Roy nodded somberly, scratched his jaw. "Now I got another one to bury."

Bobby came over. "Roy?"

"Mother-in-law," Roy said. "Out of state."

"When's the funeral?"

"Tomorrow," Roy said. "Hitting the road in a few hours. Expect my place to be standing when I get back."

"Extend my sympathies to her folks," Bobby said.

"Doubt I'll be speaking to any of them," Roy said, and turned, walking away. "Sally's mother never forgave me for her death. But I gotta pay my respects."

Roy crossed the great room without another word, stepped into the downstairs master bedroom and closed the door softly behind him.

Sam looked questioningly at Bobby. After transferring his liquor supply to the refrigerator, Dean cracked open a few beers and joined them, offering a bottle to each of them.

"Bout fifteen years ago," Bobby said in a whisper as he stared at the bedroom door, "ghoul attack in Philly. Killed Sally, wrecked Roy's arm."

"Why'd the mother-in-law blame Roy...?" Dean started to ask before putting the pieces together. "Because he took his wife on a hunt?"

Bobby nodded. "Her choice. Standing by her man."

"Guess the mother-in-law saw it differently."

"The hell knows what he told the mother," Bobby said. "After he lost the arm, he got out of the life. But losing Sally killed something inside him. For years I worried he'd eat a bullet. Kept in touch, pestered him damn near every week. Pissed him off most likely. Took a while, but I finally got it.

His son kept the light on. Roy wasn't about to check out with Lucas around. Damn proud of that boy."

"And with Lucas gone?" Sam asked.

Bobby shrugged his shoulders. "Got through four years somehow."

"Did you start calling him again?" Dean asked.

"Didn't hear about it till three months later," Bobby said. "He called me, late one night. Talked for hours, about family, getting old, hunting. Said he never missed it, not once. Too much killing, too much dying." Bobby exhaled forcefully. "Had a bad vibe about that talk. Finality written all over it. Next thing, it's dawn. He thanked me. Said the damnedest thing."

"What?" Sam asked.

"Said he never wanted to hear my voice again."

"Off his meds?" Dean suggested.

"Forget losing the arm," Bobby said. "That call? That's when he quit. And meant it."

"You were a part of that life," Sam said, understanding.

"Up till then," Bobby said. "Didn't believe him. Thought it was a matter of time. Peek behind the curtain once, damn hard to forget what's pulling the levers."

Dean took a gulp of beer. "Well, good for him," he said irritably. "He got the gold watch and a ticket out of crazy town. What about us? This job? Planning the plan?"

They settled down at the table in the breakfast nook area, as far from the master bedroom as the downstairs floor plan allowed. After some debate, they decided that Bobby would contact the police in his Fed guise, while Sam and Dean—to keep a low profile—would pose as insurance claim adjusters to talk to witnesses.

"Bobby, you'll need an angle," Sam said. "Terrorism?"

"Homeland security?" Dean suggested with a shrug.

"Something small scale," Bobby decided. "An interstate burglary ring. Gives it federal jurisdiction."

"An interstate burglary ring causing traffic accidents?" Dean asked

"No, ya idjit," Bobby said. "Distractions. Violent distractions."

"To keep the police occupied," Sam said, "before pulling off their heists."

"O-kay." Dean looked unconvinced.

"I'll make it work," Bobby said, frowning. "Somehow."

"I'll put in a good word," Roy said. He had managed to move silently into the middle of the great room with a packed suitcase. "Know the police chief. Shook my hand at Lucas's funeral."

Sam wanted to say, "I thought you were out?" But the offer seemed like returning a favor, and Sam thought of the long call Bobby had described.

"Roy, no need to—"

"It's a phone call," Roy said. "No big deal, right?"

"Sure," Bobby said. "But you're leaving."

"Time for a call," Roy said. "Make myself something to eat." He took a steak out of the refrigerator and set it on a plate on the counter to come to room temperature. "Sorry. Didn't shop for four."

"No problem," Sam said. "We already ate."

"A couple hours ago," Dean muttered and sipped his beer.

"Well, if you'll excuse me," Bobby said. "Got an identity to assume." With that, he left to swap his trucker hat, vest, flannel shirt, and jeans for his Fed suit and necktie.

Sam opened his laptop. "D'you mind if I hop on your Wi-Fi connection?" he asked Roy.

"Not at all," Roy said evenly. "If I had one."

"What? No computer?"

"Oh, I got a PC," Roy said. "Seven years old, eight, maybe. Ain't good for much. Got dial-up internet when I need it, which is rare."

"Dial-up," Sam repeated, aghast.

"Old school," Dean commented, clearly amused at Sam's reaction.

"Part of retirement," Roy said. "Don't mind waiting until six o'clock to get my news. Worst case, there's a police scanner in the basement somewhere. Haven't used that since…" His voice choked with emotion. "Not for a long time."

Sam spun the laptop around.

"What's wrong?" Dean asked.

"There's a modem jack on the motherboard," Sam said, "but I don't have an RJ12 connector."

"Sure I have a spare in a drawer with my login information," Roy said.

As he walked over to a small hutch and shuffled through the contents of the top drawer, Sam glanced at Dean and gave a small head shake.

"What?" Dean said. "Like a foreclosed house or a shack in the woods would have Wi-Fi." He tilted his bottle and frowned, climbing out of his seat. "I need another beer. You?"

"I'm good," Sam said, without bothering to check his bottle or look up at his brother.

As soon as Dean had abandoned his seat, Lucifer dropped into it. He looked around at the dark wooden walls of the sparsely furnished house and nodded appreciatively. "Hey, buddy," he said. "Cozy little tinderbox you found here. What say we light this hidey-hole up for all the comforts of home?"

Sam tried to ignore him.

"I'm the one who sees your potential, Sam," Lucifer continued. "C'mon! Let's add firebug to the Looney Tunes résumé."

"Found one!" Roy declared, holding up a tangled gray cable.

Lucifer grinned. "A good house fire really warms the cockles."

Under the table, Sam pressed his thumbnail hard into the scar on his left hand.

"You okay?" Roy asked. He stood beside Sam, hand extended with the cable.

"Fine," Sam said. "I'm fine." A quick glance across the table revealed Lucifer's absence. "Phone jack?"

"One over in that corner, by the baseboard," Roy said, pointing. "But let me call the police chief first."

Of course, Sam thought. *With dial-up, you could make a call or go online, but not both at the same time.* He considered offering the retired hunter his burner cell, but worried he might take it as an insult. Besides, with caller ID, it was probably better the call to the police chief came from the landline.

Six

"An interstate burglary ring?" Chief Donato asked as he and Bobby walked down the hall of the Laurel Hill Police Headquarters from the administrative wing to the patrol section. The place was large enough that it had an abandoned quality with so few personnel sitting at desks in offices or bullpen areas or rushing down the hall. "What's your level of confidence, Agent Willis?"

"Early stages," Bobby said while attempting to project the assured demeanor of a special agent of the Federal Bureau of Investigation. The suit and tie certainly kept him on point—dress for the role. "Seeing patterns similar to what I found during an investigation in Montana." Bobby hoped a northeastern United States chief of police would have little to no interest in crimes affecting Big Sky Country.

"What sort of patterns?"

The chief had a military bearing and the buzz-cut to match, but his hair had considerably more salt than pepper, and his midsection had expanded enough that Donato's doctor would mention diet and exercise at his next annual physical. Bobby guessed the man's role was strictly administrative, riding a desk, not a police cruiser.

Bobby considered the possibility that the police chief was a Leviathan in disguise, then dismissed the idea. The Big Mouths could be responsible for Laurel Hill's run of rotten luck, but he doubted they would have any interest in a mid-sized town in southern New Jersey. Still, these days, caution could never be overrated.

"Accident clusters," Bobby said. "First blush, appear unrelated. But they escalate. More damage, more casualties. Require more police and emergency personnel."

Chief Donato nodded, the suggestion resonating with him based upon recent events, as Bobby had hoped it would. "Draining resources." He paused in the doorway to the patrol officer section of the building.

"While you're scrambling to deal with one emergency after another," Bobby continued, "they hit your banks, jewelry stores, high-profile targets."

"We've had quite a busy day already," Chief Donato said. "Accidents that defy logic. But I have trouble wrapping my head around the idea they were deliberate… attacks."

"Sounds like the group I'm investigating. Tricky bastards. You don't make the connection until it's too late."

"Nothing's been hit yet," Donato said. "Other than a few shoplifting cases at the Laurel Hill Mall, there've been no robberies or break-ins."

"They wait for the big score," Bobby said with conviction, making the case for why no burglary ring activity had occurred yet. A stalling tactic while he, Sam and Dean investigated the true cause of the destruction. "When your department is under the most strain, they'll hit multiple high-value targets at once."

"Sounds like quite an operation."

"Unfortunately," Bobby said grimly, "they're just warming up."

"And we already have our hands full," Donato said, frowning. Then he seemed to reach a decision. "You're a friend of Roy's…"

"We go way back."

"Any friend of Roy's I'm inclined to take at face value," Donato said. "But I hope you'll set jurisdictional pissing contests aside here. Keep me apprised of anything you turn up. We've lost some good people. Hell if I know why."

"No damn reason," Bobby said sympathetically. "Collateral damage."

"Right now, yours is the best theory I've heard," Donato said. "For no other reason than that I'd love to pin these senseless deaths on somebody. Lock them in a windowless hole for a hundred years."

"You and me both."

Bobby surveyed the open patrol officer section of the police headquarters. There were two dozen desks, but only a handful of uniforms sat at them, handling paperwork or working at computer screens.

Donato led Bobby to a short row of offices and stopped in front of one with an open door. Inside, a middle-aged man wearing a uniform with sergeant's stripes sat behind a desk hunting-and-pecking furiously on a computer keyboard.

"I want to introduce you to Sergeant James McClary, Agent Willis," Donato said, raising his voice to catch the man's attention. McClary immediately looked up from his keyboard, alert. "McClary supervised Lucas Dempsey, Roy's son. He'll bring you up to speed on today's incidents. Act as liaison in case you need any support from me."

"Appreciate the cooperation, Chief," Bobby said, shaking the man's offered hand.

Once Donato left to return to the administrative wing, McClary gestured Bobby to a seat in front of his desk. "So... Agent Willis, was it? How can I help?"

"More or less what the chief said," Bobby replied. "Details on today's incidents. Whatever seems... unusual. And a list of any witnesses. Anyone who might have seen something—"

"Unusual," McClary said, nodding. "What's the FBI's interest in accidents?"

Bobby repeated the burglary ring cover story. Then, to sidestep further questions about his motives for investigating local accidents, he quickly changed the subject. "Lucas Dempsey reported to you."

"Great kid," McClary said, nodding. "Junior patrol officer. Hell of a cop. Had a lot of potential."

"Meant a lot to his father," Bobby said. "Roy couldn't have been prouder of his boy."

McClary looked thoughtful and somber.

"About today," Bobby said, changing tack again. "What kind of incidents are we talking about?"

McClary exhaled forcefully. "Three fatal accidents on one block within an hour, near as we can tell. Mother falls down the steps and breaks her neck. Anesthesiologist slips on a wet tile floor and cracks his head open. And a retired woman dies in a house fire."

"Cause of the fire?"

"Fire marshal ruled it accidental," McClary said. "Lint trap fire, believe it or not."

Bobby shook his head in a show of disbelief.

"That's not the weirdest part of the day," McClary said. "About an hour later…"

While Sam tested his patience on a dial-up internet connection, browsing various local news websites, and Roy Dempsey pan-fried a juicy steak for his solo dinner, Dean switched on the bulky twenty-seven-inch TV at low volume and caught an early newscast the old-fashioned way. The news anchor introduced footage of a house fire. In Dean's experience, television newscasts loved showing film of big fires.

"Cable?" he called to Roy.

"Basic," Roy said, flipping his steak over to cook the other side. "And they made me rent some damn digital converter for that."

"So, you've got, what, twelve channels?"

"Count your blessings," Roy said as he removed a pair

of baked potatoes from the oven. "I only got four channels with the rooftop antenna."

"That steak sure smells good," Dean said, dropping a last ditch hint.

"Just the one," Roy reminded him.

Frowning suddenly, Dean asked, "How's your supply of borax?"

"For what?" Roy asked, confused. "Steak sauce?"

"Never mind," Dean said. "We've got several gallon jugs in the trunk."

As the only effective weapon they had found against the Leviathan—though it only burnt but didn't kill them—Dean liked to know he had some of the cleaning agent on hand at all times.

Roy turned to Sam. "Your brother soft in the head?"

Sam smiled without looking up from the laptop.

On the TV, a reporter was interviewing a young woman at an airfield, a red and white Cessna framed in the shot. Still images of three faces popped up on the screen. Dean called to his brother. "Sam, three skydivers just died. All parachute malfunctions, all from the same plane."

"Got it," Sam confirmed. "Just waiting for the page to load."

"Three skydivers," Roy mused as he cut into his steak. "What are the odds? Never mind." He held his hand up and shook his head. "Forgot I don't want to know."

Dean walked over to Sam and read the on-screen information he had found over his shoulder. So far, the news site had only posted basic information: the names of the pilot and victims, the time of the incident. Not that the Winchesters would need more to discover the truth beneath the facts. Sam had also saved a few other pages, detailing three fatal accidents earlier in the day.

"No witnesses for those," Sam said, disappointed. "We could check each scene for clues. On the plus side, there's the pilot and the roofing accident homeowner."

"It's a start."

Dean looked up as Roy left his counter seat, carrying a hunk of steak between thumb and forefinger. Okay, Dean hadn't begged for scraps, but…

"Where are you taking that?" he asked as Roy turned down the short hallway that led past the staircase to the backdoor.

"The cat," Roy said.

Dean glanced around the downstairs. Had he missed a pet?

"You have a cat?"

"Not exactly," Roy said enigmatically.

Taking a few steps down the hallway, Dean leaned sideways to peer around Roy. A black cat was sitting on the back lawn a couple of yards from the door. There was something odd about the way light reflected in its eyes. Roy tossed the wedge of meat at its front paws. For a few moments, the cat simply regarded the retired hunter. Then it dipped its head, snared the meat in its teeth, and bolted across the backyard. Roy barked a laugh and closed the door.

"Stray," he explained to Dean. "Could be feral, never domesticated. Doesn't trust a soul."

"It lets you feed it."

"Kindred spirits. I lost an arm in battle, he lost an eye."

Roy rinsed his plate, glass and flatware and put them in the dishwasher. As he dried his hand, he said, "Assume you're heading out."

Dean looked at Sam, who nodded.

"Time you get back, most likely I'll be gone," Roy said. "Spare keys on the hook. Don't trash the place."

"Anything else?" Dean asked.

"Should be back Saturday," Roy said. "Friday night, maybe you could put something out back."

"For the cat?"

"You forget, no big deal. He can fend for himself."

"Has he got a name?"

"Nothing he'd answer to," Roy said, shrugging. "He's a damn cat. But, sometimes, I call him Shadow."

"Because he follows you around?"

"No," Roy replied. "'Cause he usually waits beyond the range of the backdoor light. In the shadows."

Wearing their Fed suits but carrying fake insurance adjuster IDs instead of FBI laminates, the Winchesters headed to Bedford Drive to talk to Michelle Sloney, owner of the home where the three roofers fell to their deaths. They found the address, but Sam parked the Monte Carlo several houses away and they backtracked on foot. While not an eyesore, the boosted car was obviously not a rental and contradicted the professional image they hoped to convey to witnesses.

As they walked up the driveway, Dean glanced up at the roof, not sure what he hoped to find, but trusting his eyes to notice anything irregular. Nothing jumped out at him. Yellow police tape roped off an area around a roll-off Dumpster squatting in the driveway. Dean noticed and pointed out dark bloodstains on the edge of the trash bin facing the roof.

During his online digging, Sam had discovered the homeowner was a branch manager at a downtown bank and the bank's website directory listed her telephone extension. She'd agreed to put her assistant manager in charge of the bank and meet them at her home so they could examine the site of the accident.

Sam rang the bell.

A few seconds later, a middle-aged woman opened the door and flashed a polite smile at them.

"Mrs. Sloney," Sam said. "Tom Smith. We spoke on the phone…"

Sam's voice faded with each word. Dean understood why. The woman looked like she'd gone several rounds with a welterweight—or an abusive husband. She had a nasty black eye, with bruises down her right cheek, and her right hand was bandaged.

"Ms. Sloney," she said evenly. "I'm divorced."

"From the reports," Sam said, "I had no idea you were injured in the accidents."

"Oh, no," she said, gesturing at her eye. "Clumsiness. I was rushing to call 911 and ran into the door and my hand… Pure clumsiness."

"Right," Sam said, with a quick glance at Dean. "As I explained, my partner, John Smith—it's a common name— and I are investigating some accidents in the area."

"Insurance adjusters, right?" she said. "What company?"

"We're independent contractors," Sam said. "Part of a regulatory oversight initiative to ensure against fraud by either party involved in any substantial claims."

"We just need to get a clear picture about what happened here," Dean said. "We won't take much of your time."

"When I came home for lunch all three were on the roof," she said. "Mr. Sedenko, the owner, told me they were nearly finished."

"Storm damage warranted the repair?"

"Well, that was the final straw," she said. "The roof was overdue for repair. I ran out of excuses."

"Was there anything unprofessional in their work ethic?" Sam asked. "Horsing around? Drinking alcohol?"

"Oh, no. Well, not that I ever saw," she said. "They were fast and efficient. Believe me, I did my homework, checked the company out. They're licensed, bonded and insured. Been in business for years. I even checked references, around town. No complaints."

"So, out of the blue, these three experienced roofers get clumsy and fall off your roof," Dean said, thinking aloud.

"Are you accusing me of something?"

"No, he's not," Sam said conciliatorily, flashing Dean a warning look. "It seems like a freak coincidence at the moment. Did you see them fall?"

"Only the last one," she said. "Before that, I was inside. A loose shingle flew by my kitchen window. Then I heard something crash. I assumed they were tossing debris into that trash container. Looking back, maybe the first one slipped on that shingle."

She led them from her doorway, under a small portico along the narrow sidewalk that tracked around the front of the house, to where part of a downspout had been ripped from the wall.

"After a second crash, I decided to go out and check. That's when… that's when I saw Mr. Sedenko falling off the roof. I think he tried to catch himself on the gutter. But he flipped over backward and hit the pavement face first. I heard his neck." She squeezed her eyes shut. "It was horrible. I saw the other bodies near his. I knew they were dead, but… but I had to do something, had to call someone. I called out for help, but he seemed oblivious, so I rushed back—"

"Who?" Sam interrupted. "Who seemed oblivious?"

"Oh, there was a man in a suit," she said, "walking down the street. I saw him at the curb, near my mailbox. I yelled, told him to call 911, but he had no idea what had happened. So I ran back to the house, and that's when I banged into my own door."

"This guy," Dean said, "can you describe him?"

"I don't remember what he looked like. But he was big, I mean broad *and* tall. Maybe a couple of inches taller than you." She indicated Sam, who nodded for her to continue. "He wore a black suit and one of those rounded hats with a brim—a bowler hat."

"Was that all?"

"He had a cane. He looked very… formal."

"And you never saw this guy before?" Dean asked.

"No," she said. "And something was off about him."

"How so?"

"Not all there, you know?" she said. "Or hard of hearing, maybe completely deaf. He certainly acted like he didn't understand me. I mean, I was clearly panicked, but he had this amused grin on his face, like I was the one responding inappropriately to this… this horrible accident."

"We'd like to check the roof," Dean said. "Is there a window with access or…?"

"I have an extension ladder in the garage."

"Perfect."

Ten minutes later, Dean had completed his inspection of the roof. Other than the missing shingle, he found nothing unusual. Ms. Sloney explained that the police had confiscated the roofers' generator and tools to look for evidence of foul play.

Back in the Monte Carlo, Sam said. "How does one loose shingle kill three roofers?"

"My money's on John Steed," Dean said.

"Who?"

"*The Avengers*: sixties television series. Emma Peel? That catsuit!" Dean said. "That was Steed's look."

"A catsuit?"

"No," Dean said, irritated and not sure if Sam was pulling his leg. "Diana Rigg wore the catsuit. Steed wore a suit with a bowler hat and carried a cane—actually, an umbrella, but it had a cane vibe."

Catching Sam's continued blank expression, he added, "The show aired on syndication, probably still on extended cable channels. And the bad movie version with Uma

Thurman and the Brit guy… Trust me, okay? It's a John Steed look."

"So, bowler guy, down by the curb," Sam said, moving on, "walks by her mailbox."

"Walking," Dean said thoughtfully. "I wonder if he also walked by chainsaw guy."

"No witnesses," Sam said. "Let's talk to the Cessna pilot and go from there."

SEVEN

Tora walked along another suburban street feeling like an artist in search of a bigger canvas. With the business day soon over, fathers or mothers would return from work, children would complete school assignments while waiting for dinner. Family dynamics would come into play, offering opportunities for Tora to increase resentments and elevate petty bickering to physical violence. But he had something bigger in mind.

Pausing before a home with signs of neglect, he extended his awareness and discovered an agoraphobic hoarder. An old woman with brittle bones, she squeezed through rooms piled floor to ceiling with stacks of yellowed newspapers and moldy books. He waited until she jostled a leaning tower of newsprint before giving the mound a little shove of encouragement. It crashed down, tripping her, and he heard the crunch of her hip bone breaking as she sprawled on the dust-covered floor. She wailed in pain and struggled to right herself. Instead, her tugging on the mounds of paper created a domino effect. Hundreds of pounds of paper pummeled her where she lay, pinning and eventually suffocating her.

The house a little further down the street presented no challenge. A middle-aged man on disability for a bad back lounged on a lumpy sofa as he watched ESPN highlights, a lit cigarette dangling from his fingers. In seconds, the man nodded off and the cigarette fell into shag carpeting littered with fast food wrappers. The ratty sofa was highly flammable and cooked its occupant in minutes.

As the, surprisingly, functioning smoke alarms in the house commenced a screeching chorus, Tora saw a burly, bearded man with curly black hair exiting a house halfway down the block on the other side of the street. The man wore blue coveralls with the name Frank stitched on a patch over the left breast pocket, and carried a dinged red toolbox. Frank opened the rear doors of a white commercial van with "Kiriakoulis Plumbing No Job Too Small" painted in two lines on the side panels. The plumber slid the toolbox into the back of the van and stepped back to close the rear doors.

"Frank!" Tora called.

Frank turned around, a jovial expression on his face that instantly transformed to mild confusion. "Do I know you?"

"No, but I need a ride."

"Ah, I'm sorry, mister, my insurance won't allow pass—"

In one swift motion, Tora flipped his cane up into a horizontal position, catching the midpoint in his left hand before ramming the ironbound pointed tip forward, spitting Frank like a roasted pig. He angled the point upward, shattering ribs and piercing the heart. He lifted the big man off his feet and with a hearty heave, shoved the body into the back of the van. With the heart muscle destroyed, blood loss was minimal. He reached into Frank's pockets and fished out the keys to the van. With a few quick motions, he wiped the blood and gore from his cane. Then he slammed the rear doors and hopped into the driver's seat.

Nobody witnessed the brief flurry of violence.

A few minutes later he followed the local streets that led him back to Kressen Boulevard. A fire truck and an ambulance passed him headed in the opposite direction. He slowed the van and veered toward the shoulder, giving the emergency vehicles a wide berth. Once they were beyond him, he accelerated again and followed the signs to the Laurel Hill Mall.

Before they could talk to anyone at the Haddon Airfield about the death of the three skydivers, Dean and Sam had to avoid two crews of reporters and camera operators. One crew filmed the airfield itself, most likely background footage for voiceover, while the other reporter interviewed a maintenance worker who pointed out three separate locations, no doubt indicating where the bodies had come down.

Keeping their backs to the news cameras, the Winchesters made a beeline for the Skydive Launchers hangar. They located the owner of the company, Angie Booth who, though shell-shocked by the triple tragedy, agreed to answer their questions, especially after they presented themselves as insurance adjusters and not members of the press.

"They were all experienced jumpers," she said. Hand trembling nervously, she brushed a dark strand of hair away from her face. "They had made dozens of jumps here. They brought their own gear, packed their own chutes. All three chutes failed, their reserves failed. The AADs should have opened the reserve chutes, even if they were unconscious. I don't understand how this could have happened."

"Did they pack their parachutes today?" Dean asked.

"Yes," Angie said, sweeping her hand around to encompass a broad open area in the hangar. "They packed their main chutes here, along with everyone else who jumped today."

A row of lockers lined the near side of the hangar. Offices ran along the back. Three red and white airplanes faced the entrance. Angie had informed Sam and Dean that she'd cancelled all scheduled jumps for the foreseeable future, pending a full investigation.

Dean tried and failed to suppress a shudder when he looked at the airplanes. Thinking about flying in one of those small planes was enough to make him queasy. The idea of intentionally hurling himself out the side door of one of them at thirteen thousand feet would probably give him nightmares. A belly-flop at terminal velocity onto the unyielding tarmac? *No thanks!* He'd keep his feet firmly planted on the ground.

"What about the reserve chutes, who packed those?" Sam asked.

"We pack the reserves here, every few months so they don't

get stiff," she said. "We have a certified rigger. He's in Antigua this week on a family vacation. He's due back Monday."

"Did the reserves deploy?" Sam pressed.

"Only one out of the three, apparently," she said. "I was in my office when it happened. All three men died within thirty seconds of when their chutes should have opened, maybe ten to fifteen seconds apart."

"Did anyone see the whole thing?" Dean asked.

"You should talk to the pilot."

"Is he here?"

"She," a woman said from behind them.

The attractive woman was in her late twenties and wore a brown leather bomber jacket, black top, distressed denim jeans, and scuffed brown leather boots. Naturally tan, she wore little makeup and her dark brown eyes were red rimmed, as if she had been crying.

"Luna was their pilot," Angie explained. "Luna, these gentleman are insurance adjusters investigating the accident."

"Luna Checchini," the pilot said, offering her hand to shake Sam's and then Dean's before continuing. "I took those guys up a half dozen times. Maybe more. Since they got out of college. They always jumped together. They'd hit on me on the ground, kind of like it was expected of former frat boys, but once we were airborne, they were totally focused on the jump, the thrill of it."

"Any drinking or controlled substances involved?" Dean inquired.

"No, they weren't like that," Luna said. "They got a natural high from the jump itself. I doubt they'd ever mix that with… recreational substances."

"Luna, did you see what happened?" Sam asked her. "After they jumped?"

"Mac—Bob McGlaughlin—jumped last. Just as he pushed off, the plane hit a bit of turbulence and he fell awkwardly. It happened in a split second. I came around as quick as I could. From what I could tell, he never attempted to open his chute. The AAD should've fired, but never did. He hit the ground first."

"What about"—Sam referred to his notes—"Art Polan and Dave Jackson?"

"Art's chute came out tangled," she said softly. "I knew it was his because it was red and green. Christmas colors. Dave's was red, yellow and black. From what I could see, Art tried to fix his chute, but gave up and released it. Right after that he should've pulled the reserve handle. Either he didn't pull it or it malfunctioned. Regardless, his AAD should've fired, releasing the reserve. That never happened."

"And Art?" Dean prompted.

"His main canopy opened too fast and began to tear," Luna continued. "He released it and pulled the reserve. For a few seconds, I thought he, at least, was fine. The reserve opened. But…"

"What happened?"

"His harness seemed to… to slip off him. It pulled away completely."

Sam frowned. "Those harnesses are sturdy, right?"

"Very," Angie interjected. "They have to be."

"The police recovered some of the material," Luna told

them. "One of the forensic guys said the seams came apart and the material crumbled, like it was rotted or something."

"The kind of thing you'd notice when gearing up," Dean said.

"And how do you explain three AADs all malfunctioning?" Angie said. "It doesn't make any sense."

By the time the Winchesters exited the Skydive Launchers hangar, one news van had already left the scene, but the other reporter had finished her interview with the maintenance worker and was headed their way. Fortunately, she and her cameraman were engaged in an animated conversation and failed to notice as Dean and Sam turned toward the parking lot.

Dean was driving out of the lot when Bobby called.

Sam answered and Dean only caught his side of the brief exchange.

"Hey, Bobby, what's up?

"The mall? Hold on." Sam pulled a map out of the glove compartment. Roy had left it for them on the kitchen counter, next to the spare set of house keys.

"Browning Avenue and Route 38— found it. We're less than a mile away.

"Okay."

"What?" Dean asked as soon as Sam ended the call.

"It might be unrelated," Sam prefaced, "but there's a guy waving a handgun around, threatening to shoot people at the mall."

"Wearing a bowler hat?"

EiGHT

The Laurel Hill Mall was a sprawling shopping complex extending over several blocks, with the main mall and its upscale anchor stores in the middle and smaller shopping centers and franchises scattered around it like retail ripples. The largest of the satellites was the Hillcrest Shopping Plaza on the opposite side of Route 38. Shoppers could leave their cars parked in either the mall or plaza parking lots and traverse a covered pedestrian walkway from one side to the other.

Route 38 was a major east-west traffic artery through the heart of the commercial district and convenient for drivers coming from or returning to Philadelphia. Browning Road bisected Route 38 and Dean raced through the lower volume of northbound traffic to the mall's west entrance, darting between cars and interpreting yellow lights as hints to floor the accelerator.

Early into the evening rush hour, the mall parking lot was filling rapidly with after-work shoppers. Many people were paid on Thursdays and felt the need to unburden their bank accounts before the day rolled over. Rather than seeking the closest parking space, Dean swung into the first available slot on the north face of the L-shaped mall. According to Bobby, they would find the gunman in the turn of the L.

As they jumped out of the Monte Carlo, Dean reached under his suit jacket for the automatic tucked in the back of his waistband. Sam caught his elbow and pointed. In the middle of the north face of the mall, an empty police cruiser was parked in a loading zone with its lightbar flashing. That meant at least one cop had already answered the call.

"Remember, we're insurance adjusters," Sam warned. "Not FBI agents. We can't go in guns blazing."

Dean didn't like it, but couldn't argue. In addition to that first responder, more uniforms would likely swarm the mall in minutes and the Winchesters couldn't flash phony FBI credentials this time to excuse gunplay. They had to act as concerned citizens—and as anonymously as possible. Anything to stay off Leviathan radar until they were prepared to take the fight back to the Big Mouths.

As he and Sam entered the mall through the southwest corner doors between Jamaican Nights Restaurant and Urban Apparel, Dean heard a gunshot, followed by panicked screams. People scattered away from the shooter, who stood in front of a display counter at Sparkles Jewelry, waving his gun—a snub-nosed Smith & Wesson—from the crowd to the scared saleswoman behind the counter. No bowler or cane in sight, and the guy looked too short to be the man Ms. Sloney had seen.

A mall security guard in a brown and gold-striped uniform sat slumped against the wall beside the jewelry store, unconscious. At first Dean thought the gunman had shot him, then he saw another body, obstructed by a colorful mini-train, the kind with wheels that drove toddlers in circles in open areas of the mall. Only the victim's leg extended beyond the red caboose of the train, but that was enough to reveal a charcoal gray uniform with gold piping. The leg twitched.

"Sam, he shot a cop," Dean said. "Behind the train."

From the same vicinity, a woman screamed, "Help! He's dying!"

People with wide eyes, clutching shopping bags, streamed past the Winchesters, heading for the nearest exit. Others hid behind support columns or display racks in nearby stores, afraid to move into view and risk the gunman firing at them.

"I'll take the gunman," Sam said. "Go around. Check on the cop."

Sam took a stealthy approach to close the distance to the shooter, while Dean crossed to the far side of the hallway and hurried toward the center of the mall. He looked like another frightened shopper, but with a poor sense of direction, moving away from the exit. As the gunman swiveled his arm back to the saleswoman, Dean moved forward, taking cover behind the locomotive of the train. Ducking, he ran along the arc of the train cars, hidden from view.

A young woman kneeling amid dropped shopping bags was squeezing the left hand of a trembling police officer lying on his back, bleeding from an abdominal gunshot wound. He was moaning and mumbling, eyelids fluttering.

"Please! Help him! He's dying! Do something please—please!"

Untended, the cop would bleed out in minutes, and he was going into shock. Dean peered over the caboose and spotted Sam edging toward the gunman, just on the periphery of his vision. As soon as the guy noticed Sam moving in, he would panic and start shooting in his direction.

Dean grabbed a package of three white T-shirts that had spilled out of a bag. "Listen to me," he whispered urgently to the woman, "I need you to—"

"Please! You have to help him!"

"Lady, you—"

"Hurry! Do—"

"Lady, what's your name—your name?"

"What? Mimi—Mimi Gendron. But I'm not—"

"Mimi, you can do this."

"I don't know h—"

"We need to stop the bleeding," Dean said as he ripped open the pack of T-shirts. He folded two on top of each other and pressed them against the wound

"Press your hands against this. Now!" Mimi nodded and put her hands against the T-shirts, which were already soaking up blood. "Apply pressure. Don't let up. Paramedics will be here in a couple minutes. Just hold tight. Can you do that?"

"Yes—yes!"

"Good," Dean said. "He's going into shock, so we need to keep him warm."

Dean grabbed a sweater dress and two pairs of jeans and wrapped the extra clothing around the trembling cop.

His gun must have flown out of his hand when he was shot. Dean glanced around and spotted the automatic twenty feet back, on the floor under the information counter. After he had lost the gun, the cop must have reached for another weapon from his belt—a black cylinder was slipping from his weak grip. Dean grabbed the extendable baton and snapped it open.

He looked at Mimi, who continued to hold the reddening T-shirts firmly against the cop's blood-soaked abdomen. "You good?"

Lips pressed together nervously, she nodded.

Dean turned away. He lifted his head high enough to peer over the train's red caboose.

"Stop right there!" the gunman shouted. "Or I'll blow your brains out!"

Dean froze.

But the man was facing Sam, who stood ten feet away from him, beside a mirrored support column, hands up, palms out.

"Easy, buddy," Sam said calmly. "Nobody else needs to get hurt here."

"She does," the man shouted, briefly pointing the gun at the saleswoman. "Wouldn't give me a refund for the engagement ring because I didn't have a receipt!"

"Take the money," the woman said. "Take everything you want!"

"I want what's mine," the gunman insisted. "That's all!

But you had to be a bitch about it, didn't you? Just like my girlfriend."

"She wouldn't want you to do this," Sam said, taking half a step closer.

"Lousy bitch! Says I have 'anger management issues!' The hell does she know?"

Sam edged another half step closer.

The man lunged forward and shoved his gun toward Sam's head. "One more step and I ventilate your face!"

"Hey, douchebag," Dean called from behind the gunman.

With the counter on his right, the man spun counterclockwise, bringing the gun across his body toward the new threat. But before he could complete the 180-degree turn, Dean whipped the extended baton down on his wrist. He roared in pain, the revolver falling from his numb fingers, and clutched the injured wrist to his chest. Sam immediately stomped on the back of his right knee and the man collapsed, face first, with Sam following him to the ground. Sam pressed his knee to the gunman's back to subdue him and Dean tossed his brother the pair of handcuffs he had removed from the injured cop's belt.

While the gunman wailed in protest at Sam cuffing his injured wrist behind his back, Dean checked the unconscious security guard. The man was bleeding from a lacerated scalp, but his pulse and breathing were regular. It was probably a concussion, nothing worse.

Shoppers who hadn't fled the mall after the initial gunshot raised their heads slowly from behind displays or came out of stores where they had been hiding, taking in the scene, determining if the situation was safe and, if so, who had neutralized the threat.

Too many eyes, Dean thought, *and cell phones with cameras and internet connections. We cannot be here. Might as well hang out a "come get me" sign for the Big Mouths.*

The sound of approaching sirens only increased Dean's concerns.

Then an explosion roared in the parking lot, followed by shouting and screams.

With this new threat, the cautious shoppers ran for the exit.

Dean looked at Sam in disbelief.

From the north end of the mall, several cops, each with a hand on the butt of their holstered automatic, sprinted toward Sparkles Jewelry. Two EMTs with medical kits followed close behind.

Sam stood and backed away from the moaning shooter.

With his foot, Dean swept the revolver across the floor into the jewelry store.

"Keep that away from crazy-eyes," he instructed the saleswoman, now accompanied by other store employees who had, until moments before, been keeping a healthy distance from the shooter and his intended victim.

Without waiting for a response, Dean and Sam joined the last shoppers fleeing outside.

Evidently a lot had happened since they'd entered the mall. Police at their end of the parking lot had their hands full. Several fender benders clogged the exit lanes. A speeding police car had smashed into the car of a shopper who had tried to race out of the mall lot in the wrong lane. Another car had flipped over the embankment and blown up—the source of the explosion they had heard. Gasoline spilled from several of the accident scenes, running down one of the exit ramps toward the parking lot gridlock.

As Dean scanned the area for any sign of someone wearing a bowler hat or carrying a cane, he spotted a pacing man, nervously puffing on a cigarette, which was already down to a nub. With his middle finger, the man flicked the burning stub away from his thumb. It arced through the air—

Landing in a gleaming puddle of gasoline.

"Oh, crap," Dean said.

Flame roared like an angry serpent across the asphalt and under the row of cars attempting without success to exit the parking lot. Thick smoke from burning tires billowed in the air. More screams sounded as men and woman piled out of cars engulfed from below by the spreading fire.

"Move away from the cars!" Sam shouted at a few gawkers standing around as if watching a fireworks display on the Fourth of July.

A police car rolled slowly along the west face of the mall, lights flashing. The officer inside the cruiser spoke over his loudspeaker, urging people to exit the parking lot via the south-side walkway over Route 38.

One of the cars trapped in the exit lane exploded, the force of the blast raising it in the air and blowing out the windows. When a second car exploded, people dropped any remaining bags they had managed to hold onto and sprinted across the lot as if chased by wolves. A mass of humanity funneled in one direction.

Dean couldn't find fault with the direction of the mass exodus—away from the gasoline fire and exploding cars—but something about it, beyond the potential for trampling, troubled him. A bad situation had become progressively worse with no clear end in sight. Now it seemed like they were waiting for the other shoe to drop.

"This feel… off to you, Sam?"

"Yup. Can't put my finger on why."

"Feels deliberate," Dean said. "Like somebody's pulling the strings."

Together, they trailed behind the crowd massing toward the pedestrian overpass. Everyone slowed as they entered the caged switchback stairs that climbed high enough to pass over the traffic on Route 38. The overpass was encased in cyclone fencing, like a human Habitrail tunnel, to prevent vandals from tossing objects down on the speeding vehicles below.

Before Dean reached the base of the stairs, he glimpsed a tall man in a dark suit standing at the top of the stairs on the opposite side of the tunnel, the Hillcrest Shopping Plaza side, as if waiting for the rush of people to come to him. Though Dean stood one hundred feet and an obstructed view away from the man, he had no doubt about one detail.

He wore a bowler hat.

Nine

Tora's opening gambit—inciting the gun-toting man to violence inside the shopping complex—had begun the wave of panic. But minutes after he pulled back his attention to focus on the larger plan, something or someone prematurely neutralized the enraged man. The restoration of order in the middle of the brewing chaos struck Tora like a psychic hammer blow. His extended awareness had stayed with the man long enough to see immediate law enforcement foiled. Now he paused to reach out with his mind again, and detected a pair of interlopers, wearing business suits, not uniforms. Civilians—or what humans referred to as Good Samaritans. He blamed himself. His attention had wandered. But his plan was in motion and his current situation had greater import.

Even now, the interlopers approached, but they were only

two humans among many and as powerless to stop him as all the rest. Let them witness what they could not stop.

After triggering vehicle accidents, gasoline fires, and explosions, all designed to direct the masses to him across the pedestrian bridge, he prepared to receive them.

He had already studied the myriad cracks in the concrete walkway. With his third eye open, he could trace every tiny fissure, the position and condition of every piece of rebar and, beneath the concrete, he detected every spot of rust and hint of metal fatigue within the supporting framework.

With a sure hand and clear purpose, he brought the ironbound tip of his cane down on the junction of two of the deepest cracks in the concrete. The entire pedestrian overpass shuddered from the targeted impact and, an instant later, the decay accelerated at a phenomenal rate. The cracks spread, deepened and multiplied. Chunks of freed concrete became brittle and crumbled to the consistency of sand. Concrete dust drifted down onto passing cars. Blissfully unaware of the impending danger, motorists flicked on their wipers for a few passes to clear the dust and continued on their way.

The packed crowd fleeing the mall chaos reached the top of the stairs and hurried across the overpass. Those in front soon realized something was wrong. The crumbling concrete gave way beneath their feet, tripping some and frightening others. A wide-eyed woman in a beige business suit stumbled and fell when her high heel slipped into a fissure and snapped off. A man wearing Timberland boots cursed in pain when one of his feet sank through the decking up to his knee.

As the struggling vanguard slowed, those further back yelled and pushed, encouraging those in the lead to keep moving.

From that point, the complete collapse of the pedestrian walkway happened in a matter of seconds. Jammed together and unable to retreat, the scores of people on the bridge had to ride it out, while the motorists passing underneath, preoccupied with jockeying for position in their evening commute, noticed the collapse too late to avoid compounding the tragedy.

Supporting cables buried within the concrete lost tension and began to sag. The sudden increase in weight caused the overpass to buckle, and each sagging movement added additional strain to the decaying metal framework. The whole overpass listed to the west, slowly but inexorably rolling over, like an ocean liner capsizing. With a series of loud pops, the west side of the cyclone fencing broke free from the disintegrating concrete. Those trapped in the middle of the bridge crowd pushed and kicked those in front or behind, desperate to escape in either direction. Men yelled, women screamed and several children wailed in terror.

Realizing retreat was not an option, some men in the lead rushed toward his side of the overpass. As the angle of the bridge became increasingly severe, they struggled to maintain their footing and forward momentum. The few that reached him fell before his cane as he swung it side to side like a club. His powerful blows crushed skulls and broke limbs. Some pedestrians he upended, sweeping their legs out from under them, but the treacherous footing accomplished the rest.

As the deck of the overpass reached a ninety-degree angle,

perpendicular to the highway below, strained metal supports screeched and crumpled. People fell against the cyclone fencing, only to have it give way under their weight and drop them to the speeding traffic below. A few managed to slip fingers through the openings in the fencing, only to have others slam into them from above and knock them loose.

Several who fell were instantly killed by speeding cars and trucks. Others hit the roadway below, breaking limbs, splitting their skulls open, or landing relatively intact a second or two before a car smashed into them.

Seventeen died in the few seconds it took for the motorists to react. But flooring their brake pedals in panicked attempts to halt their vehicles inevitably led to a series of multi-car crashes. A teenaged girl in the passenger seat of a sports car wasn't wearing her seatbelt and crashed through the windshield, crumpling against the side door of a black minivan twenty feet away. A portly man in distressed black leather with a wild gray beard wiped out on his Harley-Davidson, skidded across two lanes of traffic and was crushed under the wheels of a semi that had swung onto the shoulder to avoid a collision with a cement truck.

In the middle of the chaos, Tora noticed the Good Samaritans again, close to the overpass but too far away from the havoc to interfere. Nevertheless, he flicked a tendril of his power in their direction to hobble their efforts further.

People continued to fall from the bridge, slipping through the fencing and dropping violently on the hoods and roofs of cars and trucks. Wails and moans of pain and screams of fear rose like a chaotic symphony over the rush-hour traffic. The moment everyone seemed poised and safe, clinging to twisted sections of rebar or supporting cables or twisted fencing, the whole overpass finally collapsed to the highway below, crushing cars across four lanes of traffic, pinning pedestrians beneath tons of concrete and steel, puncturing arteries, severing limbs, decapitating people. The huge sections of falling steel smashed through the fuel tanks of two cars, one each in the southbound and northbound lanes. The scraping of metal against metal created showers of sparks, which ignited spilt fuel and led to more explosions. Pools of flaming gasoline spread across multiple lanes of traffic, burning pedestrians and drivers trapped in their vehicles.

With each accident, he sought to maximize the level of death and destruction. Flesh wounds became broken bones and impalements, severed limbs and decapitations. Similarly, fuel spills became fires and explosions. The radius of death and destruction spread outward like ripples from one dropped stone.

But every symphony reaches a crescendo and he felt he had wrung as much enjoyment from this opportunity as possible. While the energy he expended to create the havoc had exhausted his resources, the resulting pain, misery and grief replenished him and more.

The devastation gave him enough energy to reach out across the bustling town of Laurel Hill and claim it, his vibrations thrumming to the core of it. Those ripples would produce the desired effect. A call to violence and destruction.

The switchback stairs on his end of the overpass

remained relatively intact, held together by his will to facilitate his exit. Ignoring the cries behind him, he descended the stairs with a buoyancy in his step he hadn't experienced in a long time. He crossed the parking lot of the Hillcrest Shopping Plaza, climbed into the plumber's van and navigated several back streets to avoid the gridlock he'd created.

Sam pushed his way through the frightened crowd, Dean at his side, as the pedestrian overpass crumbled and collapsed. Then Dean vanished, replaced by Lucifer, who cheered and clapped as pedestrians fell to their deaths.

"Hell of a party you got here, Sam," Lucifer said. "I should know. Right?"

Sam edged forward, but Lucifer caught his arm.

"Watch this one, big guy."

In the middle of the highway, a man in a tan blazer, face bleeding, fell to his knees a moment before the grill of a white Ford pickup crushed his head against the rear bumper of a Mazda Tribute.

"Woo, boy! That skull burst like a ripe melon!"

Shut up, Sam thought intently. *Shut up!*

"Little help here, Bunky," Lucifer said as he grabbed an elderly woman by the nape of her neck. "Let's make pancakes together."

Lucifer pushed the woman forward, ignoring her hysterical screams, and shoved her under the wheels of a speeding commercial van.

Sam squeezed his eyes shut, flinched when he heard the

wet thud, and speared his right thumbnail into the scar on his left palm.

Through the press of rushing, shoving bodies, Dean saw the tall man in the bowler hat slam something downward. Instantly, the overpass shuddered, as if in the throes of an earthquake. Many people had crammed into the caged switchback staircase, with those in the lead already nearing the top. Nervous shouting followed. Several people yelled, "Hurry!" or "Move!"

As another car explosion sounded from the parking lot behind them, the crowd pushed forward with renewed urgency. Dean wanted to reach the guy in the bowler, but the mass of humanity flowing up the staircase blocked him. With the nearest traffic light a couple of hundred yards away, dodging cars across four lanes of speeding traffic was the next best option.

"Sam! It's Frogger time."

When he got no response, he turned and discovered his brother had fallen several steps behind. Sam stood motionless, staring off into space, his left hand gripped in his right.

"Sam!"

Dean ran back and shook Sam's shoulder. "Sammy!"

Sam, startled, focused on Dean's face. "I'm okay. Fine. What?"

Dean pointed to the far side of the crowded overpass. "Bowler!"

Sam looked where Dean pointed. "Where? Oh, I saw the hat—for a moment."

"We'll lose him in the crowd unless we cross the highway," Dean said.

"Right." Sam nodded. "Good idea."

"Sam, are you with me?"

Dean had a horrible fleeting image of his brother freezing halfway across the highway, staring off into space as a pickup truck bowled him over like a tenpin, shattering every bone in his body. "On second thought, you wait here. I'll cross. We can trap him between us."

As Dean ran toward the highway, the overpass deterioration accelerated. The whole caged tunnel began to roll over like a log in a stream. Chunks of concrete dropped to the highway, followed by falling people, slipping through the loose fencing. When a few attempted to exit the far side of the bridge, the man in the bowler struck them down. Everyone who had reached the bridge was trapped, screaming, falling and dying. Cars smashed into falling pedestrians or slammed into other vehicles, creating fuel spills, ruptured fuel tanks and more explosions. If racing across the highway had been a dangerous proposition before, now it was certain death.

Dean hesitated for a fraction of a second, then trotted briskly back to his brother. "Plan B."

Unable to assist the fallen, they guided people away from the overturned stairwell.

"This way," Sam shouted, directing people east, parallel to the fires and explosions.

Dean nodded and steered people west. By splitting the crowd into two groups, they minimized the potential for trampling.

For a quarter-mile on either side of the overpass collapse, wrecked and burning vehicles jammed all lanes of traffic. Because many drivers had swerved off the road to avoid major collisions, the shoulders were also packed with vehicles. Several ambulances approached from the east and west on Route 38, but their drivers had to stop well short of the injured and proceed on foot with emergency kits and stretchers. Other emergency vehicles—fire trucks and police cruisers—entered the mall parking lot from the east and north entrances to tackle the fires and treat the injured.

After the crowd from the caged staircase had dispersed, Dean and Sam approached the wreckage. Movement on the other side of the highway caught Dean's eye. Metal creaked and twanged as the staircase on the far side tilted forward, performing a slow-motion collapse onto the road surface. Dean tried to remember when he had lost track of the man in the bowler. He had seen the man striking down pedestrians who tried to make it across the bridge, immediately before it collapsed. Somehow Dean doubted the stranger had suffered the same fate as his victims. His staircase had stood long enough for him to retreat to the south, and the smaller shopping center on the other side of Route 38 would provide cover for his escape. By the time they crossed the highway, the man in the bowler would be long gone.

"Dean!" Sam called.

This time Dean had been the one staring off into space.

Sam scrambled over the toppled staircase and edged into the remains of the smoking demolition derby. Within seconds, he was coughing uncontrollably.

* * *

With the cruiser's siren wailing and lights flashing, Sergeant McClary drove with controlled recklessness through the streets of Laurel Hill. Initially, the mall shooting had been the destination, but reports soon came in about the collapsing pedestrian overpass, along with an impromptu demolition derby on Route 38. Riding shotgun, Bobby realized before McClary that the logjam ahead posed a real problem to any further forward progress.

"Looks like we hoof it from here."

McClary shook his head. "Not just yet."

With short, strategic blasts of his siren, the sergeant managed to coax several drivers far enough out of the lane for him to squeeze through. But he gained only a hundred yards at best and the pace was so deliberate Bobby wondered if walking would have been faster.

He saw the overpass ahead, in the final stages of a violent collapse, and spotted one lone tall, dark figure escape on the right side. Bobby leaned forward for a better look, but the man slipped between parked cars in the Hillcrest Shopping Plaza.

"Let's go!" McClary said, now out of the cruiser and already moving toward the mall.

Bobby nodded, then turned back to where he had last seen the tall man, but he was gone.

Tires had exploded, sending chunks of burning rubber in all directions. Radiators had burst, and car upholsteries continued to burn, releasing toxic fumes over the area in a sickening cloud. Before following Sam onto the highway,

Dean rifled through several dropped shopping bags and found a cotton dress. He ripped it to form a long strip of cloth that he tied like a kerchief, covering his nose and mouth, to cut down on the amount of noxious fumes he inhaled. After ripping another strip, he passed it to Sam.

"Wear this," Dean said. "Maybe you won't get lung cancer by next Wednesday."

They looked like Wild West bank robbers.

The masks helped with their breathing, but offered no relief for their eyes. As Dean squeezed through the wreckage, looking for survivors, his eyes burned and swam with tears. A mass of bodies lined the west edge of the collapsed overpass. Dean lost track of the number of severed limbs, but noted three decapitated heads. In the jumble of corpses they found no survivors, so they worked back away from the bridge, checking cars.

They searched for several minutes before finding a survivor, a young man buckled in the back seat of a car in which three other passengers had died. The rear passenger door had crumpled in the frame, pinning it shut, but Dean reached in through the broken window and, with Sam's help, pulled him clear and carried him to the side of the road. He looked like he had broken both ankles and the wrist of the arm he had flung out to brace himself.

Firefighters on both sides of the collapsed pedestrian bridge were spraying foam over the gasoline fires, working their way inward. Paramedics eased wheeled stretchers in between wrecked and disabled cars, seeking injured to treat. By this time, police from the mall and both sides of Route

38 had made their way into the heart of the destruction. Once the official first responders had control of the vast accident area, one of the cops ordered Sam and Dean off the highway.

Sam started to protest, to insist that they could help, but Dean caught his arm and whispered, "Low profile, remember?"

So they nodded and returned to the side of the road.

"I wonder if the junker survived," Dean said.

"What?"

"The Monte Carlo," Dean explained, "stuck in car hell back there."

Sam noticed a couple of men approaching them, one in an overcoat, a thick folder under one arm, hurrying to gain separation from the other in a charcoal gray police uniform. He pointed them out to Dean.

"Bobby. About time he showed up."

When Bobby was close enough to whisper to them, he said, "Sent you boys to stop a lone gunman, not blow up an overpass. The hell happened here?"

"The perp in the bowler hat," Dean said. "We saw him on the bridge."

"Spotted someone on the other side. Too far away to do diddly," Bobby said.

"Agent Willis!" the cop, a sergeant, called.

"Go on ahead, McClary," Bobby called back to him. "Getting a statement from these witnesses. I'll catch up."

McClary waved and strode out into the highway to assess the situation.

"What's up with Sergeant McClary?" Sam asked.

"Assigned to me by the chief," Bobby said. "Supervised Roy's son."

"Are those police files?" Dean asked, indicating the folder under Bobby's arm.

"Back up," Bobby said. "'Bowler hat'?"

Sam briefed Bobby on Michelle Sloney's account of the three roofers and the man in a dark suit and bowler walking past her house at the time of the accident.

"You definitely both saw him here?" Bobby asked.

"Dean saw him," Sam said. "I… missed him in the crowd."

"Hold on." Bobby opened the Manila folder and flicked through pages of reports and photocopies of crime scene photos. "Here," he said, finding a grainy still image and pulling it out to show Dean. "Taken from a traffic cam feed."

Dean looked at the photo of a tall man in a dark suit standing at an intersection. Because the traffic camera focused on vehicular traffic and not pedestrians, the man was almost out of the frame and most of his body was obstructed by the traffic light pole. But Dean had no doubt that the hat obscuring his face from the camera's eye was a bowler.

"Gotta be the same guy," Dean said. "Where was this taken?"

"Ground zero at this morning's rush-hour pile-up."

Tora settled onto a bar stool at Dale's Fireside Tavern with a frosty glass beer mug and ordered a round for the house. He was in a celebratory mood and the burst of appreciative cheers and applause almost made him regret what he planned next. A flat-screen TV mounted on the wall showed a news bulletin with helicopter footage of the overpass collapse. He tried not to stare. A smile would have been as unavoidable as it was inappropriate in a sympathetic environment. But the audio was turned down and nobody among the after-work crowd seemed to notice the human tragedy.

"What's the occasion?" the bartender asked.

After a sip of draft beer, he smiled and said, "I gave a killer presentation today."

"Good for you."

The beer was an excuse to mingle in a crowded environment. When the bartender drifted away to take an order, Tora left his stool and walked into the men's room. Alone, he opened his third eye just enough to see what lived on the surfaces of door handles, counter, faucets, and the towel dispenser. Within a few seconds, he located a common strain of flu virus on the edge of a stall door and proceeded to make it uncommon and highly virulent.

Because the personal touch was so important, before he left the bar, he circulated for a few minutes, shaking the hands of some of those enjoying their free drink—and spreading the virus on multiple surfaces for maximum impact.

As he crossed the parking lot to his stolen van, he imagined he heard the sound of dry coughing from within the tavern. If the incubation period for the viral strain he mutated was that brief, he really had outdone himself. A stellar day.

TEN

Sam stood in the Laurel Hill Mall, beside the mirrored support column near Sparkles Jewelry. Against his own advice to Dean, he took out his gun and aimed it at the head of the crazed gunman. For the moment, the man hadn't noticed Sam. He faced the frightened saleswoman, waving his own gun around while demanding a refund for the engagement ring.

Instead of returning the diamond ring in its padded jewelry box, the gunman had brought it back on the ring finger of his fiancée's severed left hand. Blood dripped from just behind the wrist. It looked like the hand had been chopped off with an axe.

"I put it on her finger," the man said, spraying spittle as he raised the severed hand. "But apparently *this* doesn't count!"

He slapped the severed hand onto the glass countertop for emphasis.

The saleswoman shrieked.

"Gotta put him down, Sam. He is one sick puppy," Lucifer whispered in Sam's ear. He patted Sam's shoulder. "Takes one to know one, right?"

The automatic trembled in Sam's hand.

"In five seconds, that saleswoman's brain is tapioca," Lucifer said. "But, hey, I love me some tapioca."

"No!" Sam said, drawing the man's attention.

The gunman's head whipped around. Sam fired the automatic, blasting a hole through his forehead. At the exact moment his head snapped back, the face changed, became Dean's.

Dean collapsed to his knees, staring vacantly at Sam as blood trickled down either side of his nose. Then he fell over sideways.

"Oops," Lucifer said. "Did *not* see that coming."

Sam started forward, in shock, but stopped as someone rushed toward him from the right. He spun to face the crazed gunman again.

"Who the hell are you?" the man shouted, raising his gun.

In reply, Sam raised his own gun in a smooth, practiced motion and fired three rounds into the man's chest.

Stopping abruptly, the gunman looked down and pressed his hand against the fabric of his shirt. Blood welled over his fingers, oozing downward in thick streams. When he looked back up at Sam he wore a trucker hat and his face belonged to Bobby.

"Son, why…?" he asked, before pitching forward.

"Oh, my," Lucifer said. "What are the odds?"

"No," Sam said, shaking his head violently. "No! This is not happening."

Lucifer smiled, arms spread, palms up. "Bright side, buddy," he said. "Just the two of us from now on." He crossed the index and middle fingers of his left hand. "And we're like this."

"No!" Sam shouted again. He lunged forward—

And almost fell off Roy's sofa.

He breathed deeply in the predawn light and ran a trembling hand through his hair. *So much for a restful night's sleep*, he thought.

Of the three of them, Dean woke last on Friday morning. Sam stood over the breakfast nook table, papers and photos spread out, while Bobby had covered every square inch of space on the kitchen counter with more police files. Dean stretched, looked from one man to the other. "Tell me that's coffee I smell."

"A fresh pot," Sam confirmed.

"Help yourself, Mr. Van Winkle," Bobby said without looking up.

"Hey, I still got harpy smackdown aches and pains." Dean poured himself a mug of coffee and downed about half of it before speaking again. "Anything make sense yet?"

Before Dean had nodded off the night before, they had gone through the police reports, accident scene photos and witness statements until his vision blurred. After hours of analysis they had come to the conclusion that Laurel Hill was an unlucky town. Incredibly unlucky. If it hadn't been for the presence of the man in the bowler hat near all the accidents,

Dean might just have advised the mayor to start passing out rabbit's feet and four-leaf clovers to all residents.

"Like something telling us where to find Waldo?" Bobby asked. "No. Nothing like that."

"These witness statements," Sam said, thinking out loud, "maybe the police are asking the wrong questions."

"Do the victims have anything in common?" Dean wondered.

Bobby picked up a legal tablet filled with handwritten notes. "First known incident, three experienced roofers fall, one after the other."

"The woman who owned the house gave herself a black eye running back to dial 911," Sam added. "Then injured her hand."

"Plain old clumsiness," Dean suggested.

"Maybe," Bobby said. "The timing of her clumsiness, though... Some kind of after-effect of whatever made the roofers fall?"

"It was just after she saw Steed," Dean said. "Bowler guy."

Bobby read from his notes. "Few blocks away, David Boyce chainsaws his femoral artery, bleeds out."

"Close enough for bowler guy to have walked there," Dean said.

"Thursday morning rush-hour pile-up is next," Bobby continued. "Everyone in the accident died. From the traffic cam, we know bowler man was there." He flipped through several pages. "McClary gave me a list of witnesses. Bystanders. Few drivers far back enough they weren't involved in the chain reaction."

"Okay, but if it is him, what's his M.O.? Was there anything helpful on the traffic cam footage?" Sam asked.

"Stands there like he ain't got a care in the world," Bobby said. "Walks away when the emergency vehicles show up."

"The bus accident's next," Sam said. "Excluding the fitness center casualties, the bus driver died and one passenger. But is there a connection to our guy?"

"Hold on," Bobby said. "Got a transit map here.

"Yup. Intersection of the pile-up is a scheduled stop for that bus."

"So he saw the bus passing or—"

"He was on the bus," Sam finished for Dean, "and got off at that stop."

"Do we have names for the other passengers?"

"That we do," Bobby said, holding up a page. "When the police questioned them, nobody mentioned our tall stranger. But, like you said, maybe they didn't ask the right questions."

"Sam and I can question them," Dean suggested.

Bobby nodded. "After the pile-up and bus crash," he said, "we have a series of accidents: Deanna Roe, married mother of two boys, trips down the stairs carrying a laundry hamper, breaks her neck. Hal Norville, divorced anesthesiologist, falls stepping out of the shower and splits his head open. Suffers massive stroke. Gertrude Finney, retired spinster, dies in a lint-trap fire. Only pattern so far is no pattern."

"How far apart were the accidents, geographically?" Sam asked.

Bobby checked his notes, rubbed his eyes. "Same block. Parry Lane. Location is the pattern."

Dean frowned. "Being round this guy is like having a black cat cross your path, times a hundred."

"Better watch out for Roy's stray, then," Bobby commented.

"Actually, having a black cat cross your path is considered lucky in some cultures, like Britain and Japan," Sam said.

"Anyway, the skydivers were friends back in college," he continued quickly, seeing Dean and Bobby's blank expressions.

"Reeks of wrong plane, wrong time," Bobby said, shaking his head. "Could've been three strangers."

"The three roofers knew each other, too," Dean said.

"Wrong roof," Bobby countered. "Victims of opportunity."

He lifted a page from a neat stack. "Two more incidents before the mall: Roger Basely fell asleep on the couch while smoking, and Mildred Dottery suffocated under newspapers."

"Suffocated?"

"Newspapers from Jimmy Carter's heyday," Bobby explained. "Hoarder. Both victims lived on Lafferty Lane."

"The mall shooter," Dean prompted.

Bobby picked up his notepad. "Shaun Benton," he said. "McClary checked him for priors. Couple domestic disturbance calls, bar fights, assault and battery."

Dean frowned. "McClary—d'you trust him?" he asked Bobby suddenly.

"Reason I shouldn't?"

"No reason," Dean said. *When the Leviathan can look like anybody,* he thought, *anybody could be a Leviathan.*

"This Benton guy admitted he had anger management issues," Sam said, "but something pushed him over the edge."

"Or someone, pushing his buttons," Dean said. "Bowler

guy was definitely there, at the mall."

"So, maybe instead of pushing the shooter physically, he pushed him mentally," Bobby suggested,

"Could be this guy has no pattern," Dean said. "No plan. Just create random friggin' havoc."

"Distracted and sleep-deprived drivers," Sam said, thinking out loud again, "careless chainsaw operator… It's like that expression: an accident waiting to happen."

"Except bowler guy's tired of waiting."

"We can't predict when, where or who. So maybe we can figure out how, or why."

"He enjoys it," Dean said grimly. "When he was swinging his cane on the bridge, I swear he was smiling."

"We'll get this sumbitch," Bobby said. "I'll ask McClary to check every video feed he's got. Guy in a bowler hat with a cane should stick out like a stretch limo at a muscle car convention."

"Good," Dean said, "because we got no clue what's next."

ELEVEN

"Bomb threat," Ryan Bramble scoffed. "Load of crap, more like."

The entire student body of Laurel Hill High School—the beige brick monstrosity, as he thought of it—had been evacuated to the open field across the street from the school and its parking lot. Each teacher tried to keep his or her students corralled in a separate area, matching faces to names on their attendance sheets to make sure everyone had left the building, but friends inevitably strayed across the imaginary lines to talk to one another.

Standing with his balled fists shoved into the pockets of his black jeans, Ryan faced the entrance of the school, where two regular cop cars and two K-9 SUVs occupied the bus lane, and couldn't help feeling irritation at the intrusion.

"What's your theory, Ryan?" Sumiko Jones, his girlfriend,

asked as she pointed her cell phone camera up at him. They shared a government class that period so they wouldn't catch any flak for hanging out during the evacuation.

He flipped a strand of cobalt-blue hair out of his eyes and raised a hand in front of her camera lens. "Don't record me for your blog."

"Okay, Mr. Crankypants," she said, smiling. "You'll be an anonymous source. Tell me what's going on?"

"Isn't it obvious?"

"Bomb-sniffing dogs searched the perimeter of the building and now they're checking inside," Sumiko said and pursed her lips. The fire-engine-red lip gloss matched the outer layer of her black and red top. Her pitch-black hair was styled in a pixie cut, though he preferred her hair long, as it had been when they first started dating in junior year. "I'm going out on a limb here, but I'm gonna say they're searching for a bomb."

"That's what they want you to think," Ryan said. "Actually, it's a drug sweep."

"Why search the exterior?"

Ryan placed his hands on her shoulders and looked down at her with a shake of his head. Even wearing her three-inch black platform boots with all the buckles, she was almost a foot shorter than his six-five frame. He had always been taller than her, but had gone through a six-inch growth spurt in the last year, while her height had probably maxed out. Sometimes he felt like a clumsy ox around her. Coaches for the various Laurel Hill Lions sports teams took notice of his size, but he wasn't graceful or athletic. "They want to keep us off guard."

She arched an eyebrow. "Are you worried about something in your locker?"

"You'd know if I had anything."

"Ha!"

"Like I can keep secrets from the Lion Truth blogger."

"Shh!"

"What? It's not a secret. Your name's on the blog. You're live-blogging the evacuation now, aren't you?"

"True, but if I keep reminding everyone, they get nervous and stop talking." She typed furiously on her cell phone as she spoke to him. "And... posted!"

"Writing about me?"

"No," she said. "And I'm not posting your theory either. I don't buy it, Bramble."

"Why not?"

"Haven't you been reading my blog?"

"Who can keep up?" he said. "You know, you could write for the school paper."

"Nah," she scoffed. "Too structured. Nothing but puff pieces. I write what I want when I want to write it. And you haven't been reading it. All the strange accidents happening around town the last couple days. Totally bizarre."

"I don't watch or read the news," Ryan said. "I've got my own problems. Besides, why do you even care about that stuff?"

"Maybe it's happening here, now," Sumiko said, jerking her thumb over her shoulder toward the school.

"We could use some excitement," he said sullenly.

"Wow," she said, shocked. "I thought you were joking, Ryan. But you really don't have a clue."

"I don't want to talk about it, okay?"

"Wait, there's Rachel Barish," Sumiko said. "I heard she was in the principal's office when the bomb threat call came in."

Ryan trailed after her, exasperated. "How could you know that?"

Sumiko held her phone up over her shoulder and waved it toward him, as if he could read the display while she jogged away. "Kassidy Barish, her sister, texted me. Rachel signed in late. Orthodontist appointment."

"Mr. Bramble, where do you think you're going?"

"Nowhere," Ryan said, stopping in his tracks.

Mr. Detrick, his government teacher, was a real hard ass, especially where Ryan was concerned. Sometimes it was like he was looking for an excuse to have Ryan suspended. In fact, all of his teachers watched him as if they expected him to go postal. With his size and dyed blue hair, he would never be inconspicuous. Maybe that was part of the problem. Sumiko, on the other hand, could run laps around the entire student body or jump rope in the middle of the street and none of the teachers would raise an eyebrow. She always seemed like she had a purpose. At one time, Ryan thought he might be college bound. Up until this year, he'd had good grades and attendance. He hadn't aced every course like Sumiko, but he held his own. Lately, though, his academic efforts had come up short. As and Bs had drifted down to Cs and now a few Ds. He tried to study longer, reviewed material repeatedly, but that only produced tension headaches, not better grades. Sumiko tutored him in the classes they shared and that helped to a degree, but he continued to fall behind. Maybe he knew, subconsciously, that it was futile. His father worked two jobs, but could never afford to send Ryan to college. More likely, Ryan would need a job to help out with household expenses. Or maybe the thought of losing Sumiko had triggered a defeatist spiral. He simply couldn't keep up with her. After this year, she would attend some prestigious university somewhere far from Laurel Hill, leaving him behind to flip burgers for minimum wage, completely forgotten.

Adding to his growing isolation, he hardly ever saw his father lately, and when they were together, they never talked. Not really. Ryan could feel his life slipping away and each day the frustration grew inside him, building up so much pressure he wanted to scream and pound his fists against the wall. Maybe his teachers sensed it. Maybe they were right to be wary of him.

Sumiko slipped back beside Ryan the moment Detrick looked the other way.

"You're like a ninja," he whispered.

"Are you being racist?" she asked, smiling to take the sting out of it.

"Cat burglar, then," he said. "Get anything bloggable?"

"Nothing good. Rachel was there when the call came in. They called the principal to the phone. She heard some whispering. One of them grabbed a procedural manual off a shelf. Someone else called the police."

He leaned over so he could talk to her privately, without

the rest of his government class eavesdropping. "Miko, do you think…?"

"What?"

"I mean, is something wrong with me?"

"Well, if you don't stop growing, I'll need a stepladder to kiss you."

"I'm serious." He looked around nervously. "Ever feel like you don't belong?"

"It's called being a teenager, doofus."

"Do you—?"

The sounds of angry shouting were coming from two classroom groups away. Ryan saw somebody shove someone. "Get away from her, creep! No! I don't care! That perv was sniffing her hair!"

Of course, Sumiko was instantly filming the skirmish.

In the blink of an eye, she had turned her attention somewhere else. Maybe it was just as well. He doubted he could have told her what he was feeling, because he wasn't sure himself. Trapped and desperate summed it up.

"That's Tyler Shackleford, one of the Lion's linebackers, shoving and shouting at Dalton Rourke, who's been suspended more often than a busload of avid bungee jumpers," Sumiko said, speaking for the microphone, not for Ryan's benefit.

"Bungee jumpers travel in buses?" Ryan wondered aloud, knowing she would ignore him while she was live-blogging.

"And the strawberry-blonde tresses in question belong to the statuesque Jennifer Martin, who's been dating young Tyler since last year's Holiday Ball."

Tyler pushed Dalton again, then a third time, shaking off gym teacher Mr. Gadsen's restraining hand. At first Dalton, who was at least Tyler's equal in size and build, took the abuse, but his face was rapidly turning beet red from his neck to his buzz-cut red hair. Looking at him, Ryan knew Dalton was about to explode.

"Don't do it," he whispered.

But, as Ryan had expected, the next shove triggered Dalton's retaliation. He roared and lunged forward, striking Tyler high on both shoulders while hooking one of his ankles with a heel. Tyler fell back onto the grass and, in a second, Dalton had dropped to a knee beside him and raised a fist to punch him in the face.

Mr. Gadsen hooked Dalton's elbow before he could strike. Then Mr. Detrick grabbed Dalton's other arm. Together they pulled him away. As Tyler climbed to his feet, looking abashed at having lost the upper hand, Gadsen barked, "Both of you report to the vice principal's office when we're done here."

"It's his fault," Tyler said, placing a possessive arm around Jennifer's shoulders. "That freak was sniffing her hair like a dog. Right, Jen?"

Looking embarrassed, Jennifer hugged her elbows tight against her body and nodded slightly.

"This is bullshit," Dalton said. "I was defending myself."

"True that," agreed zombie-pale Jimmy Ferrato, one of Dalton's few friends.

"The vice principal's office," Gadsen repeated, pointing at Dalton and Tyler, his hands cocked like six shooters.

"Both of you."

The teachers made them separate, but Tyler looked back and pointed at Dalton, mouthing the words, "You're dead, punk."

When his back was turned, Dalton flipped him the bird.

"Posted!" Sumiko said. "That will generate a lot of hits tonight."

"And that matters because…?"

"If I get enough hits, I can monetize," Sumiko explained. "Feed my tech needs, clothes, car, exotic vacations." She shrugged with an impish grin. "The sky's the limit."

"That's what you care about?"

"No, Bramble," she said. "I want to get the worrying-about-finances part of my life out of the way, so I have time for the stuff I really care about."

"And what stuff is that?"

"I'll have the rest of my life to figure that out!"

Everyone started talking at once. Ryan looked up and saw the police and K-9 units come out of the school. One of the cops spoke with the principal and vice principal, who had been standing in the school parking lot during the search, before heading to his cruiser. The principal waved to the students to return to the building. The mass slowly walked forward, waiting for a cop to stop traffic while they crossed the street.

"Jackrabbit," Sumiko said.

"What?"

She pointed.

Dalton Rourke and Jimmy Ferrato were sprinting in the

opposite direction, turning out of sight behind a row of houses. Of course, Sumiko caught their escape with her cell phone camera.

The moment they were gone, Sumiko bumped into Ryan with her hip and nodded toward the far side of the crowd, where a young man with a shaved head and earrings, wearing a battered leather coat, jeans and black boots, was watching the students and teachers. He winced as he massaged his temples. It looked like a bad hangover. As the students returned to the school, he took a perpendicular course toward the row of houses, away from the cop at the intersection, head bowed.

"That's Jesse Trumball," Sumiko said, intrigued.

"Yeah. So?"

"So, he dropped out months ago," Sumiko said. "Why's he at a school evacuation?"

"Because he misses us?"

"As if," Sumiko said, simultaneously tapping away on her touchscreen keyboard. "Nope. Mr. Trumball called in the bomb threat."

"Miko! You can't post that on your blog," Ryan said. "That's slander."

"*Written* defamation is libel," Sumiko explained. "What I just *said* was slander." She reached up and wrapped her hand around the back of his neck, tugging him down for a quick kiss on the cheek. "But you won't turn me in, will you, sweetie?"

"Of course not," he said, but she had already turned back to her cell phone.

He hardly ever had her attention anymore, and even then she divided her focus between him and the phone. Every day the scale seemed to be tipping further out of balance with her and he felt helpless to stop it.

They walked back inside together, but Ryan might as well have been alone.

TWELVE

Bobby called ahead and met Sergeant McClary in his Laurel Hill Police Department office. McClary leaned back in his office chair, one hand clicking on a mouse as he scanned his computer monitor, the other holding a clear plastic cup containing a banana-strawberry smoothie, which he sipped through a thick straw. When he saw Bobby, he grinned sheepishly and waggled the cup. "To ward off low blood sugar."

"That'll do it."

He motioned Bobby to a seat in front of his desk. "What can I do for you, Agent Willis?"

"Couple things," Bobby said. He opened the folder he was carrying and removed the grainy traffic cam photo of the man wearing the bowler hat from the top of the stack. "Consider this gentleman a person of interest."

McClary leaned forward in his chair. "I remember him. He stood there during the massive pile-up. The guy might be guilty of retro fashion sense and incredible apathy toward human suffering, but nothing illegal, surely." McClary took a long sip of his smoothie while Bobby stared at him. "What? You think he's part of the burglary ring?"

"Same guy walked by the triple roofer accident."

McClary set his cup down. "Really?"

"According to Michelle Sloney," Bobby said, neglecting to mention that the Winchester boys had been the ones to interview her, and leaving Dean out as a witness on the overpass. "My advice, pull every video feed you've got. See how often this guy shows up near trouble."

"Good idea," McClary said, nodding. "Maybe we've got evidence of him doing... something to set these things in motion. You know what's weird?"

"All ears."

"We had all kinds of makes and models of vehicles involved in that hellacious pile-up —foreign and domestic, models spanning fifteen years, give or take— and not one airbag deployed." McClary said. "Not a single damn one. Logistically, how is that even possible?"

Unless every airbag in town is a malfunction waiting to happen? Bobby thought. Not a theory he wanted to test personally— or suggest to McClary. He'd lose all credibility with the man.

"Maybe some kind of EMP device that disables impact sensors."

"Who knows? I'll get this cleaned up if we can't find a better photo," McClary said, indicating the traffic cam shot.

"Release it to the press. Bring him in for questioning, if nothing else. What's the other thing?"

"The bus crash," Bobby said. "I'd like to interview a couple of the passengers."

"That crash happened about a half-mile away from the pile-up," McClary said. "D'you think they're related, other than by timing?"

"That bus stops at that intersection," Bobby said significantly.

"But it wasn't involved in the…" McClary stopped mid-thought. "Maybe the guy in the hat rode the bus to that stop."

"It's a thought."

McClary exhaled forcefully. "I don't know," he said. "The bus was checked for mechanical failure. The brakes worked fine. The driver simply keeled over. I don't see how they connect."

"Not a big fan of coincidences, sergeant."

"Okay," McClary said. "We're spinning our wheels—no pun intended—so I'll ask the county M.E. to treat the bus driver as a possible homicide. They'll check the body for punctures or anything that might not show up on a routine tox screen."

"I'd like to talk to a few of his passengers, and covering our other bases, anyone who witnessed the pile-up."

"Sure," McClary said. "We got statements from a few people who were closest to the driver. It seemed like another unfortunate but unconnected accident at the time. As far as the pile-up, we talked to one woman walking her Yorkie, but she took cover pretty quick." McClary clicked his mouse a

couple of times, typed briefly on his keyboard. "Hold on…
Printing the names now. Be right back."

Bobby waited while McClary stepped outside his office to
pull a page off one of the network printers. When McClary
returned, he handed Bobby the printout before returning to
his chair. "For what it's worth, anyway," McClary said. "Keep
me posted if it pans out."

Bobby stood and had turned to leave when McClary's
phone rang. With a nod of thanks, Bobby backed out to
give the man some privacy. But McClary held up his hand,
signaling Bobby to wait.

"Yes, I did," McClary said into the phone. "Yesterday
evening. Sure." Snatching a pen out of a desk caddy, McClary
wrote down some information in sloppy cursive. "Thanks."
He hung up the phone and shook his head. "I'm really
starting to hate coincidences."

"What?" Bobby asked, his turn to be intrigued.

"A missing person report came in yesterday from one"—
he paused to check his notes—"Liana Bekakos, bookkeeper-
slash-receptionist for Kiriakoulis Plumbing. It seems the
owner, Frank Kiriakoulis, never returned from his last job.
The uniform who took the report assumed Frank decided to
spend a long weekend in Atlantic City, blow off some steam."

"Meaning Frank's vehicle is missing as well?"

"White van, commercial plates," McClary said, smiling like
the cat who'd swallowed the canary. "Kiriakoulis Plumbing
painted on the side panels."

"Either I'm slow," Bobby said, "or you've got one hell of
a hole card."

"I put an alert in the system for anything else unusual related to the streets where we've had these bizarre accidents. And yesterday we had two fatalities on Lafferty Lane."

"Guy burned on his sofa and the hoarder."

"Care to guess the street address of Frank's last job?"

"Find that van," Bobby said, "maybe we find Mr. Chapeau."

"Tie him to grand theft," McClary said. "Possible kidnapping."

Bobby suddenly looked solemn. "I've got a bad feeling Frank's no longer among the living."

"Look, I wasn't hungry, okay?"

"I'm not criticizing, Dean," Sam said. He was sitting in the passenger seat of the miraculously unscathed Monte Carlo, looking over the list of bus passengers Bobby had passed to them. "It's commendable you gave up your last breakfast sausage to a feral cat."

Led Zeppelin's "Immigrant Song" faded and the classic rock station began a block of commercials. Dean lowered the volume on the radio.

"He's not feral," Dean said, bristling. "He's got a name. Shadow."

"Right."

"He's more like an outdoor cat," Dean continued, frowning. "Look, Roy guilted me into it. We took over his house. We can't let his damn cat starve."

"I agree."

"Fine," Dean said. "Where to?"

"A twofer," Sam said, tapping the list. "Janice Cummings and Felicia Akop rode the bus together. Both work at Salon Colette."

He checked his map and relayed the directions to Dean.

Dean noticed a slight tremor in Sam's hands.

"Everything okay in Sammy-land?"

Sam shot him a quick glance, then looked away, as if worried Dean might see something in his eyes. "I'm—fine. Fine."

"Which you would say even if you weren't?" Dean asked.

"No," Sam replied. "Just the usual, you know. There's a baseline…"

"A baseline of crazy?"

"Of stuff I need to deal with," Sam said, "every day."

"Your new normal?"

"Right," Sam said with a hint of a smile. "This and that. I deal."

"And that doesn't change?" Dean asked. "Ever?"

"Sometimes it… catches me off guard."

Sometimes Dean worried that Sam's mental rollercoaster was one Lucifer ticket stub from flying off the rails. He couldn't know the amount of crap Sam had to fight through each day to function without the benefit of a straightjacket and padded walls. He only knew what Sam told him. Fortunately, Sam seemed willing to admit to and discuss these mental battles. Maybe he couldn't spare the effort required to maintain secrets while fighting for his daily dose of sanity.

"Don't worry, Dean," Sam said. "It's under control."

For now, Dean thought grimly. *But for how much longer?*

Ten minutes later, they stood in a beauty salon in a strip mall. Underneath "Salon Colette", painted in broad gold cursive letters on the plate-glass windows, were the words "Walk-ins Welcome!"

The interior of the salon was functional, with a long rectangular floor plan. Open, mirrored hair styling stations lined either side, with hair dryers and shampoo sinks in the rear. A tall glass and chrome rack filled with hair care products separated the reception area from the cutting floor, but a half-dozen female customers and stylists were visible from the entrance. Hanging ferns spaced at irregular intervals and glamorous headshots of models with assorted hair styles were the only decorative touches.

The bottle-blonde receptionist looked up, startled, when Dean and Sam approached her desk. "Do you have, um, appointments?"

"Sign says walk-ins welcome," Dean said.

"We're not here for haircuts," Sam explained.

"Right," the receptionist said, visibly relieved. "We don't get a lot of guys."

Sam gave her their insurance adjusters cover story. "We have a few questions for"—Sam checked Bobby's list—"Janice and Felicia."

"Janice Cummings?" she asked, eyebrows rising. "That's me."

"Great," Sam said. "And Felicia?"

Janice craned her neck. "She's finishing up with a client." Speaking louder, she said, "Felicia, when you get a minute."

She returned her attention to the Winchesters. "How can I help?"

"It's about the bus accident," Dean said.

"Oh, my God," Janice said. "That was awful. Scared the hell out of me." She frowned, abashed, and lowered her voice. "I thought we were going to die. When we crashed through that place—the fitness center—I don't know, I thought the ceiling might fall down or the bus would explode."

"How about this guy?" Sam asked, showing her the grainy photo of the man in the bowler hat. "Was he on the bus?"

Janice took the photo, regarded it carefully, her brow creasing, then finally shook her head as she handed it back to Sam. "I can't really see his face. But I would have remembered that outfit. Sorry."

A tall brunette with frosted tips, wearing a white blouse and a short black skirt under a black hairdresser's apron, approached them, scissors poised in her upraised hand. "What's up, Jan—?" Then she noticed Dean and Sam in their suits and smiled. "You boys looking for a trim?" she asked provocatively. "I'm sure I could fit you into my schedule."

"They're here about the bus accident," Janice explained.

"Oh." The hairdresser's smile evaporated. "That was a nightmare."

"Felicia Akop?" Sam asked.

"The one and only," she said. "Are you two cops? Because we already—"

"Insurance adjusters," Dean interjected. "John and Tom Smith. Unrelated."

"We were just asking Janice if she saw this man on the

bus," Sam said, showing her the picture.

Waste of time, Dean thought, *they rode together.*

Felicia nodded. "Oh, yeah, I remember that guy."

"You do?" Janice looked surprised.

"He got on the stop before yours," Felicia said to Janice. "The guy was huge, the bus creaked under his weight. He walked hunched over. As soon as he got on, he walked to the back of the bus. He must've gotten off before the accident."

"He didn't pass you on the way out?" Dean asked.

"He must've used the back door," Felicia said. "It was closer to where he was sitting."

"Did he... interact with the bus driver?" Sam asked.

"Other than paying his fare? No."

"No bumping or jostling?"

"Nope," Felicia said. "Never said a word to anyone that I recall."

"Can you describe his face?" Dean asked. "Was there anything unusual about him?"

Felicia pursed her lips as she stared at the grainy photo. "I didn't make eye contact. Something about him gave me the willies, you know what I mean?"

Sam nodded, waiting. Dean kept quiet too, hoping something would pop to the surface. The guy had walked right by her bus seat, an arm's length away.

"The hat—a bowler—and the dark suit and cane. That's kind of all I remember." She closed her eyes, as if reliving the brief memory. Then she frowned. "His forehead, even with the hat..."

"What about his forehead?" Sam inquired.

"Frown lines," she said, scrunching up her face. "Deep creases, like… furrows. I remember thinking he could be the 'Before' photo in a Botox ad. That's it. It was a quick glance and then I looked away. He made me nervous, but I don't know why. Maybe his size freaked me out. Does that help?"

"Maybe," Sam said.

Dean couldn't think how the information was meaningful beyond adding a slight detail to their physical description, but he kept quiet.

"Do you think he was responsible for the accident?" Janice asked.

"We're looking into all possibilities," Sam said. He turned to Felicia and said, "Thank you."

"Anytime," she responded, smiling broadly again. She reached into an apron pocket, produced a business card, and tucked it into the breast pocket of Sam's jacket. "Any other questions you want to ask, anything at all, call me."

Sam cleared his throat. "Okay. Thanks."

Ryan came home after school to an empty house. His father wouldn't be back from his construction job for a couple of hours, then he'd have a one- or two-hour pit stop before heading off to his second job on an office cleaning crew. Ryan dropped his overstuffed backpack on the dining room table and tugged out his textbooks and notebooks. He took a cursory glance at his assignments, with little motivation to work on any of them, and noticed the top edge of his calculus exam poking out, returned to him today with a big fat red D that looked as if it had been scrawled with gusto by Mr. DeGraff. Beneath the damning grade, his teacher had written, "Work harder!" Snatching the exam out of the notebook pocket, Ryan crumpled it into a tight ball and tossed it toward the kitchen trashcan—and missed. Naturally.

His temples throbbed, another tension headache coming on. He had to remember not to clench his jaw so hard or he would crack his teeth. *Calm down,* he admonished himself. But controlling his stress level never came easily.

It didn't matter how hard he worked, the calculus textbook and the practice exercises might as well have been hieroglyphics for all the sense they made to him. He had always managed Bs in math—geometry, algebra, trigonometry—with an occasional A in a marking period here and there. Now, he struggled to make sense of it. He'd read that you reach a limit on what your brain can learn. At some point, the brain refuses to comprehend something, no matter what you do. Calculus gave him headaches. The harder he tried to make sense of it, the worse the headaches became. He might as well have been allergic to it. Or maybe he was making excuses for having no interest in math anymore. He didn't want to learn it, so it became too hard. He could move onto something more interesting. People got psychosomatic illnesses, imaginary illnesses that felt real to them. Maybe he was sabotaging himself.

His father was never home, and he had never known his mother. Sumiko would probably run off to a distant college. He would be all alone. Stupid and alone. Worthless. Nothing seemed to matter anymore. Maybe life had no real meaning. Anyone who believed otherwise was kidding themself.

His cell phone buzzed in his pocket, startling him. Normally, he switched it from vibrate to ring mode straight after school, but with all the excitement he had forgotten. A glance at the face and name on the display made him smile.

"Hey, Sumiko," he said. "What's up?"

"Want to come over?"

"No homework?"

"I finished it in study hall."

"Lucky you," he said, glaring at the stacked pages of his own assignments. He tried to remember where his father kept the matches. He'd like to burn the entire mound. Why not blow it off? It wasn't like his father would care, or even notice.

"Too much work?"

"Nothing that can't wait," he said. "I'll be over in ten."

"Great," she said. "See ya, big guy."

"I'm not calling you 'little lady'," he said. She wanted that to be their thing. "Feels like a bad John Wayne impersonation."

"John who now?"

"You're hopeless," he said, laughing.

THIRTEEN

Barbara Nice-Miller led Bobby to a seat in her living room after he explained he was with the FBI. She even offered him a cup of tea, which he declined in the unspoken interest of expediting the interview. She sat across from him with her Yorkie—"Little" Sebastian—in her lap, as if Bobby might need to interview the dog as well. The tiny dog had yipped at him from the moment he walked into the house until she picked him up. Then it settled down and watched him warily.

Maybe the dog knows my FBI credentials are fake.

"So, what do you want to know about that horrible day, Agent Willis?"

"Notice anything unusual?"

"I was talking to my little Sebastian during our morning walk," she said, staring lovingly at the dog as she scratched it behind the ears. "At first I thought it was an explosion. Then

I saw all the cars out of control and crashing into each other. I picked up little Sebastian and ran behind the bank sign, the one that shows the time and temperature. Sebastian was shaking like a leaf. I closed my eyes during all the explosions and wanted to scream. Actually, I might have screamed, a little. Not that I could hear myself."

Bobby showed her the traffic cam photo of the man in the bowler hat. "Notice this man?"

"Oh, yes, the crazy man!"

"Crazy?"

"At first, I noticed him because he was dressed so formally," she said. "He stood there the whole time. Of course, he didn't have a little doggie to protect, did he, Mr. Sebastian?" Her voice climbed a few registers as she addressed the dog.

Bobby cleared his throat, hoping to redirect her attention to the other human in the room. "Crazy like he was fearless?"

"Or paralyzed with fear," she said. "To be charitable. Maybe he was too ill to take cover."

"Why would you think he was ill?"

"Before the accidents started, he was massaging his temples," she said, "like he had a bad tension headache. My aunt Wilhelmina had migraines so bad she would throw up. Maybe the poor man was too sick to run."

"And after the accident? Did you see him leave?"

"He must have felt better after the shock," she said. "He walked away before the police could talk to him. I hung around to help—I took a first aid class fifteen years ago—but it was so awful… There was nothing I could do before the paramedics came."

"Thanks for your time, ma'am."

"You're welcome," she said as she walked him to the door. "Say goodbye to the nice FBI agent, Sebastian."

The little dog resumed yapping at Bobby until he was back in his Chevelle.

His next stop was at the small storefront of Kiriakoulis Plumbing to talk to Liana Bekakos, who had reported her boss, Frank, missing after his last job on Thursday. She hadn't witnessed anything in person, but he hoped she could shed some light on Frank's habits.

She addressed him from the other side of the store's counter, nervously twisting ringlets of her black hair between her thumb, index and middle fingers.

"No, Frank isn't like that at all. He's very responsible. He certainly wouldn't run off to Atlantic City on the spur of the moment. He *is* the business. If he doesn't do the work, it doesn't get done. It's his reputation. I've been calling customers to cancel. I don't know what to do."

"When was the last time you spoke to him?"

"He called to tell me when he arrived at Kerry Gillard's house on Lafferty, to do a new toilet installation," she said. "Routine stuff."

"Never called after?"

She shook her head. "Usually he calls on the road, if he's stuck in traffic," she said. "Otherwise, he'll check in when he arrives at a job. I called his cell, but no answer. It just goes to voicemail. Same for his home number."

"He got family? Wife? Kids?"

"He's a widower," she said. "His wife died five years ago. Breast cancer. There're no children. He lives alone, but I have a spare key. I checked his home. There's no sign of him."

"You call this Kerry person?"

"Yes, when Frank was late for his next appointment," she explained. "To check what time he'd left. She said he'd been gone for an hour. There was no sign of the van." She had been speaking quickly, as if in a rush to get the facts out so the investigation could continue. "Do you think he's been kidnapped?"

"It's a possibility?"

"Who would do such a thing, and why? For ransom? He's a working man. Not rich by any means. I would know, I'm the bookkeeper."

"Wish I knew," Bobby said sympathetically. He suspected Frank had been killed for his van, nothing more, but didn't have the heart to tell her. Who was he to destroy any hope she harbored for his safe return? He could be wrong about Frank. It was certainly possible.

But not likely.

Dalton Rourke couldn't go home until after school dismissal, so he hung out with Jimmy Ferrato at the basketball court behind the old Barkley Middle School. They were hidden from the street by the shuttered school in front and by the woods in back. A small pocket of sanity. They sat on the cracked court, tugging out tufts of grass that were trying to reclaim the space for Mother Nature.

"Got any weed?" Dalton asked.

"I wish," Jimmy said. "Mom found my stash Saturday morning. I've been tapped out since then."

They smoked their remaining cigarettes instead, about a dozen between them, marking time. The crumbling, abandoned school with its deteriorating playground was one more piece of evidence convincing him that life was meaningless. No matter what you tried to accomplish, how much you strived for anything, it all went away, like the Kansas song, "Dust in the Wind." In a hundred years, who would care that he had failed classes, skipped school, tripped Tyler Shackleford, lived and died? In a world where nothing mattered, you could do whatever you wanted. Unfortunately, he still had to live through the short-term consequences.

After the initial rush of ditching school during the bomb threat evacuation, Dalton realized he was simply postponing the inevitable verbal beat down. Just because nothing mattered, didn't mean they couldn't make his life miserable in the meantime. His escape had not been well thought out. He'd left his books on his desk and his backpack on the chair.

"Did you really sniff her hair?" Jimmy asked.

Dalton took a long puff from the cigarette, shrinking it down to a nub, which he flicked across the court after lighting another one. "Yeah."

"Why?"

"I was hungry," Dalton said. "Her hair smelled like dessert."

Jimmy laughed until he started coughing. "What?"

"The shampoo or conditioner or whatever," Dalton explained. "It smelled like strawberries, honey, almonds. My stomach was growling."

"You're crazy."

"Girls wash their hair with all that scented crap and expect you not to smell it?" Dalton said. "C'mon, man! Chocolate, caramel and green apples."

"No way!"

"Pineapples, too. Coconut and a hint of marshmallow."

"You are so full of crap!"

"Maybe that was her perfume," Dalton said, grinning. "Like a freaking buffet, man."

"You're sick, dude."

"Maybe," Dalton said. "But now I'm starving. What time is it?"

"You see me wearing a watch?" Jimmy said. "And I lost my cell phone privileges after the stash grab."

At least he'd had a cell phone to forfeit. Dalton had nothing of value—unless you counted thrift store clothes and a hand-me-down stereo.

He stood up and felt lightheaded, staggering before catching his balance. He crushed his last cigarette butt underfoot and started coughing, his throat dry and burning. *Too much nicotine*, he thought. After the coughing spasm, his head throbbed. He adjusted his knit hat, pulling it down to his ears, then pressed his palms against his temples while dark spots swam across his eyes.

To avoid another coughing fit, he spoke softly. "Let's head back."

Thirty minutes later, when he stepped through the front door of his grandparents' house, he acted as if it had been another normal school day he didn't want to talk about. He opened and closed the hallway closet door, as if he were stowing the backpack he didn't have with him.

"I'm home," he called.

"You're late," his grandmother said from the dining room.

"Busy," he said, avoiding specifics.

He stepped into the dining room and saw his grandparents finishing their dinner. They seemed to eat earlier every day. Soon they would eat dinner at noon. It was nothing special, some frozen microwave chicken meals. They never cooked anything fancier than mac and cheese or fried eggs. There was no meal or plate set out for him. How many ways could they tell him they never wanted to raise him, that he was a burden foisted upon them, a mistake his mother made and left for them to clean up after she died in childbirth?

"I'm hungry," he said.

"Throw something in the microwave," his grandmother responded, as if talking to a simpleton.

Closing his eyes for a moment, he imagined shoving her curly-gray-haired head into the microwave and cooking it on high until her eyeballs popped out of her head like champagne corks on New Year's Eve. Or maybe they would boil in the microwave and drip down her cheeks like scalding milk.

Before he could come up with a smartass comment, his grandfather asked, "Where's your homework?"

And so the grilling begins, he thought. "Don't have any."

"How would you know," his grandmother asked, "since you left your backpack in school?"

Had they seen him come in empty-handed? "Yeah, forgot it. After this bomb scare we had."

"The vice principal called," his grandfather informed him. "Again. You're suspended for a week. And they're considering expulsion."

"Like I give a rat's ass about school."

"Get up to your room!" his grandmother shrilled. "You're grounded."

"I'm hungry."

"Now, Dalton," his grandfather said, rising out of his chair.

Dalton eyed the butter knife on the table, wondering if it was sharp enough to slice open the old man's throat. Five seconds and he could drop the old bastard. His fingers trembled and twitched as he stared into the angry man's face. His grandmother had the portable phone in her hand, ready to call 911. They would love to be rid of him. The thought of giving them what they wanted calmed him enough to turn his back and walk away.

"How dare you embarrass us," his grandmother yelled after him. "You are an embarrassment to this family—just like your tramp mother!"

That was all that mattered to them, how he made them look in the eyes of the neighbors and school administrators. They didn't care if he was happy or fed or healthy, unless it reflected on their so-called parenting skills.

He thundered up the stairs, giving each footfall extra weight, hoping something would break and cost them money they didn't have for repairs. He strode into his bedroom, the smallest room in the house, and slammed the door so hard it rattled on the hinges. The room was a mess, but he didn't care. There were clothes piled on every surface, plus a tide of candy and fast food trash. He wanted the room to be a canker sore in their house, the more despicable the better. Lately, they only stepped through the doorway to conduct drug searches.

With his door closed, they wouldn't check on him. Out of sight, out of mind was how they dealt with him. They had banished him to his tiny corner of the house. Mission accomplished. Now they could enjoy their evening without having to see him again.

Fine. He grabbed his black hoodie out of the closet, slipped on a pair of dark jeans and black boots and climbed out the window, crept along the porch roof and dropped to the ground next to the driveway. He would meet up with Jimmy Ferrato, assuming his friend could sneak out after whatever punishment his folks gave him, and they'd hitch a ride east, shake down some Summerdale teens for walking around money. He needed an outlet for his frustration and Summerdale kids had very punchable faces.

Disappointed with the fallout—*ha ha!*—from his fake bomb threat, Jesse Trumball returned home at four o'clock in a foul mood. Sure, the cops showed up with their bomb-sniffing dogs, and he had cleared the building, but then… boring. Just everyone standing around like they had missed their bus and couldn't remember how to walk home. Granted, he hadn't thought out his plan in terms of ultimate entertainment value.

Running a hand across his shaved pate, he squeezed his eyes shut for a few seconds, wondering if they might have some aspirin in the medicine cabinet. Ever since the evacuation, he'd had a headache that wouldn't quit and it was about to get worse.

Idly, he wondered how difficult it was to build a real bomb, a fancy one with a timer. Not that he actually wanted to kill any of the dumbasses in school, but he would love to see the expressions on their faces when the building went up like Krakatoa. He had heard the internet had bomb-building information anyone could access. If only he had a computer. Of course, he could always visit the library. Maybe the prissy old librarian would have a heart attack when he walked in. That would be good for a few chuckles. But even if he found bomb-making instructions, he would have to sneak into the school to plant the damn thing in a restroom or somewhere. Maybe in Miss Garrity's desk drawer. The bitch had driven him crazy like it was her life's mission. Dropping out of that hellhole was the best day of his life. Now he would like nothing better than to sneak back in for ten minutes to plant his farewell present.

Someday, maybe.

He sighed when he saw his old man's primer-spackled piece of crap sitting in the driveway, dreading the inevitable confrontation. Resignedly, he walked into the kitchen and found his father there, sitting at the table drinking a forty-ounce bottle of beer.

Alert the media, he thought.

It was probably his second or third one of the day, if he hadn't dipped into the hard liquor yet. At least he was still standing. By four o'clock there was a fifty-fifty chance Jesse would find him passed out somewhere in the house; slumped over the bowl or sprawled in the hallway, lying in a drying pool of vomit. *Good times.*

Occasionally his father failed to make it home after one of his benders. Whether he shacked up somewhere or passed out in an alley, he never said. He would stumble home, mumbling and cursing, his clothes looking like he dove out of a moving car and rolled down a muddy embankment. Sometimes he would come home bloody. He'd probably been fighting over the dregs in empties with some homeless wino.

"Where you been?" his father asked, his speech already slurred.

"Out," Jesse said, pulling open the refrigerator door as if he expected to see actual food on the shelves. Best-case scenario, he'd find some leftover takeout or a slice of pizza from the last delivery.

"Looking for a job?"

"What? I can't live off disability, like you?" Jesse asked.

"Got a bad back," his father said. "Injured on the job."

"Tell that story to someone who believes it, Pop."

Jesse's father stood unsteadily. "Don't get smart with me, boy!"

"Right," Jesse said softly as he scanned the barren shelves. A crumpled-up brown paper bag offered the possibility of something edible inside. "I wouldn't want to confuse the few brain cells you have left."

"Turn around and say that to my face."

Jesse stood up straight, closed the refrigerator door and counted to ten silently. Then he turned around to face his father. The man was big and beefy, about an inch or two shorter than Jesse's six-foot-five frame, but he outweighed Jesse by about forty pounds. He was a brawler, a street fighter. When Jesse was younger, and smaller, his father had no hesitation about hitting him when he "stepped out of line." Hands, belt and suitably blunt and weighted objects were fair game for delivering punishment. Once their heights had equalized, however, his father's abuse became more selective—he picked his moments to remind Jesse who was in charge. Right now, his old man was gripping a half-filled forty-ounce glass bottle as if he meant to test its battle worth against the side of Jesse's head. Jesse figured he could take his old man, drunk or sober, but it might get ugly fast, for both of them.

"Never mind," Jesse said, walking away.

"That's right," his father said, "walk away, tough guy."

"I'm taking your car," Jesse said, "to grab something to eat."

"I need it."

"You're too drunk to drive," Jesse said, taking the keys off the wall hook. "Sleep it off."

"Get off your high horse. You're lucky I put a roof over your head," his father said. "More than your mother ever did. Took one look at your sorry ass and walked out. Smartest thing she ever did."

Jesse froze. He curled his hands into fists, squeezing so hard his fingernails bit into his flesh. Talk of his mother was a sore spot with him. He couldn't defend a woman he had never known, but the attacks always felt intensely personal. Throughout Jesse's life, his father had insisted that Jesse's mother had abandoned him as a baby, that as soon as she recovered from giving birth to him, she had left without so much as a glance over her shoulder. His father told him that her pregnancy had been like a disease she had to overcome and afterward she couldn't bear to look at the result. The newborn meant so little to her that she had abandoned her loving husband so she wouldn't have to spend one more day with their boy.

For most of Jesse's miserable childhood, he fantasized that she would return and whisk him away to a better life, an existence without his father around—the only way he would ever be happy. But the years passed without a phone call or a note or any attempt by her to contact him. Finally, as he entered his teen years, he started to believe what his father had said over and over again, that she hated her son and couldn't bear the sight of him.

Though he now accepted his father's pronouncements about his mother, Jesse couldn't stomach his father using her abandonment to provoke him. Jesse felt himself balancing on a precipice: regain his balance and walk out the door, or fall and… his father would never insult him again.

"Don't stand there like a moron! What's the matter with you?"

As if sensing Jesse's murderous indecision—or completely

blind to it—his father slapped him across the back of his head, hard enough to sting but not wound.

Jesse imagined his father clutching the forty-ounce bottle, waiting.

FOURTEEN

"Answer me!"

Jesse clenched his jaw, refusing to speak. A clock ticked in his head, counting down the days, hours, minutes, and seconds until... Was he ready? It would be so easy and he ached to put an end to his father's abuse. But if he acted now, he would face the consequences unprepared. On the other hand, if he waited until he had saved enough money and had prepared an exit strategy, he might avoid those consequences. He would have disappeared to Mexico or South America somewhere long before anyone found the body.

Through gritted teeth, Jesse repeated, "Sleep it off!"

He rushed out of the house, grabbing his hooded jacket off the coat rack without breaking stride, muttering a string of curses under his breath.

Opening the trunk of his father's beater, he took out a

tire iron and tossed it on the passenger seat before burning rubber out of the driveway. The problem with bottling up his rage at home was that he needed to vent somewhere on something—or someone. Driving the car into a brick wall might provide momentary satisfaction, but he needed the car for his own special brand of income generation. For that, he also needed the cover of night, so he took care of his hunger first, navigating the drive-through lane of the nearest burger franchise. He ordered three of the largest patties, then tossed the sesame rolls out the window, scarfing down the condiment-smeared meat as he drove.

Bart Larribeau and Keith Kulback were standing outside the Food & Fuel mini mart, eating chips from snack bags as if they never intended to leave. The owner wouldn't let them loiter unless they bought something, so each minor purchase gained them a half hour without harassment. They would pay the tithe until Jesse showed up to avoid any confrontation with the police. Jesse continually reminded them to stay off police radar as much as possible. Attention was bad in their line of business.

As soon as he pulled up in a handicapped parking space in front of the mini mart, they pushed off the wall, tossed their snack bags toward the overflowing trashcan and slipped into the car. Bart beat Keith with rock over scissors and rode shotgun, holding Jesse's tire iron across his lap.

"Where to?" Bart asked.

"The Cheshire," Jesse said. "It's been a couple weeks."

"Sounds good," Keith said.

Jesse drove east and parked in an alley near the Cheshire

Theater. The marquee read "Fiddler on the Roof" and listed matinee and evening performance times.

"How long?" Keith asked.

"Less than an hour," Jesse said. "It's close to show time."

He leaned back in the driver's seat and worked his way through two large cardboard containers stuffed with French fries after giving the third to Bart to split with Keith. Though they were a couple of years older than him, he outweighed each of them by fifty pounds and had assumed the role of leader.

The crowd outside the theater thinned as the smokers moved inside to take their seats before the show began.

Somebody always ran a little late, parked a little farther away, hurried to reach the theater.

Finally, Jesse spotted a middle-aged man in a dark suit holding his wife's hand, urging her without much success to walk faster in her shimmery evening gown and high heels. When the couple were within thirty feet of the theater, Jesse grabbed the tire iron and opened his door.

"Show time," he said. "Wait here."

"You sure?" Keith said.

"I shouldn't need backup," Jesse said, and hurried along an intercept course, pulling up his hood to hide his bald head and obscure his face. He kept the tire iron flat against the back of his leg.

The woman spotted him first and whispered something to her husband.

As Jesse closed the gap between them, he said, "Sir, do you have the time?"

The man stopped, stepping slightly in front of his wife, as he assessed the threat. "Sure, it's—"

Jesse couldn't wait another second. Usually he would simply threaten violence and the money and jewelry gushed forth into his possession. But the rage that had threatened to explode at home, the anger broiling beneath the surface all evening, found its outlet. He swung the tire iron in an overhand arc and broke the man's wrist.

He cried out in pain.

Jesse swung the metal rod low, smashing it against the side of the man's left knee. He crumpled to the ground, curled up in agony, gasping for air. The woman, her hair layered over her head in a fancy hairdo that must have taken hours to prepare, opened her mouth to scream. He grabbed her hair and yanked her head back, the tire iron poised over her face. "Scream and I smash your teeth in."

The woman gulped and a tiny whimper escaped her throat.

"Cash and jewels," he said. "Now! Or I take them from your dead bodies."

In a few seconds, he had the man's wallet, wristwatch and cash, along with the woman's pearl necklace and rings. He stamped both their smartphones into shards.

"We gave you what you asked for," the woman pleaded. "Now go. Please."

"Don't give me orders," Jesse said.

The man was still curled up, moaning. Annoyed, Jesse brought back his foot and drove his steel-tipped boot into the man's belly.

As the man gagged, the woman cried out, "No! Stop hurting him!"

"What the hell did I just say to you?" Jesse demanded, his face flushed with anger. Lunging forward, he backhanded the woman so hard he split her lip open and she fell on her ass, crying. "You wear too much makeup, bitch!"

He raised the tire iron over his head, clutched so tightly his knuckles were white. He was panting, his arm trembling with the urge to cave in her skull.

Somebody grabbed his shoulder from behind. "Dude!"

Jesse spun around, enraged, but caught himself when he saw Bart staring at him as if he were insane. "What...?"

"Let's go, man!" Bart whispered urgently.

"Right," Jesse said. "Yeah, right. Don't know what got..."

With Bart tugging him, they ran down the alley and jumped into the car.

Jesse's last glimpse of the couple was encouraging. The wife was huddled over her husband, not trying to get the make and model of their car or memorize the license plate number.

"That was messed up, man," Bart said, shaking his head. "What happened to intimidation?"

"Yeah, Jess," Keith said. "What the hell...?"

"Bad day, that's all," Jesse said. "Wrong place, wrong time."

"Are you sure, man?" Bart said. "If you start breaking bones, nearly killing people, we're looking at serious jail time. You'd better let us handle the next one."

"I'm okay now," Jesse assured him. "It won't happen again."

"Good," Bart said. "Should we take this stuff to Mickey's? Cash in?"

Mickey owned a pawnshop and had a back door arrangement with them—completely off the books and the security cameras. He probably gave them ten cents on the dollar, but it was a simple way to convert jewelry and other valuables into quick cash. After converting the goods to cash, they would split the haul three ways.

"Sure," Jesse said, massaging his forehead. The damn headache wouldn't go away, not after he ate and not after he vented his frustrations on a couple of easy targets.

"Jess, me and Bart had an idea," Keith said hesitantly.

"Really?" Jesse said, amused. Combined, they had the equivalent of half a brain. The simpler the operation the better. "What's that?"

"Burglary," Keith said. "Parents working two jobs, kids at school. Why not hit some homes? Go in the back door, out of sight, walk out with the good stuff. Quick and easy. No fuss, no muss."

"Less chance of the cops catching us in the act," Bart said. "Out in the open is risky, you know?"

"Yeah," Jesse said. "I'll think about it."

Now that he had a chance to look back on his violent actions, Jesse was surprised to realize how much he had enjoyed the display of power. Power gave him control. Fear bent others to his will. And what an incredible rush! He wasn't sure he wanted to give that up. Ever.

Maybe he wouldn't need Bart and Keith backing him anymore. With their lack of ambition, they held him back from his true potential. Let them sneak into houses and make Mickey rich while the pawnbroker doled out scraps in return. Jesse would keep the power.

Soon everyone would fear him.

Ryan rang the doorbell at Sumiko's house and heard her yell to her mother that she'd get the door. Her father, some sort of corporate consultant, traveled by airplane as frequently as most people commuted by car or train, and was rarely home. Ryan guessed that in ten years Roger Jones would consult primarily via video conferencing calls. But maybe he needed to tour facilities to recommend manufacturing renovations or massive layoffs. Usually Sumiko and her mother had the house to themselves. Sometimes Ryan ate dinner with them, but he was careful not to become too dependent on their generosity, too needy. He liked to retain the appearance of self-sufficiency, even though he often felt as if his world had jumped the rails and was careening out of control. Lately, panic nibbled at the corners of his day-to-day existence and he had the sensation—premonition?—that he would soon lose everything that meant anything to him. He was self-aware enough, however, to pin his anxiety on the imminent end of his senior year of high school. Every day it became harder to see a meaningful future.

Sumiko yanked the door open and beamed at him.

"You made it!"

"I only live ten minutes away."

She hadn't changed out of her red and black school clothes, but she had ditched her boots and stood in bare feet with her toenails painted crimson. Without footwear, she appeared even smaller and more fragile next to him.

"Come in," she said, tugging him into the house by his hand before pushing the door closed with her foot. Of course she was clutching her smartphone in her other hand. By this time, he pretty much considered it to be surgically attached to her palm. "I've got something to show you."

"In front of your mom?" Ryan joked.

"Ha!" she caught the back of his neck and tugged him down for a quick kiss on the mouth. Her lip gloss tasted like strawberry.

"Hi, Ryan!" Mrs. Jones called from the kitchen, which had a counter with a pass-through opening to the dining room. "Are you staying for dinner?"

"Thanks, but…" He felt his stomach rumble. "I really shouldn't…"

"Nonsense," she said as she filled a pot with water to boil on the stove. "I'll set a plate for you. We're having pasta with meat sauce."

"She was gonna make *yakitori*," Sumiko whispered, "but forgot to buy skewers."

"I'll eat anything that isn't squirming on the plate," Ryan said.

"Eww!" Sumiko said. "Gross."

"Do you two have homework?" Mrs. Jones called.

"No, mother," Sumiko said. "I want to show Ryan my blog."

"Is that what the kids are calling it these days?"

"You're so very funny, mother." Sumiko rolled her eyes.

She tugged Ryan's hand again. "C'mon!"

"Door open. Two feet on the floor!" Mrs. Jones commanded with the weight of parental authority.

"Two feet each," Sumiko asked as they climbed the steps, "or combined?"

"You're so very funny, daughter," Mrs. Jones said.

"Daring," Ryan said to Sumiko.

"I'm flexible," she replied with a wink.

"And bawdy," he added.

"I can't help it," she said. "I'm excited."

"And I'm right behind you," Ryan said, patting her rear for emphasis.

She let out an involuntarily squeal and raced up the last few steps.

FIFTEEN

Sam opened the door to Roy Dempsey's cabin and Dean walked through ahead of him carrying the grease-stained brown paper bag containing their sandwiches and an order of fries from Famous Andy's. While the sandwich shop boasted a healthy takeout business with a quick turnaround, the cramped interior featured only three small, circular tables and no counter seating. So rather than wait a couple of hours for a table to become available, Sam and Dean had followed the consensus and taken their order to go.

Dean removed the wrapped sandwiches from the bag along with a fistful of napkins and spread them out on the breakfast nook table. With anticipatory gusto, Dean unwrapped his sandwich: a foot-long roast-beef sub, dripping with gravy. Sam's grilled chicken on a multi-grain roll was positively Spartan in comparison, other than the few spots where the roast-beef juices had seeped through the paper into his roll.

Sam watched as Dean patted his hands dry with a couple of paper napkins, then picked up the dripping sandwich and soaked them all over again.

"Do you need a bib?" he enquired.

"This," Dean said, nodding toward his sandwich, "is 'famous.' What you have there is… unknown and best forgotten."

"Famous last words."

As Dean took an ambitious bite out of his sub, Sam raised his roll to his lips and paused, about to open his mouth.

Lucifer sat across from him, next to Dean.

"Sam? C'mon, buddy! I specifically asked for the meatball sub."

Ignoring him, Sam took a bite of his sandwich.

"Now that's just rude," Lucifer said, "eating in front of company. I thought we were pals, down in the foxhole, toasting our tootsies."

Sam set his sandwich down and lowered his hands under the table.

"Tell you what, Bunky," Lucifer said, "pop a cap in Deano here, and I'll finish the roast beef. Deal?"

With his thumbnail, Sam pressed the scar until pain flared.

"Sam," Dean asked, "something wrong with your boring-on-a-bun special?"

When Sam didn't reply right away, Dean put down his sandwich and leaned forward. "Sammy! You in there?" He waved a gravy-smeared palm in front of his brother's face.

After pressing his eyes closed, Sam shook his head. Lucifer was gone.

"Yeah, I'm fine, Dean," he said. Then to cover, he added, "I was just wondering how the bowler guy triggered the bus driver's heart attack. They had no contact on the bus, then the heart attack happens blocks away from where our guy gets off."

"Contact's unnecessary," Dean said. "The guy just needs to be in the general vicinity."

"So how does he pick his victims?" Sam said. "Hell, why pick Laurel Hill?"

Dean took another generous bite out of his sandwich and mulled over the questions as he chewed. Then he patted his hands dry again and stood. "I'm getting a beer. You want one?"

Sam nodded. His two questions represented the roadblocks to completing the job. Unless they could determine where the guy in the bowler would strike next, they had to depend on serendipity to find him. Laurel Hill was not a small town and he could be anywhere.

"The worst part is, we may need to wait for another big attack, like the pedestrian overpass, to have a shot at him."

Dean placed an open beer bottle in front of Sam before returning to his own seat.

"Random attacks in a random town," he said, shaking his head at the futility of it. "And we don't know what he is, how he operates, or how to gank him."

"We haven't ruled out bullets." Sam took a swig of beer.

"We were close," Dean said, referring to the overpass

collapse.

His cell phone rang. "Bobby," he said after a glance at the display.

"Hey," he said into the phone.

"Roy's cabin."

Dean listened for a moment then said to Sam, "Turn on the news. Channel ten."

Sam powered on the television set and changed channels. A blonde anchorwoman spoke, a reproduction of the grainy traffic camera photo of the bowler guy in a graphic over her shoulder. Sam raised the volume.

"…wanted for questioning by the police concerning the recent spate of severe accidents. If you see this man, do not approach him. Contact police immediately. He is considered extremely dangerous.

"In other news, an explosion rocked the Cedarbrook truck station when this Haddonfield man"—a photo of a middle-aged man wearing a Phillies cap appeared over her shoulder—"Alex Bryant, drove away from a fuel pump while the hose was still pumping gasoline into his fuel tank." Footage of the fire, as seen by a news helicopter, replaced the anchor's face on the screen for the rest of the story. "Five people were killed in the explosion, including Bryant. Two others suffered third-degree burns."

The anchor looked up from her monitor and back into the camera lens with a sympathetic shake of her head. "Another fatal accident today involved twenty-eight-year-old Corey Tourand, who fell ten stories when his window-washing platform collapsed outside the Laurel Hill Towers corporate office building. A spokesman for Tourand Clean cited the company's impeccable safety record and promised a full investigation to determine the cause of this tragic accident. Martin Tourand, father of the victim and owner of the twenty-year-old company, was unavailable for comment."

The camera switched to her perfectly coiffed male co-anchor, who stared earnestly into the lens. "On the medical front, the staff of the Laurel Heights Medical Center have their hands full. Over three dozen adults have been admitted with a deadly strain of the influenza virus—with five deaths reported already. In addition, at least eighteen children with life-threatening MRSA infections have been admitted to the hospital. Authorities are tracking the source of the outbreaks. Meanwhile, additional patients have been shuttled to nearby Evesford General.

"Coming up later in the broadcast, our very own Dr. Charlotte Kinzie has some important tips you won't want to miss on how to protect you and your family from these…"

Sam turned the volume low and rejoined Dean at the table.

Dean, who had been listening to Bobby during the news reports, finally disconnected the call. "Bobby's headed to the hospital with McClary. He'll stop back later."

Sam jerked his thumb over his shoulder in the direction of the TV. "No mention of the missing plumber or the van?"

"McClary's worried civilians might approach the van," Dean explained, "get themselves killed. And he doesn't want to tip off bowler guy that we know about the carjacking. But every cop in town is on the lookout."

"If somebody spots bowler man," Sam said, "maybe we can get the jump on him."

"It certainly improves our odds," Dean said. "Bobby talked to the plumber's bookkeeper. She says he's dependable. Not the type to blow off work with no explanation."

"Anything else?"

"He talked to a lady walking her dog who witnessed the pile-up," Dean said. "She saw our guy. Said he seemed fearless at the accident scene. No ducking for cover, no jumping out of harm's way."

"So, not worried about personal safety."

"Maybe. She did say he looked sick." Dean picked up his sandwich again. Sam noticed he had gathered some loose strands of roast beef into a little pile on a napkin and had a good idea why, but kept silent. "Or in pain. He was massaging his temples."

"There'd be lots of moving pieces in a pile-up," Sam said. "Maybe he was straining? Or maybe that's how he flexes his bad-mojo muscle?"

He had heard the pulse-pounding bass of Club Elektric from the street outside and the urgent rhythm called to him. The name of the nightclub flashed in red and purple neon script above the open door. Red was his favorite color. People in their twenties and thirties flowed freely in and out of the club, which offered no pretense at exclusivity in the form of a forbidding bouncer.

Inside, Tora found a woman in a slinky black dress at a reception counter collecting an admission fee in the form of a two-drink minimum. She handed him two coupons redeemable for drinks inside. Briefly, her warm hand brushed against his and he considered cutting his night short and taking her, but he had time. After his recent success, he was in the mood to celebrate before commencing the second part of his plan.

He sat on a padded stool at the corner of the bar, redeeming his first coupon for a mojito, and took several sips, nodding his approval. Then he spun the stool around to face the growing crowd. Colorful neon tubes snaked around the walls of the multi-tiered nightclub, which included several lounge areas with black banquettes, mirrored columns, and three large black parquet dance floors. Chrome and glass predominated, reflecting the neon tubing in dizzying fashion wherever he looked. Cocktail waitresses in short, iridescent blue dresses circulated through the lounges, balancing drinks on clear trays. The throbbing music called to mind ancient tribal rhythms and he imagined the frenetic dancers as primitive supplicants praying to their gods for rain or a bountiful harvest. Or fertility.

As he watched, the distillation of the dancing and mingling as a courtship rite became obvious to him. No longer hunters and gatherers, these humans were driven by their mating instinct to one degree or another, whether the intent was purely recreational or a step toward a long-term commitment or something between those extremes. Some small groups of men and women discussed business, ostensibly networking to enhance their financial status, but in a place where the music's volume overwhelmed and discouraged prolonged discourse, the mind's focus shifted to visual information and the not so subtle cues of gyrating body language.

He found himself at ease in a place that welcomed frank observation, his mind set to a similar purpose, to find a suitable candidate for a unique bonding ritual. Unfortunately, he had ignored his own imperative for too long, and this particular female selection carried more meaning than any before. He needed to proceed with caution and choose carefully.

His gaze traveled methodically across the nightclub, shifting from small groups of conversing women to candidates on each of the dance floors. Eventually, his attention settled on one dancing shape, a seductive young blonde woman wearing a revealing, red sequined dress that fell to mid-thigh. The snug material glimmered in the reflected light, appearing almost liquid, as if the woman's body was drenched in fresh-spilled blood, and she awaited him on a sacrificial altar.

He found her mesmerizing.

For a few carefree moments, Ryan forgot about his directionless future and enjoyed the present. But the feeling of buoyancy couldn't last. By the time he joined Sumiko in her bedroom, his forehead was throbbing in pain. He thought that by getting out of his lonely house and away from the damning grades and ponderous textbooks, he could relieve the pressure weighing on him, but his mind circled back in desperation.

Sumiko led him to the chair next to her computer desk and instructed him to sit. Aside from the folders and piles of paper stacked on her desk, her bedroom was neat, no clothing slung over chairs, doorknobs or bedposts, and no trash on the floor. She had decorated her walls with a bunch of movie posters, including *Tron*, *War Games*, *The Matrix*, *Source Code*, and *Inception*. Several framed watercolors of flowers interrupted the movie theme, but Ryan knew Sumiko's mother had hung those years ago.

"Have you got any aspirin?" Ryan asked before she could call up her blog. He didn't want to face it without a pain reliever in his system. Though he tried to muster enthusiasm for the Lion Truth blog, he would never be as excited about it as she was. He had hoped it would be a passing fad with her, but the hobby had morphed into an obsession. "I can't shake this headache I've had since the bomb threat evacuation."

"Sure," Sumiko said. "I'll be right back."

With her gone, he sagged in the chair, bowing his head and cupping his temples in both palms. The skin across his scalp was pulled tight, as if from a nasty sunburn. His pulse throbbed insistently and the pressure seemed to swell behind his eyes. An insane idea crossed his mind, that if he cut his flesh and let some of his blood escape, he could relieve the pressure.

"You're in luck, big guy," she called from down the hall. "We're down to our last two Excedrin."

"Great, thanks," he called, pushing himself against the chair back.

A moment later, she entered the bedroom with two

aspirin in one hand and a paper cup of water in the other. He swallowed the aspirin and finished the water, crumpling the cup and tossing it toward her trashcan. Of course, he missed.

"You're a lifesaver," he said.

She pushed his knees apart and came close, placing her hands on his shoulders. With him sitting and her standing, their heights were almost equal. "Are both your feet on the floor, Bramble?"

"Yes."

"Are both my feet on the floor?"

"Yes."

"Good," she said. "Then I can do this."

She leaned forward and kissed him. This time, she lingered and their mouths opened and the taste of strawberry lip gloss gave way to the sensation of her tongue darting across his lips.

Ryan's hands encircled her waist and began to drift down, seemingly of their own accord.

She pulled her head back and frowned. "I forgot what I was doing."

"I'll remind you," Ryan said, a little breathlessly.

"The blog," she said. "I wanted to show you what I've done."

"Of course," Ryan said, "the blog."

"Oh, don't be grumbly," she chided. "My mom's fifteen feet away!"

"I thought we were good with all four feet planted."

"I guess I'm not as daring as I thought."

She slipped from his grasp and sat in her chair, spun

to her computer screen and brought up her blog. "So, I've expanded the blog," she explained. "Before it was all about school stuff, which is fine, short term. But we'll be gone soon and that will be irrelevant."

As will I, Ryan thought darkly.

"The bomb threat got me thinking," Sumiko continued, ramping up to full blog engagement, "with all the bizarre accidents happening around town, I thought maybe there's a pattern."

"A pattern? To accidents?"

"Granted, the sample size is small," Sumiko said, "but this is not a normal distribution pattern: too many accidents, too many fatalities. I think some kind of force is at work here. Maybe it's man-made, or a government experiment, or a terrorist cell."

The pain in Ryan's head was driving him to distraction, and Sumiko's voice was a harsh counterpoint to the throbbing in his skull. He felt his hands trembling, and clutched them together to stop the involuntary movement.

"Terrorists? Don't you think that's a stretch?" Ryan reasoned. "The bomb threat was a fake."

"Right," Sumiko conceded. "Jesse Trumball called it in."

"You know that for sure now?" Ryan's right eye had begun to twitch. He pressed his fingers against it. His forehead felt clammy to the touch. Stress compromised the immune system. That made sense.

"It's the only explanation for why he was there," Sumiko said. "Big bozo."

"What?"

"Jesse. A bozo."

"Oh." For a fleeting moment, Ryan had thought she was insulting him and his fists had clenched. *I was about to hit her,* he realized. *What the hell is wrong with me?*

"So it was a hoax. How do you get terrorists in Laurel Hill out of that?"

"Terrorists are one option," Sumiko said. "They're not the only option. Remember the big pile-up on Wednesday?"

Ryan nodded. "You mentioned it before. So?"

"Well, you know Teresa Pezzino? Her brother is a junior patrol officer. Get this—he told her that none of the vehicle airbags deployed during the pile-up. Not one. You don't think that's bizarre?"

"It's… it's unusual, yes. But…"

A sharp pain knifed across Ryan's forehead. He staggered to his feet, knocking the chair over. It fell to the floor with a muffled thump. Ryan stood with his legs spread, hands clutching his forehead.

"Ryan? What's wrong?"

"Nothing," he mumbled. "Headache."

"Oh, okay," Sumiko said. "I can explain the rest of this later."

"I don't give a damn about your blog!" Ryan suddenly exploded. "That's all you talk about, all you care about. I'm sick of it. Screw the damn blog!"

He swung his arm out and swatted her flat-screen monitor so hard it tumbled off the desk and collided with the metal armrest of her chair. The screen cracked before tumbling toward the floor, suspended by its power and data cables.

"Ryan!" Sumiko yelled. Her eyes were wide, her normally pale face flushed. "Get out! Now!"

"Sumiko—"

"Out!"

"I'm—"

"We're done," she shrieked, shoving him repeatedly toward the door. "I never want to see you again!"

Ryan stumbled out of the room, staggered down the stairs, one hand on the railing as he pressed the other against his forehead, trying to contain the throbbing. He turned toward the front door and heard Mrs. Jones calling after him.

"Ryan? What's going on? What happened up there?"

"I don't know," Ryan said. "I really don't know."

Mortified, he ducked out of the front door and ran down to the sidewalk, feeling alone and completely lost. Sumiko had been his last anchor, the last thing holding him in place, and he'd screwed it up, pushed her away.

Now he had nothing.

Sixteen

Breathless, Dawn Nyberg returned from the dance floor of Club Elektric to the chrome and glass table occupied by several of her coworkers. She fanned her face with both hands to cool off before picking up her glass of club soda and draining it. Because she planned on drinking later at her cousin's bachelorette party, she wanted to pace herself here. She glanced at her smartphone lying on the table and saw a text message from her older sister, Summer.

"Summer's on her way," she said to her coworkers. "I wish I could stay with you guys."

"How well do you know this cousin?" Rebecca Walsh, her manager at Price Group Communications, asked with an arched eyebrow, teasing.

"I haven't seen her much since we were kids," Dawn admitted. "But she's family. I can't bail on her."

"Just say your car broke down," Khristine Butler suggested. She had been temping for PGC for nine months and had become friends with everyone at the company.

"Stop pressuring her," Meg Price, the company's owner, told the others. She was only a few years older than her employees and always sought to build a sense of camaraderie in the workplace, a team atmosphere that eschewed backbiting and petty jealousies. "She already feels guilty."

"But she might change her mind," Khristine said, "because she has a not-so-secret admirer."

"What?"

"Uber-formal guy," Khristine said with a slight tilt of her head toward the bar. "Bowler hat and cane. Looks British. He just ordered a mai tai. He couldn't take his eyes off your sweet dance moves."

"Shut up, Khris," Dawn exclaimed, giving Khristine a playful shove. She felt her face flush with embarrassment.

"Oh, my, he's huge," Rebecca said as she took a sip of her margarita timed to sneak a peek at the bar. "Maybe Jeeves is scouting this place for the royal family."

Khristine giggled.

Dawn raised her hand to her chin, tossed her hair aside, cast a subtle glance toward the bar, and looked away immediately. The man was staring at her as if expecting to make eye contact. Something was off about him. And it wasn't just his out-of-place clothing. "Please tell me he's not coming over here," she whispered urgently to her coworkers.

"Warning, Ms. Nyberg," Khristine said with her hand shielding her mouth, "he's downing that glass of liquid courage with a gleam in his eye."

Dawn's phone vibrated against the glass table, startling her. The music was so loud, it masked the sound, but the shimmying movement unnerved her. Dawn grabbed the phone and read the display. "Thank God. Summer's outside."

Khristine shuddered involuntarily. "It looks like he could hide silver dollars in that forehead."

"He's not that bad," Rebecca said. "If you like them massive."

"He's all yours," Dawn said, dropping her phone in her small clutch purse and hurrying away from the table. She eased through the crowd and apologized to those she inadvertently jostled. With each step, she begged herself to not look back. By the time she reached the hostess counter at the front of the nightclub, the urge to glance over her shoulder had become unbearable. She had been holding her breath so long her chest hurt. When she finally shot a glance behind her, the large man was ten feet back and closing.

As she stepped outside, cool air chilled her flushed skin and she shivered.

For a panicked moment, she stood there alone, wondering where her sister was. She had nowhere to go now. Knowing she would be riding with Summer to the bachelorette party, she had carpooled to work with Khristine, so there was no car waiting for her. She dared not turn around and walk toward the strange man.

She heard a heavy footfall behind her. The hair on the nape of her neck rose.

Summer's Prius zipped across the fire lane and came

to an abrupt stop in front of her. Without looking back, Dawn stepped off the curb, grabbed the handle and yanked, praying the door was unlocked. The door opened and she jumped into the passenger seat with a frightened squeal.

Only after she engaged the lock did she look out the window.

She screamed with fright as a large hand reached toward the glass.

"Go!"

"What the hell, Dawn?"

"Just go, damn it!"

Summer floored the accelerator and the car shot away from the curb. After they had pulled out of the parking lot, Summer frowned at her.

"What was that about?"

"A freaky guy," Dawn said, her hands trembling uncontrollably on her knees. She took several deep breaths to calm down.

After they had passed a few traffic lights, Dawn said softly, "I can't explain why, but that man scared the hell out of me."

So close! She had been within a few strides of him when the car pulled up at the curb. Though Tora hurried, she slipped into the car a moment before she would have been within arm's reach. He blamed overconfidence for botching the abduction.

Inside the nightclub, she had made brief eye contact with him and then abandoned the relative safety of her companions. Foolishly, he had believed she might be drawn to him, to his aura of power, and had decided to meet him outside the club for a brief assignation. He had been lulled by the apparent ease of the hunt, his prey willingly separating herself from the herd. Alcohol had not dulled his senses, hubris had.

He had allowed a prime specimen for his own courtship ritual to escape his clutches when a small show of his real power could have brought her down easily. A broken high heel, a stumble, a collision with another nightclub patron at an inopportune time and he would have had her in his grasp.

Fortunately, there was no shortage of suitable human females in Laurel Hill. But with only two days until the new moon, the time for subtlety had passed.

Walking briskly toward his van, he decided to try a less crowded location. And this time he would leave nothing to chance. With his other plans already in motion, quick, decisive action was called for.

As he opened the driver's door of the van, he caught a whiff of the decaying plumber in the back. He would need to acquire another vehicle soon. The company name was painted on the side panels and somebody would have reported the plumber missing by now. Tora saw no reason not to dump the van and the body at the same time.

He climbed in and drove out of the parking lot, looking left and right for an out-of-the-way location to abandon the van. Someplace where it might escape notice for a few days. The colder the trail he left, the less he would have to deal with human interference.

Ahead, movement caught his eye.

A fit young brunette with a ponytail that exposed a long, graceful neck, wearing a light jacket and black yoga pants was attempting to lock the exterior door of Sunrise Yoga Studio. She struggled with the keys, fumbling for the lock she couldn't see as she balanced two boxes crammed and overflowing with colorful pamphlets on her hip.

Perfect, he thought. She had come to him as good as gift-wrapped.

He steered the van toward the curb and slowed to a gentle stop.

The fingers of his right hand drifted to his temple.

The keys slipped from her fingers.

As she crouched to pick them up, the top box overbalanced and dozens of brochures spilled across the sidewalk.

Sumiko muttered a string of curses under her breath as she unplugged and untangled her damaged flat-screen monitor. It had cracked right down the middle.

Ryan, she fumed, *that selfish son of a bitch!*

"What gives him the right?"

There was a knock on her doorjamb.

For a split second she thought Ryan had come back to apologize and she fought the urge to hurl the monitor at him before he could utter a word. But she sagged in relief—and a little disappointment—when she saw her mother standing in the doorway with a concerned look on her face.

"What happened?" she asked. "Did Ryan do something… inappropriate?"

Sumiko laughed. "Yes," she said, shaking her head. "He

broke my monitor!"

"Oh," her mother said, confused. "You had an argument."

"After he broke it," Sumiko said. "Before that…" She set the damaged monitor on the carpet and sat dejected on the edge of her bed, forearms against her thighs. "Apparently I was boring him."

Her mother sat beside her and wrapped an arm around Sumiko's shoulders.

"The blog?"

"How did you know?" Sumiko asked.

"Well, you, ah, mention it quite often."

Sumiko dropped her chin to her palms, totally deflated. "Great. I bore my own mother."

"I'm happy with anything that excites you," her mother said supportively.

"That's mom-speak, right?"

"It doesn't mean it's not true," her mother said, smiling.

"It doesn't mean he's not a jerk for breaking my monitor," Sumiko said.

"That was uncalled for, yes."

"He's been acting, I don't know, weird lately," Sumiko said. "Complaining about headaches. And I know he's having trouble at school."

"Trouble?" her mother asked, her tone becoming less supportive and more concerned. Mother alarm bells ringing.

"His grades," Sumiko explained. "He's struggling with his class work. I've tried to help him, but… What am I going to do?"

"What do you want to do?"

"I don't know," Sumiko said. "I told him it was over—*we* were over."

"Are you?"

"I don't know. But I'm still mad at him."

"Maybe you should sleep on it."

"I guess so."

"It looks like you're out of the blog business," her mother observed.

"Hardly," Sumiko said, finally smiling. "But I'll need your help with the monster in the closet."

"Monster?"

"The beast," Sumiko said, rising to pull open her closet doors. Placing her hands in the middle, she slid her rack of clothes apart, pushing the hangers to either side, to expose the floor littered with retired computer parts. She pointed to her old nineteen-inch CRT.

"Sumiko," her mother said, "that's as big as our dishwasher."

"Probably heavier, too," Sumiko said. "Hmm… If Ryan comes back, I could drop it out the window on his head."

"Sumiko!"

"Just joking, Mom."

Together they carried the old CRT to her desk and Sumiko connected it to her computer.

"And we're back in business," she said, slapping her hands together to brush off the accumulated dust.

"Have you heard about the hospitals?" her mother asked.

Sumiko sensed something to take her mind off the fight with Ryan. "No. Spill!"

Her mother told her about the deadly flu virus spreading through Laurel Hill, along with the outbreak of MRSA afflicting nearly two-dozen children. "Wow," she said, stunned by the news. "This is Lion Truth material, Mom. Thanks!"

"I thought your blog was about school stuff."

"Past tense, Mom," Sumiko said. "Something big and bad is happening in this town. I thought today's bomb threat was part of it, but that was a false alarm."

"Sumiko, maybe it would be better, and safer, if you stayed focused on school activities," her mother suggested.

"Mom, I have to get the word out about this," Sumiko said. She had already pulled up her blog dashboard and begun typing her next post. "Somebody needs to stop this. They need to know what's happening."

"The evening news is handling that, dear."

"Nobody waits for television news anymore, Mom. It's all about the blogosphere. Instant access to all the information. Did you hear any names?"

"Names of victims? No, but some of these other accidents…"

"That's okay," Sumiko said. "I'll make some calls. I'll know somebody who knows somebody who is affected by this."

"Well, I'm glad you're feeling better," her mother said as she backed out of her daughter's room.

Sumiko had compartmentalized her anger toward Ryan, setting it behind a kind of mental firewall that protected her from the fallout of their fight. While she kept busy with blog business, she could deal with it by not dealing with it. Later, at night, in the dark, the firewall would come down and she would need to process her feelings, to decide if she wanted a future with Ryan or if she had meant what she'd said in the heat of anger. And if Ryan wanted nothing more to do with her, she would have to deal with that later.

With her post's introduction finished, she picked up her cell phone and fired off two dozen rapid text messages, some to groups of recipients, others to individuals. Over the past year, she had built up a network of sources. One group message was to girls she knew who babysat, or whose sisters or friends were babysitters. Since they all had cell phones and obsessed over texting, the replies would start coming in within minutes, if not sooner. If a connection linked the kids with MRSA, she was confident she would find it.

"No frigging way," Julie Parelli said as she watched her carefully labeled and stamped brochures spill across the sidewalk like a paper avalanche. The rubber bands on at least three of the bundles had snapped. *What were the odds?*

Heaving a sigh, she set her boxes down so she could lock the yoga studio doors. The last thing she needed was to forget to lock up and find the place trashed in the morning. Tucking her keys in her jacket pocket, she kneeled on the sidewalk and reached out to pull the farthest brochures toward her, forming mounds she could cram and restack in the boxes. She had spent ninety minutes putting labels and stamps on them so she could stop at the post office on the way home and drop them in the night box outside the lobby.

They would go out first thing in the morning and, she hoped, drum up some business for her new enterprise. As her father always said, cast out enough fishing lines and you're bound to get a few nibbles. Besides, with her current capitalization, she could only afford small ads in the local free paper and they held no more information than a business card. With the tri-fold brochures, she could list all her classes and services along with her experience.

A shadow fell across her outstretched arms, startling her.

"Excuse me, young lady," a man with a deep voice said, "It looks like you could use some assistance."

Julie looked up, and up—the guy was tall, NBA basketball center tall. He looked formal in his rounded hat and carrying a cane. Definitely not the first mental impression she would have had if someone had said, "Mugger" or "Rapist." But she had an independent streak—her mother called it a stubborn streak—a mile wide.

"No, thanks," she said, flashing a polite smile. "I've got it covered."

"Nonsense," he rumbled in a Barry White baritone. "What kind of gentleman would I be if I let a young lady crawl around on the sidewalk unassisted and merely walked by?"

One who listens to a young lady's wishes, Julie thought, but instead said, "It's no big deal, just a few spilled brochures."

Before she had finished speaking, he was on one knee, gathering brochures with his free hand. Julie gave an inward sigh, pushing back the stubborn streak. Even so, she redoubled her own efforts so she could finish up as quickly as possible and be on her way to the post office.

The man tucked a wad of brochures into one of the boxes, patted them down, then straightened up and stood over her, both hands resting on the handle of his cane, while she finished repacking the rest of the brochures.

Waiting for a tip, maybe?

She hadn't wanted his help in the first place and now she wanted him gone, because he was starting to freak her out, regarding her from above, his forehead looking like the loose folds of a shar pei's hide.

"Thanks," she said as she climbed to her feet while balancing the overflowing boxes again. "Have a good evening."

"I shall," he said, tipping his hat slightly before walking down the sidewalk.

Julie turned down the side of the building to her parked Camry and placed the boxes on the hood of the car so she could take out her keys. As she pressed the button that unlocked the doors, she heard the crunch of a footfall on gravel.

A frightened glance to the side revealed a tall shape looming over her.

"Stop or—"

Her head whipped back painfully, her scalp on fire. She started to fall, then her body jerked to a halt and she was pulled back toward the front of the building.

She could just see the tall guy in the hat above her, dragging her viciously by her ponytail.

Julie screamed and pressed down on her key fob's panic

button, but for too short a time to activate it. The man swung her sideways with no apparent effort, slamming her into the side of the building. The impact jarred the keys loose from her grip.

Trying to regain her feet, she twisted around and caught sight of a van, his apparent destination. With a spike of dread, she knew that if he succeeded in getting her into the van, she was as good as dead. Kicking and twisting, she screamed for help.

Her body rose off the ground, yanked up by her bleeding scalp, burning agony flaring white spots across her field of vision. Then he flung her down hard, as if he were cracking a whip. Something snapped within her, a crunch that vibrated through her body before she slipped into darkness.

She would not shut up. First he tried to soften her up by slapping her against the wall, but that only inspired her to greater volume. As he emerged onto the street, he became impatient with her caterwauling, so he jerked her by her hair and received blessed silence.

A moment later, he sighed. Her body hung completely lifeless, dangling from the fistful of hair he clutched. Judging by the angle of her head in relation to her shoulders, she was no longer a viable candidate for his ritual. She was nothing more than food now, if he became peckish, or more trash awaiting disposal.

Twice in one night, he had failed in his simple mission.

He swung open the rear doors of the van and tossed the lifeless body on top of the ripe plumber. With her spine completely shattered, the torque created by flinging her into the van almost dislodged her head from her torso. It was so easy to forget how fragile human bodies were.

Again, he had been careless.

Climbing into the driver's seat of the van, he noticed a police car traveling in the opposite direction. The pale blur of the occupant's face seemed to stare at him for a moment and the cruiser's brake lights flared.

He pulled into traffic, but glanced in the rearview mirror. Sure enough, the police officer had switched on the cruiser's red and blue lights as he made a U-turn and began pursuit of the van, siren wailing.

He had waited a few hours too long to dispose of the van. Yet another mistake to record on the night's ledger.

SEVENTEEN

After Dean finished his sandwich, he placed the small pile of leftover roast beef on a paper plate and waited.

Sam had borrowed Roy's dated computer system to print out a map of Laurel Hill. For the street-level detail they needed, he visited a mapping site, zoomed in and printed out the visible map over multiple pages in a grid pattern. With strips of clear adhesive tape, they made a map large enough to cover the breakfast nook table. Sam called up his incident file and fed the addresses to Dean, who marked each location with a red X.

Even with the television at low volume, Dean could hear the soothing voice of the news station's resident medical expert, Dr. Charlotte Kinzie—wearing a white doctor's lab coat over a black and gold top—as she rattled off tips for protecting children from MRSA: children should be encouraged to wash their hands with soap and warm water for as long as it took to sing "Happy Birthday" twice. Clean hard surfaces with a bleach mixture. Cover cuts… This was the second time she had given the same tips. Dean wasn't paying close enough attention to tell if the news station was rebroadcasting her initial report from the earlier telecast or if she was on live again. In a minute or two, she would switch gears and talk about flu prevention. One of the anchors commented that since authorities hadn't released the source of either outbreak, everyone should take appropriate precautions.

"That's everything," Sam said after providing the last address.

Dean stared at the map, frowning.

"Do you see a pattern?" Sam asked.

"Is random a pattern?" Dean said. "Put on a blindfold, throw twenty darts in the air, and you might get this pattern."

"Random," Sam repeated, while clicking around online.

"Okay, there are short spikes," Dean said, "where he walks along a street and several people die in weird accidents. Then the next cluster… But basically, random is what I've got."

"We should chart the outbreaks," Sam suggested, "see what that tells us."

"Medical stuff?" Dean asked doubtfully. "It doesn't fit the M.O., does it?"

"Two different fatal outbreaks in one town, while bizarre fatal accidents are occurring? I think we should put it in the mix."

"The news hasn't reported Patient Zero for either outbreak," Dean said, "and no call from Bobby. So how do we mark it on the map?"

After a few seconds of silence, Dean looked at Sam, who was deep in thought as he stared at his laptop screen.

"Sam? Are you there?" Dean tried not to imagine Sam was staring into the bowels of hell or that the graphics on the screen had begun to melt onto the keyboard, mesmerizing him. His brother said he had his reality meter under control, despite continuing hallucinations, so Dean wanted to give him the benefit of the doubt. But his concern for Sam's sanity was not something he could switch off.

"What? Oh, yes," Sam said, glancing up, "I'm fine. Something caught my eye."

"That's how it begins, Sam," Dean said, affecting a Public Service Announcement tone. "Something catches your eye, and before you know it, you've got an online porn addiction."

"Speaking from personal experience?"

"*I've* got all my vices under control," Dean replied, taking a sip from his flask. "More or less."

"Keep telling yourself that," Sam said. "Anyway, it's not porn. I found a local blog. It turned up in my search results. It catalogs all the crazy accidents. Do you know there was a bomb threat at the local high school?"

"It wasn't on the news."

From outside came an insistent meow.

It's time, Dean thought, scooping up the paper plate with the pile of roast beef.

"The bomb threat was a hoax," Sam said. "But this

blogger… She seems to be a student at the school, and she's floating some theories of her own, dismissing the normal stuff, terrorists…"

That Sam had missed an opportunity to needle Dean about feeding Roy's feral cat was a clear sign of his preoccupation with the blog, and that was enough to intrigue Dean.

"So what's her theory?" he asked over his shoulder.

As Dean opened the back door and glanced across the short wooden deck into the darkness beyond the pool of light, he saw Shadow's good eye reflecting yellow. He set the plate down carefully on the deck.

"When Roy gets back, make sure you tell him I didn't let you starve."

Knowing the cat wouldn't eat with him standing close, Dean backed into the house, but kept his eyes on the dark silhouette. He caught a good look at the cat when it stepped into the light. "Whoa," he exclaimed, startled.

"That cat's like a friggin' refugee from *Pet Sematary*," he said, walking back into the living room.

"What?"

"Nothing," Dean said. "What about blogger girl's theory?"

"To anyone else, it might seem like a schoolgirl's wild imagination."

"But not to you?"

"No," Sam said. "Sumiko Jones believes—"

"That's the schoolgirl?"

Sam nodded. "She believes the cause is supernatural in origin."

"That girl wins a kewpie doll."

"That's not all," Sam said, sitting up straighter. "She pinpointed—"

Dean's phone rang. He crossed to the table and checked the display. "Bobby," he said as he answered the call. "Whaddya got?"

The connection was bad, more static than words. He pressed the phone to his ear and strained to hear each word. "Bad connection. Speak up," he shouted.

"…left hospital… —geant McClary… patients… parents… kids… most go… preschool. First Step Forward…"

Dean turned to Sam. "No Patient Zero for the MRSA, but Bobby's found ground zero. It's—"

"First Step Forward Preschool," Sam finished.

"Dude, you're psychic now?"

"No," Sam said, "but maybe Sumiko is."

Over the phone, Dean heard a police siren begin to wail.

"Bobby, is that you and McClary?"

"—rolman spotted… —er's van… in pursuit…"

"Bobby! You're breaking up! What about the van? You're in pursuit? Where?"

Static filled the line.

"I'll call back," Dean shouted, disconnecting and dialing Bobby's number.

"They located bowler man?" Sam asked.

"A patrolman spotted the plumber's van. McClary flipped on the siren. That's all I heard."

The phone beeped and disconnected. "Crap!"

Dean looked down at the map spread across the table and

located Laurel Hill Medical Center. "They left the hospital. No idea which way…"

Sam typed on the laptop keyboard. "There, I subscribed to her feed. Sent her a message."

"Cruising schoolgirls now?" Dean said. "There are laws against that, man."

"I checked the preschool's website," Sam explained. "The staff members are listed, but no email addresses or phone numbers, and there's nothing in online White Pages. They must be unlisted."

"And the preschool's number?"

"After hours," Sam said. "I tried on my cell while you had Bobby on the line. No answer."

"So you asked blog girl for the phone numbers?"

"First I congratulated her on scooping the newscasters, asked how she knew about First Step. Then I asked for the number."

The laptop pinged. Sam smiled. "She wants to know why I want to know."

Sam typed a message.

"And?"

"I told her I had the same idea: supernatural origin."

"Spilling family secrets now?"

"I'm getting an anti-establishment vibe from her," Sam explained. "If she sees me as a kindred spirit, maybe she opens up."

"Dude, *you're* giving off a sexual predator vibe."

Focused on the information, Sam ignored the jibe. "Her 'sources' gave her the names of eight of the kids," Sam said.

"All go to First Step. And there it is—the cell number of the owner and manager, Lethia Williams."

"See what you can get out of her," Dean said. "I'll keep trying Bobby."

While Dean dialed Bobby's phone again and again with no success, he heard Sam talking to the preschool owner, giving her the insurance adjuster spiel. Moments later, Sam switched into sympathetic listener mode. Dean imagined the woman must have tremendous guilt issues if her business was the source of the staph outbreak.

In frustration, Dean slammed his phone down on the table.

"…anything unusual in the last couple days?" Sam was saying. "Anything that felt odd?"

A pause.

"Really. A tall man with a cane and a bowler hat. A ball…?"

Good job, Sam, Dean thought. *If bowler man caused one dangerous outbreak, it's a good bet he caused the other.*

And Bobby was in pursuit.

Think, Dean!

The static had begun when the call came in over McClary's radio. McClary activated his siren and the cell phone reception unceremoniously went to hell. Surely the siren wasn't the cause… but maybe bowler guy could interfere with communications. If he could disable dozens of airbags, maybe he could create cell phone interference. Dean considered it half a miracle they worked under normal circumstances.

He slapped a palm on the table top. "Police scanner!"

Sam held up his hand. "Thank you, Ms. Williams. I appreciate your assistance."

Dean hurried down the basement stairs.

EIGHTEEN

After leaving the hospital, Sergeant McClary and Bobby were heading to the police building, where Bobby had left his Chevelle. During the drive, Bobby decided to call Dean to tell him the MRSA outbreak had originated at the First Step Forward Preschool and that the deadly influenza strain may have started in a local bar.

"I thought you were here alone, Agent Willis," McClary said, an edge of suspicion creeping into his voice. Either suspicion or fear of an impending jurisdictional pissing contest.

"Couple of specialists in town I've worked with before," Bobby said casually before the call connected. "Studied the M.O. of the burglary ring."

Dean's phone rang with a garbled tone.

The poor cell phone connection prevented Bobby from

giving Dean all the information he had. By the time he had managed to tell Dean about the preschool, a request for backup had come over the police radio. A patrol officer had spotted the plumber's van and was in pursuit of the suspected kidnapper. As they were passing through the commercial district, McClary was closest to the scene, on a perpendicular course.

Bobby's connection dropped completely a few moments after McClary turned on his siren and lightbar.

Bobby double-checked his seatbelt. McClary noticed the motion. "Don't count on your airbag," Bobby reminded him.

"Right," McClary said, nodding. "EMP jammer."

"Or whatever the hell it is."

McClary spoke on his radio to ask the patrol officer, Tom Gravino, if he had a visual. Gravino confirmed and gave his location: traveling south on Queen's Boulevard.

"I'm on West Ellis Pike," McClary said. "I'll cut him off."

McClary tapped his brake and swerved around cars in the last two intersections before Queen's Boulevard. The cruiser roared onto the boulevard, making a wide right turn, and moments later Bobby spotted the speeding white plumber's van. Several blocks behind, another police cruiser raced in pursuit, Gravino's Crown Vic.

"Got him," McClary said, flashing a satisfied grin.

The van swerved right, jumping a curb on the west side of the highway and barreled across a vacant parking lot. Then the driver made a sharp right and headed back north up the alley behind the shopping center.

"Gravino, take the north entrance," McClary barked into

his microphone. "I'll block the south. Over."

McClary floored the accelerator, cutting across three lanes of traffic before hitting an entrance ramp into the parking lot. With his left hand braced on the dashboard and his right gripping the upper window frame, Bobby held on throughout the bumpy ride, trying not to think of everything that could go wrong in a high-speed pursuit when the odds were stacked in favor of the other guy.

"There's no outlet from that alley until the other side of the shopping center," McClary said. "He's trapped between us."

One side of the alley was lined with the backs of strip mall stores, one abutting the next at varying heights. The other side consisted of a long eight-foot high retaining wall topped by a ten-foot chain-link fence.

Calls from other units crackled over the radio. They were seconds away. Bobby had a bad feeling his fate would be decided before they arrived.

They saw the rear of the van as the driver raced north on a slight incline, toward Gravino's cruiser. The alley was wide enough for a semi to back into the loading docks behind a few of the larger stores in the strip mall; enough space for two cars to pass side by side. But Gravino wouldn't allow that to happen. For the next few moments, Gravino and the driver in the van were engaged in a game of chicken—a game that was fair only if both drivers had to worry about the outcome of a collision.

At the last moment, Gravino slammed on his brakes and spun his wheel hard to the left to present the broadside of his cruiser to the front of the van.

The van never slowed, never veered.

The collision sounded like an explosion. The van crushed the passenger side of the cop car and pushed the cruiser twenty feet backward. The back wheels of the van rose two feet off the ground, before slamming down.

A split-second after the initial impact, a woman's body came flying out through the van's windshield, slamming into the lightbar on the hood of the cruiser and partially dislodging it, before rolling limply down the rear window.

The rear doors of the van swung open and Bobby saw a blur of movement inside, somebody bending over, lifting something.

"Look out!"

A man's body sailed through the air toward McClary's approaching cruiser.

"What the hell!?" McClary exclaimed.

He slammed on his brakes and tried to veer to the right.

The large corpse—Bobby realized it must be the plumber's body, with a ring of dried blood around his chest—crashed into the windshield. The safety glass crumpled with a thousand fractures and the lifeless body pressed down on the dashboard.

McClary's evasive action steered the car down a loading bay ramp where it slammed into the concrete wall. As Bobby suspected, no airbags deployed as he was flung against the seatbelt's shoulder strap. Only after he fell back against the seat did he release the breath he had been holding. His hands trembled as he unbuckled the seat belt. In the instant before the impact, he had convinced himself the seatbelt would fail as well.

With the cruiser's front end crumpled, Bobby's door screeched as he forced it open. McClary's door seemed jammed as well, but his side window had shattered, so bracing himself against the window frame, he hoisted himself through. Bobby squeezed through the tight space he had made and circled around to the back of the cruiser.

They had lost less than thirty seconds, but they were too late to save Gravino.

At the top of the ramp, with McClary a step behind him, Bobby saw the tall figure in the bowler hat walking toward the smashed police cruiser, an iron-tipped cane clutched in his right hand. There was no mistaking who he was, even if Bobby hadn't figured out exactly *what* he was.

Gravino was out of the ruined police car, his gun in a two-handed grip pointed at the imposing figure, who strode forward as if unconcerned. "Stop! Or I'll shoot!"

Quick as a striking cobra, the cane batted aside the gun. To Gravino's credit, he held onto his handgun, but before he could bring it to bear again, the tall man thrust the cane forward, like a fencer lunging with the tip of an épée.

The cane pierced Gravino's throat with so much force that it shattered his spine, the iron tip bursting through the nape of his neck. Then, as if sensing Bobby and McClary behind him, the tall man grabbed Gravino's belt with his left hand and effortlessly hurled him bodily over his head toward them.

As soon as the cane tip pulled free of Gravino's throat,

blood spurted and gurgled from the opening. For a few moments, Gravino's heart kept beating as his body tumbled through the air. McClary broke to the left, while Bobby ducked to the right. Both men had their guns drawn, but their target loped away from them.

Several police cruisers arrived as reinforcements, three at the north end of the alley and two more from the south. Without warning, McClary fired several rounds at the retreating figure. None seemed to connect. Bobby tracked the man, arms extended, his gun in a double-handed grip, waiting for the right moment and wishing he had a rifle instead.

The tall man veered to the right and leapt onto the closed lid of a dark Dumpster. As he turned toward a utility pole braced against the back wall of a store, Bobby fired three quick shots. At the second shot, the tall man jerked and Bobby believed he had found his mark. The bowler hat, already askew, tumbled off the man's head.

"D'you see that?" McClary asked, stunned, as they ran to close the distance to their target.

"Yup."

"How is that possible?"

"Bad genes," Bobby said, and instantly regretted it.

The tall man scooped up his bowler from the Dumpster lid and jammed it on his head again, slipped his cane through his belt, and leapt toward the utility pole. With inhuman strength and speed, he climbed the pole, hand over hand, and reached the roof even as McClary and Bobby emptied their magazines at the ascending target.

McClary spoke into the microphone clipped to his epaulet. "Officer down! Perp's on the roof! Armed and extremely dangerous! Move units to the front of the shopping plaza. Now! Go! Go!"

The last police car at each end of the alley reversed course to circle around to the front. Bobby looked back at McClary's cruiser, Gravino's, and the van. All vehicles disabled. If they'd had an opportunity to stop him, they had missed it. The odds were in his favor, always in his favor. And Bobby now seriously doubted conventional ammo would slow him down, let alone put him down.

Nevertheless, Bobby broke into a sprint, or what passed for a sprint at his age, to the alley's north entrance. All three police cruisers had backed out now. McClary ran beside him, his breathing not nearly as labored as Bobby's. Reports on McClary's radio came back negative, one after another. Nobody had spotted the fugitive.

"I hit him at least twice," McClary said. "You?"

"Four, easy," Bobby said, matter-of-fact. "Three in a row while he climbed that pole like a damned monkey."

"What the hell is he?"

"Don't know," Bobby said honestly as they reached the entrance and turned toward the front of the plaza.

"But that—what I saw—on his head," McClary said. "It was, right?"

Bobby nodded. "Horns."

"Jesus!"

They stopped in front of the first store. Police cruisers roamed the vast empty parking lot like sharks hoping for chum. One patrol officer trained his car's spotlight toward the store windows as he drove slowly past each business.

Too much glare, Bobby thought. *Never see a damn thing in there.*

McClary stared at Bobby. "You're not nearly as freaked out as I am."

"No," Bobby admitted. He peered into the night, hoping to catch some movement. Streetlights provided enough illumination to prevent the tall man from hiding anywhere outside the plaza. Maybe he had doubled back, once they abandoned the alley. The way he climbed the utility pole, he'd have no problem scaling the chain-link fence above the retaining wall.

Bobby shook his head. "We lost him."

"Not yet," McClary said. Squeezing the radio microphone again, he deployed the cruisers in a widening grid. Two stayed at the shopping plaza—if the search failed, he and Bobby would need a ride back to the police station.

McClary turned to Bobby, hands on his belt. "So what was that? Genetic mutation? Some kind of circus freak?"

"If I knew, I'd tell you," Bobby said, and almost believed he would. "Whatever it is, it ain't normal."

"Not by a long shot," McClary declared. Then, quieter, he said, "Maybe I've read too much Stephen King, but I'm starting to doubt it was even human."

"Certainly a possibility."

"*What?* If I were you, I'd be calling me crazy."

Bobby smiled. "No," he said, "I wouldn't—and neither will they."

The blue Monte Carlo swung into the lot, veered toward

the storefront and pulled up to the curb in front of Bobby. Dean climbed out of the driver's side a moment after Sam exited the passenger side.

One of the two remaining cruisers swooped in with a short siren blast.

"They're with me," Bobby informed McClary. "My specialists: Tom and John Smith."

McClary waved off the support, then spoke into his radio. "Hernandez, wait around back with the bodies. Call an ambulance and notify the county coroner."

"B—Agent Willis, you okay?" Sam asked, catching himself just in time. "The cell phone was useless."

"But we remembered Roy's police scanner," Dean finished. "Followed the chatter here."

"Tom, John," Bobby said, "this is Sergeant McClary, Laurel Hill P.D. Friend of Roy's. Supervised Lucas Dempsey. Already explained you're specialists I've worked with previously."

They shook hands and McClary seemed to take their measure. Bobby was confident McClary had no reason to doubt him after what they had been through.

"Got our work cut out for us, boys," Bobby said. "Sumbitch shrugged off bullets like they were paintball pellets."

"Specialists," McClary said to the Winchesters. "So you've dealt with this sort of thing before."

"Um, what sort of thing, exactly?" Sam asked, looking from McClary to Bobby and back again, wondering if McClary had peeked at their hunter playbook or read a few chapters.

"Leaps buildings in a single bound," McClary said. "Throws human bodies around like beach balls at a summer concert. Has a pair of horns growing out of his head. That sort of thing."

"Oh," Sam said, and cleared his throat. "Then yes, more or less."

McClary's radio crackled to life.

"Sergeant, I'm behind the shopping plaza," Hernandez said, "and we have a problem."

"Speak."

"I found two bodies."

"Two?"

"Yes, sir," Hernandez said. "Gravino is missing."

NINETEEN

"Balls," Bobby exclaimed for the third time since he and the Winchesters had returned to Roy's cabin from the shopping center by way of the police station. Bobby wanted his car on hand in case they needed to split up.

"Stop kicking yourself, Bobby," Sam said. "You couldn't know."

"An obvious ploy," Bobby said. "Gets the cavalry to chase his shadow and doubles back. Hell, I had a hunch and didn't follow it. Now Gravino's body's missing."

McClary had stayed at the crime scene, upset with himself as well, but he had caught Bobby's arm before he left with Sam and Dean and whispered fiercely, "We need to talk. Off the record. After I'm done with the official paperwork."

Bobby had nodded and gripped the man's shoulder. "Whenever you're ready."

"You're sure the cop was dead?" Dean asked.

"Course I'm sure, ya idjit," Bobby said, irritated. But Dean could tell Bobby's anger was directed inward. "Horned sumbitch skewered his throat with that cane."

"Even if you had gone back," Sam reasoned, "you couldn't have stopped him. You said so yourself. You shot him four times, McClary hit him twice."

"Why take a corpse?" Dean asked. "Why that corpse?"

Bobby glared at him for a moment, then nodded slowly. "Fresher."

"For food?" Sam wondered.

"Maybe," Dean said, shrugging. "Maybe it animates corpses."

"Hasn't played that tune so far," Bobby said, considering.

"The point is," Dean continued, "we don't know. We can't guess where this thing will strike next, or why, because we don't know what the hell it is."

"Dean's right," Bobby said. "We're twisting in the wind."

"I guess we can rule out the Leviathan at least," Sam said.

"For a bright side," Bobby observed, "that ain't sayin' much."

"We know he creates bad luck, causes accidents," Sam said.

"Makes bad situations worse," Dean added, "spreads sickness."

"Sickness?" Bobby asked. "You tied him to the outbreaks?"

Sam filled him in on the preschool owner's account of a tall man with a bowler and a cane handing a ball back to the young boy who became Patient Zero.

"McClary and I were in the emergency room," Bobby

said. "Place was overflowing, like a plague ward. Heard talk among the staff about four cases of West Nile virus, for Pete's sake. So, accidents, disasters, illness, disease. Look hard enough, bet we find reports of crop failure."

"Any suspects come to mind?" Sam asked as he plugged the laptop into a phone jack to use Roy's dial-up internet service. He winced as if in pain as the modem squawked and dinged its way to a slow connection.

Bobby frowned. "My collection of lore's locked in a storage unit. Puts me at a disadvantage. Let's run it down... Even if I hadn't seen the damn thing, we're a few hours from the Jersey coast, so rule out merpeople or sirens."

"'Merpeople'?" Dean asked.

"Lured sailors to their destruction," Bobby said. "Bad omens. Foretold disaster, but some believed they also caused it."

"A duwende?" Sam suggested, skimming an article. "They can cause bad luck."

"Too small," Bobby said. "We're looking for something triple-XL."

"Same deal with the mothman," Sam said. "Its appearance supposedly foretold disasters, including the '67 Silver Bridge collapse at rush hour. Forty-six people died. Maybe he does more than predict disasters."

"Mothman had large wings," Bobby said. "Explains the moniker. This guy had horns, not wings, unless he had a pair tucked under his suit..."

"And why climb when you can fly?" Dean pointed out.

"No mention of weapons, either," Bobby said. "This

thing swung its cane like a sword… or a club. Carries it in plain sight."

"A club," Sam said thoughtfully, "bound in iron…" He clicked a few keys, read quickly and looked up at them. "I know what it is."

"Don't keep us in suspense," Bobby said.

"It's a creature from Japanese folklore," Sam said. "An oni. Humanoid, gigantic, described as an ogre or troll, two horns growing out of its head, sometimes an odd number of eyes or fingers, carries an iron club—a *kanabo*. Sounds like very bad news. It's described as invincible, causes diseases and disaster, is associated with bad luck, misfortune, and known to consume human flesh."

"Gravino," Bobby said. "Fresh meat."

"So we've got an oni on our hands," Dean said. "And it's invincible."

"Need an invincibility loophole," Bobby said.

"Any tips on how to gank it?" Dean asked.

Sam frowned, scrolled around, and clicked another link. "There's something here about a demon gate, warding off the oni."

"Horse left that barn," Bobby said. "I recall something about a ceremony to expel an oni."

"The *oni-yahari* ceremony," Sam said, and raised his eyebrows, "involves villagers throwing soybeans out of their homes and chanting 'Oni go out, blessings come in.'"

"All the earmarks of whistling past a graveyard," Bobby said, disgusted.

"Right," Dean agreed. "I am not fighting this thing with a

bag of beans. We've gotta find something else."

Tora walked along the produce aisle, ostensibly checking bundles of carrots, heads of lettuce and assorted apples, but his attention was focused on the young woman with dark brown hair ten paces ahead of him. Five minutes before, the oni had followed her into Robertson's Market. From her navy blue skirt suit, he assumed she had an office job, one with some responsibility, as she had apparently worked late on a Friday and had yet to change into more casual clothes. She wore no engagement ring or wedding band and, rather than pushing a shopping cart and stocking up for a family, she carried a plastic basket containing a few small items. She was young and appeared healthy enough for his plans—and without the attachment of a spouse or family who might report her missing before the oni had time to finish the ritual. Unless she worked weekends as well, her coworkers would not note her absence until it was too late.

He had no intention of buying anything from the market and he walked the aisles primarily to assess the woman, but he couldn't resist nurturing strains of salmonella, e-coli and listeria, increasing their potency and resistance to antibiotics while spreading them to every surface and each item he touched.

Once he had convinced himself the woman was a good candidate, he proceeded toward the exit. As he passed a partially enclosed office behind an information desk, he spotted a grainy photograph of himself being displayed on a small television set. A news bulletin was warning civilians to contact police if they saw him. Sometimes he forgot how efficiently humans in this age disseminated information.

As he was not yet ready to tip his hand, Tora must remember to fade from human perception when his power was not otherwise engaged. Though hidden electronic surveillance cameras might capture his image, he could channel his power so that humans focused their attention elsewhere, overlooking him, despite his imposing size.

He left the supermarket empty-handed and waited next to the woman's silver Nissan Altima in his blue and white Chevy conversion van.

He had acquired the vehicle behind a store from a shop owner who had the misfortune to run into the oni while locking up for the night. With the dead police officer slung over his shoulder, the oni convinced the proprietor that he needed to get the cop to the emergency room immediately. The man wanted to call 911, but the oni persuaded him that driving to the hospital in the van would save time.

"Oh, but I'd be keeping you from your family," the oni said, as if reconsidering the emergency call option.

"I'm recently divorced," the man said bitterly. "I live alone."

"Well, I could wait here for the ambulance..." the oni said.

"No, you're right. This is faster." With that, the owner opened the rear doors of the van.

But when the oni laid out Officer Gravino on the carpeted interior, the shopkeeper finally saw the mortal wound in the cop's throat and slowly backed away.

"That man's dead," the shopkeeper whispered. "What have you—?"

Tora shoved his cane under the man's jaw and drove the point up through the roof of his mouth and into his brain with such force the man's feet left the ground. For a few seconds his arms and legs twitched and his eyes rolled back in his head. Then his body slumped, lifeless, suspended in mid-air by the cane. With his free hand, the oni opened the back door of the store wide enough to heave the corpse into the room. After locking that door, he closed the rear van doors and drove away.

En route to his hideaway, Tora stopped at a traffic light and noticed the young woman in the car next to him. On a whim, he followed her a few blocks and waited until she parked in the supermarket lot before he pulled in beside her car.

To keep the storefront in view, he had backed the van into its parking space. Through gaps in the windows between large posters proclaiming double coupons and other special offers, he watched her enter an express checkout lane near the exit. Before she left the store, he started the van and drove to the far side of the parking lot, pulling into a space where he could watch her car through his side-view mirror.

She opened the car door lock with a key fob button and climbed in with two small plastic bags of groceries that she placed on the passenger seat before buckling her seatbelt. A moment later, she started the car, turned on her headlights and drove from the lot. He followed at a discreet distance.

Within a half-mile, she left the commercial district and turned onto a state road with longer gaps between traffic lights and a limited number of streetlights. Tora gradually accelerated, closing the gap between her Altima and the van to several hundred feet. Before he had climbed back into the van, he had nicked the base of the valve stem on her rear driver's side tire with his hardened and darkening thumbnail. Pressing his right index finger to his temple, he focused his power, reaching out to apply pressure to the compromised valve stem. This was about fine control. He must create enough damage to drain the tire, but not so much that it triggered a blowout, which might startle the woman and cause her to crash. If she suffered a serious injury, she would be useless for his ritual. Of course, he could keep her body for its food value, but he already had a fresh human corpse for his larder.

Her tire began to thump and wobble, the metal rim digging into the flattened rubber. After a few seconds, she noticed the problem, coasted onto the shoulder and turned on her hazard lights. Two hundred feet behind her, he slowed his approach, giving her time to react to the roadside inconvenience. As he neared, he noticed the telltale glow of an activated cell phone near her cheek.

Of course, wearing formal clothes she would want to avoid the grimy task of changing a flat tire, which is why he planned to offer assistance. But if she had the services of an automobile club, she might decline the offer of help from a stranger.

Focusing again, he interfered with her cell phone operation. The transmission would become too garbled to give her location.

From a hundred feet back, he saw the exaggerated

pantomime of her frustration with the phone. This was exactly the type of situation in which a portable, personal communication device could prove invaluable. If it worked.

As she exited the car and walked to the trunk, he pulled onto the shoulder, coasting the rest of the way to avoid startling her. She opened the trunk, hands on her hips as she stared down into the interior, her body language a study in frustration. After a few moments, she managed to haul out the spare tire and lean it against the rear side panel of the Altima.

He climbed out of the van, intent on playing the role of Good Samaritan. As he swung his door closed, the sound startled her. She looked up, eyes wide, staring into the glare of his headlights, and probably saw him in silhouette.

"Good evening, madam," he said, tipping his hat. "May I be of service?"

"Got a cell phone I can borrow?"

"Unfortunately, no," he said. "But I know how to change a flat tire."

"You some kind of male chauvinist? Think a woman can't change a flat?"

"You would soil your clothing."

"What about your suit, pal?"

"It is of no concern to me."

"Thanks for the offer, but I can handle this on my own."

"As you wish," he said and tipped his hat once more before returning to the van. He climbed into the driver's scat and waited, unmoving as she wrestled with the lug nut wrench. First she broke a fingernail and cursed loud enough for him to hear it in the van. Then the wrench slipped and gouged her foot above her navy shoe, prompting a louder torrent of curses.

Once more he left the van and walked toward her.

"I said you could leave," she barked at him, a convenient target for her frustration.

"I thought you could use the illumination from my headlights."

"Your headlights are giving me a migraine," she snapped. "Now go. Please! Before I call the cops."

"How will you call them?" he said. "Your phone doesn't work."

"What?"

"How will you call for help?"

She raised the lug nut wrench defensively. "I'll scream, you bastard. Get out of here. Now!"

"Nobody will hear your scream."

With a flick of motion, he swatted the wrench out of her hands with his cane. It clanged on the asphalt on the far side of the road. Startled, she stared at him for a moment, her eyes wide in terror. Then she backed away, preparing to run, but he flipped the cane around and hooked her ankle with the handle, tripping her.

She fell to her knees, crying out in pain.

When she reached for the door handle with her right hand to pull herself up, he grabbed her hair and rammed her head into the side panel of the car. This time he took extra care not to kill the woman in the process of subduing her. Dazed, she fell backward onto the hard surface of the road, moaning in pain and confusion, struggling to rise with limbs that had not regained sufficient coordination to complete the task.

He grabbed her upper arm and dragged her to the back of the van. Holding her upright, he opened the doors. Though her head lolled to the side and her eyelids fluttered, she became aware of the police officer's body sprawled across the carpeted floor and her moaning became shrill. She tried to pull away from him, but lost her footing and dangled from his tight grip. Unceremoniously, he tossed her into the back of the van where she landed on the corpse and immediately pushed herself away.

While she struggled to sit up and escape from the van, he opened the toolbox he had discovered earlier and removed a large roll of silver duct tape. She tried to push herself off the floor of the van, but he shoved her back, hard enough to knock the breath out of her. Again he cautioned himself to moderate his use of force. It was so easy to break their bones. He caught one ankle, pressed it against the other and quickly wrapped a few loops of tape around them.

"Stop! Get away from me! HELP!"

He slapped her face hard enough to bring tears to her eyes.

In a moment, he wrapped tape around her face, covering her mouth but leaving her flaring nostrils exposed so she wouldn't suffocate. He reached for her wrist, but she slapped his hand away, pushing herself deeper into the van to remain out of his reach. Catching one foot in his grip, he yanked hard, pulling her to him.

"I do not plan to kill you," he assured her.

Immediately her eyes tracked to the corpse sharing the back of the van with her.

"That was self-defense," he said, which was a partial truth. The cop had pointed a gun at him. "I have other plans for you."

That information seemed to alarm her more than he had anticipated. She thrashed as if suffering a violent seizure.

With a sigh, he grabbed her head and banged it forcefully against the floor of the van, hoping to incapacitate her without crushing her skull in the process. Again her eyes fluttered, rolling up in her head, and her limbs sagged as she drifted toward unconsciousness. While she remained docile, he rolled her onto her stomach and taped her wrists behind her back. A moment later he slammed the van doors and returned to her car to clean up the scene.

She had stopped the Altima on a lonely stretch of road, with a thin border of trees on either side. Unfortunately, there wasn't enough depth or darkness in the woods to conceal the vehicle, which left one other reasonable option.

After tossing the spare tire and the lug nut wrench back into the trunk, along with her two bags of groceries, he removed a grimy white T-shirt and left it tucked in the driver's window. Passing motorists would assume a mechanical malfunction had caused the driver to abandon the vehicle until it could be towed or repaired. He took her purse and cell phone with him, as leaving those items behind would arouse suspicion.

After he climbed back into the driver's seat of the van, he looked in the back and saw that the woman remained semi-conscious. No broken bones, no serious tissue injuries, and she was young and healthy, a perfect candidate.

He shifted the van into gear and drove away. Soon the Altima's blinking hazard lights faded in the distance.

Despite his earlier frustrations, his plans remained on schedule. Already, the calling had begun. Now he could perform the demon gate ritual with the woman.

TWENTY

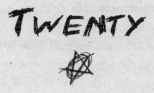

Ryan Bramble slipped in and out of consciousness, plagued by a series of disturbing nightmares.

In one dream, he was lost in a jungle of Amazonian proportions, the type of place where explorers might find cargo cults or discover new plants or species of animals. He dangled over a precipice, clutching coarse vines and roots as his feet sought purchase. Glancing over his shoulder, he couldn't see the bottom of the cliff; the greenery descended into an encompassing darkness. In the distance he heard animal grunts, and strange birdsong filled the air. Strain as he might, he heard no human sounds, no voices and not the slightest hint of technology. The place was strange and alien to him, as if he had been transported into the setting of a Jules Verne novel.

He wanted to call for help, but some instinct warned

him against revealing his location. A sense of foreboding pressed like a weight against his awareness. The unseen predators rustling through the bushes possessed a ferocity he was unprepared to face. For his own survival, he must stay hidden from them. Dream certainty told him so. But his position was untenable. His tight grip on the vines that supported his weight was causing them to excrete sap, and that moisture was loosening his hold. Inch by inch, he slipped farther down from the edge, farther from potential rescue.

When the vine in his right hand snapped, he swung wildly to the left and almost lost his grip on the other vine. With his right arm flailing, he snagged a dry root protruding from the cliff face and stabilized himself. Panting from fright and exhaustion, he sucked in the sickly sweet smell of the treacherous sap and the heavy jungle air. How much longer could he grip his meager lifeline? Isolated from civilization, what were the odds of rescue? A grim certainty took hold in his mind, that he would slip and fall, plunging into the darkness below, and die alone, unnoticed and forgotten.

With hope slipping away and his arms trembling with exhaustion, he glanced up when a shadow fell over him and couldn't believe what he saw. Sumiko! Standing on the edge of the precipice, staring impassively down at him, arms crossed.

"Sumiko, help me!" he whispered fiercely. "Get something to pull me up!"

"Help you?" she asked incredulously. "Oh, I have something right here," she said, turning away to lift something by her feet.

He waited nervously. A glimmer of hope flickered to life.

She would save him. Sumiko would save—

A dark rectangular shape swept into view and at first he couldn't understand what it was, but then he saw the large crack down the middle, the power cord dangling behind like the tail of a stingray. It was the flat-screen monitor he had broken.

"Miko?"

She hurled the monitor at him.

One corner smashed into his right hand and he lost his grip on the root. Spinning from the vine, he felt sap ooze between his fingers and slipped down several inches.

"What the hell?" he yelled at her. "You could have killed me!"

Now she was holding a countertop microwave in both arms. She dropped it on his head.

"Nooo—!"

Ryan thrashed in bed, muscles convulsing as the nightmare turned to instant darkness.

Then he stood in a long hallway in what looked like an elegant hotel gone to seed. Every ten feet, on both sides of the hallway, doors with chipped gold paint awaited him. He ran from one end of the hallway to the other, but found no elevator or stairwell exit, only the hallway and the doors.

He picked a door at random and tried the doorknob. The door swung inward and he almost stepped into a pitch-black void that chilled him to the bone. He slammed the door and backed away, bumping into the door on the other side of the hall.

Tentatively, he tried that door. It opened on a single

room with gray brick walls and warped floorboards; no windows or closet or bathroom. The room seemed like a cell, or a root cellar, not a place to spend much time. He turned in a circle and again felt a chill. Glancing at the door, he saw it was slowly closing. A fierce premonition overwhelmed him—if the door closed it would vanish, leaving another brick wall. He would never escape. Below the warped floorboards, nothing but a grave waited for him. Lunging forward, he caught the edge of the door an inch before it reached the doorjamb. Without a backward glance, he fled the room and slammed the door. He was trembling and soaked with perspiration.

The third door opened onto the hallway itself, as if he was peering into a mirror. When he walked through the doorway he simultaneously stepped into the hallway again.

A fourth door opened into a room with pulsing gray walls, glistening as if wet, but he couldn't bring himself to touch them. Stepping closer, he felt heat radiating from the throbbing walls, as if they were part of a diseased organ. He noticed tiny pores or spiracles covering the surface and they appeared inflamed. As he watched, black goo, like some sort of toxin, began to ooze from the tiny holes, running down. Following the course of the black liquid, he looked down for the first time and realized the floor was made of the same living material as the walls. As soon as he noticed it, the floor began to undulate beneath him. Twice he almost fell before catching his balance. The second time, his hand nearly touched the floor. He saw with horror that the black ooze had begun to pool in several spots around him.

Stumbling, he worked his way toward the exit, and with each step his shoes pulled against the tacky, glistening floor. He felt like an insect caught in the petals of a carnivorous plant, like one of the flies his seventh grade science teacher had fed to the Venus flytrap on his desk. Somehow he fought his way out to the hallway and pulled the door shut.

Unwilling to try any other rooms, Ryan stood helplessly in the middle of the hallway and tried to formulate a plan to escape. At least one room must have an exit. How else could he have gotten into the hallway?

Sooner or later, he would have to try the other rooms.

He took a step and his foot broke through the floor. Yanking it free, he took another step and felt the floor collapse beneath his weight again. The building that contained the hallway—whatever the building was—began to tremble, slightly at first, but gradually increasing until cracks appeared in the walls and spread to the ceiling. Domed light bulbs popped or flickered out, one by one, and darkness claimed the hallway. Plaster rained down on his head and the flooring shook so violently he fell down. He knew that if an earthquake rocked the building and he couldn't leave, the next best option was to huddle in a doorway, but that meant he would have to open another door.

A violent explosion shook the hallway. Ryan flinched and made a decision. Lurching forward, he fumbled in the dark until he found a doorknob and pushed the door open. Though he braced himself in the doorway, another violent tremor cost him his balance. He swayed forward and stepped into the dark room—and toppled into thin air to the sound of people screaming.

Ryan landed with a thud, his left arm and legs bound.

His eyes opened to morning light, but he fought violently against the sweat-soaked bed sheet that ensnared him as if it were alive. Trembling, he sat against the edge of his bed, head in his hands. *Nightmares,* he told himself. *That's all.*

He had fallen out of bed.

His muscles were taut as piano wire. His skin felt feverish and he wondered if he had caught one of those diseases, the epidemics he had heard mentioned on the radio. He had a killer headache. He pressed his fingers and palms against his forehead and felt his pulse raging, straining against his flesh. The heat radiating from his forehead convinced him he had a fever. If he had to guess, it was well over a hundred degrees, maybe as high as brain-cooking levels, although he felt wired, rather than wiped out. His head was sore and he found a couple of lumps, as if he'd been whacked over the head with a club... Of course, he had fallen out of bed and reacted violently to the nightmares. He would probably find half a dozen bruises on his body in a few hours.

He pulled off his sweat-soaked T-shirt and put on a fresh one, then a pair of sweat pants. He walked down the hall to his father's bedroom. Saturday morning meant he had a slim chance of actually seeing his father in person. However, when he reached the master bedroom, his father was already showered, shaved and dressed, and was combing his hair. From the determined look on his face, Ryan assumed he was heading out.

"Hey, Dad," he said.

His father glanced his way briefly while rinsing his hands. "You look like hell."

Ryan was several inches taller than his father and broader across the chest. He dyed his hair blue, but its natural color was red, no match to his father's black hair. Based on photos, Ryan favored his mother more than his father and he thought maybe that resemblance brought back bad memories and was the reason his father avoided him. Maybe the simple act of being born had forever damaged the father-son bond.

"I had a bad dream," Ryan said. "Where are you headed?"

"Errands," his father said. "In case I'm not back for dinner, I'll leave a twenty on the counter. Order pizza or something."

"I was hoping we could talk…"

"Later," his father said, slapping his shoulder as he slipped past him. "Gotta run."

"Of course," Ryan said to his father's retreating back as he hurried downstairs and, less than a minute later, left the house. "It's always later."

Ryan noticed a photo on the floor, its edge sticking out from the closet door. He pulled the door open and found two photos he had seen recently—Ryan as a toddler on his first tricycle, with red, white and blue ribbons dangling from the handlebars, and a picture of him a few years later, cannonballing into a neighbor's above-ground swimming pool. Sumiko had organized a birthday party for him a week ago and had borrowed a bunch of childhood photos of Ryan from his father to display on a sheet of poster board titled "Ryan Through The Years." She had included one photo from each year of his life, from birth to his seventeenth birthday, the last taken the morning of the party.

Looking up, he saw a dark wooden box on the shelf, its lid held partially open by a stack of photos hastily put away after the party. Ryan took the box down and laid it on the foot of his father's bed, intending to put the fallen photos back inside and secure the lid's latch. Instead he took more photos out and placed them in two rows on the bed. Even in the photos Sumiko hadn't selected for the poster, he was almost always alone. He had no siblings and his mother had died giving birth to him. His father had taken most of the photos, so he was behind the camera, not pictured with his son. Always alone—that was how Ryan saw himself, and the photos documented a solitary existence. From the moment he'd been born, his life had become derailed. The story of his life was "what might have been." No relationship with a mother he couldn't know. The happy memories expected of a normal childhood switched out at birth for years of silent grief. Many of his classmates came from broken homes, children of divorce or of parents who never married, but his family had never been whole. Not for a single day. What should have been his family was nothing more than a broken promise.

He closed his eyes and sighed. His pounding headache was not conducive to philosophical contemplation and he really had no stomach for wallowing in self-pity. Shaking his head, he gathered the photos into a neat stack and shoved them into the laminated box.

He noticed his fingernails and paused. They had darkened

from the beds outward, as if bruised, but when he pressed on them they weren't sore. Had he banged them in his sleep? Both hands? All ten fingernails? Again, he feared some mystery illness coursed through his veins.

When he stood up, lifting the box in one hand, a surge of pain flashed across his forehead and, for a moment, darkness enveloped him. The box fell from his numb fingers and struck the floor.

Disoriented, he swayed on his feet and tasted blood. His lip was split and bleeding where a canine had jabbed into the flesh. Seizure victims could bite their tongues. Was it possible he had experienced a brief seizure?

His father couldn't afford an emergency room bill, especially for a false alarm. Ryan would wait and see if it got worse before visiting an E.R.

Bending carefully, he picked up the wooden photo box—and discovered a hidden panel in the base. The fall had jarred it loose, less than a quarter-inch, but he found a hidden latch to release the tray and pulled it out. Tucked carefully inside the narrow compartment was a folded piece of loose-leaf paper filled with a swooping, feminine cursive: a handwritten note from his mother that his father had never shown him.

Leaving the box on the bed, he walked slowly out of his father's bedroom as he read the letter.

In his dream, Dalton Rourke punched Summerdale kids in the face, over and over. He would knock them down and they would rise up again, their faces bloody but ready and willing to take more punishment. At first he enjoyed the continual violence, the grim satisfaction of inflicting pain, unleashing his rage on all the kids who had it easy, had more than him, who looked down their noses at him. He would beat the crap out of every one of them and shake them down, like a tax for having it too good. Teach them that life was anything but easy, then let them crawl home, bawling for their mommies to make it all better.

But the dream suddenly became weird. When one kid's cheek split open, something hard and twisted grew out of the blood, like a diseased shrub. Another teen, with the bridge of his nose split, clawed at his face as vines sprouted from beneath the torn flesh. A third one doubled over, coughing up blood from internal injuries one moment, then spewing fast-growing vines the next. Wooden spikes erupt from the fourth teen's eye sockets.

Staring at their transformations in horror, he backed away. "What's wrong with you?" he asked. "What the hell are you?"

"We are what you made us."

"You're—you're not human!"

The kid with spikes for eyes turned to the others and said, "Look who's talking, boys!"

"You're crazy," Dalton whispered.

The others laughed hysterically, pausing to grunt uncomfortably as vines and branches erupted from their flesh and splashed him with their blood, before resuming their laughter. Their blood sprayed his eyes, and his vision blurred and swam as he tried to blink it away. The more he tried to see, the darker everything became, first blood-red, before descending into darkness, where their laughter followed him in a series of distorted echoes.

He awoke in his narrow bed in his cramped bedroom overflowing with his intentional clutter, soaked in his own sweat, panting as if he'd run a four-minute mile. His head throbbed and it felt like a steel band was tightening around his skull. After a few moments, he tasted blood in his mouth and he thought crazily that the splatter of dream-blood had crossed over from nightmare into reality, that the blood of his victims contaminated him even now that he was awake.

Lurching out of bed, he stumbled to his trashcan and emptied the contents of his stomach, retching so hard he felt muscles cramping in his side. His lips were cut, swollen and bloody. Droplets of blood speckled his forearms and hands. He curled his right hand into a fist so hard that his arm trembled. With a savage grunt, he drove his fist into the wall, his knuckles smashing a hole through the plaster.

Jesse Trumball raised the tire iron over the man's head and this time nobody stopped him. He swung the rod down, like it was an axe and he was splitting wood. The metal crushed the man's skull as the woman screamed. He swung it again, pulping the man's head. Lifeless eyes hung loose in their shattered sockets. By the third swing he noticed bits of fractured molars sticking to the tire iron, which was tacky with blood.

The woman kneeled beside the dead man, her face gripped in her hands, wailing inconsolably. Taking position in front of her, he hoisted the tire iron again. Before he swung it, she looked up at him, hair wild, her eyes wide with grief and terror, tears streaking her mascara so that he had the impression her face had begun to melt. He waited for the inevitable plea for life. Actually, he wanted her to beg for mercy so that for one moment she would understand how pointless that was, that she had wasted her life believing the wrong things. He edged the rod slightly higher, jaw clenched, preparing to split her skull open with the first blow.

She took a deep, trembling breath. "You're a monster," she said. "You know that now, don't you?"

Jesse screamed and swung the tire iron—

His body jerked awake.

His eyes flew open, his heart racing as he took a moment to recognize his bedroom. Memory merged with the dream. He fought to separate reality from fantasy. Had he killed the man? And the woman? Or had he spared them? No… he'd wanted to kill the man, but Bart had stopped him. Bart had been absent in the dream version.

Was the dream a vision of what would have happened if he'd attacked the theatergoers alone? Or just his subconscious playing games with him? He grabbed the bed sheet to toss it aside and noticed that it was slashed in several places, as if someone had gone nuts with a box cutter. As he stood, a pounding headache overwhelmed him and he swayed on his feet, catching the headboard to stop himself from tipping over.

With a little help from Bart and Keith, he'd polished off a case of beer before coming home. That could explain why most of the night was a blur and maybe account for the weird dream and the morning hangover. He wondered if his father felt this way every day of his life. Staggering toward the bathroom, he rubbed two raised bumps on his scalp. He couldn't remember banging his head. Maybe he'd passed out and Bart and Keith had given him a taste of his own weapon for scaring the crap out of them.

If they had messed with him while he was unconscious, he'd break their arms, then shove their heads through the nearest brick wall. Either way, they were dead to him.

TWENTY-ONE

Kim Jacobs came to her senses, gradually aware of a series of body aches, as brief images from recent memory flashed across her mind: working late to finalize her company's financial statements, leaving the supermarket after picking up ingredients to cook herself dinner, the flat tire, her attempt to change the flat tire, the tall man in the van who wouldn't go away. Then everything came back to her, the attack in the street, banging her head against the side of her Altima, lying in the back of his van with duct tape wrapped around her legs…

Even before she willed her eyes open, the pain in her head was throbbing in time with her heartbeat. She assumed she had suffered a concussion in the attack, possibly a fractured skull. Pressed together, her wrists burned, and she couldn't move her legs, though her bare toes rubbed against thin carpeting. Her shoulders ached as if someone had tried to pull her arms out of their sockets. In a moment, she understood why. Her body was suspended vertically, all her weight supported by her wrists held high overhead.

When she looked up, she saw rope looped around her wrists and tied to a large eyebolt screwed into the ceiling. Her toes brushed the ground, but couldn't support much of her weight. Instead, she twisted in a slow rotation, glimpsing an unlit neon sign of letters spelling out the word ARCADE. Beneath the sign was a room with a large display window, but no pinball machines or coin-operated video games. Anything that had been in there had been stolen or sold. Turning a bit farther, she saw a three-tiered rack holding a dozen chipped bowling balls, then a series of polished wooden bowling lanes fronted with standard consoles and attached plastic seats, ringed by plastic benches for those not keeping score. She saw no pins at the ends of the lanes, just dark holes beneath the pin-setters. She recognized the place. The bowling alley had been closed for several months. Years ago, she had bowled at Laurel Lanes with her coworkers in a casual league on Tuesday nights. Now she was a prisoner here.

Turning farther, she recoiled in horror as she almost bumped into the body of a dead man hanging upside down by his ankles, wearing only a white t-shirt and boxers. Rectangular sections of flesh on his thighs and upper arms had been carved out with a sharp instrument, the wounds raw and red.

The cop in the back of the van, she thought immediately. Her gaze lowered to check his face. She screamed.

His body ended at the bloody stump of his neck. He'd been decapitated.

Shrieking, she lurched against her bonds, twisting and pulling with all her strength, hoping to break free of the ropes or dislodge the eyebolt in the ceiling. After thrashing helplessly for what felt like ten minutes, she sagged in exhaustion, panting as the white spots in her vision disappeared one by one.

"You are strong," he said. "Good. That strength will help you survive the ritual."

Pivoting on her big toe, she twisted so she could see her kidnapper. He sat on a high stool behind the shoe counter. The cubbyholes behind him held a half-dozen unmatched shoes, abandoned just like the damaged bowling balls, too worthless to sell.

With his hands positioned on either side of a scuffed red bowling ball bag, the tall man smiled at her. "I wanted you awake for this."

"Are you—are you planning to… kill me?"

"If I wanted you dead, you would be dead."

"Then what?" Kim asked, horrible possibilities rising to the surface of her mind faster than she could push them back down.

"I have special plans for you," he said gravely. "I want to bring you through the demon gate."

"What—what does that mean?"

"In time," he said. "First, I want you to witness this."

He reached into the bowling bag and she braced herself, sensing what was in the bag. For a moment, she squeezed her eyes shut, but then she had to look—

—at the severed head of the dead cop.

"Oh, God—oh, God—oh, God," she whispered.

She felt her gorge rise and gagged as bile burned her throat.

"You see," he said slowly, raising his fingers toward the cop's head, "they must shed their human face. That is the first step."

His fingernails were angled into sharp points and seemed unnaturally thick, like animal claws. With the fingernail of his index finger, he dug into the top of the cop's forehead and peeled a long strip of skin away from the face. Then another one. And another.

She screamed until her voice failed.

Dean stood watching the television news at low volume, tapping the red marker against his palm. Dr. Charlotte Kinzie, the news station's medical expert, was explaining to the anchor that the Burlington County Health Department had declared additional outbreaks of food poisoning, mentioning salmonella, listeria and e-coli, traced to a local supermarket. In addition to the new outbreaks, the influenza and MRSA cases were reaching epidemic proportions, with over a dozen deaths. While she spoke, the station aired footage of a packed emergency room, doctors and nurses hurrying through the hallways, followed by a brief interview with an elderly doctor who declared the situation to be the worst he had experienced in his forty years in medicine. He mentioned that the new strain of influenza was deadlier than the one Laurel Hill experienced eighteen years ago, only three years into his tenure at Laurel Hill General.

Sam had had his nose glued to the laptop all morning, spending half his time checking for new accidents of a bizarre nature and relaying the incident locations to Dean so he could update their oversized town map, and the other half seeking additional lore for ways to defeat the oni.

"A guy fell cleaning his gutters," Sam said. "Died."

"Normal accident?"

"He impaled his brain on a garden hoe."

"I'll add it with a question mark."

Bobby, dressed in his Fed suit and ready to roll, hung around long enough to take an old-school approach, calling hunters he had worked with over the years, looking for anyone who may have crossed paths with an oni.

"The town's scheduled to have a fiftieth anniversary parade tomorrow. We could try the soybean casting-out ceremony," Sam suggested.

"Definitely Plan B," Dean said. "Maybe Plan C."

Knuckles rapped impatiently on the front door.

"Did somebody order pizza?" Dean asked.

"For breakfast?" Sam said.

"Well, it ain't Roy," Bobby said as he covered his phone. "It's his place."

"Maybe he lost his key?" Dean wondered aloud. But his internal paranoia meter had started ticking.

Bobby walked toward the door as he ended his call. "Thanks, Digger," he said into his cell phone. "Find anything, call me pronto. I'll owe you."

Dean looked at Sam and mouthed "Digger?" Sam shrugged.

Bobby glanced through the curtained window beside the door. "It's McClary."

Dean frowned. "Were you expecting him?"

"Didn't schedule a play date, if that's what you mean."

Bobby reached for the doorknob.

"Hold up a second."

Dean hurried to the kitchen, grabbing Sam's arm on the way. "Back my play."

Sam looked confused, but withheld his questions.

Dean set a meat cleaver on the countertop and gave Sam a meaningful nod. Then he pulled a jug of borax from beneath the sink and poured the liquid over a striped dishtowel. He wrung it out just shy of sopping. With his hands wet from the cleanser, he moved toward Bobby, dishtowel in hand.

"Now."

Bobby shook his head. "This ain't—"

"Think about it," Dean said. "If he's a Big Mouth, this is how he'd gank us. Isolated. No witnesses."

Outside, McClary knocked again, louder.

"Naturally, he'd knock first," Bobby said dryly.

"Catch us with our guard down," Sam said, swayed by Dean's argument.

Dean nodded to the door, ready.

Bobby shook his head. "You're starting to remind me of Frank."

As soon as Bobby pulled the door open, McClary, in uniform, burst into the room.

Dean stepped in front of him, pretended to dry off with the soaked towel, and extended his right hand.

"Welcome, Sergeant."

A distracted frown flickered across McClary's face, but he reflexively shook Dean's offered hand, then looked down at his own—now dripping harmlessly with borax.

"I think you missed a spot," he said.

"Yeah, sorry," Dean apologized, feeling the tension leave his body. He had been ready to spring into action at the first sign of burning, melting Leviathan flesh. "I'll grab a fresh towel."

Before turning his attention to McClary, Bobby shot Dean an "I told you so" glare. Dean responded with a minuscule "better safe than sorry" shrug.

"I'm here unofficially," McClary said, "about as unofficially as unofficial gets."

"I expected a call, Sergeant," Bobby said to the agitated cop, "not a personal visit."

"Sorry. I haven't slept," McClary said, pacing around the small room. "I'm kinda wired."

"We hadn't noticed," Dean remarked as he offered the man a fresh towel from the kitchen.

"About last night…" Bobby said.

"Want to know what I wrote in my report?"

"Okay."

"Absolutely nothing about horns."

"Wise omission."

"I suggested the assailant *may* have been wounded," McClary said. "Know why?"

"I'll bite."

"The only blood found at the scene belonged to the

victims."

"Makes sense," Bobby said.

"Sure. If you weren't there," McClary said. "And Chief Donato was not there. But I hit the guy. You hit him too."

"This is true."

McClary threw up his arms in frustration. "But I can't write that bullets bounced off this guy."

"Maybe he wore a Kevlar vest," Sam suggested.

McClary snapped his fingers. "Bulletproof vest. Good one. I can use that."

"Happy to help."

"But it's not true," McClary said, turning to Bobby. "Because I'm guessing guys with horns sprouting from their head don't shop the Kevlar aisles."

"Probably not," Bobby said.

"So… those were real horns?" McClary asked. "Not some kind of appliances or implants, like those fake vampire teeth fetishists get anchored in their jaw?"

"You could write that in your report," Bobby suggested. "Cover yourself."

McClary plopped down on the sofa and sighed. "Yeah, if anyone else saw what we saw. But that doesn't explain the other stuff."

Bobby walked over to the man and sat in the armchair perpendicular to the sofa so he could address McClary on his level. "Comes a time, Sergeant, when you have to decide."

"Decide what?"

"Live the comfortable lie," Bobby said, "or face the hard truth."

TWENTY-TWO

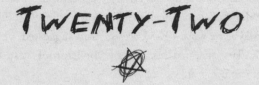

Sumiko stood in front of Ryan's house for five minutes, trying to decide if she wanted to walk up to the door or go back home. After a night to sleep on their argument, she tried to decide if she'd been fair to him and, conversely, if he'd been fair to her. If she was honest with herself, she had to admit she had been a bit self-absorbed about the blog. All the crazy stuff happening in town fed into her need to post updates, to try to find a connection that might explain all the oddities. She'd graduated from posting current events at school—tongue-in-cheek investigative reports about the mystery meat in the school cafeteria, and speculation about the identity of the perpetrators of various school pranks—along with hearty helpings of libidinous gossip, to writing posts about people dying in horrifying accidents and outbreaks of deadly diseases. At some point, the information flow had overwhelmed her.

Now that her emotions were at a low boil, instead of seething, she tried to see things from Ryan's point of view. She had been a girlfriend consumed by information and events that had little relevance to her blog's professed subject matter or to them as high school students. Maybe she hadn't made enough time for him. Setting aside her own interests for a moment, she knew he worried about his grades and about his future, and that he had little support from an absentee father. That was something they had in common. Ryan would need scholarship help and a boatload of loans to have a shot at college, any college. He probably had more stress in his life at the moment than he could handle. So, maybe he needed to talk to someone, and she had been the only person willing to listen—except she was too busy rattling on about all the weird stuff she was documenting on her blog.

She took a deep breath.

Okay, she admitted. *I was kind of a jerk. But,* she reminded herself, *he crossed a line by destroying my property.*

Was the destruction intentional? He had grown several inches in the last year, and sometimes he was ungainly, to say the least. She hadn't really given him time to explain.

We were both wrong, she concluded.

With a sigh, she walked up to his door and knocked.

Ryan opened the door, wearing an old blue hoodie pulled over his head, and quickly stuffed his hands in the pockets. He seemed a bit twitchy, his eyes looking as if he'd seen a ghost. If she didn't known him so well, she might assume he was using illegal drugs.

"Sumiko?"

"Ryan," she said. "Are you okay?"

"Yes—I don't know," he said, shrugging. "I'm not sure what 'okay' means anymore."

"This is hard for me," she said, looking down at her feet for a second, "but I want to apologize. Not for yelling at you when you broke my monitor. You totally deserved that. I want to apologize for not listening to you—"

"I'll pay for the monitor," Ryan said. "It was my fault."

"Thanks. I'm using my old CRT for now. So, no rush on paying me back. I'll see if I can have it repaired. It'll be cheaper than buying a new one. Maybe."

"Okay," Ryan said absently. "Send me the bill."

"Ryan," Sumiko said, "what's wrong? You seem... odd."

"Look, I gotta go."

"Where?"

"You were right about us breaking up," Ryan said. "You're busy and I... I need some time alone, you know? You should stay away from me. Seriously."

"Ryan, are you blowing me off?"

"It's a bad time," Ryan said, looking past her. "That's all."

"You're breaking up with me?"

"It's inevitable, right?" he said. "You've got your pick of colleges. You'll be gone, new worlds to conquer, and I'll be here. It was just a high school fling, right?"

"Ryan, that's not how I see us."

"Maybe you should face reality, Sumiko," Ryan said. "This has to end. No sense prolonging the pain. Just... rip off the

Band-Aid, right?"

"It was a stupid fight, Ryan," she pleaded. "Couples have fights all the time. They get over it. Why are you acting this way?"

"It's a bad time, Miko," he said, reaching for the door. "I've gotta go."

As she stood on the doorstep, her jaw practically unhinged in surprise, he stepped back and closed the door in her face. For a few moments, she stared at the door in disbelief. Waiting. But he left her standing there, dumbfounded. Obviously something was wrong with him, the way he huddled inside the hoodie, his lack of eye contact, his twitchiness. An idea began to form, that Ryan had somehow become part of the craziness infecting the town. Yes, the bomb scare was a hoax, but that didn't mean Ryan's weird behavior wasn't part of the general madness.

Finally, she turned and walked away, in the general direction of her home. "What the hell was that?" she asked herself aloud.

At that moment, she had no idea, but she was determined to find out.

Ryan leaned against the closed door, sensing Sumiko's presence on the doormat outside. Certain she had seen through him, he tried to remember what he had said or what signs he'd exhibited. He was sure he'd been infected by something, and he couldn't bear the thought of infecting her. Or of admitting to her that he might be dying. Best to push her away.

As soon as he lowered his guard, he felt the rage bubbling up inside him and his muscles trembled with the urge to smash something or hurt someone. Talking to Sumiko had exhausted him. Pushing her away had been painful, but necessary. It was the only way to protect her from whatever was happening.

Inside the pocket of his hoodie, his right hand clutched the letter his mother had written to his father weeks before he had been born. The idea that his father kept that letter secret from him all these years made him want to scream. Once more he unfolded the paper and stared at the words as if they were a puzzle and its solution would explain his life.

He found himself sitting at the kitchen table looking down at the sheet of paper. The letter spoke about commitment despite what had happened to his mother. Without getting into specifics, she hinted at a terrible event that his parents had endured, a tragedy his father had kept hidden from him. His fists trembled on either side of the letter. A fever burned within him. His forehead continued to throb with a dull ache, itching as if he had a rash. His fingernails, now completely dark, had coarsened, with pointed tips so sharp he had been able to carve his name in the wooden tabletop with one of them, as if it were the blade of a penknife. He had hidden his nails from Sumiko, even as a sick desire to wrap his hands around her throat surged within him like a dark tide.

When he heard a key in the front door lock, Ryan jumped out of his chair, worried that Sumiko had come back. But she didn't have a key. Only his father…

"I forgot some letters I wanted to mail," Ryan's father

said when he spotted his son standing in the kitchen. He twirled his car keys around his index finger as if he couldn't wait to get back on the road.

"What is this?" Ryan asked, feeling anger rising inside him again.

His father stopped by the sideboard, his hands on a stack of stamped bills to be mailed. "What are you talking about?"

"This letter mom wrote you before I was born."

"Where did you find that?"

"Answer the question!"

"Ryan…" His father looked away, trying to compose himself. "You were never meant to see that."

"What does it mean?"

"Your mother and I were going through a rough patch when she wrote that," his father said. "Trying to deal with… to get ready for parenthood."

"What about the attack?"

"Ryan…"

"She writes, 'Honestly, I didn't know how we could survive together, after the attack. In different ways, it was incredibly hard for both of us. My decision to keep this child was the hardest decision I've ever made, knowing you might not choose to walk this path with me. I know this is nothing like how we envisioned raising a child together. So thank you for supporting my decision to have this baby and to raise him as if he were ours. Together, we are so strong, my love. I know we can handle this and create something positive out of what has, until now, only been horrible.'"

Ryan stopped reading and stared at his father.

"You've always hated me."

"That's not true."

"My whole life, you've avoided me, never wanted to spend any time with me."

"I've had to work two jobs," his father said, "to keep a roof over our heads."

"That's always been your excuse," Ryan said. "But you don't look at me like a son, not really. I'm like a neighbor's kid you've had to watch for too long." He laughed bitterly. "All these years, feeling like I wasn't good enough for you, that I was somehow lacking. No matter how hard I worked, how good my grades were, nothing made a difference."

"You have worked hard," his father said. "Maybe I didn't tell you often enough."

"Are you kidding? You never said 'good job' like you meant it. Any compliment, any scrap of praise, all I felt was your disappointment. I assumed I wasn't good enough. I changed the way I looked!" Ryan grabbed a hank of his dyed blue hair. "Every time I looked in the mirror, I thought something was wrong with me. Because of the way you treated me!"

"You're not a neighbor's kid," his father said, but he continued to look past Ryan's shoulder, finding something more interesting about the kitchen cabinets than his child. "Every morning I wake up, I tell myself you are your mother's son."

"But not yours," Ryan said, finally voicing the truth. He dyed his hair to hide its natural color, because it marked him as different from his father, his only surviving parent.

"Not mine," his father conceded. "I tried to give you a good home, a safe place to live, a chance to grow and learn…"

"This house isn't a home," Ryan said angrily. "It's a motel, with two strangers renting rooms."

"Your mother was the strong one," his father said. "I tell myself that you are her son, but when I look at you… all I see is him."

"My real father?"

"The man who attacked your mother," he said. "I'll never forgive him."

"Who—Where is he?" Ryan asked.

"They—The police never found him," his father said. "Your mother and I decided we'd raise you, but on that one day she wasn't strong enough."

"The day she was attacked?"

"The day you were born," his father said, and now a tear rolled down his cheek. "She hemorrhaged so badly, the doctors tried everything…" His voice became strangled with emotion for a couple of moments. "Before she died, she made me promise… promise I would take care of you."

In that moment, Ryan finally witnessed genuine emotion from his father, the love for the mother Ryan had never known. Throughout Ryan's life, his father had been a stoic, distant man, never showing emotion. He had watched over Ryan, given him a place to live, but had never shown him real affection. Never a tear shed in pride or joy. He had taken care of him, kept his promise to Ryan's mother, but nothing more.

Watching his father moved to tears, but not for him—never for him—Ryan felt rage boiling inside again. He had received more affection from teachers, and from his friends' parents, even from complete strangers, than he ever had from this man before him.

"A lie," Ryan shouted at him. "From the minute I was born, my life has been one big fat lie!"

With a roar of anger, Ryan grabbed the edge of the table and flipped it over.

"Ryan!"

He grabbed the dish drainer, lined with drying glasses and bowls, and threw it against the wall. Glass and ceramic shattered and the dish drainer knocked the calendar off the wall.

"All these years, I've hated my life," Ryan yelled, striding toward his father with clenched fists, "and now I know why. Because I've hated you!"

His father stood there, stricken, hardly reacting when Ryan punched him in the face. Beneath his knuckles, he felt his father's nose crunch and shift. Blood streaked down his face. Ryan punched him in the face again, knocking him to the ground. When he fell, Ryan drew back his right foot and kicked him in the gut.

His father doubled over, helpless.

Ryan pulled back his foot again and aimed the toe of his boot at his father's head. As the rage burned within him, he imagined his father's face pulverized, his skull fractured, and the mental picture made him smile in anticipation. He trembled with the need to crush the life out of the man who had made his whole life a sham.

At the last moment, something stopped him from delivering a fatal blow, something fought against the rage inside him and won.

"You're not worth it!" he whispered fiercely and ran outside.

Standing in front of his house—never his home—he bent over, hands on his knees, panting as he waited for his heart rate to return to normal. When his head began to clear, he realized what had stopped him—Sumiko. She was the only thing that had ever truly meant something in his life and deep inside he knew that if he murdered his father, he would lose her forever. For a moment, he had stared into the abyss and finality had stared back at him.

Even though he had pushed her away for her own safety, he couldn't accept a future without the possibility of her in his life. She had saved his father. But he wasn't sure if anything could save him.

TWENTY-THREE

Disoriented, Jesse assumed the previous night's beer consumption had dehydrated him, because something was definitely wrong with his body, other than a standard-issue hangover. He thought food might settle his stomach, make the pounding in his head go away or simmer down. He staggered down the hall to the staircase and grabbed the banister railing with his right hand while massaging his brow with the left. The raised bumps at the top of his forehead—just behind where his hairline would be if he didn't shave his head bald—felt dry and scaly, as if he had some kind of rash. His probing fingers found a split in the skin, like a cut, but without blood.

His father climbed the stairs, clutching a forty-ounce beer bottle in his hand but paying attention to little else. Jesse, distracted by the bloodless slit in his scalp, bumped into his old man and knocked the bottle loose. It hit the stairs and toppled over, spilling the rest of the beer.

"What the hell!?" his father groused, his speech slurred. "You some kind of moron, boy?"

Jesse shoved him against the wall. "I must be," he said angrily, "to have stood your drunken bullshit all these years."

"You got it wrong, buddy boy," his father shouted, spittle flying freely. "*I've* had to put up with *you* all these years. Now make yourself useful—get me another beer and clean up this damned mess!"

"Do I look like your servant, Pop?"

His father leaned in so close Jesse had no choice but to inhale the sour mixture of booze and dried vomit steaming out of his mouth. "No," his father said. "You look like something I scraped off my shoe."

Jesse grabbed his father's chin and shoved him backward, hard, slamming his head into the wall. A framed picture of his father standing with a few fishing buddies at some lodge fell off the wall and clattered down the stairs. Before his father could react, Jesse slugged him in his big gut, then grabbed him by the shoulders and hurled him sidewise, down the stairs.

His father rolled awkwardly, his foot splitting two balusters on the way down. At the base of the stairs, he swayed on his hands and knees, fighting for the strength or balance to rise.

Jesse charged down the stairs and grabbed his father by the hair, lifting his face up high enough for a punch.

"Go ahead, tough guy," his father slurred. "Do it, you stupid son of a bitch. Kill me, just like you killed your own mother!"

Jesse released him and stepped back, staring at his father as if he had sprouted a second head. "What?"

"You killed her," his father repeated. "So go ahead and kill me. A matched set."

"What the hell are you talking about?" Jesse yelled angrily. "Mom ran away. She couldn't take living with you. And who could blame her?"

Jesse blamed her. For leaving him with this worthless human being, for abandoning him. His father liked to blame Jesse for her leaving, saying she couldn't take raising a kid and left to avoid the responsibility, but Jesse knew she left because her husband was a worthless drunk. The only doubt that had ever crept into his mind was trying to understand why she would throw out the baby with the beer-drenched loser.

"It was you," his father said, pointing at him, "you freak. You killed her."

His father climbed awkwardly to his feet, clutching the edge of the kitchen table for support. In his inebriated state, standing and regaining his balance required all his remaining wits and stamina. Panting, he staggered back until he bumped into the counter. Jesse stalked after him, fists clenched at his sides.

"You're a worthless liar," Jesse said. "She ran away from you!"

"Want proof, smartass? I'll take you to her grave!"

"Liar!"

All his life, the idea that Jesse's mother might come back for him, might contact him and offer him an escape from this worthless excuse for a father, had kept him sane. A tiny scrap of hope that somewhere life made sense. He hated that she had abandoned him, but he thought he could forgive her... if she came back for him.

"She died giving birth to you, jackass," his father said. "Bled out on the table. Worst part is, you're probably not even mine. I loved your mother, but she was no saint. Sure, I'd go on my benders, but she'd shack up with a different guy every other week, always looking for something else, something better. Never satisfied with what we had. And in the end, it caught up to her. She gave birth to a freak bastard and it killed her."

"You're a worthless drunk and a lousy liar," Jesse said, his lips drawn tight. "Why should I believe a word out of your mouth?"

"Believe what you want," his father said. "But you know it's true." He raised his hands over his head and laughed. "Hell, I'm a hero! Raising somebody's bastard. I should get a medal."

"Shut up!"

"Know why I never told you she died, where she was buried?" his father asked, his slobbery mouth hanging open. "Because I was afraid you might piss on her grave, that killing her wasn't good enough for—"

Without thinking, Jesse had grabbed the largest butcher knife from the wooden block on the counter and shoved the blade up to the handle into his father's chest. Only after he released the handle did Jesse comprehend what he'd done.

His father looked down, taking several seconds to understand what had happened. Then he looked up at Jesse again.

"Had to have the…"

He dropped to his knees.

"…matched… set."

He toppled forward, driving the knife a bit deeper, before slumping on his side in a growing pool of blood.

Backing away, Jesse grimaced at the pain burning through his scalp. He pressed his palms against the twin bumps and it seemed to him that they had grown larger in the minute or two since he rushed down the stairs.

He grabbed his jacket and his father's car keys and ran out of the house.

Dalton Rourke sat on the edge of his unmade bed and stared at his dark, pointed fingernails. After punching a hole in his wall, he had washed the plaster dust off his hand and rinsed the vomit out of his mouth. But no amount of scrubbing removed the darkness from his fingernails. Some kids his age painted their fingernails black, but he hadn't done anything of the sort. The darkness seemed natural somehow—if not normal—possibly from a vitamin deficiency. If that were true, he thought it should be a slow process, starting at the beds of the nails. But the weird coloring and coarsening had happened rapidly. Maybe it was a symptom of a disease. His grandparents never turned off the television, even when they weren't watching it, and he had heard them talking about a bunch of epidemics in town. Could he have been infected? The really weird part was that his nails seemed stronger than before. After lashing out and punching a hole in the wall, he'd have expected bruising on his hand, too, but it felt fine.

His head continued to throb and the two bumps above his hairline felt dry and scaly. Probing with his fingers, he felt a cut in his skin but, strangely, no blood. Beneath the slit, something hard pressed upward, almost like adult teeth erupted from the gums, pushing out baby teeth.

Grabbing his gray knit hat off his headboard, he walked down the hall to the bathroom. He paused mid-way to listen to his grandparents below.

"…punish him if we're not here?" his grandfather asked.

"I'm certainly not going to let *Fiddler* tickets go to waste," his grandmother replied.

He nodded to himself, recalling that they had purchased tickets for *Fiddler on the Roof* at the Cheshire Theater months ago. If that was for tonight's show, he'd have the house to himself. He wouldn't have to listen to them bitch about how he was a disappointment as a grandson, an embarrassment to the family name, a juvenile delinquent headed for life in jail, yadda, yadda, yadda.

"We've got less than a year left to put up with his nonsense," his grandfather said.

Of course, he thought. *They'll be kicking me out as soon as I turn eighteen.*

That had been their threat for the last three years. Not that he should straighten up his act or they would throw him out—they weren't offering an either-or proposition. They had simply told him that at eighteen he would have to find somewhere else to live, their obligation would be finished. Nobody could speak ill of them after that. In the end, all that mattered to them was their reputation.

His grandfather had suggested on more than one occasion that he join the military at eighteen: "Maybe they can whip a loser into shape."

Dalton grimaced as a spike of pain shot across his forehead. He stumbled into the bathroom and stared at his head in the mirror. Normally, his buzz cut revealed his scalp, but his red hair seemed longer, as if it had grown a half-inch in the last twenty-four hours. With the fingers of both hands, he pushed his hair away from the bump with the split skin over it. He saw something bone-white underneath. He prodded it with his index finger, expecting something loose, embedded under his skin, but it felt sturdy and hard as bone. "What the hell is that?" he whispered to himself.

He reached into a drawer under the sink and removed a pair of scissors, spreading the blades as far apart as possible. Holding one of the blades in his hand like a miniature ice pick, he shoved the point into the cut in his scalp and pressed against the hard substance. If he could wedge the blade under the obstacle, he thought, he could pry it out of his head. But as much as he probed and prodded, he couldn't find an underside to the hard object. Grimacing, he dug deeper, then yelped when the blade slipped and gashed his scalp.

Letting the scissors fall into the sink, he reached up with his palm to press on the fresh cut. Blood flowed between his fingers and down one side of his face. He grabbed a clean towel from the small closet in the bathroom and pressed it against the open wound. The throbbing in his head accelerated, accompanied by steady waves of excruciating pain. Now it felt as if something with sharp claws had crawled under his scalp and wanted to burrow into his brain. Grimacing again, he rammed his head against the mirror over the sink. The blood-soaked towel cushioned the blow, but the mirror was thoroughly fractured. His vision swam and he thought he might pass out. With his free hand, he clutched the edge of the sink while biting on his lower lip, hoping the sudden burst of fresh pain would help him focus and stay upright.

From outside the bathroom, he heard the plodding footfalls of his grandfather coming up the stairs. "Dalton!" he called.

"Yeah," he mumbled. Then, louder, "What?"

"Where the hell are you?"

Dalton hurried to the bathroom door, opened it and leaned out. "Bathroom," he said. "I'm cutting my hair."

His grandfather squinted in his direction as if trying to make sense of the image of the teenager leaning through a doorway. "You're bleeding."

"It's just a nick."

"What kind of dumbass nicks his scalp while cutting his own hair?"

Dalton shrugged. "I sneezed. Jabbed myself with the scissors."

"You're paying for that towel out of your allowance."

"Sure," Dalton said. *What friggin' allowance are we talking about, you senile tightwad?*

Dalton tried his best not to mouth off to the old man. Between the thundering pain in his head, the blood running down his scalp, and the blood pooling in his mouth from where he'd bitten his lip, he just wanted the old bastard gone. Arguing would only prolong the encounter.

"Your grandmother and I will be attending a play tonight."

"*Fiddler*," Dalton said. "I heard."

"So you're eavesdropping now?"

"Whatever," Dalton said. "Like I give a rat's ass about your social calendar."

Well, he'd tried to keep it civil. *Screw them.*

"That's the type of disrespect that gets you in trouble," his grandfather said, waggling a wrinkled finger at him. "We're going out tonight. You are still grounded. You will remain in this house and stay out of trouble. No visitors. I better not find out you let that creepy Ferrato kid in this house. He's a no-good thief."

"Whatever," Dalton said again. "That all?"

"If I find out you crossed any lines, I'm taking away all your privileges."

Guy's delusional, Dalton thought. *What friggin' privileges?*

"Yeah, whatever," he said. "I got a head wound to treat."

"So it's settled?"

"For the third time, old man."

"I'd lose the attitude if I were you, boy," his grandfather said, his face livid.

Now he had gone too far and provoked the old timer simply because he wanted to get rid of him.

"We let your mother run wild and see what happened to her. A no-good tramp who got herself knocked up and gave birth to a troublemaking bastard."

Dalton flung the door aside and let the bloody towel fall to the floor.

"Shut the hell up about my mother!"

"What do you know about her, boy? She was a whore with no self-respect and she died giving birth to a worthless piece of—"

Dalton was on him in a second, wrapping his hands with their dark, sharp fingernails around his grandfather's wattled throat, ready to squeeze the life out of the old bastard's frail body. "I should rip your head off!"

Movement from the bottom of the stairs drew Dalton's attention. His grandmother was staring up at him with a cold loathing that was almost palpable. "Put one mark on your grandfather and I swear to God I will have you charged with assault and battery and locked away."

Not if I kill you both, Dalton thought. *I could get away.*

She raised the telephone clutched in her hand. "One call and your life is over."

Dalton glared at her for a moment, looked at his grandfather who seemed much too calm for having two powerful hands wrapped around his scrawny throat, and back at his grandmother. Suddenly, he realized they wanted him to lash out. That was the only excuse they needed. Raising a delinquent, trying to set him on the straight and narrow, might look noble in the eyes of their neighbors and the members of their church. If he assaulted them, nobody would blame them for having him locked up. If he was dangerous to his own family, his grandparents got a free pass. They would be off the hook.

How long have they been waiting for me to hit one of them, to inflict a bruise or broken bone, something worthy of a long jail term?

He couldn't give them the satisfaction.

With a muttered curse he dropped his hands and backed away. Blood flowed freely down his face, dripping on the front of his shirt.

Oh, if they want violence, I'll give them violence, he thought. *But I'll dish it out on my terms, when I'm ready...*

TWENTY-FOUR

Dean took the wheel of the Monte Carlo, which allowed Sam to review information on the laptop. The Who's "Won't Get Fooled Again" crackled through the car's crappy speakers. The enlarged map spread out on Roy's breakfast nook table had, so far, proved to be a dead end. Once Sam had determined from witness statements that two weird fatal accidents occurred two minutes and five miles apart, they had to face the possibility that the oni's malevolent effect no longer required his physical presence. Unless he had access to a vehicle traveling 150 miles per hour, the effective radius of his power had expanded to include both locations. Another disturbing possibility was that he may not have been local at either accident, which would make him that much harder to locate. Their new plan was tenuous at best. Sam and Dean would patrol the town, like a police cruiser but without supernatural blinders, while Bobby and McClary reviewed traffic and security cam footage on the chance they would spot something suspicious, then direct the Winchesters to the trouble zone.

"Needle in a haystack time, Sam," Dean said.

"He's building toward something," Sam said. "He came here for a reason."

"Maybe this is oni vacation time," Dean suggested. "Show up in a medium-size town, create havoc for a week, kill a few dozen locals, go back into hibernation."

"Hibernation?"

"Well, some kinda disappearing act," Dean said. "We haven't been able to find a trail of destruction leading here."

After a few quiet moments, Sam said, "You really thought McClary might be one of them?"

"A Big Mouth?" Dean said. "Sure."

"Why him?"

"Why not?" Dean shot back. "We don't know their numbers or what they're planning. They were *us*, Sam. They painted a friggin' bull's-eye on our backs in neon colors. So how do I trust a stranger without knowing?"

"Right," Sam said.

He looked down at the laptop, frowning in thought. "Skip the residential neighborhoods," he said. "Let's assume small stuff doesn't require his presence anymore. But maybe he still needs to be hands-on for the big stuff."

Dean nodded. "Like pile-ups and overpass collapses."

"If he's planning something big," Sam said, "he needs lots of bodies in one place."

"Right."

"I downloaded the community events calendar," Sam said. "It might give us some possibilities."

Bobby helped Sergeant McClary move three computer workstations to one desk in the open patrol area of the Laurel Hill Police Department. McClary logged into the security software to pull up a grid of traffic and security camera feeds on each monitor. As Bobby soon discovered, the feeds varied tremendously in quality. Most cameras had stationary views or limited tilt and zoom. Others produced blurry images or were mounted too high on traffic or utility poles to show any detail. But the oni was distinctive enough, assuming he retained his bowler and cane, that even a distant image would suffice.

McClary seemed nervous, his hands shaky as he juggled data and power cables around to set the monitors side by side. Back at the cabin, he had opted for the hard truth rather than the comfortable lie. The first thing he'd asked after Bobby told him that the weird accidents were the work of a supernatural being known as an oni was, "Does Roy know about this stuff?"

"Yes," Bobby said, "but he's retired."

"Retired from what?"

"Hunting," Bobby replied, explaining that Roy had lost his wife and his arm to another type of supernatural creature.

"What about Lucas? Did he know?"

"Not sure how much Roy told him," Bobby said, figuring it was Roy's prerogative to go into those details. "But I know he wanted to keep the boy out of this life."

"So instead of becoming a... hunter," McClary said, "Lucas goes into law enforcement."

"Apples don't fall far."

McClary lowered himself onto a stool beside the kitchen counter. "The weird thing is, the roadside accident that killed Lucas fits the same profile as this... oni."

"If the oni was around then," Dean said. "Second car rams the first, gas tank explodes, both drivers and Lucas die."

"How do you hunt something like this?" McClary asked. "How do you stop it?"

"We find its weakness," Dean said, "and gank it."

"'Gank it'?" McClary asked. "You mean, kill it?"

"No due process for monsters," Bobby said. "It's them or us."

Now McClary was committed to helping them find a supernatural creature.

Once all the monitors displayed a full grid of camera feeds, McClary rubbed his jaw thoughtfully and looked at Bobby. "On any given day, forty percent of our video surveillance cameras don't work. Of those that do, some can't move at all, most can only focus in one direction and, at night, the images are too dark to provide much detail. The best images come from private surveillance cameras, those mounted inside stores or along the perimeter. They're better because those cameras are closer to the subjects."

"All we need to see is a tall man in a bowler with a cane."

"That's what I'm counting on," McClary said. "Tell me something?"

"Okay."

"Do you ever get used to this stuff?"

"Not in a way that it ever becomes easy," Bobby said. "But live long enough, you become competent."

"Different kind of perp," McClary said. "Different set of rules."

"Mortality rate for hunters ain't something to brag about."

"I don't imagine it is," McClary said solemnly.

"Speaking of the hard truth," Bobby said. "You decide how much to tell the chief?"

"I sure as hell can't tell him what you told me," McClary said. "I'll need to filter this. He's old school down to the bone. If I tell him we got an oni on the loose, he'll personally escort me to a psych eval. Probably want me committed." He shook his head. "I feel like a tax cheat."

"Come again?"

"Keeping two sets of books," McClary explained. "One for me, another for the chief."

"First we gotta find this bastard."

"I'm working the stolen car angle," McClary said. "We have two cruisers rigged with ALPR systems—automatic license plate recognition. They can check thousands of license plates per hour in high-traffic areas. They get any hits, the patrol officers will notify me immediately."

Bobby had a moment of concern about the Winchester boys tooling around town in the stolen Monte Carlo, but had to hope the neglected car hadn't been reported stolen yet. More often than not, they dumped a car long before the owner reported it missing.

"How current are the records?" Bobby asked.

"We download a fresh database each morning."

"If the oni stole another vehicle," Bobby said, "it might not be reported yet."

"True," McClary said. "But we forced his hand, made him abandon the plumber's van before he was ready. Maybe he'll get careless."

As she dangled from the eyebolt in the ceiling of Laurel Lanes, Kim Jacobs' shoulders were on fire. She had stopped breathing through her nose hours ago because the smell of the headless corpse hanging upside down beside her threatened to make her physically ill. She stared up at the ceiling until her neck cramped, because the other options horrified her. She couldn't bear to look at the body hanging beside her or the changing face of the inhuman monster calling itself an oni. She found it hard to believe he had ever looked human.

After the oni had peeled all the skin from the decapitated cop's head, he had tossed it in a trashcan. He had seemed pleased with the completion of his gruesome ritual, but promised more to come.

"I will transform you," he said. "Make you more than human."

"I'm good, thanks," she said, trying to keep her eyes averted.

She had first noticed his transformation while he flayed the cop's head. Since she couldn't watch the deliberate desecration of the human remains, her gaze shifted to the murderer. He had taken off his bowler hat to reveal ridged horns protruding from above his forehead at a low angle. As he worked on his grisly task, the horns seemed to lengthen. At first, she thought she might be hallucinating, but soon she noticed his close-cropped hair lengthening, becoming bright red. When she dared to glance at his hands, she saw that his fingernails were dark and pointed, like the claws of some predatory animal. Now and then he would look at her and smile. Gradually, during the flaying, his teeth lengthened and became pointed, like flat, thick fangs.

"What's happening to you?" she finally asked.

To her dismay, he smiled more broadly, exposing an expanse of his shark teeth. "As I shed my human face, so too will they shed theirs."

Kim had to swallow before she asked, "What about me?"

"You will pass through the demon gate," he said, "to stand as my mate."

"No," she said, horrified. "That's not possible. You're not even human."

"Your path is more difficult," he said, sounding almost sympathetic. "You must shed your humanity."

"You're crazy," Kim said, making a renewed effort to pull her taped ankles apart even as she twisted her wrists to try to loosen her bonds. "Let me go! I don't want this!"

"After your transformation, you will look back on this resistance as foolishness," the oni said. "I will show you the way."

"I'll die before I become a monster!"

"I will protect you," the oni said calmly, "from yourself."

She glared at him, determined to kill him or die trying.

"But I must leave for a short time," he said, climbing off the stool behind the shoe rental counter and walking across the bowling alley to the pro shop. "I must complete the calling," he told her, raising his voice so she could hear him, "and it requires a substantial ritual of blood."

If he leaves, I can escape, she thought wildly. *I have to find a way out of here.*

He emerged from the pro shop and walked toward her, carrying coils of rope, a roll of duct tape, a burlap sack, and a pair of handcuffs. "I need to prepare you for my absence."

"I'm tied up and taped already," she protested. "Where can I go?"

"I have no doubt you are resourceful. I will protect you from yourself," he repeated. "But I must warn you—if I return and discover you tried to escape, I will cut off your head and feast on your flesh."

"I thought you needed me?" she asked nervously. "The demon gate thing."

"What do you humans say?" he asked mischievously. "There are plenty of fish in the sea. Disappoint me at your peril."

Over the last several hours, she had worked some play into the tape binding her ankles. Though she'd had less success with her rope-bound wrists, given time, she might work her hands free. But he was about to wipe out all of her progress.

"Please," she said desperately. "I promise I won't try to escape. I'll wait here until you get back."

"I wish I could believe you."

"You can. I promise," she said. "But these ropes are killing my shoulders. Could you tie me to a booth or a ball return—anything on the floor?"

"You'll keep for a few hours."

"Please!"

Peeling off a six-inch strip of duct tape, he slapped it across her mouth. Then he knelt at her side and knotted ropes around her ankles, over the worn tape. She wanted to complain that the rope was too tight, but he wouldn't have listened, even if he hadn't effectively gagged her. Next he tied additional rope around her wrists, which were already chafed raw. Then he reconsidered and untied the extra rope.

She breathed a sigh of relief—until he slapped one of the handcuffs around her right wrist.

What the hell?

He pulled her forward and in a flash of intuition she knew what he intended and she thrashed wildly, her screams muffled by the duct tape.

No! No! Nooo!

He closed the other cuff around the ankle of the upside-down corpse. Reaching down, he picked up the burlap sack and slid it over her head, plunging her into darkness. Her nostrils flared as she breathed rapidly, skirting the edge of mindless panic. When she felt rope tightening around her throat, to secure the burlap sack in place, she renewed her frantic—and muffled—screaming and writhing. But when she bumped into the headless corpse and recalled the sections of flesh gouged out of the body, she became still, eyes squeezed shut in the darkness. With a supreme effort of will, she calmed herself. If she hyperventilated with the bag over her head, she would suffocate and become another hanging corpse in the abandoned bowling alley.

Something pressed against the front of the sack, near her mouth.

She arched her back, twisting her face away from the unknown threat. Then the sack ripped and she understood— it was a breathing hole, in the form of a small tear opened by one of his claws.

"Wouldn't want you to suffocate while I'm gone."

A moment later, he bumped into her and she froze.

Jostling her arms, he pushed her aside a few inches as he seemed to reach up to the ceiling. But her hope that he'd had a change of heart and was lowering her to the floor was short-lived. Instead, she felt a slight easing of the pressure on her shoulders. She could now touch the floor with the toes of both feet simultaneously, removing some of the burden from her shoulders, arms and wrists.

He lowered the eyebolt, she thought. *Maybe I can work it loose now.*

The possibility gave her something to focus on in the dark instead of obsessing about the headless, decaying and partially eaten corpse to which she was handcuffed.

"That should ease your immediate concerns," he said. "Now I must go."

By this time, she realized suddenly, she should be hungry, but having a monster shackle you to a corpse apparently was an effective appetite suppressant. In fact, the thought of food made her feel ill. But her thirst was more persistent.

Her throat burned, more so after her screaming. And now that she was gagged, she couldn't ask for a sip of water.

"Remember my warning."

She nodded quickly, unsure the motion translated outside the sack, but he seemed satisfied. She listened as his footfalls receded to the back of the bowling alley. After several seconds, a metal door swung and then banged shut. She waited, motionless, thinking it might be a trap. She could picture him standing quietly inside the bowling alley, his back to the rear wall, watching her, waiting to see if she would attempt to escape. If she tugged on the ropes binding her ankles or wrists once, he would charge across the bowling alley and lop off her head with a meat cleaver.

Holding herself unnaturally still for what felt like an hour but was probably no more than five minutes, she listened for the slightest sound of his presence, a rustle of clothing, a squeak of his shoe against the floor, a sigh or the clearing of his throat.

The only sound she heard was her own shallow breathing, amplified inside the darkness of the burlap bag.

When she was confident he had left the building, she yanked her arms furiously back and forth with two goals in mind: If she could work the eyebolt loose from the joist in the ceiling, she should be able to remove the hood and work the wrist knots loose. And if her wrists started bleeding before the eyebolt came loose, she might be able to use the lubrication of her own blood to pull her wrists out of the ropes. Of course, she had to deal with the handcuffs securing her to the cop's corpse, but one step at a time.

* * *

Tora parked on the street outside the gated parking lot of the Gafford Sports Arena, a rundown semi-pro baseball stadium scheduled for demolition after one farewell sporting event, an exhibition soccer game between two semi-pro teams, the Denver Dragons and the Jersey Devils. With construction of a new multipurpose facility two miles away nearly complete, the locals had come to bid farewell to a venue that held many fond memories for them. Nostalgia had provided a boost to the expected attendance for the final event and the soccer teams were reaping the benefits of playing before a full house.

Inhaling the mixed scents of hotdogs, French fries, funnel cake and popcorn, Tora stood beside the fence and raised his left hand to his temple. He allowed his third eye to open wide. Unseen by human eyes, waves of his power wafted across the parking lot and seeped into the cracked concrete and fatigued metal struts of the arena.

For added power, he raised his cane several inches above the ground, paused to focus the effect, then slammed the point down on the concrete sidewalk. Tremors shook the ground, flowing in a straight line toward the stadium.

The oni was well versed in demolition.

TWENTY-FIVE

When Bobby called Sam's burner cell to report that multiple emergency calls had come in from the Gafford Sports Arena at the intersection of Ellisburg Pike and Cuthbert Avenue, Sam checked a cached onscreen map and told Dean they were only four blocks away.

Dean gunned the accelerator. "Sporting event, huh?"

"According to the community calendar, an exhibition soccer match." Sam read something then looked at Dean, alarmed. "Seating capacity is 5,600. It's the last event at the stadium. They're tearing it down in two weeks."

"Crowded and old," Dean said. "Low-hanging fruit."

Sam consulted his map. "Turn right up ahead."

Once Dean made the turn, he saw the first responders, two police cars and an ambulance, speeding to the parking lot entrance, so he followed them. Even from that distance, they could hear the yelling and screaming of thousands of people.

As the Monte Carlo roared up the entrance ramp, Dean had to pump the brakes to avoid a rush of people, many of whose faces or arms were streaked with blood and dust, flowing out of the stadium in a mass panic.

"A target this size," Sam said, "there's a good chance he's close."

Dean hoped that was more than wishful thinking on Sam's part. Of course, they still had no idea how to gank the bulletproof oni. At least they could try to minimize casualties. Beyond that, Dean had suggested they "give fire a chance." Since New Jersey's legislature didn't trust drivers in the state to pump their own gasoline, Dean had the listless attendant fill a two-gallon container with regular, which they now kept in the Monte Carlo's trunk alongside their cache of conventional weapons. Of course, if the New Jersey legislature knew Dean planned to douse the oni with two gallons of regular and light him like a tiki torch, they might not trust drivers to buy gasoline either.

Dean double-parked away from the hundreds on foot who had already escaped, jumped out of the car and ran toward the shaking stadium, Sam at his side. A three-story red-brick structure faced the parking lot, stairs on either side leading to upper-level seating. Even from the parking lot, Dean caught glimpses of the stadium's layout. The outdoor stairs rose to a row of enclosed upper box seats that overhung the second of two staggered tiers of outdoor seating. The first level looked like individual stadium seating, while the second level consisted of long rows of aluminum bleachers.

Behind that back row, tucked under the upper box seats, was a promenade with a row of vendor stalls and kiosks.

Dean heard the prolonged creaking of straining metal, a series of explosive pops, and glass shattering. As he neared the ticket window and the ramps leading up to the first level of seating, he saw that the section of upper box seats closest to the parking lot had collapsed, tossing box ticket holders through shattered windows and crushing several people in the back rows of the bleacher section.

Against the mass exodus of the scared and wounded, Dean and Sam fought their way up the ramp. The whole stadium shook, as if in the throes of a powerful earthquake, and the next section of upper box seats collapsed. One middle-aged man in a business suit was thrown through the window, but managed to catch the upper box seat walkway railing long enough to slow his momentum before dropping awkwardly to the aluminum benches below.

Amid the crush of people on the ramp, several reacted to the ominous sounds of destruction behind them by pushing and elbowing their way toward the parking lot. A mother carrying her crying two-year-old daughter and pulling her frightened four-year-old son by the hand, fell down awkwardly. She tried to shield her daughter, but lost her grip on her son, who began to cry.

"Stop!" she screamed. "You're hurting my babies."

"Whoa!" Dean said, planting the palm of his hand on the chest of a large man intent on ignoring the woman's pleas as he strode over her.

The man looked down and shook his head as if the

woman's plight didn't matter in his rush to save his own ass. "Outta my way," the man mumbled, but slid sideways before continuing his descent.

Dean caught the woman's arm and helped her up, while Sam scooped her son up and lowered him to the ground on the other side of the guide rail.

"Wait for your mom," Sam told the kid.

Dean steered the woman to the railing, helped her over and handed her daughter down to her. All three of them jogged to the parking lot.

The Winchesters worked their way into the stadium and immediately came to the bottleneck. The collapse of the first upper box section had brought down slabs of concrete and twisted rebar from the ceiling of the promenade, destroying two vendor stalls and almost completely blocking the exit. The air was heavy with concrete dust sifting down from the damage above. Narrow cracks in the floor, walls and ceiling continued to multiply. The stadium was literally crumbling around them.

While some people continued to stream through the cramped exit aisle, the police who had arrived on the scene a couple of minutes ahead of the Winchesters were directing people down to the field and across what would have been the infield—if the grass had been marked for baseball instead of soccer—and back to outfield depth, well clear of the toppling row of box seats. Frightened fans waited with uniformed soccer players from both teams in bright gold and red uniforms. A cyclone fence wrapped around the outfield, decorated every few feet with brightly painted plywood sponsor signs. Dean's attention was drawn to a cop who stood outside the fence, all the way down the third base line, with a pair of bolt cutters, improvising a new exit.

Dean scanned what seemed like a sea of bobbing baseball caps looking for a man in black wearing a bowler. "I don't see him, Sam," he yelled over the chorus of frightened voices around them. "You?"

"Nothing."

Dean turned to Sam. "If he's here, how close—"

A woman with frizzy red hair grabbed Dean's arm and said urgently, "A man is pinned back there, bleeding and dying!"

The lights in the ceiling of the promenade had burnt out. With the partial collapse of the upper box seats, the promenade looked more like a tunnel. Vibrations continued to shake the walls and the floor under their feet. To Dean, it felt like a ticking bomb. If they weren't careful, the whole friggin' shebang would come down on their heads.

The first vendor stall looked like it had gone a couple of rounds with an auto compactor. A white-aproned burger-flipper had the misfortune of leaning over his grill when the first slab of concrete fell, striking his back and pulping the upper half of his torso. Flames burned his clothes in the few patches not soaked with blood. Sam crouched and stepped through the gap that led to the remainder of the promenade. Dean followed, looking nervously over his head a half-dozen times, expecting the next slab of death-dealing concrete to fall the moment he became inattentive.

The next several stalls had suffered damaged from falling

debris. One contained a dead woman whose head had been crushed by a massive chunk of concrete. By another was a lifeless man who had been impaled through the eye by an exposed piece of rebar that still held him upright. Everywhere Dean looked, blood had spattered the walls and floor. Closer to the exits than the fans, the other vendors had probably been the first to flee when the destruction began.

A pronounced shudder shook the stadium. Several chunks of dislodged concrete fell around them. Above them, frightened cries rang out from people in the upper box suites. Belatedly, Dean wondered if the first responders had turned off natural gas lines feeding into the stadium. That should be standard protocol, but with the oni's powers in the mix, crucial details might have been overlooked.

"We're courting disaster here, Sammy," Dean said.

"I know."

As the promenade opened up, beyond the collapsed upper box sections, they moved down to the upper tier of seats. They found a swarthy man on his knees with his right arm pinned against the back of the last row of bleachers by a slab of concrete wedged against one of the support struts. His eyes squeezed shut in pain, the man moaned softly. Blood ran down his arm and dripped from his fingertips.

Sam pulled Dean aside.

"Arm's a goner," Sam whispered.

"So we go *127 Hours* on him, 'cause I left my penknife in the car."

"No," Sam said. "But that concrete might be the only thing stopping the next section from coming down."

"Shove and run?"

Sam nodded. He crouched beside the man. "Buddy, can you hear me?"

The man's eyes fluttered open and took a moment to focus. "What…?"

"Can you hear me?"

The man nodded. Dean feared he was slipping into shock.

"Mister—Sir, what's your name?" Sam asked.

"Ruben," he said softly, attempting a weak smile. "Ruben Cordova."

"Ruben, we have a situation here," Sam said evenly. "Are you with me?"

The man nodded again.

"When we shove this concrete block out of the way, I need you to head down to the field. Got it?"

Again the man nodded, then gave a hesitant thumbs up with his free hand.

Dean stood next to Sam against the concrete slab, closer to the support strut than to the pinned man. They would try to push it away from the strut, releasing the pressure on the man's pinned arm.

"On three," Dean said. "One… two… THREE!"

The upper tip of the slab screeched against the strut, shifting a couple of inches, but not enough to fall. Ruben cried out in pain. "*Dios mío!*"

"That woke him up," Dean said grimly.

"Again," Sam said.

On the next count of three, the slab of concrete scraped away from the strut and fell with a thunderous impact, breaking in half. The sound of shrieking metal filled the air. Ruben climbed awkwardly to his feet, his ruined arm limp against his body. Sam caught him under his good arm and helped him upright and into the aisle.

The three of them rushed down the rows of bleacher seating, some of which contained the sprawled and bloodied bodies of those struck and killed by flying debris.

Behind them, steel screeched and large chunks of concrete fell like mortar rounds. Glass popped and shattered, pelting them like hail. Alarmed cries rang out from above. Turning back, Dean saw groups of people flailing around inside the box enclosures. Their only exit was the walkway that ran in front of the box seats and it had become a treacherous incline.

A paramedic hurried over to Sam and Ruben and led the Hispanic man across the field to where the others had gathered. The police had begun to lead people, single file, to the cutout in the cyclone fencing.

"Sam, we've got people trapped up top!"

A frightening tremor shook the ground beneath them. Cracks raced under their feet and the rows of bleachers started to collapse into the foundations below.

On the far side of the field more metal shrieked, demanding Dean's attention.

"That's not good."

Suspended on two stilt-like metal struts, a Jumbotron and scoreboard overlooked the outfield and the fans who had sought shelter there. The large screen tilted forward as one of the struts buckled.

"Run! Get off the field!" Sam yelled, waving them toward

the third base line fence.

Many stared at Sam as if he had lost his mind, but a few looked up and saw the massive screen leaning over them. The sound of screaming people joined the screeches of the metal. Explosive pops, like gunshots, rang out, as the bolts supporting the structure snapped one after another. One side of the Jumbotron swung like a trapdoor, seconds from dropping to the field below.

A man in a chambray shirt and jeans ran to his young son, who was sitting on the field, pulling up blades of grass and blowing them off his open palm. The man scooped up the kid and ran toward the infield. A police officer ran to intercept him.

"Look out!" Sam shouted, pointing frantically overhead.

The screen broke free and dropped, narrow end down. Its long shadow fell across the cop's path. Stunned, he looked up, too late to move. The massive screen crushed his skull and shattered his spine. The running man covered his son's eyes and veered toward the hole in the fence.

Dean turned back to the collapsing row of upper box seats.

The nearest section pressed against the backs of the aluminum bleachers. Some of the people climbed over the railing and dropped down on to them. Dean waved to the people in the far section to follow the walkway down to the upper tier bleachers. They needed to get everyone down before the next suite section collapsed.

"Anybody trapped up there?" Dean asked every third person who passed him. Most shook their heads, watching where they placed their feet. Whole sections of the bleachers had become treacherous as well. The concrete on which they were mounted continued to crumble. Once survivors had climbed over the upper box walkway railing, Sam directed them to the picnic patio area where the concrete steps leading to the field hadn't begun to erode yet.

As the last few people reached the railing, another tremendous shudder shook the stadium. "Run!" Dean shouted. "To the field!"

Something about the stadium felt malevolent to Dean, like it was making the most of its last chance to take more lives. But he dismissed the notion as nonsense. The malevolence he sensed surely came from the oni, infecting the building with its mojo, or whatever the hell it called its destructive power.

The Winchesters were the last to reach the field. As they hurried toward the hole in the fence, Dean glanced at the red-brick ticket office and administration building. The rolling tremors were tearing it apart. Brick by brick it crumbled. By this time, Dean hoped fervently, the place should be empty. From the parking lot, he heard new waves of emergency vehicle sirens and the harsh blare of fire truck horns. Sam slipped through the fence before him. As Dean ducked through, the ground shook beneath him and he almost fell flat on his face.

The parking lot was crowded with cars bunching up near the exits and people wandering around looking for lost family members, trying to remember where they had parked, or seeking medical attention from one of the half-dozen ambulances with overworked paramedics. Another tremor hit and one of the cars seemed to tilt at a crazy angle. Dozens of people stumbled and fell, and twice that number screamed in terror. Car alarms joined the chorus of emergency sirens and human misery.

"What the hell?" Dean said.

Sam saw it too. "The ground's opening up."

Fractures and cracks snaked across the asphalt parking lot, expanding into crevices wide enough to capture car tires and human legs. What worried Dean was the logjam of cars whose drivers inched impatiently toward the exits.

"Dude, I've got a bad feeling," Dean said grimly. "All those cars."

Sam nodded. "Oni bombs."

As Sam spoke, a car's rear end dropped a foot. Metal screeched as the axle broke, spraying sparks.

Dean raced across the parking lot, yelling, "Leave your cars! Get out! Run!"

Sam ran in the other direction, shouting similar instructions.

A cop caught Dean by the arm. "Hey, buddy!"

Dean whirled to face him. "Get everyone out of this lot now!"

"Yes, in an orderly—"

"No time for that!" Dean said. "These cars are gonna blow!"

"We're trying to avoid a riot here, pal."

"Use your loudspeaker," Dean insisted. "Get them out now!"

"Listen here—"

With the sound of tortured metal, another car fell into a new crevice. Someone yelled, "Fire!"

An instant later, a gas tank explosion lifted the car in the air with a roaring fireball.

The cop released Dean and raced for his cruiser. A moment later he was instructing everyone over the loudspeaker to abandon their vehicles and run from the lot.

About friggin' time, Dean thought.

He flinched as another explosion roared thirty feet away. A burning piece of car shrapnel whistled past his face. "Son of a bitch!" he exclaimed, ducking instinctively.

That was lucky, he thought. *Another inch or two and...*

Dean scanned the surging crowd intently.

"Where the hell are you?" he whispered. "Come out, come out, wherever..."

Everyone was running and stumbling toward the exits, a sea of panic and raw fright. Against that wave of frantic motion, one tall, calm figure stuck out like a sore thumb. The oni stood on the far side of the gated parking lot, near a blue van with a broad white stripe, the handle of a cane held under his overlapping hands. He no longer wore a bowler hat. Dean could clearly see a wave of bright red hair with two bone-white horns angled backward over a lumpy forehead. And in the middle of his forehead—

"Okay, that's new."

Dean's cell phone was ringing. With all the other human and mechanical sounds washing over him, he almost missed it. After checking the number on the display, he pressed the connect button.

"Bobby!" he exclaimed. "Where the hell are you?"

Static warped the voice on the other end.

"…with McClary at stadium… see the sumbitch… the fence…"

"Yeah, he's hard to miss," Dean said. "Two horns and three eyes."

"…meet… stop…"

The call dropped before Dean could answer.

He cupped his hands over his mouth and called Sam, pointing when he had his brother's attention. They sprinted toward the fence.

Dean saw an abandoned cherry-red Ford F-150 pickup truck with the driver's door wide open and had an idea.

TWENTY-SIX

Bobby rode with McClary in his cruiser, buckled up and hanging on in the cramped front seat as McClary raced through red lights with his siren blaring and took turns so sharply the car's suspension was pushed to the limit. With the oni's power at work, Bobby worried a catastrophic accident was inevitable. At the speeds McClary was attaining, a fatal head-on collision or multiple rollovers were distinct possibilities.

Once the extent of the stadium collapse had become evident, based upon the progressively dire string of emergency calls coming into the station, McClary abandoned the traffic and security cam feed monitors, placing greater importance on his presence at the disaster scene. For him, the decision was a no-brainer. Why examine camera feeds looking for the oni when it had basically announced where it was? Bobby agreed, but wanted to arrive in one unbroken piece. Though McClary had accepted the supernatural nature of this particular perp, Bobby doubted he fully appreciated the consequences of dealing with a creature that could tilt the odds so drastically in its favor.

When McClary swerved into oncoming traffic to get around a line of cars blocking the passing lane and nearly slammed into a Chevy Silverado before darting back, Bobby spoke up. "We're playing with rigged dice here, Sergeant."

McClary frowned. "What's that supposed to mean?"

"This oni specializes in bad accidents," Bobby reminded him, "and you're dealing him face cards."

McClary eased up on the accelerator a bit and nodded nervously. "Right. Right. The crazy stuff. I keep forgetting."

His NASCAR tryout would have been interrupted in a couple of blocks anyway, as panicked drivers exiting the stadium snarled up traffic in all directions, maneuvering through the congestion as if blindfolded. The harsh crunch of metal on metal sounded repeatedly as erratic driving led to a string of fender benders. Nobody stopped to exchange insurance information. By some unspoken mutual agreement, their only concern was fleeing the disaster area as quickly as possible.

If McClary hadn't been forced to slow down, Bobby might have missed the oni, standing calmly outside the parking lot fence on Ellisburg Pike near a blue van with a white stripe. He still wore the dark suit and held his ironbound cane in a two-handed grip, but the bowler hat was gone, revealing the twin bone-like horns, which Bobby judged had grown longer since their last encounter.

"We got him," Bobby said, pointing.

He called Dean's cell, but the connection crackled with static and became fainter the closer McClary's cruiser came to the oni. Bobby caught the sergeant's arm and nodded toward the tall figure.

"Look how focused he is."

"Like he's in a trance," McClary observed.

"Let's not spook him."

McClary nodded, turning on his lightbar without sounding his siren as he edged across three lanes of traffic and parked at the curb a hundred feet from the oni.

Bobby followed McClary to the trunk of the cruiser.

"Let's change this up," McClary said, switching out the magazine in his automatic. "Armor-piercing rounds," he explained. "These might cut through that impenetrable hide of his." He handed Bobby the shotgun. "Try this on him."

"Well, I won't miss," Bobby said as he hefted the shotgun, "that's for damn sure."

They hurried along the curb, McClary giving Bobby a wide berth.

Inside the parking lot, another car exploded in a prodigious ball of flame, the roar rising briefly over the sound of emergency sirens and car alarms. People screamed and staggered toward the exit, squeezing between and climbing over abandoned cars. Beneath them, the ground vibrated with fluctuating intensity, like waves breaking on the shore, retreating, and surging again. Bobby wondered if the oni could create destructive harmonic patterns in the earth.

When they were within twenty feet of the oni, McClary

stopped and raised the automatic in his right hand, braced with his left palm. Conscious of the real possibility of friendly fire in this situation with this particular opponent, Bobby stepped several paces to the side.

The crumbling stadium held the oni's attention, seemingly to the exclusion of all else.

Now or never, Bobby thought.

"Die, you motherless bastard," McClary said an instant before he squeezed the trigger. Bobby followed a split-second later with a blast from the shotgun.

As Dean had guessed, the driver of the red pickup had abandoned the truck in such a rush that they had left the keys in the ignition. Dean unlocked the passenger door for Sam—who jumped in a moment later—before trying to start the engine. His first attempt failed. On his second attempt, the engine turned over briefly, then stalled.

"No, no, no," Dean said bitterly. "This is small potatoes."

"Dean?"

"It's a theory."

"I'm all ears."

"A disaster this size, I'm betting the oni is redlined," Dean said, "maxed out. He might be vulnerable now, if we hit him fast."

"You know this how?"

"A piece of shrapnel whizzed by my ear."

"And…?"

"It didn't hit me," Dean said. "An inch to the left and I'd have a skull skylight. I was *lucky*."

Sam nodded, understanding. "You think he's spinning too many plates."

"In his case, juggling too many hatchets."

"Dean!"

Dean saw it. Bobby and McClary were on the other side of the fence, sneaking up on the oni as he focused on orchestrating the stadium collapse and exacerbating the ensuing mayhem. McClary aimed high and took a head shot. From where the brothers sat, it looked like he hit the oni, whose head twitched to the side, but inflicted no apparent damage, before Bobby hit him with a shotgun.

They finally had the oni's attention.

The oni turned toward its attackers and McClary proceeded to empty his magazine, aiming high with no evident effect. One of the bullets ricocheted, gouging a furrow in the side panel of the van. Another ricochet sprayed sparks off the ground.

The oni walked toward the two men, raising his cane. Bobby worked the pump-action shotgun and sprayed him from head to toe as he advanced.

Dean tried the ignition once more and this time the engine turned over, running roughly for a few moments then roaring to life as he gave it gas.

"Buckle up!"

He glanced up and saw the oni catch McClary by the wrist of his gun hand and squeeze. As McClary grimaced in pain, Bobby pressed the shotgun muzzle under the oni's chin and fired his last shell. The oni released McClary, who dropped to his knees, and swung his cane in a backhanded blow, dislodging the shotgun from Bobby's hands. With his free hand, the oni grabbed the front of Bobby's suit, lifted him bodily off the ground and hurled him into the highway. Bobby slammed lengthwise against the windshield of a gray Subaru Outback, fracturing the safety glass, and rolled down the hood of the car.

Dean shifted the pickup into gear and floored the accelerator, racing toward the spiked iron fence and gaining speed every foot of the way. He aimed the front of the pickup at the small gap between two sections of fence closest to the oni.

Sam braced his hand against the dashboard.

Time seemed to slow down.

Looking at the tips of the spiked fence, Dean tried not to think about all the ways the collision could go wrong. He hoped his theory of the oni maxing out his mojo was sound, and tried to coax a little extra bit of speed out of the pickup.

Two seconds before impact, the oni turned toward the truck, his back to the blue and white van. He raised the ironbound cane in both hands and swung the pointed tip toward Dean's head.

The pickup slammed into the iron fence and, after a brief moment of resistance, the two sections swung apart and down like a mangled gate. As the pickup burst through the gap, Dean ducked his head below the dash, unimpeded by airbags that, naturally, failed to deploy.

The pickup seemed to slam into a wall. Dean and Sam were hurled bodily against their seatbelts then fell backward in unison.

Groggily, Dean looked up and saw what appeared to be a bullet hole through the windshield directly in front of where his face had been. The center of the hood had crumpled in a U-shape.

"Where's the…?"

Sam rubbed the side of his head and looked around. "Bobby?"

The Ford's engine had stalled. Dean shifted the transmission into park and climbed gingerly out of the cab.

McClary was kneeling by the side the road, doubled over in pain as he clutched his injured wrist against his chest. Walking past him, Dean scanned the street. The gray Subaru hadn't moved after Bobby smashed the windshield. Dean's gaze traveled forward several yards, his heart in his throat, until he spotted Bobby, lying motionless in the middle of Ellisburg Pike.

Bringing down the stadium from several hundred yards away had taken all Tora's concentration and power. In comparison, the pedestrian overpass collapse had been simple. He had been in physical contact with the overpass and the structure was simplistic. With the stadium, he had attacked from a distance to avoid interruption by the fleeing masses and to give himself, appropriately enough, a larger playing field on which to wreak havoc. His third eye guided his destructive power to where it would cause the greatest damage, and his *kanabo*, currently molded into the shape of a cane with an ironbound handle and tip, directed the waves of force to the intended targets.

While his third eye became dominant—and he reveled in the destruction it facilitated—his other senses lost priority. A human might have described his state of consciousness as a trance. As a result of his inattention, the two men he remembered from the previous night's car chase snuck up on him. The one in the uniform fired bullets at close range that actually stung the oni. Though they couldn't break his skin, they did break his concentration. Then the other man fired the shotgun at him, another distracting annoyance.

He broke the wrist of the lawman and would have ripped the offending gun hand off that wrist if the other man hadn't fired his shotgun—as if the weapon could harm him, even with the muzzle pressed against his skin. After batting away the toy, he tossed the older man aside like an impudent child.

Finally, two young men—the Good Samaritans from the overpass collapse—had tried to run him down with a pickup truck. He had given a moment's thought to disabling the truck, but its momentum would carry it forward regardless, even if he'd had time to create a fuel line leak, generate a spark and have it blow up in a glorious fireball. His second option was to spear the head of the driver like a fish in a slow-moving stream, but the man had already ducked out of sight in anticipation of such an attack. As a result, the tip of his cane stabbed air beyond the windshield.

The oni took the brunt of the collision, which damaged the bumper and hood of the truck, but not his body. He was slammed unceremoniously into the side of his van, but the damage to his vehicle was cosmetic and minimal.

Fortunately, his large-scale ritual of blood had already

been a resounding success. The calling would become undeniable, a beacon drawing them to his side. Everything had been prepared. Once they were together as a family, he would complete the demon gate ceremony with the human woman on the new moon.

Tora had no need to remain at the site of the stadium collapse, so he shoved the pickup truck back an arm's length while the humans inside were too stunned or cowed to interfere, and walked around to the driver's side of his van.

He had briefly considered killing the interlopers there and then, by hand, one after the other, but the ritual's success had lifted his spirits while simultaneously draining him of his stored energy. The waves of fear, grief and misery wafting out of the stadium parking lot were slowly replenishing him, but he needed some time alone, without distractions, to recharge. Moreover, he had left the woman alone for too long and she could not be trusted while she remained human. She would not believe his promise to let her live if she made no attempt to escape, and she was also too unenlightened to desire the fate he had in store for her. A death threat was effective only when the alternative had greater appeal. Losing her now would delay his plans, whether he attempted to retrieve her, locate and execute her, or seek another woman for the ceremony. Because the new moon was tomorrow, he had to complete the ceremony tonight. By dawn, she would be remade in the oni's image.

He started the van and drove to the bowling alley.

TWENTY-SEVEN

"Bobby, you are not dead!" Dean said, shaking Bobby's shoulders where he lay in the middle of Ellisburg Pike. He had scraped his face, but otherwise, Dean saw no obvious injuries.

Internal bleeding wouldn't... No! "D'you hear me?"

Bobby opened his eyes. "Thanks for clearing that up."

Sam walked up beside Dean. "Bobby, are you okay?"

"Eggs are scrambled, but the shell ain't broken," Bobby said, wincing as he tried to sit up. "On second thought..."

The driver of the gray Subaru, a young mother with a toddler gripping her hand, approached. "Is he okay? He came out of nowhere, hit my windshield before..."

"Dean, where's the—?"

"The van!" McClary exclaimed.

Dean and Sam, distracted by Bobby's plight, had assumed

the oni fled on foot after the collision. They both turned around, reaching for their concealed automatics, as the blue van raced away from the curb and slipped into the rush of traffic skirting around multiple fender benders.

"Son of a bitch," Dean whispered.

He and Sam put away their guns and helped Bobby to his feet.

"Not an invalid," Bobby groused, despite looking unsteady. "Don't need help crossing the street. Get after him!"

"We catch him," Dean said dejectedly, "then what?"

"He's right, Bobby," Sam said. "You shot him point blank. Dean hurled a pickup truck at him. Nothing hurt him. Nothing slowed him down. We've got nothing."

"Find his lair, wherever he goes to ground," Bobby said, helping McClary to his feet to prove he'd recovered from the windshield collision. "We'll figure something out."

Dean and Sam hurried back to the pickup truck. When it wouldn't start, Sam looked back into the parking lot.

"Forget it," Dean said. "Even if it didn't blow up, you'll never get it out of the lot."

But Sam had already jumped out. He called back over his shoulder, "We made our own exit."

Less than a minute later, the Monte Carlo rumbled over one of the flattened sections of fence and Dean hopped into the passenger side before Sam brought it to a complete stop. Once they were in the flow of traffic, Sam drove aggressively, ducking in and out of lanes to gain ground. Dean scanned left and right, checking each side street they passed.

"D'you think Bobby's okay?" Sam asked.

"It's not like he'd say if he wasn't," Dean replied.

"Yeah."

"The windshield probably cushioned his fall."

"Seriously?" Sam asked incredulously. "How?"

"Compared to asphalt," Dean said, shrugging. "Sure."

Sam thought about it and nodded.

"Of course, he ain't gettin' any younger," Dean said. For a moment back there, staring at Bobby's unmoving body, Dean thought they'd lost him. Dean had watched too many people he cared about die, and wondered how many more he would lose before his own number was up. *How many heavy losses can you face before you stop caring if your own ticket gets punched?*

"Dean, you okay?"

"Yeah," Dean said as he craned his neck to see around a New Jersey Transit bus. "Yeah, I'm fine."

"Good call," Sam said, "on the lucky break."

Dean smiled. "Now and—Whoa! Blue van, up ahead. Turned right at the intersection."

As Sam accelerated, the Monte Carlo gave a shudder, as if it might stall, then it surged forward and he maneuvered around the slow-moving transit bus, cutting in front of it just in time to turn at the intersection.

"Easy, Bullitt," Dean cautioned. "Let's not tip our hand."

"Right," Sam said. "Reconnaissance."

Sam stayed back, leaving a couple of cars between the blue and white van and the Monte Carlo. The oni had no reason to suspect they were in the old car. He'd only seen them driving the red pickup truck. If he did suspect a tail, he might trigger a blowout or engine failure to lose them.

Eventually, he led them to an abandoned bowling alley. When the van turned into the parking lot, Sam initially passed the ramp, then made a U-turn to cross to the other side of the street when the oncoming lanes were clear. As Sam neared the bowling alley's parking lot, Dean saw that the van had bypassed the front lot to drive behind the building.

"He went around back," Dean said. "Service entrance maybe."

"There's a fence back there," Sam said. "No outlet?"

He turned onto the lot, coasting toward the front door, where a realtor sign taped to the window indicated the property was for sale. Sam parked the Monte Carlo next to a chain-link fence, away from the front doors and windows, all of which were covered with plywood, on the chance that the oni might peek out through a gap.

They exited the car quietly and crept along the front of the bowling alley, ducking below the level of the windows. Before they reached the doors, Sam leaned forward and peered into the building through a small gap between the plywood covering the plate glass windows and the edge of the doorframe.

"Two bodies hanging in there," Sam whispered. "Like a meat locker."

"Its pantry," Dean said, recalling Sam's oni research. "It eats human flesh."

"Dean," Sam said. "We've got a problem."

Sam looked at his brother, his eyes wide.

"One of the bodies is alive."

"So much for surveillance duty."

* * *

When the oni returned to the bowling alley, he found the woman where he'd left her, hanging from the hook in the ceiling. She had managed to shake off the burlap sack he'd tied around her head. Her dark hair was matted against the sides of her face, her skin covered with perspiration. Her wrists looked raw above and below the ropes that bound them. Her arms and legs trembled with exhaustion. If he cut her down now, she probably couldn't stand on her own.

"I warned you," he said, glancing down at the burlap bag at her feet.

"I couldn't breathe with that over my head," she said quickly, her voice raspy. "Even with the hole."

"This will be over soon," he promised, slipping his cane through his belt as if it were a scabbard. "The calling is almost complete. By dawn tomorrow, you will pass through the demon gate."

He unfastened the handcuff that had shackled her to the upside-down corpse and she visibly shuddered as she swung a few inches farther away. Reaching up, he unscrewed the eyebolt suspending the headless cop and carried the body to the shoe rental desk.

"Take me down," the woman said. "Please. My arms are coming out of their sockets and my legs are on fire."

"Soon," he said. "First I must complete the calling."

He crossed the bowling alley and retrieved his duffel bag from the counter in the pro shop. Except for a few chairs and a filing cabinet, nothing of value had been left behind. Placing the duffel bag on the counter near the dead cop's feet, he unzipped it and removed a gleaming meat cleaver. With one powerful whack, he lopped off the cop's right arm below the shoulder.

"Oh, God," the woman gasped. "What are you doing?"

Another whack of the cleaver separated the humerus from the radius and ulna. He removed a curved knife from the duffel and stripped the bone clean of decaying flesh, muscle, tendons, and nerves.

"Normally, this is a hilltop ritual," he explained as he worked. "The roof of this building will have to suffice. The calling ritual is complete when I break the human bone in half, signifying their break from their humanity. They will have no choice but to come to me, Tora, father of all, and together, we will celebrate." He turned to leave, but paused as a thought occurred to him.

"Do you wish to observe the ritual?"

"No, not at all," she said quickly. "I've… I've seen enough."

"Then I'll leave you as you are until I return."

Behind the bowling alley, next to where he had parked the van, stood a dinged brown Dumpster. Tora jumped up and landed on the lid of the trash bin, then jumped to the roof of the van, and from there he leapt the remaining distance to the gently sloped roof of the bowling alley. Walking to the center of the roof, he sat cross-legged and began the final stage of the calling ritual.

Sam watched the oni take down the headless corpse, lay it out on the shoe rental counter, then return with a duffel bag and a meat cleaver to lop off the arm and strip the bone clean. He talked to the woman the entire time as if she were a willing participant. Though Sam couldn't hear a word either of them said, he gave Dean the play-by-play without attempting to guess at the meaning behind the oni's actions.

While Sam stayed by the door, Dean opened the trunk of the Monte Carlo and filled two bottles with gasoline from the two-gallon jug and stuffed rags inside each one. Since bullets were ineffective against the oni, they would each have a Molotov cocktail at their disposal.

When the oni walked out of the back door again, carrying the gleaming bone over his shoulder, Sam whispered to Dean, "He's leaving. Without the woman."

"It might be our best chance to get her out."

"If he sees our car—"

A metallic clang sounded, followed by a muffled thump.

"He jumped on the roof," Sam guessed, "with the arm bone."

"Ours is not to reason why," Dean whispered. "Let's go."

Dean rushed by Sam, running along the side of the bowling alley, his prepped Molotov cocktail down at his side. Sam followed with his own gasoline grenade, glancing upward a couple of times, expecting a trap or sneak attack. Since they couldn't guess at the purpose of the human bone, they had no idea how long the oni would stay on the roof.

When Dean grabbed the handle on the back door, Sam placed his palm against the steel to stop him and whispered, "Quiet."

Dean nodded, understanding. Squeaky hinges would alert the oni.

One inch at a time, Dean eased the door open until they could slip through the gap and hurry to the woman.

"Thank God, thank God," the suspended woman whispered hoarsely. "Get me out of here. Please hurry! He's performing a 'calling ritual' on the roof."

"How long?" Dean asked.

Sam reached above the woman's hands and sawed through the ropes with a pocket knife, while Dean untied the ropes binding her ankles.

"I don't know. He said 'they' would have no choice but to come to him, the father of all. Called himself Tora. Earlier, he peeled the skin off that cop's face and said, 'They must shed their human face.' It was horrible!"

With her wrists released, the woman's full weight came down on her feet and her legs buckled. "I—I can't stand. My legs, too weak."

"I've got you," Sam said, wrapping a hand around her waist after picking up his Molotov cocktail with his other hand. "Anyone else here—alive?"

"No," she said, trying to walk, but stumbling. "Is he some kind of—? He's not human? Is he—a demon? The horns…"

"Something like that," Dean said without elaborating as they hurried toward the back door. "Did he mention his plans? A goal?"

"Something about taking me through a demon gate," she said, shaking her head. "Said I wouldn't be human anymore, that I would be… like him somehow."

"Why you?" Sam asked, wondering if the oni wanted a mate.

"I think he tried before," she said. "Ended up killing them. He said he'd kill me if I tried to escape. Pick somebody else."

When they reached the door, Dean leaned close and listened. "All quiet."

"Let's go," Sam said, still supporting the woman.

Sam took the lead while Dean watched their back, Molotov cocktail in one hand, a Zippo lighter in the other. As they crept along the building, moving as quietly and efficiently as possible, Sam thought he heard chanting from above, in a guttural language he didn't recognize. *A few more minutes,* he thought. *That's all we need.*

Dean opened the driver side door and climbed in with extra care.

Sam eased open the passenger side door, fearful that the metallic squeak of the hinge would alert the oni, and almost dropped his gasoline-filled bottle in the process. He helped the woman slide across the bench seat. As he turned to climb into the car after her, the heel of his boot struck an empty soda can and it clanked across the parking lot. Sam froze, staring toward the roof of the bowling alley, one hand holding the bottle, the other ready to snatch his own lighter out of his jacket pocket.

After a moment, Sam got in the car and pulled the door shut with a soft click.

"Are you police?" the woman asked.

"Consultants," Dean said, watching the bowling alley roof through the windshield as he reached down to start the car. "Tom and John Smith."

"Kim Jacobs," she said. "Thanks for rescuing me."

"We're not out of the woods—"

A dark figure dropped from the sky with a roar and landed beside the car.

Kim screamed, her tortured voice raw.

Dean grabbed his Molotov cocktail off the dashboard and pushed his door open. "Sam…"

Dean's voice faded away and Sam shook his head to clear the cobwebs.

He was sat in a truck stop diner, in a red booth across from Lucifer, who was slapping the bottom of a ketchup bottle over a plate of scrambled eggs. Instead of ketchup, blood dripped out of the bottle.

"Hello, Sammy!" Lucifer said. Putting the bottle down, he snapped his fingers in front of Sam's face. "You in there, Sam? Pay attention. This is our sharing time."

Sam reached for the scar on his left hand, but he was holding a beer bottle in his right hand and for some reason he couldn't release it.

"C'mon, don't be a party pooper," Lucifer said, frowning. "Eat up! Everyone's watching."

Sam looked down at his plate.

A dozen gleaming white eyeballs stared up at him.

"Tastes better with a little salt," Lucifer said, and slid the salt shaker across the table with the tip of his index finger.

A man on a stool spun around to face Sam. His eyes had been gouged out, the sockets dark and empty, leaking tears of blood.

"They're to die for."

* * *

Tora snapped the arm bone in half, completing the calling ritual. Then he heard a *plink* of metal against asphalt, followed by a metallic click. Opening his third eye, he looked beyond the building, seeing three people in the car, the woman seated between—the two interlopers! Rising to his feet, he dashed across the roof and launched himself off the edge.

The human on the driver's side came out of the car with a gasoline-filled bottle and a lighter, attempting a fire-bomb attack. With a flick of his power, the oni disabled the lighter long enough to throw the man against the wall of the bowling alley, where he struck his head and fell to the ground, dazed. The bottle shattered, spraying gasoline across the ground and the wall of the building.

The other man sat in the car, in some kind of trance, his right hand holding another fire bomb as he pushed it against his left. The woman cowered against him, screaming herself hoarse. "No! No! No!"

Catching her kicking leg, Tora dragged her from the car and wrapped his large hand around the back of her neck. "Struggle and I crush your spine."

She froze.

"Move!" he said, pushing her ahead of him.

If these two infernal men knew his location, others might follow. With the calling complete, the three would come to him, but until they were transformed by the ritual of blood, they would remain vulnerable. Fortunately, they would come wherever he was, and he had scouted alternate locations as a precaution. The decision to abandon the bowling alley was simple.

He ripped the plywood off the front door, punched through the plate glass and turned the deadbolt. After he shoved the woman inside, he scooped up the Zippo and ignited the gasoline on the wall. Then he tossed the lighter through the open car door onto the front seat, igniting the upholstery.

The two incapacitated men had attempted to run him down at the stadium. They didn't act like any traditional law enforcement officers he had ever encountered. He wondered if they were hunters and decided they must be. He grabbed his duffel bag, then dragged the hysterical woman to his van parked in back.

Let the interfering bastards burn!

Dean regained his senses, and felt a flash of heat.

He rolled onto his back in time to see the blue van race out of the parking lot.

He remembered the oni's attack, his lighter malfunctioning—

Something was burning.

Flaming gasoline had ignited the sleeve of his jacket. He whipped the coat off and stomped on the sleeve, extinguishing the fire.

Black smoke streamed out of the Monte Carlo.

Sam!

Skirting the flames around the broken bottle, he rushed to the car and saw the bench seat smoldering around the Zippo lighter. Tossing his ruined jacket over the seat, he smothered the flame.

Sam stared through the windshield, the unused Molotov clutched in his right hand. As soon as Dean plucked the bottle out of his hand, Sam reached for his scar.

From the trunk of the car, Dean retrieved a portable fire extinguisher and sprayed the burnt seat cushion for good measure.

How can we win with the deck stacked against us?

"Dean?" Sam said, looking around before focusing on his older brother. "What happened? I saw the—Where's Kim?"

"We lost her."

TWENTY-EIGHT

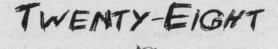

"I really wanted to toss the old bastard down the stairs."

Dalton Rourke sat beside Jimmy Ferrato on the grassy incline that overlooked the high-speed rail line. Escaping the house had been as simple as opening his bedroom window. As soon as his grandparents started to dress for an early dinner before seeing *Fiddler on the Roof* at the Cheshire Theater, he slipped out. There was no chance they would ruin their big night trying to track him down. Hell, they might not even open his bedroom door to check on him before they left.

He and Jimmy often visited this embankment to watch the trains zoom past, so fast the faces in the windows were indistinct blurs. The rush of the trains promised instant escape from the town. It didn't matter that the people on the trains were mostly commuters, coming from or returning to Philadelphia, maybe New York. The idea of escape was all that mattered. Getting the hell out of Laurel Hill, New Jersey. He hated his life and that made him hate the town that had trapped him within its borders. Once Dalton got out, he would never return.

"I could picture it in my head, Jimmy," Dalton continued. "I heard his bones crunch and him wailing in pain. It was so sweet. But then I saw the look in my grandmother's eyes. She wasn't afraid. No, man, it was like she was daring me to hurt him, daring me to take that next step, like that's what they'd been waiting for all these years, baiting me to commit a crime serious enough to have me locked up."

"Sick way to live, dude," Jimmy said, chuckling darkly.

"But if I killed him and her," Dalton said, "I'd be free. There'd be nobody to turn me in. I could hop a train and be gone like the wind."

"Dream on, D-man," Jimmy said, chuckling again. "I've seen you lay a righteous beat-down on dudes looked at you cross-eyed, but no way you're gonna kill your g-parents."

"You think it's funny?" Dalton asked, climbing to his feet to tower over his friend, fists clenched. "You think I'm funny?"

Jimmy scrambled back and jumped up. "C'mon, man," he said. "It's a joke, you know. A whatchamacallit, reality check. Right?"

Sudden fury surged in Dalton and he swung his right fist into his scrawny friend's gut, doubling him over. "My life is not a joke!"

Jimmy sputtered, holding up a hand to stall Dalton. "What the hell—!"

"You think I'm a joke?"

"Not what I meant, okay…"

Dalton felt the familiar rumble of an approaching high-speed train. He had read once that they traveled up to 150 miles per hour and they blew through many train stations without slowing down.

"You want a reality check?" Dalton asked.

He grabbed the back of Jimmy's shirt collar and a belt loop and ran him down the incline while Jimmy staggered to keep his balance. Out of the corner of his eye, Dalton saw the silver blur flashing toward them, glittering in the late-afternoon sunlight.

"Here's your reality check!"

Using Jimmy's forward momentum, Dalton hurled him onto the train tracks. His arms flailing, one of Jimmy's feet touched down between the rails a split second before the high-speed train struck his body. The bone-crushing impact was muffled by the roar of the train.

Dalton dropped to his knees, closed his eyes and lifted his face to the sky as the wind from the train's passage whipped his clothes and cooled the fire burning under his skin.

A voice from inside his head spoke to him. "*Come to me!*"

Suddenly, he knew there was a place for him.

"So, Jesse," Bart Larribeau said as the three of them walked along the paved bike path that wound behind the elementary and middle schools, "Keith and me been talking about this and we decided—"

"You decided?" Jesse interrupted, feeling anger bubbling

up, again. After he had stabbed his old man, he thought he'd cured himself of his anger issues. After all, his father had always been the problem in his life and Jesse had finally shut him up for good. His next order of business: hit the road and never come back. But why rush? Nobody would miss his father. He had no job, no coworkers, no family or friends who wanted anything to do with him. The man was toxic and anyone who knew him would experience relief at his absence. Jesse could take his time and gather enough funds to hit the road in style.

Then Bart and Keith had requested a meeting, said it was important. He thought maybe the cops knew something, so he had agreed to meet them back in the woods, away from prying eyes.

Jesse wore a gray hoodie with the hood pulled tight over his bald head to hide the weird lumps that had started to break through the skin. He needed to see a doctor, but that could wait until he set himself up in another town, far from here.

"We got this sweet home burglary routine now," Bart continued. "Low risk, high reward. And you… you're not interested and that's fine. You're too hardcore for us, Jesse. That tire iron beating… You nearly killed that dude. So, me and Keith, we decided we should go our own way. You got your thing, we got ours. No harm, no foul, right?"

Jesse stood with Bart on his left and Keith on his right. He looked back and forth between them, incredulous. "You both decided this?"

"Yeah, man," Keith said, shrugging. "Different strokes."

Jesse raised his right arm swiftly and rammed his elbow

into Keith's throat. Gasping for air, Keith dropped to his knees. Then Jesse grabbed both sides of Bart's head in his hands and pulled his face down as he brought his knee up, shattering Bart's nose. Bart staggered backward, stumbling off the asphalt path and down the dirt embankment toward the streambed below.

Jesse followed Bart.

"You want to kick me out of your pathetic gang?" he said. "You think I need you two losers?" He grabbed the back of Bart's head and slammed his face repeatedly into the nearest tree trunk. "You're pathetic."

He dropped Bart to the ground, climbed the embankment and found Keith lying on his side, choking and slobbering helplessly. Grabbing Keith's wrist, Jesse dragged him down the slope and dropped him beside Bart's lifeless body. While Keith sputtered and wheezed, Jesse found a nice hefty rock.

Keith stared up at Jesse, his eyes widening in panic when he saw the rock raised above him. He sputtered some more. "Nuh-nuh-nuh!"

"You had your say," Jesse said and slammed the rock down on Keith's face.

After the third or fourth crushing impact of stone against flesh and bone, Jesse stopped.

Neither of his former friends was recognizable. That seemed appropriate.

He spared a few moments to swipe their wallets and cash. Then he covered their bodies with dead leaves, twigs, clumps of moist dirt, and bits of brush—enough camouflage to conceal them for a while from any bikers or pedestrians who might pass by on the trail above.

Relieved rather than remorseful, he said, "Good riddance."

A voice spoke, not from without, but from within: "*Come to me!*"

Ryan Bramble sat on the ground behind the small shopping center consisting of Sal's Sandwich Shop, LH Liquors, Tattoo U, and Tony's Pizzeria, hidden between two of the four Dumpsters. Rocking back and forth, his hands pressed to the sides of his head, he tried not to think about the secret his father had kept from him his whole life. Because each time he thought about it, he wanted to kill his father. He debated walking the three miles back to his home and finishing what he'd started. As much as he tried to calm himself, the anger boiled up inside him.

He had pushed Sumiko away and was afraid to go near her now. Her computer monitor had been the first casualty of his insane rage, and he couldn't bear the thought that he might hurt her.

What's happening to me?

The sour tang of garbage filled his nostrils, but the unpleasant odor fitted his mood. At the moment, he didn't trust himself to be around anyone.

Movement registered on the periphery of his vision. Glancing down, he saw a rat's head poking out from under the Dumpster on his right, its nose twitching excitedly. The same smells that disgusted Ryan probably filled the beady-eyed rodent with delight.

He sat still as the rat edged closer. Maybe it was going to challenge him. This was the rat's turf and Ryan had intruded. Its pink paws took a couple more tentative steps toward him.

Ryan was unaware that he had bared his own teeth until he flicked out his hand and caught the rat, wrapping his fingers around its back and attempting to squeeze the life out of it. His dark fingernails cut into the nearly boneless flesh. The rat squealed and clawed at him, its sharp teeth nipping into Ryan's fingers, drawing blood. No matter how hard he squeezed, the damn thing wouldn't die.

He slammed the rat's head against the blacktop so hard he bruised his knuckles. Then he rammed it against the side of the Dumpster. Still it twitched in his grip. Uttering a string of obscenities, Ryan brought the rat to his mouth and ripped a chunk of flesh out of its belly. Then, disgusted with himself, he spat out the hunk of raw flesh and fur and hurled the rat against the back wall of the tattoo parlor. He trembled with rage.

As rat blood dribbled down his chin, he ran his hands over the twin lumps protruding from his scalp. Some of his dyed blue hair had fallen out round the lumps, and its natural red color was showing near the roots.

Without warning, bile surged up his throat. Leaning sideways, he vomited against the side of the Dumpster, blotting out the smeared rat blood.

He stumbled away from the smell of his own vomit and dropped down next to the last Dumpster, tucking himself into the corner. Now he was almost certain he had caught something, probably something fatal, like mad cow disease or something else that made you crazy before you died.

Fumbling in his pocket, he took out his cell phone and called Sumiko.

"Hello?" she said. "Ryan?"

He had only wanted to hear her voice, he'd forgotten that his name, number and photo would show up on her phone's display. "Hey, Miko."

"Where are you?"

"It doesn't matter," he said. "I wanted to hear your voice."

"What's happening, Ryan?"

"Have you—What have you heard about the diseases, the epidemics?"

"The flu, MRSA, food poisoning—that's what you want to talk about?"

"No," Ryan said. "I mean... I wondered if anything really bizarre was affecting people. Crazy stuff. I figured, for your blog, you might..."

"To hell with the blog, Ryan," Sumiko said. "What's happening with you?"

He laughed bitterly. "My dad told me he isn't, you know."

"Isn't what?"

"My father," Ryan said. "He was—My mother was... Some guy attacked her."

Sumiko was silent for a moment. "Oh, Ryan, I'm so sorry. I had no idea."

"You and me both."

"Can we talk? Where are you? I'll come to you."

"Not a good idea," Ryan said. "I... need to be alone. For now. To process."

"Okay," she said. "Understood. But I'm here, any time you want to talk."

"I'm sorry," Ryan said, "about your monitor. I don't know what came... I mean, I'm sorry. No excuses. And I wanted to say thanks."

"For what?"

"If it hadn't been for you," Ryan said, "I would've... You were—*are* a good influence."

"Ryan, I'm worried about you," she said. "Don't do anything stupid. Okay? You'll get over this. Things will get better. I promise."

"Thanks," Ryan said. "I gotta go."

He heard her calling his name as he disconnected the call. When she called back, he let it go to voicemail. Something bad was happening to him, and whatever it was, he had to face it alone.

A voice spoke to him. "*Come to me!*"

TWENTY-NINE

Sumiko jabbed the disconnect button and stared at her phone. "Voicemail," she said in disbelief. "Seriously, Ryan?"

Putting the phone down, she tapped her fingernails on her desk, a nervous habit she had when undecided about what to do next.

Ryan had dropped a bombshell on her about his parentage and then refused to talk about it. To be fair, Sumiko was the talker in the relationship. Ryan brooded. And he'd just found out he wasn't related to the man who had raised him, and that he had been born as the result of a sexual attack on his mother.

She grabbed the phone, noting but not reading the multiple text messages from friends and Lion Truth sources about the stadium collapse, then set it down again.

He said he needed time to process the information. She

had to respect that. Right? At the same time, he'd sounded awfully depressed, maybe dangerously so.

What if he tries to...?

No, she wouldn't think like that. If he needed time to process, she would give him time to process. But she could be his safety net, just in case. Waking up her computer, she logged into her Show My Pals account and a map popped up with several thumbnail-sized profile photos attached with arrows to green dots. Her photo overlapped with her mother's, since their GPS locations were both in their house at the moment. A couple of her other friends, with whom she had swapped location access privileges, showed up at various addresses around town. She located Ryan's dot a few miles from her house and zoomed in on his location, checking the street names. "Tony's Pizzeria," she said. "He likes it there. Comfort food. Probably a good sign."

Unless that's his last m...

"Stop it," she scolded herself.

Then the dot started to move.

After a few minutes, she wondered where he was headed. Past Tony's was a commercial area that had gone steadily downhill as the mall siphoned business away. A lot of stores had gone out of business. Nearby, an extensive home community project had stalled after the economy tanked and credit dried up. The land had been bulldozed and later fenced in to prevent accidents and lawsuits. "Coming Soon" signs bolted to the fence had become ironic, advertising a date almost a year in the past.

"Why that part of town?"

Her internal worry meter started to tick upward. She picked up her phone and ran the Show My Pals app. She grabbed up her laptop, ran down the stairs and asked to borrow her mother's Honda Odyssey.

I can't be his safety net five miles away.

"What the hell, Sam?" Dean said as they walked through the door into Roy Dempsey's log cabin, with Roy once again at home, judging by the silver Dodge Ram in the driveway. "You go on hiatus with Lucifer the second we're attacked? He almost burns us alive, and takes the woman again."

"Dean, I—"

Roy sat at one of the kitchen stools, chowing down on what looked like a two-foot-long hoagie, which required a lot of focus when you only had one arm. That Dean's stomach was growling in protest added to his irritation over the oni fiasco. Roy scratched his grizzled chin and stared at Dean.

"Don't look at me like that," Dean grumbled. "I fed your creepy cat."

"Whatever this is," Roy said, waving his hand between the brothers, "leave me out of it."

"Right," Dean snapped. "Wouldn't want to spoil your meal."

"I bought three extra," Roy said evenly. "In the fridge."

"You did not," Dean said, brightening instantly.

He opened the fridge. "You did! I totally misjudged you."

"You didn't wreck my house," Roy said. "Figure I'm ahead of the game."

Dean took the sandwiches out of the refrigerator. "Know what would make this perfect? Pie."

Handing one of the wrapped sandwiches to Sam, he said, "I thought you had Lucifer-vision under control."

"I do," Sam said, frowning, "usually. This time was worse."

Dean took a bite of the overstuffed hoagie. "It's the bad luck mojo!" he said between mouthfuls. "My lighter fails, you visit *The Twilight Zone*. The guy throws banana peels under our shoes. How do we fight that?"

Sam picked at his sandwich, removed a few items that didn't meet his seal of approval, then ate with a thoughtful expression on his face. "The lore mentions holly guarding against the oni," he said. "What if…?"

Roy gave Sam an odd look.

Dean removed a few bottles of beer from the fridge and passed them around.

"What? You got something?" he asked Sam.

"With all the information on expelling the oni from a town—"

"The soybean confetti?"

"Right. I figured holly guarded against him coming," Sam said, "and since he's already here, what's the point? But what if it guards against the oni's mojo."

"And evens the odds," Dean said, nodding. "Could give us a fighting chance."

"But he's still invulnerable."

"So we can't gank him."

"Holly?" Roy asked, so softly Dean almost didn't catch it.

"What?"

"You need holly for an oni?" Roy said. Both Dean and Sam nodded. "There's a holly bush out back."

"You just happen to have holly growing out back?" Dean asked.

"This doesn't mean I'm involved," Roy said.

"No," Sam said. "Of course not."

"Eighteen years ago," Roy said after a sip of beer, "before Sally died and…"—he raised his half-arm—"I thought we might have an oni here in town."

"What?" Sam asked incredulously.

"You're telling us this now?"

"Look, I had no idea what you were hunting and I liked it that way," Roy said. "We had a bad flu epidemic, train derailment, factory explosion, some other weird stuff, all in a few days. I researched the lore, but then things went back to normal. Still, I bought an American holly shrub from a local nursery and planted it out back. Boy scout mode back then."

"Always be prepared," Dean said, nodding. "That saves us some time."

Bobby came through the front door, if anything, looking worse than he had after bouncing off the windshield that afternoon. Wincing, he eased his way into the kitchen. Dean handed him the third hoagie from out of the fridge.

"Appreciate it, Roy."

"Singer, you look like ten pounds of crap in a five-pound bag."

"Feel like a rodeo clown with a hangover."

Sam brought Bobby up to speed on the holly and Roy's

account of possible oni activity eighteen years before.

"Might be the same one," Bobby said. "But why come back?"

"Just tell me how to gank it," Dean said, looking back and forth. "Anybody?"

Bobby sighed. "Wish I had my books. Let me see the laptop. Maybe I'll spot something we overlooked."

"What happened, Singer?" Roy asked. "You can't walk without wincing. Better sit this out. Or are you nuts?"

"Certifiable," Bobby said with a wry chuckle. "But the job ain't done."

Roy heaved a sigh. "I must be as crazy as you, Bobby."

"So it's Bobby, now?"

"Oh, shut up before I lose my nerve," Roy said. "Don't know if this helps, but the oni comes outta Japanese lore, and the various branches of that monster family tree don't get along. The *obake* are Japanese shape-shifters, take animal forms, sometimes even *protect* humans. They and the oni don't trust each other."

"He's afraid of animals?" Dean asked incredulously.

"If he thinks that animal might be a threat," Bobby said, nodding, "an *obake*."

"Could McClary bring in some K-9 units?" Sam asked.

"They might scare him away, but they won't kill him," Dean said.

"If he leaves my town," Roy said, "that's good enough for me."

What about the next town? Dean thought grimly. *We gotta end this once and for all.*

* * *

Ryan arrived first at Hawthorne's, the locally owned department store that had become yet another casualty of the economy. The derelict building had been on the market for a while with no buyers on the horizon. Graffiti marred the plywood covering all the windows. Inside, the place was an empty shell. Whatever hadn't sold during the bankruptcy sales had been auctioned off afterward.

Ryan had no idea why he had been summoned to this location. He became increasingly mystified minutes later when Dalton Rourke walked up to him. But when Jesse Trumball drove up in a red Dodge Durango and climbed out to stand beside them, the reason became clear. Ryan noticed the bumps on their heads—even though they had made minimal efforts to hide them with a knit hat and a hoodie, respectively—the red hair coming in at the roots, the darkened nails. As they stood side by side, their near-uniform height, several inches over six feet, was the final piece of the puzzle.

"Brothers," Ryan said softly.

"What?" Dalton asked.

"You're my brothers."

"He is correct," a deep voice said.

A tall man in a dark suit was leaning against one of the landscaping trees decorating the perimeter of the building. Ryan hadn't noticed him until that moment, but when he stepped forward, out of the shadows, Ryan saw the horns sprouting from his head.

Those are growing in us! he realized.

"My three sons," their father said, "by three different

mothers. I am Tora."

Ryan stepped forward, fists clenched. "You—You raped my mother!"

"That is a human concern," Tora said. "The time has come for you to rise above your humanity. The process has already begun—I'm sure you have each noticed your physical changes. You must, however, voluntarily complete the final rite of passage to become oni."

"What if we don't want to become oni?" Dalton asked.

"Speak for yourself," Jesse said belligerently.

"You have no choice," Tora said. "If you fail to complete the rite, you will die stillborn, half human, half oni. It is an agonizing end." He paused to let that sink in. "Instead, I offer you power above human sheep, to achieve your rightful destiny."

"We'd be as powerful as you?" Ryan asked. Then he could channel the rage inside him and focus on killing the man— this oni—who had killed his mother, even if her death was the reason Ryan existed.

"One day, yes," Tora assured him. "But our time is short and first I would introduce you to the woman who will become my mate and your oni mother, who will replace the frail human mothers you never knew. Tomorrow we will be complete, a family. But tonight, my sons, you will become oni!"

Like hell, Ryan thought bitterly.

As the oni led them through a door he had jimmied open, Ryan noticed Dalton and Jesse nodding, smiling at each other.

Oh, God, he thought, appalled, *they actually want this!*

* * *

Parked across the street from Hawthorne's in her mother's Odyssey, Sumiko had been about to climb out of the minivan after Ryan stopped in front of the department store when Dalton Rourke joined him, followed by Jesse Trumball in what must have been a stolen SUV. Instead, she snapped a few photos with her smartphone, but couldn't get a clear shot of the man who spoke to them.

On seeing Ryan, Dalton and Jesse together, her first thought was, *Those three have nothing in common.*

The only time Sumiko had seen them relatively close together was during the bomb threat evacuation at school. Other than that, as far as she knew, they were complete strangers. But seeing them standing next to each other, she realized that not only were they the same age, they were also about the same height and build. A suspicion began to form.

She opened her laptop, scrolled through pictures in her blog and checked photos from scanned yearbooks. Certain physical features were very similar. They had the same brow, nose and chin. Ryan dyed his hair blue, but it was naturally red. Jesse's too, judging by old photos of him before he shaved his head. Switching on her portable Wi-Fi hotspot, Sumiko looked at social media profiles, ran searches on their names and found out they were born within the same week. She knew Ryan's mother and Dalton's mother had both died in childbirth.

That's a weird coincidence, she thought. *What about Jesse?*

She called her friend Brennan Kennedy, who worked part-time at the Laurel Hill Library, and asked her to look up old newspaper records of their birth week. Twenty minutes later, Brennan called back and confirmed what Sumiko suspected—Jesse's mother had also died in childbirth. Sumiko had entertained the idea that they were triplets born of one mother then separated at birth, but there had been three mothers.

So, what if they were secretly related as half-brothers? That means one man is their father. That man they just met outside Hawthorne's?

She brought up her blog dashboard and typed a headline: "What do these three have in common?" She positioned three photos of Ryan, Jesse and Dalton, side by side, which displayed their physical similarities.

If that man is Ryan's father, he's a criminal.

A criminal meeting his sons in an abandoned building. Sumiko had a bad feeling Ryan was involved in something dangerous. She wondered if it was somehow related to the fatal accidents happening all over town. How could she protect Ryan without betraying him?

She posted the blog entry.

Then she remembered the investigator who had contacted her through her blog and hadn't scoffed at her supernatural theories about the weirdness in town. He might listen without suggesting an extended stay in the loony bin. He might even be taken seriously if he reported it to the cops. She had started to type an email to him when she noticed movement across the street.

Jesse Trumball, hunched over in a gray hoodie with his hands stuffed in the pockets, walked briskly to the red Durango. Before he climbed in, he looked back and forth across the parking lot, causing Sumiko to duck down out of sight.

Though it was dusk and the light was fading, shadows losing their definition against the encroaching darkness, she could have sworn she saw blood smeared on his chin.

Is this some kind of fight club?

Jesse drove the Durango in a loop and parked beside the door. Sumiko watched as the tall man climbed into the passenger seat, Dalton opened the rear door behind him, and Ryan, his head bowed, walked around the back of the SUV and climbed into the seat behind Jesse. A moment later, the red SUV darted out of the lot and drove away from the depressed commercial district.

After a few seconds, Sumiko started the Odyssey, made a U turn and followed.

Ryan, what the hell have you gotten yourself into?

THIRTY

Ryan sat behind Jesse with his elbows on his knees and his face in his hands, trying to contain the roaring in his skull. It felt like ten thousand bees buzzed under his skin. It was hard to sit still, to try to think, to even remember who he was. For the sake of revenge—to avenge his dead mother—he had allowed himself to taste the oni's blood. Now it burned inside him, driving away rational thought and replacing it with bloodlust.

When he'd entered Hawthorne's dark interior with the others, his only goal had been to find a way to kill the stranger who could somehow speak into Ryan's mind and had compelled him to show up on his doorstep. But he wasn't a man, it wasn't human. It was an oni, whatever that meant, some kind of mythical being that was apparently not so mythical after all.

"Cool car, Trumball," Dalton said. "Stolen?"

"Borrowed," Jesse said. "My neighbor's on vacation. I let myself into his house and grabbed the keys. He won't miss it until Monday."

Ryan tried to hold onto his identity—his old identity, not the monstrous hybrid he had become—and not think about the promise of violence and the overnight transformation to come. He tried to remember what had happened in Hawthorne's so he could fight the driving urge to kill…

After the oni led them toward the back of the department store, Ryan saw the disheveled woman tied to one of the support columns on the lower level of the store. The woman looked battered and hopeless, almost unconscious on her feet. Ryan wondered if his mother had gone through a similar ordeal. When Ryan stepped forward, intending to untie the woman, the oni caught his shoulder in one massive hand and squeezed hard. It smiled and said, "She is no concern of yours, young one."

"But she's—"

"Though it would grieve me," Tora said evenly, applying more pressure until Ryan winced, "I would rip your spine from your body."

Then the oni lined the three of them up in a row and explained the ritual of blood needed to complete their transformation from hybrid to oni. "A taste of my blood will imbue you with strength beyond that of humankind," the oni said while pacing in front of them, rubbing his bare hands together while his cane dangled from his belt. "Thus fortified, you will go to a human gathering to proclaim your dominance with a slaughter. You will have weapons to aid you, but at least one killing blow must come from an oni trait you now possess, your nascent fangs or your hardened fingernails. When your skin runs red with the blood of your victims, your body will begin the final stage of transformation. With the dawn, you three will be reborn."

"And if—if we don't do this by dawn?" Ryan asked.

"Your body will reject your dual nature. It will literally tear itself apart," Tora explained. "Your muscles will constrict until your bones snap. One by one your organs will shut down. You will experience excruciating seizures and your brain will hemorrhage. But, with my guidance, I am confident none of you will fail."

The oni chanted in a guttural language and then, with one inhuman fingernail, sliced open his opposite forearm.

"With a taste of my blood you will experience some of my power and invulnerability," the oni continued, "enough to sustain you through the violence of the ritual. Succeed, and with the dawn, the power will rise from within you."

One by one, he smeared his blood across their lips. First Jesse, then Dalton, and finally Ryan tasted oni blood—and it was like a contact high. Ryan felt a surge of power, like he could run through a brick wall and feel no pain.

As disgusted as he had been by the idea of tasting the oni's blood, Ryan wanted the power it offered. Anything to give him an edge against the inhuman creature that had violated his mother. But at the moment the blood touched his tongue, Ryan had to admit to himself that he craved the power the way a hungry man craves food. His physical transformation had already started and with it his temper had run wild, almost beyond his control, a powder keg ready to explode. Now he *wanted* to explode.

But I won't kill, he told himself. *I won't become a monster.*

Ryan shook his head and tried to focus on his current surrounding, in the Durango. He couldn't change what had happened in Hawthorne's, but he could keep the promise to himself. He had to stay alert for any opportunity to fight back.

"We need a gathering?" Dalton asked. "Lots of people in a confined space?"

"Yes," the oni said. "Do you have something in mind?"

"Damn straight," Dalton said, grinning. "The Cheshire Theater."

Jesse laughed for some reason. "I know it well."

Ryan looked back and forth between them and tried not to stare at the oni, worried that his hatred for the monster would be visible in his eyes.

The oni opened the duffel bag at his feet and handed them each a long curved knife. "Keep these concealed until we are inside," he said. "Then kill as many as you can. But remember to save at least one for your fangs or claws."

"Almost there," Jesse said.

Ryan took his knife and stared at the gleaming blade. He imagined plunging the blade into somebody and trembled with excitement. He squeezed his eyes shut.

Don't become the monster. Don't... become the monster...

Trailing the red Durango, Sumiko slowed when Jesse parked the SUV on the right side of the street. When all four of them got out of the Durango and walked down the sidewalk, she had to make a decision. Ryan would never hurt her, but that left three extremely large males with violent backgrounds, while she was one slender teenaged girl who was too nosy for her own good. She stayed in the Odyssey and drove past them, raising her right hand and forearm in front of her face in case they looked as she passed.

As she crossed the intersection, she glanced in the rearview mirror and was surprised when they walked into the Cheshire Theater. According to the marquee, *Fiddler on the Roof* was the featured play, two shows daily.

Oh, Ryan, no! She made an illegal U-turn and drove back to the theater, parking on the opposite side of the street.

Please tell me you're not helping them rob the place.

She darted across four lanes of traffic, eliciting a strained chorus of car horns.

When her hand fell on the handle of one of the ornate wooden doors of the theater, she paused, uncertain of her next course of action. She could talk Ryan out of criminal stupidity, but not those other three goons. Maybe she could drag Ryan out and to hell with—

Screams erupted from inside.

Sumiko jumped back from the doors as if she'd been shocked.

Too late. God, I'm too late…

Continuing to back away, she patted her hip pockets, remembered she had left her phone on the passenger seat of the Odyssey, and ran back across four lanes of traffic as the light turned yellow. A driver intent on running the yellow light had to stomp on his brakes to avoid hitting her. The car screeched, its bumper striking her leg, almost knocking her down. Laying on his horn, the driver spewed curses out of his window in between questioning her mental capacity. She barely heard him as she jumped in the Odyssey and dialed 911.

The cell reception was horrible. Static overwhelmed the operator's voice, swallowing whole words. Sumiko shouted, "Robbery at the Cheshire Theater! Hurry!"

She rocked back and forth in the driver's seat, hands gripping her phone tucked between her knees, muttering, "Ryan, what have you done? What have you done?"

After Roy showed them to his American holly shrub, Bobby and Dean took two pairs of pruning shears and collected two dozen sets of leaves with red berries. Bobby planned to have McClary pass the extras out to the patrol officers assigned to him. Protection against supernatural accidents, clumsiness and mechanical malfunctions would level the playing field a bit and, they hoped, reduce casualties the next time they encountered the oni. But the holly wouldn't defeat him.

Sam stayed inside the cabin, re-examining the lore, looking for something he might have missed or something that allowed for a reinterpretation of the lore. While online, he noticed a couple of new items on the RSS feed for the Lion Truth blog. The first related some information about the stadium collapse and gave the names of some of the victims—no information Sam didn't know or hadn't experienced firsthand. The newest item caught his attention because it seemed out of place. Three faces, all young men, side by side, almost like mug shots. He skimmed the entry. All three had been born within the same week, seventeen years ago, to three different women who all died in childbirth.

A bizarre coincidence, Sam thought. *Unless it wasn't.*

Sam reviewed the facts: Half-brothers; different mothers, one father. All conceived approximately eighteen years ago.

"Eighteen years…" Sam tapped a pen on the table and recalled what Kim Jacobs had told them about the oni's plans. *"No choice but to come to him, the father… They must shed their human face."*

"Dean! Bobby!" Sam shouted.

He met them as they came through the back door with Roy and a couple of bags filled with holly.

"He came back for his family," Sam told them.

"Wait. What?" Dean said, frowning. "There's an oni family in town?"

Sam explained his theory that when the oni visited Laurel Hill eighteen years ago he impregnated three separate women.

"The teens are hybrids. They must come of age in their seventeenth year. He's back to collect them or to guide them through a transformation."

"So it really was an oni all those years ago," Roy said. "I'll be damned."

"What about the woman he kidnapped?" Dean said. "Is she meant to become his mate?"

"The demon gate ceremony must change the woman," Sam said. "It looks like human women don't survive the birthing process."

"Great," Dean said. "An oni who's ready to settle down."

"And oni family values involve slaughtering humans by the truckload," Bobby said grimly.

His cell rang.

"McClary," he told them, then answered.

"Yup. Sore as hell. How's the wrist?" He listened for a few moments. "Aw, hell... No, it's gotta be him. No, no magic bullet yet. Just holly... And send some K-9 units. I'll explain later."

"Where?" Dean asked.

"Cheshire Theater," Bobby said. "Sounds bad."

"That's ten minutes from here," Roy said. "Five if we ignore red lights."

"Roy," Bobby said, "this ain't your fight."

"Hell it ain't," Roy said, grabbing his keys. "Should have killed the bastard eighteen years ago."

Ryan was losing the battle against his inner demon.

The oni had led them into the lobby of the Cheshire Theater. Wielding his cane like a deadly combination of a sword and club, he struck down the startled theater workers loitering in the open area.

"Once inside," he told his sons, "block the exits. Allow no one to leave."

"I'm all over the balcony," Dalton said with demented glee.

Doors on either side of the lobby led into the theater, so Tora instructed Jesse and Dalton to enter through the right before grabbing Ryan's arm and pulling him through the left. He must have sensed Ryan's hesitation because he pressed his face close to Ryan's, baring his sharp teeth, and said, "By my blood, I command you. Allow no one to leave by the fire exit."

The mention of the oni's blood and the memory of it on his lips and tongue had galvanized Ryan, as if the phrase had triggered a post-hypnotic suggestion. When the others fanned out, he rushed down the left aisle and took a position blocking the fire exit.

With the lights down in the theater, the audience of several hundred hardly noticed their arrival and deployment. Most of the actors were on stage for the big wedding celebration near the end of the first act.

The screaming had begun when Jesse jumped on stage with his knife and started slicing throats, one after another. A few people tried to stop him, without success. By that time, the audience had risen en masse from their seats to rush for the exits, where the oni awaited them with his deadly cane in one hand and a meat cleaver in the other. When they tried to reach the other door to the lobby, dead bodies rained down from the balcony, courtesy of Dalton, striking the backs of seats or the burgundy carpeting.

After slaughtering the orchestra, Jesse waded through the crowd, slashing left and right with deadly abandon until he blocked the door opposite the oni.

Until then, Ryan had stood in mute shock by the fire exit, his own hands unsullied. But he felt the fire burning inside him so fiercely that he feared what would happen the moment someone approached him. His need to lash out at something, someone, was being held in check by the thinnest of threads.

"The fire exit!" a burly man in a dark, blood-spattered three-piece suit yelled, leading a dozen people down the left aisle toward Ryan.

The men wore suits and ties and the women wore fancy evening gowns, formal attire now at odds with the slaughterhouse the theater had become.

"Out of the way, boy!" the man shouted at Ryan.

"*Stand your ground!*"

The voice was like a drumbeat inside his head.

Ryan braced himself.

"I—can't," Ryan said. A part of him, human-Ryan, wanted to run as far away from the theater as possible. But another part of him, a dark urge rising to the surface of his consciousness, wanted to fight... and to kill.

"Move!" the man shouted, and charged—

Right into the tip of the sharp blade that Ryan had raised reflexively.

As the heavy man crashed into him, Ryan felt the knife sink into the man's flesh, almost too easily. Warm blood gushed over Ryan's fist. He pushed and the man fell back and collapsed.

"You bastard!" a woman in an emerald dress screamed and rushed Ryan, her hands lashing out, trying to rake his face with her fingernails.

In self-defense, he caught her with his free hand around her throat and, before he could stop himself, he squeezed. His dark fingernails sliced through her neck as easily as his knife had pierced her husband's chest. Blood sprayed from an artery, washing over Ryan's face. He knew in that moment he was lost.

His head burned as his horns nudged through his scalp and, when he grimaced in pain, his sharper teeth sliced his bottom lip. In the middle of his forehead, a dull ache began to throb and recede. Human-Ryan, if any part of him still existed, succumbed to despair. The stronger darkness surged up through him and lashed out at anyone who approached him.

The next several minutes were a blur, with brief flashes of the carnage resolving into horrifying clarity before sinking into the fog of brutality. Jesse ripped out several throats with his claws and a few more with his teeth. Dalton's victims continued to fall from the balcony. At some point, a theater worker started to turn the house lights up, before Jesse found him. Now the theater had a twilight cast to it, as if light could never overcome the darkness.

People were too cowed to approach the exits. Screaming had turned to sobbing, with many of the wounded moaning and writhing on the floor or sprawled across seats. Some tried to call for help on their cell phones, but found none of their phones would complete a call.

The oni impaled anyone within arm's reach with his cane or lopped off heads and arms with powerful swipes of the blood-drenched cleaver.

Over a hundred people were dead or dying before the first contingent of police officers arrived. The first few stood in uncomprehending shock, but soon had to recover to fight for their lives. They fired guns at the oni, some point blank, but could not injure him.

A shot hit Jesse. He yelped, staggered backward a couple of steps, and looked down at his chest. He laughed. The bullet had ripped through his hoodie and shirt over his heart, but he seemed more startled than hurt. He rushed the cop and stabbed him in the gut, ripping the blade upward, killing him.

Ryan remembered what the oni had said about his blood conferring some of his invulnerability to his sons, at least for several hours. He jerked as a bullet struck his own upper arm. He inspected the point of impact and saw a red welt, nothing more. The bullet hadn't penetrated his skin either. More bullets followed. Most hurt about as much as a wasp sting.

The oni stalked the police officers who had fired on them, cutting them down one by one. Others inadvertently killed each other with crossfire or deadly ricochets. Guns jammed. They tripped or slipped in blood and fell. One knocked himself out when he fell against the back of a theater seat. Some tried calling for backup, but their radios crackled with static and squeals.

Ryan understood that the oni was responsible for the accidents, the clumsiness of the cops, the malfunctioning cell phones and police radios. Human-Ryan, voiceless and dwindling into irrelevance, knew that the people were doomed. No one in the theater would survive the massacre.

THIRTY-ONE

Dean had kept the Monte Carlo's windows rolled down since leaving the bowling alley to try and rid the vehicle of burnt car seat smell. So far, it hadn't helped.

Dean and Sam heard the police sirens long before they arrived at the blocked intersection with an ambulance and at least seven police cruisers parked at odd angles in the middle of the street, their flashing lightbars painting everything within sight blue and red. One cop had been left outside to reroute traffic and order pedestrian gawkers to vacate the area.

From the opposite direction, two black and white police SUVs with the K-9 designation on their side panels arrived, weaving through the police cars to approach the theater entrance.

"I guess we hoof it from here," Dean said to Sam, who was riding shotgun, looking anxious.

Dean swung the Monte Carlo to the curb before the police blockade. Bobby and Roy followed in Bobby's Chevelle, which he slipped into the closest parking space behind the Monte Carlo. The four of them jogged toward the theater. Bobby took the lead, moving like a shopping cart with a bad wheel, on the lookout for McClary, who could clear them with the traffic cop. They each carried holly leaves and berries in a trouser pocket. Bobby held the extras in a paper bag for McClary to distribute to his officers.

As they crossed the intersection, Sam stared across the street, apparently distracted.

"Sam!"

"What?"

"Lucifer-vision?" Dean asked softly.

If the holly worked, the oni's mojo couldn't trip up Sam with an ill-timed Lucifer visit. Of course, Dean knew Sam's mind might wig out all on its own.

"No," Sam said. "A young Asian woman peeking out of that minivan. Our blogger, maybe?"

"Could be," Dean said. "She's definitely got her finger on the pulse of the weird."

McClary had ridden to the theater in one of the K-9 vehicles. He approached them, a fresh cast on his right forearm, as the drivers of the two units opened the rear doors and led out two German shepherds on leashes.

As Bobby's group reached the sidewalk, the traffic cop yelled, "You can't go in there!"

"Stand down, Becker!" McClary called. "They're with me."

McClary lowered his voice and said to Bobby, "It's

worse than we thought. It's a bloodbath in there. Details are sketchy. Radio reception keeps dropping out. But that—The oni—he's not alone."

"Right," Dean said. "Dad's got Mike, Robbie and Chip with him now."

"What am I missing?" McClary asked, confused.

"The oni came back to claim his three sons," Sam said. "Half-breeds."

They hurried into the lobby. The two K-9 officers waited with the dogs, one at either door. Six other officers split up with them, three to a side, guns drawn, looking nervous. One fresh-faced cop gripped a shotgun, which caught McClary's eye.

"Winemiller, you can't fire a shotgun in there!"

"Right, sir," the junior patrol officer said, and turned toward the outer door.

"Winemiller! Go round back. Tell Louden we go in sixty seconds."

"Wait." Bobby held a sprig of holly out to the junior officer. "Put this in your pocket.

"That's an order," he added, when Winemiller gave him a disbelieving look.

McClary nodded his confirmation, then turned to Bobby as Winemiller jogged away. "I'm supposed to be on desk duty, but I can't sit this one out, no matter what the chief says."

"Where is the chief?" Bobby asked.

"Calling in a SWAT team from the FBI's Philly field office and pressing the mayor to have the governor call in the National Guard," McClary said. "I expect he'll be here soon.

We're calling everyone. All hands on deck." He handed Bobby a gun. "Loaded with armor-piercing rounds. So's mine, but I'll only risk point blank range with my left hand. These will go through soft targets, so watch your aim. Ricochets are a bitch."

Bobby nodded and then reached into the bag for the holly. "Have your men carry these. Could stop the bad luck hoodoo. Maybe improve radio reception."

"Got any rabbit's feet in there? Four leaf clovers? Horseshoes?"

"Can't hurt," Dean said. "We're packing."

"If nothing else," Sam added, "it might give us time to find a weakness."

"Maybe the weakness," McClary suggested, "is his three sons."

As the sergeant quickly passed out the holly, brooking no complaints, Dean looked at Sam, who nodded and said, "He's got a point."

"Roy, you're with me," Dean said, moving to the right door. "Agent Willis, go with S—Tom."

The Winchesters had discussed their deployment in the car. Bobby continued to walk with a limp, grimacing with each step. Roy had one arm and had retired from hunting with good reason. Both men were too stubborn to sit out the battle, but too much of a liability to each other to team up.

McClary checked his watch. "Go!"

The K-9 units went through the doors first, followed by the other officers and McClary, with the Winchesters, Bobby and Roy bringing up the rear.

* * *

Sumiko had stayed hidden below the window of her mother's Odyssey when the police cars arrived and blocked the intersection. She kept hoping and praying that Ryan would come out of the theater unharmed. But nobody who went inside the theater came out and she feared a robbery had turned into a hostage situation. She heard occasional gunshots and screaming when the outer doors opened and tried not to let her imagination run wild.

She could picture Ryan holed up with hostages, along with the criminal who had assaulted his mother, and the two juvenile delinquents. A horrible family of outlaws, and Ryan had let himself get pulled into their orbit. There was nothing she could do now. Ryan was in too deep.

When she saw the other men arrive, the ones not wearing police uniforms, she wondered absently if one of them was the investigator who had contacted her.

She blamed herself for driving Ryan away with a stupid argument right when he needed her most. Finding out his father had lied to him all his life had been too much for him to handle alone. Despair overwhelmed her.

Knuckles rapped on the window.

Sumiko nearly jumped out of her skin.

A flashlight shone in her face. "You can't stay here, miss! Move along!"

Heart racing, she started the Odyssey and drove along the shoulder until she could swing into the street. She couldn't leave Ryan, but she had to move the car. She turned left down the nearest side street, made a U-turn and parked near the curb where she could see the police cars but not the traffic cop or the front of the theater. She left the car and walked to the corner, looking toward the intersection. That's when she saw the speeding car, weaving back and forth across two lanes of traffic.

The car never slowed. The traffic cop bolted out of the way just in time and rolled across the hood of a cruiser. The speeding car smashed through the angled cop cars in a rapid series of destructive impacts before veering into and splitting a utility pole. EMTs rushed from the parked ambulance to the driver.

Sumiko hugged herself, wondering what else could go wrong.

Everything went to hell five seconds after Dean walked through the doorway into the theater. He allowed himself a frozen moment to take in the extreme level of carnage before him, dozens of broken bodies, severed limbs everywhere he looked, blood running down every surface. Walls, chair backs, support columns, and wall sconces dripped with gore. Survivors huddled together, small islands of life in an ocean of death. In the left aisle, the oni sported a wild head of red hair around the two bone-colored horns. His arms spread, a cleaver in one hand and his cane in the other, he stalked more victims. Farther down the left aisle, near the fire exit that had been rammed open by McClary's men, Dean spotted Ryan, one of the three teenagers pictured on the blog page. Ryan fought the cops with a knife, screaming "No!" every time he lashed out at someone. In the right aisle, the largest son, Jesse, ripped out an old man's throat with his dark fingernails.

Jesse had horns now, half the size of the oni's.

The K-9 officers released the German shepherds on entry and both dogs bounded toward the oni with rumbling growls and hackles raised.

When the oni whirled to face the new threat, Dean hoped to see fear in his inhuman eyes, but nothing registered. He swept out his foot and kicked the first dog in the chest, sweeping it aside so hard it flailed through the air and struck a blood-wet wall with a whine of pain. He drove the cleaver blade into the second dog's head. It dropped to the floor, unmoving.

"So much for that theory," Dean said grimly.

McClary yelled, "Agent Willis and I have armor-piercing rounds. Get the sons!"

Sam and a couple of McClary's men angled toward the left aisle, closing on Ryan. Bobby stood near McClary to get a bead on the oni. That left Dean and Roy, along with the remaining cops, to tackle Jesse in the right aisle—

Wait! Where's the third son? Dean wondered.

The disemboweled body of a man in his sixties dropped in front of him with a heavy wet splat. From above, a woman screamed, "Dalton! Stop!"

"Shut up, you worthless bitch!"

"Balcony!" Dean said to Roy.

They scrambled up the stairs and found Dalton by the balcony railing, covered in blood, with one arm wrapped around an old woman's neck, his sharp-toothed mouth close to her throat, a blood-drenched knife in his other hand pressed to her abdomen. Twin horns had erupted from his head, protruding more than an inch, and the center of his forehead was unusually lumpy. Something squirmed under the skin.

"He killed my husband right in front of me and laughed," the woman said, "after killing all these people. My evil grandson—"

"I told you to shut your mouth!"

Dalton's dark nails bit into her fleshy neck, drawing blood.

Roy stepped forward, the gun in his hand lowered, nonthreatening. "Dalton, listen to me," he said. "You don't want to do this."

"Why the hell not?" Dalton said. "The way this bitch treated me my whole life."

"I had a boy. He was a few years older than you when he died," Roy said, taking another tentative step forward.

"What the hell, Roy?" Dean whispered fiercely.

Roy ignored him. "It's hard raising a boy, son. Sometimes parents are strict, maybe too strict. Doesn't mean they don't—"

A rapid series of car crashes erupted from outside.

Dean half expected a cement truck to plow through the wall of the theater.

Dalton raked his claws across his grandmother's neck, ripping her throat apart, and hurled her body sideways over the edge of the balcony, trailing an arterial spray of blood.

"Oh, no…" Roy said, raising his gun.

Before he could get off a shot, Dalton lunged toward him, knife raised.

Dean fired twice as the blade came down. Both bullets

hit Dalton square in the chest, but neither penetrated his skin. He merely twitched from the twin impacts as his dagger plunged into Roy's chest.

Roy dropped to his knees, the knife handle protruding from his torso.

Dalton raised his blood-soaked hands, smiling. "Bullets can't hurt me," he boasted, "and I don't even need a knife to slice your throat open."

The lumpy flesh on Dalton's forehead parted and—as Dean had suspected—revealed a milky-white third eye just as he lunged toward Dean, flashing his dark claws. Dean reacted instinctively, shooting the third eye. Blood burst from the gaping hole and white fluid spilled over Dalton's nose. His human eyes rolled back in his head and he collapsed face first.

"Aim for the third eye! Weak spot!" Dean shouted down from the balcony.

A moan escaped Roy's lips. He pitched sideways, caught himself briefly on his arm, then tipped over. A moment before his face could strike the floor, Dean caught him.

"Roy," Dean said. "You're gonna be okay."

"No… I'm not," Roy said, gasping for air. "Thought I could get her clear."

"I know," Dean said. "Hold on."

Roy shook his head. "Finish this."

"I will."

"Tell Singer… Tell Bobby he's too damn old for this work," Roy said. "And… don't ever un-retire." He coughed up blood and closed his eyes. "Never… ends well."

Dean could say the same for most hunters' lives.

He felt the moment Roy died, and laid him gently on the floor.

Now that he had discovered the chink in the oni armor, Dean had to hope he could keep that promise to Roy, and end the reign of terror. He hurried down the curved staircase to join the fight below.

THIRTY-TWO

When Dalton died, the severing of the blood-bond staggered Tora, as if he had been dealt a physical blow. For long moments he had trouble breathing. His rampaging bloodlust, shared with his transforming sons, had clouded his better judgment. Because of the nature of his abilities, he often had to soak up the fear and grief he caused from a distance. The completion of the oni rite of passage into adulthood had, however, allowed him to sink his claws into the gloriously violent celebration. But they had stayed too long.

The last group of police officers had come with the two infernal hunters, and they must have discovered that holly leaves neutralized his direct influence over human behavior and actions. He noticed the difference immediately—it was as if they were invisible to his third eye. And while he could withstand the force of the armor-piercing bullets, those rounds could injure his sons, though not mortally. He should have signaled a retreat earlier. Because he waited, his nascent family had suffered an irreparable loss. Moreover, the hunters had discovered the one fatal weakness in his sons. Dalton and Jesse had developed their third eye already and Dalton had died because of it. Ryan's hadn't formed yet, but could at any moment, placing him at risk.

"*We leave now!*" he ordered through the blood-bond. "*Out the back!*"

Sam and the other police officers fighting Ryan and Jesse discovered that, in addition to being impervious to bullets, the oni's sons were endowed with inhuman strength. When Sam's group got a clear shot at Ryan, they took it, but direct hits produced nothing more than a grunt, a flinch or the occasional stumble. Though scores of theatergoers had been killed, with twice as many wounded and slowly bleeding to death, Sam estimated one to two hundred survivors. Some cowered on the floor between rows of seats, others lay prostrate under seats or feigned death to escape the attention of their attackers. Small groups huddled together, inaccessible for the moment because of a veritable barricade of corpses. The survivors, uniformly too terrified to flee, were also potential victims of stray bullets. Even when Sam urged them to run for the exits, they wouldn't budge. They had seen one horrific outcome after another for anyone who ventured into the aisles.

So far, neither the police nor the hunters had done

anything to instill hope in the survivors. They waged a war of attrition in which only one side suffered losses. With the exception of Winemiller, the half-dozen officers who had rammed open the rear door of the theater had already fallen, victims of physical battery or knife wounds from Ryan or friendly fire. One had slipped in blood and split his head open on an armrest.

With their armor-piercing rounds, Bobby and McClary had interrupted the oni's killing spree, but they would run out of special ammo soon and they had to dodge his attacks with the cleaver and cane.

In the right aisle, three officers had fallen, victims of Jesse's knife or claws. The remaining police officers were retreating, taking shots when they had a clear line of fire, but their bullets could have been made of modeling clay for all the damage they inflicted.

Sam took a shot at Ryan and hit him in the throat without opening a wound. Undeterred, Ryan stepped over the body of a dead policewoman toward Winemiller, slashing his knife back and forth. Winemiller jumped back, almost fell, but regained his balance.

We can't stop them, Sam thought grimly. *They'll kill everyone here.*

They were only a few minutes into the battle, but a dire outcome seemed inevitable.

Then Sam heard his brother shouting. "Aim for the third eye! Weak spot!"

Sam immediately drew a bead on Ryan's head, but Ryan's third eye wasn't open yet.

Behind him, Sam heard a commotion. As he whirled, he

saw the oni backhand McClary with the flat of the cleaver. The force of the blow hurled the sergeant across a half dozen theater seats.

Jesse stabbed a cop in the chest, pulled the gun from the man's weak fingers and shot the other two cops near him. Then he loped across the seat backs in the middle seating section toward the oni in the left aisle. Bobby tracked him and fired a shot that whipped back Jesse's head. He crashed between two rows of seats.

Bobby spun, sighted on the oni's head and got off one shot. The oni's head jerked back, but he recovered quickly. With his cane, he clubbed Bobby, who managed to turn away from the brunt of the blow, but fell in a heap. A moment later Jesse was up again, a line of blood along his temple, his blossoming third eye intact.

Based on Dean's experience, Sam wouldn't need an armor-piercing round if he could score a direct hit. He took aim at Jesse.

The lumbering oni closed on him, his cane raised like a spear. Sam had no choice but to face Tora. Sam got off one shot, his last, but it struck the oni's right horn and ricocheted. He swung his gun hand up to deflect the iron tip of the cane. The automatic was knocked from his numb fingers and he was airborne, brushed aside by the oni's powerful arm, and crashed into seats, landing atop two sprawled corpses. The side of his jacket had been sliced open and a line of blood trickled down his abdomen, the result of a close call with the cleaver. Wincing, Sam pushed himself up in time to see Winemiller take a shooting stance.

"Winemiller!" McClary called weakly. "Stand down!"

"I got th—"

The tip of the oni's cane skewered the junior officer's throat. While his body twitched, gushing blood, the oni embedded the cleaver in an armrest, then shoved his clawed hand, palm flat, claws aligned, through Winemiller's torso and ripped out his beating heart.

Dean strode down the aisle, firing round after round at the oni, whose bulk shielded his two remaining sons. The oni hurled the cleaver toward Dean, who ducked as it whistled past his head. While Dean dodged the cleaver, the oni picked up Winemiller's body and flung it at him, knocking him over.

By the time Sam managed to disentangled himself from the corpses, the oni and his two sons had slipped out of the fire exit.

Sumiko sat huddled in the Odyssey and tried to call her mother, but her phone kept dropping signal bars whenever she dialed. The ambulance had left with the injured driver who had been too drunk to find his brake pedal and nearly killed the traffic cop. The street was deserted.

Movement caught her eye. Instinctively, she ducked, peering over the edge of the door. Three dark figures ran through a backyard, hunched over.

The streetlight on the nearest utility pole had died when the DUI driver crashed into it. But she recognized one of the men, Ryan, and he appeared to be injured. He was with the tall man and Jesse. They must have left Dalton behind. But why? Had he caused the crisis at the theater? Surely the cops wouldn't have let the others go that easily. They would be questioned.

When they piled into the red Durango, drove slowly away from the theater blockade area and turned down a side street, she made up her mind. She tossed her useless phone on the passenger seat, started the Odyssey and followed them. If Ryan hoped to salvage anything out of this disaster, he had to turn himself in. Maybe he had been coerced into helping the vile man who was his real father. She refused to believe he would willingly take part in a holdup or hostage-taking situation. This might be her last chance to help him.

To avoid answering questions all night at police headquarters, Dean, Sam and Bobby left the theater after helping McClary back on his feet. The sergeant took charge of the situation, but winced continually, having suffered several fractured ribs in addition to dealing with a broken wrist. Patrol sweeps of the area had turned up nothing and, as they might have predicted, traffic cameras in the area had malfunctioned.

Sam's cut was several inches long but shallow and had stopped bleeding. Bobby's torso was one large bruise, but he didn't believe he'd cracked any ribs. If he had, he refused to admit it. He took the news of Roy's death hard.

"Aw, hell," he said. "Told the stubborn bastard this wasn't his fight."

"It never ends well," Dean said, recalling Roy's final words.

"At least we found a weakness," Sam said. "We got one of them, and I almost hit the Big Daddy's third eye."

"Almost?" Bobby said. "Hell, I nailed it. Point blank."

"No damage?" Sam asked.

"By the look of it, sure hurt like hell," Bobby said. "It gripped that cane something fierce."

Sam frowned. "The cane," he said. "According to the lore, an oni wields a club."

"A *kanabo*," Bobby said. "Reshaped for modern times?"

"The expression 'oni with an iron club' means something's invincible in Japanese, right?" Sam said. "So, what if the club enhances its abilities. What if the third eye is a weakness that's protected?"

"Right. Protected," Dean said. "So we're screwed. No Achilles' heel. No chinks in the armor."

"No, Dean," Bobby said, nodding. "Sam's onto something here. That cane's not just a weapon, it's an amulet, a protective shield."

"We take the cane, then shoot the eye," Sam reasoned.

"Fine," Dean said. "But we gotta find him first."

"There is someone who might know." Sam glanced across the street. "If I can find her."

"The blogger?"

"She knows those kids, the oni's sons," Sam said. "Probably tracked them here. Her car's gone now. Maybe she followed them when they left, too."

Sam took the laptop from the Monte Carlo's trunk and discovered a message from Sumiko, stating that she suspected something was wrong with Ryan and had followed him and the others to the theater. She was worried, but didn't know what was happening. "She sent this after we arrived."

"Say where she is now?"

"That was the only message," Sam said, a look of concern on his face. "She's not replying to email. We need to call her, but I don't have her number."

"I'll call McClary," Bobby said, reaching for his phone. "Should have access to her home number. If it's unlisted, someone at the high school should have it."

Sam turned to Dean. "If she went after them," he said, "she's following them blind."

"With no idea she's chasing a bunch of cold-blooded murderers."

THIRTY-THREE

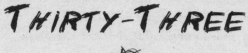

Sumiko parked a block and a half away from Hawthorne's. She waited until the three of them slipped inside the shuttered department store before leaving the minivan. She planned to pull Ryan aside and convince him to ditch the other two. Once they were away, she would urge him to contact the police, tell them how he'd been forced to go along with the others. There was no other explanation in her mind for his behavior. She knew Ryan too well to believe he would willingly commit a serious crime. If he gave evidence against the man who attacked his mother, the obvious ringleader, the police might give Ryan a reduced sentence, maybe probation or house arrest. She had to help him make it right.

She examined the door into Hawthorne's and discovered the lock had been forced and the hinges damaged. It almost swung open when she grabbed the handle. She paused, reaching into her jacket pocket to mute her phone—not that she'd had a reliable signal all night—but couldn't find it. Either the phone had fallen out of her loose jacket pocket or she had left it on the passenger seat again. Regardless, she needed to get Ryan away from the others as soon as possible, before the police found them all together.

Taking a deep breath, she eased the door open and stepped into the dark department store. All the merchandise was long gone, but some broken mannequins remained, like ghosts on eternal guard duty, along with empty clothing racks with plastic and metal hangers. Glass counters remained, but all the cash registers were gone. In the center of the store, the dust-matted up and down escalators crisscrossed each other, forming an X. High above, a long row of skylights, spattered with months of bird droppings, allowed starlight to filter down to her, multiplied by reflections in metal, glass and mirrored surfaces. As she crept deeper into the department store, her eyes adjusted to the darkness well enough to avoid bumping into counters and empty display racks.

She heard voices coming from what had been the home theater section of the store and peered ahead, straining to penetrate the darkness. As she passed the escalators, she saw flickering candlelight dancing on the walls. A little farther and she saw Ryan standing in profile, recognized his voice and that he was angry.

"—made me do those—those horrible things!"

"This is your true nature," a deep voice replied. "By dawn your transformation will be complete. You will cast aside human weakness and human concerns. Now, we finish the demon gate ritual so that she too will become oni and share our strength."

Sumiko froze when she heard a woman sobbing.

To her right, a dark shape rose from the motionless escalator stairs, hurdled the railing and landed behind her. She shrieked as one powerful forearm wrapped around her neck, the other around her waist. She had glimpsed his familiar face. Even though blood streaked his forehead and cheeks, she recognized Jesse Trumball.

He lifted her off her feet and carried her bodily toward Hawthorne's home theater department. She punched and kicked, clawed and screamed, but her awkward blows landed without force and he outweighed her by a hundred pounds. Seconds later, he set her down before the ringleader and Ryan without releasing his hold on her.

"You were right," Jesse said to the tall man, "we had a spy."

"Soon your third eye will give you the ability to see beyond, too."

Before she could fully register the paired horns on their heads, the swollen lump in the center of their brows, or their rows of shark teeth, her gaze was drawn to the dark-haired woman bound with rope to a support column. The woman's wild eyes darted around frantically without focusing, tears streaked her cheeks and her lips looked raw, as if she'd gnawed on them until they bled. Sumiko feared the woman had gone insane. When she noticed the brass bowl on the floor and the glistening red, fist-sized lump it held, she began to understand why.

Oh, God, no!

"For the demon gate ritual, I needed a fresh human heart," the tall man said. "Now my son brings a beating heart to replace my silent offering. Excellent!"

Ryan turned to Sumiko. For a moment, he seemed confused, as if he didn't recognize her, then his gaze locked on her face.

"Ryan?" she said, her voice quavering with fear. "What's happening?"

"No!" Ryan shouted at the oni. "Let her go! She has nothing to do with this."

"The moment she walked in here, she forfeited her life," the oni told Ryan. "You are oni, of my blood. You will do as I command." With his cane hanging from his belt, the oni took rope from a duffel bag, tossed it on the seat of a molded plastic chair with metal legs and shoved the chair across the floor to Jesse. "Tie her to the chair until I require her heart."

Jesse picked up the rope and shoved her down into the chair. As he wrenched one of her arms behind her, she twisted free and flung herself from the chair on to her hands and knees. She tried to push off from that position, but stumbled, her heel sliding on the scuffed tile floor.

Jesse caught her arm and yanked hard. A bone snapped in her forearm, delivering a sharp burst of pain. She cried out as he hauled her back to the chair.

Ryan roared and launched himself at Jesse.

Sumiko saw Jesse pull a knife from the back of his belt.

"Ryan, no!"

Releasing Sumiko, Jesse shoved the point of the knife

into a strange lump that had formed in the middle of Ryan's forehead. The blade sank several inches into Ryan's skull. Sumiko screamed. Jesse twisted his forearm then tugged the knife free. Ryan gurgled and pitched forward, then fell sideways, curling into a fetal position.

The oni strode forward and caught Jesse by the throat, a murderous look in his eyes.

"How dare you!"

Sumiko scrambled to Ryan's side and lifted his head awkwardly with her good arm. Blood and white fluid trickled across his face. His eyes darted back and forth but gradually stopped tracking, seeming to lose focus. "Ryan!"

"Miko. So sorry," he gasped. "I've done… terrible things."

"It's okay, Ryan," she said, her voice breaking as she brushed locks of hair away from his face. Most of the cobalt blue had faded, replaced by natural red. "What happened to you… It's not your fault."

But he was gone, his eyes staring blankly past her.

Conscious of the oni gripping Jesse by the throat, she backed away on her knees from Ryan's body as quietly as possible, but her heel struck the chair leg, which squeaked against the floor. In a flash, the oni caught the elbow of her broken forearm and lifted her upright. White-hot pain flared within the already swollen arm.

"You had no right to kill a son of mine," he said to Jesse.

"He was weak," Jesse said, refusing to cower. "You saw it."

"Ryan was stronger than all of you," Sumiko said defiantly.

"If she speaks again," the oni said, "rip out her tongue. I need her heart. Nothing else."

Jesse pinned her to the chair.

The oni approached the bound woman. He sliced open his inner forearm with one of his dark fingernails, creating a cut several inches long. After a few moments of guttural chanting, he held the dripping wound up to the mouth of the woman.

"Drink of my blood," he commanded. "Then you will consume the girl's heart. By dawn, you will be oni."

The woman tilted her head forward.

The oni smiled, nodding encouragement.

She snarled and sank her teeth into his open wound, almost growling as she gnawed, tearing at his flesh with no intention of letting go. With his free hand, the oni shoved her head backward. The defensive reflex was sudden and entirely too forceful. The back of the woman's head smashed into the support column and her skull collapsed like the shell of a raw egg dropped on the floor. She died instantly.

That's what she wanted, Sumiko thought. *She had no hope left.*

The oni roared, enraged. He drove his fist into the woman's face, pulverizing her nose and eye sockets so the bloody mess was no longer recognizable as a human face.

"My plans," he lamented. "She ruined everything!"

"Use her heart," Jesse suggested. "It's still warm."

"Her heart?" Tora turned to Jesse, who still stood behind Sumiko, his large hands holding her down in the chair. "Her heart! Of course. I need a healthy, adult human female for the ritual. Any female."

His gaze dropped to Sumiko and he smiled, revealing his rows of razor-sharp teeth. "How fortunate for me you came here tonight."

Dazed and grief-stricken, Sumiko needed a few seconds to comprehend the meaning of his words.

"No, no, no," she said. "Not me. I refuse!"

"Your consent is unnecessary."

"But, I'm not healthy," she said desperately, her mouth suddenly dry. "My arm! It's broken!"

"The demon gate transformation will heal your arm," he said as he approached her, offering his bleeding forearm, "make you stronger. More than human. Better than human."

Sumiko screamed.

THIRTY-FOUR

Once Bobby had the number of the vice principal of Laurel Hill High School, the man looked up Sumiko's home contact information. Bobby, using his FBI cover, talked to the girl's mother, who hadn't seen her or heard from her since she borrowed the car. Calls to her cell phone went to voicemail or the connection dropped. After the third attempt, Sumiko's mother remembered a tracking app Sumiko had installed on their phones. She ran the app and located her daughter's phone. The green indicator dot was stationary but appeared sporadically, forcing her to refresh the display. She gave them the approximate location and Bobby promised to call when they had found Sumiko.

With Dean and Sam in the Monte Carlo and Bobby following solo in his Chevelle, they found the Odyssey empty, parked on the side of the road in a rundown commercial district. Sumiko's phone had fallen to the driver's floor mat.

"She followed them and parked here," Dean said. "That means the oni are within walking distance."

"If you were an oni who wanted to perform a ceremony," Bobby asked, "where would you hunker down?"

"Another abandoned building," Sam said. "No interruptions."

They returned to their cars and drove slowly in the direction the Odyssey had been headed. A couple of blocks away, Dean saw Hawthorne's department store and pulled into the parking lot.

Near the entrance, he saw a red Durango, inconclusive by itself, but a short distance later, as he followed a curve in the parking lot, Dean spotted another vehicle, hidden from street view, tucked back beside a fenced area for Dumpsters: the blue and white van.

"Bingo!"

Their plan was simple and direct. Dean's favorite kind; less chance of something going sideways. Assuming the holly still protected them from tripping up or tipping their hand, Sam would occupy the oni, attacking with armor-piercing bullets provided by Sergeant McClary. Dean would sneak in close with a crowbar to dislodge the cane-club from the oni's hand. At that point, Bobby would take the shot with his rifle. If he hit the bull's-eye—the oni's third eye—he'd gank the bastard. Ryan and Jesse were wild cards in the plan, but without the protection of an iron club, their third eyes were completely vulnerable.

As Dean stepped out of the car, a dark shape darted past

his legs and disappeared into the shadows.

"Did you see that?" he asked Sam across the roof of the Monte Carlo.

Sam shook his head.

Bobby approached from the Chevelle, carrying his Browning rifle with the light mounted but switched off. Lightning flashed, followed by an encroaching rumble of thunder as dark clouds rolled in, blotting out the stars.

They approached the Durango carefully. It was empty, but the hood was warm.

One of the doors into Hawthorne's had been jimmied and hung open several inches. Dean gripped the handle and eased it open in case the damaged hinges creaked. Again, he saw a shadow dart by his feet. It vanished into the gloomy store.

"See that?" he whispered.

Both Sam and Bobby shook their heads.

Dean was sure he hadn't imagined it. Whatever it was, it was quiet and much smaller than an oni or a human.

A raccoon, maybe, he thought. *Looking for a trashcan to tip over.*

Once inside the dark department store, they fanned out. Bobby planned to hang back for a clear shot.

They hadn't gone far when Dean heard a deep voice talking.

Then a woman screamed.

Lightning flashed again, through the skylights, and cast harsh shadows across the skeletal interior of the department store.

Dean abandoned stealth and rushed toward the voices. Sam angled in from Dean's right, handgun raised at eye level, braced with his left palm. A glance back revealed Bobby scrambling up the motionless escalator, seeking high ground from which to take his shot.

Details revealed themselves by candlelight.

The corpse of a woman was bound to a support column, her face a ruin. They had failed to save Kim Jacobs.

Once again, Dean thought bitterly, *we're too damn late.*

Sprawled on the floor, forehead bloody, was Ryan's body. Jesse stood behind Sumiko, pressing down on her shoulders to pin her to a chair. The oni loomed over her, cane in one hand as he held his other forearm, dripping blood, near her face.

With Kim dead, he's performing the demon gate ritual with Sumiko.

Dean looked toward Sam, but his brother had come to the same conclusion and fired two armor-piercing rounds at the oni. Raising his head, the oni peered into the darkness and, a moment later, the folds of flesh on his forehead parted, revealing the third eye. Bobby didn't fire. The oni still held his protective *kanabo*.

Dislodging the club was the only item on Dean's to-do list.

Racing forward, he twisted away from a clothing rack lined with hangers without making a sound, which gave him confidence the holly was working. Otherwise, he would have given away his position prematurely.

As if following a silent command, Jesse released Sumiko and charged into the darkness toward them. Hunched over, he held his forearm like a shield in front of his forehead. Nevertheless, Sam took a shot and jarred Jesse's elbow. The oni hybrid yelped in pain and veered away from Sam.

Dean slid low and swung the crowbar below Jesse's

knees. The force of the blow spun Dean around, but he held onto the crowbar and had the satisfaction of watching Jesse perform an involuntary forward flip. Unfortunately, Jesse recovered first. He scrambled up, lunged forward and pounced at Dean, clawed hands reaching for his throat. Dean had witnessed the oni claws in action at the theater— they were like a fistful of box cutters. Before the claws could clamp on his throat, Dean twisted the flat end of the crowbar up. As Jesse fell on top of Dean, the steel tip sunk into Jesse's mutated forehead, piercing the third eye and sinking into his brain. Jesse writhed in pain above him, claws twitching inches from Dean's face. Heaving upward, Dean shoved the body off him and yanked the crowbar free.

Sam was firing round after round.

"Dean!"

Dean pushed himself upright and looked toward the candlelight. The chair was empty. Lightning flashed, revealing the dark, hulking shape of the horned oni charging him.

Backing up, Sam continued to fire, pausing to replace an empty magazine, but the enraged oni shrugged off the impacts.

Dean tossed a clothing rack in the oni's path to slow him down, but he swatted it away with the cane. Empty hangers clattered across the floor. A small dark shape raced away from where the clothing rack had been. Out of the corner of his eye, Dean saw Bobby changing position on the escalator stairs, carefully sighting along the rifle barrel in the relative darkness without switching on the mounted light. Ducking under a backhanded sweep of the cane, Dean gripped the crowbar in both hands and waited for an opening to strike the Tora's wrist. Sam hit the oni with two more rounds as a distraction, but the oni caught Dean's shoulder in his right hand while holding the cane in his left, safely out of reach of the crowbar.

Mm-rroww.

Dean turned toward the unexpected sound as the oni's grip on his shoulder tightened painfully.

Near ground level, one glowing yellow eye peered out of the darkness.

Mm-roww.

Lightning flashed, revealing Roy's freaky cat, with his blind, milky-white eye.

"*Obake?*" the oni gasped in disbelief. "No. Not here."

Sam took another shot and hit the shaft of the cane. Instinctively, the oni yanked the cane closer to his body—and closer to Dean.

The gloom flowed back, but the oni continued to stare at the cat's one bright, reflective eye as if hypnotized. Dean swung the crowbar in a short arc. The steel smashed into the oni's hand above his thumb. With a second, quicker blow, closer to the fingers, Dean dislodged the cane from his grasp.

The oni staggered backward as a rifle shot rang out.

Bobby switched on the mounted light, revealing the oni's face.

A nasty gash had been ripped into the third eye. White liquid and blood trickled down either side of the oni's nose. He staggered.

"Impossible…"

Bobby fired again and the oni's head whipped backward, still framed in the harsh light.

Blood and brain matter pulsed out of the gaping hole. The oni dropped to his knees. His mouth sagged open as he reached forward, his trembling hand stretching toward the protective *kanabo*. Before his fingers could close around the handle, Bobby fired a third shot, widening the hole in the middle of the oni's forehead.

Tora swayed slowly from side to side before toppling over backward with a heavy thud. The hand that had reached for the cane twitched once. Then the body lay still.

Lightning lit up the sky, followed immediately by a crash of thunder. Rain fell in a sudden downpour, drumming on the skylights like the roar of a thousand distant voices.

Sumiko emerged from a dark corner where she had been hiding since Jesse left her unattended to attack them. Tears streaked her face.

"Sumiko," Sam said. "Are you okay?"

Dean noticed she was cradling her forearm.

"She's hurt."

"Broken arm," she said. "Not so bad."

Her tears continued to flow.

Roy's cat walked up to her and rubbed against her calves, purring.

Must've been in the back of the car all night, Dean surmised. *I left the windows open to air out the burnt car seat smell and the cat moved in.*

"He likes you," he said to Sumiko.

She dropped to one knee and stroked the cat's head with

her good hand.

"He saved us," she said. "I'll call him Lucky."

THIRTY-FIVE

The town of Laurel Hill would need weeks to repair the damage, longer to recover from the myriad wounds and process the grief at so many lost lives. Out of respect for the dead and in consideration of the grieving families, the mayor had decided to postpone the town's fiftieth anniversary parade indefinitely. Fortunately, after the oni's death, the various epidemics lost their virulence and those afflicted seemed to be recovering.

McClary told Bobby he would be riding a desk for weeks and it would probably take at least that long for him to complete all the paperwork. In return, Bobby filled him in on everything that had happened at Hawthorne's and left it to McClary to deal with the bodies and filter the information for his official report.

Sumiko adopted Lucky, who seemed happy enough to

swap the feral lifestyle for steady meals, a warm bed and human companionship. The Lion Truth blogger dealt with her grief over Ryan Bramble's death, in part, by removing all posts related to the oni's swath of destruction. She also decided that wherever she attended college and whatever major she chose, she would take plenty of electives on mythology and folklore. The information might come in handy some day.

Bobby decided to stay at the cabin for a few days, long enough for Roy's out-of-state family to make funeral arrangements for his old friend. Roy would be buried in a plot next to his wife and son.

Bobby walked out of the cabin with Sam and Dean to say goodbye before they headed to Maine to investigate a series of flayed human corpses.

"If we hadn't showed up on his doorstep," Dean said, "Roy would still be alive."

"Hunters don't retire, not knowing what we know," Bobby said. "Roy was… on an extended sabbatical. If not the oni, something else would've brought him back."

"He tried to get Dalton to see things from his grandmother's point of view," Dean said. "That set the kid off."

"He was too far gone," Sam said. "Maybe even doomed from the start."

"Not a day went by, Roy didn't think about the family he'd lost," Bobby said. "Family held power for him—the presence of it, and its loss. But family is what you make of it. When it works, you hold onto it, because you never know when your ride'll be over."

After their goodbyes, Sam and Dean climbed into the Monte Carlo, Dean behind the wheel and Sam kicking back in the passenger seat. As Dean backed out of the gravel driveway, Sam glanced over at him.

"How are you dealing with… everything?"

"The life?" Dean asked and shrugged. "Hundreds died, but stopping the oni, I figure we saved thousands. So, yeah, it's a grind and it never ends, but that has to count for something."

"I almost forgot," Sam said and removed something from his jacket pocket. Ripping off the cellophane wrapper, he hung a cardboard pine tree air freshener from the rearview mirror.

"It won't help," Dean said. "I'm ditching this car first chance we get."

Sam smiled, enjoying the moment.

Though Dean wearied of the unending series of battles and the futility of trying to achieve a lasting victory, Sam was determined to enjoy his life on the road for what it was. He wouldn't let the daily struggle to maintain a vise-like grip on his sanity define him. A short life wasn't the only possible bad outcome to the hunter life. Some things were worse than death.

Dean switched on the car's radio. As if echoing Sam's thoughts, the classic rock station was playing "Don't Fear the Reaper."

ACKNOWLEDGMENTS

In the UK, thanks to my editor, Jo Boylett, and Cath Trechman at Titan Books for bringing me back to write another *Supernatural* novel. Thanks to my US editor, Christopher Cerasi, at Warner Bros. Entertainment Inc. for the vote of confidence and for wrangling this project between continents. Thanks to Nicholas Knight for summarizing the *Supernatural* monster list during a time crunch. And thanks to Rebecca Dessertine for her early feedback and support. The guidance all of you provided is much appreciated.

Thanks to Greg Schauer, owner of Between Books in Claymont, Delaware, for years of support and encouragement. Thanks to everyone who entered the "use my name for a character" contest. Your enthusiasm for *Supernatural* is inspiring. Special thanks to my Twitter followers who helped me focus and re-focus during (seemingly) endless nights of writing. And continued thanks to the Logan Township New Jersey police department.

Finally, I wouldn't have the pleasure of writing *Supernatural* novels if not for show creator Eric Kripke and the entire cast and crew for bringing his vision to life.

ABOUT THE AUTHOR

John Passarella won the Horror Writers Association's prestigious Bram Stoker Award for Superior Achievement in a First Novel for the co authored *Wither*. Columbia Pictures purchased the feature film rights to *Wither* in a prepublication, pre-emptive bid.

John's other novels include *Wither's Rain, Wither's Legacy, Kindred Spirit, Shimmer* and the original media tie-in novels *Supernatural: Night Terror, Buffy the Vampire Slayer: Ghoul Trouble, Angel: Avatar, Angel: Monolith* and *Grimm: The Chopping Block*. In January 2012, he released his first fiction collection, *Exit Strategy & Others*.

A member of the Authors Guild, Horror Writers Association, Science Fiction and Fantasy Writers of America, International Thriller Writers, International Association of Media Tie-In Writers, and the Garden State Horror Writers,

John resides in southern New Jersey with his wife, three children, a dog and a cat. He is also a web designer and webmaster for a few *New York Times* bestselling authors.

John maintains his official author website at www. passarella.com, where he encourages readers to email him at author@passarella.com, and to subscribe to his free author newsletter for the latest information on his books and stories.

ALSO AVAILABLE FROM TITAN BOOKS

SUPERNATURAL
FRESH MEAT
BY ALICE HENDERSON

A rash of strange deaths in the Tahoe National Forest
bring Sam, Dean and Bobby to the Sierra Nevada
mountains to hunt a monster with a taste for human
flesh. Walking corpses, bodies with missing organs, and
attacks by a mysterious flying creature lead the trio to
a cunning and deadly foe which can assume a human
form and will do anything to survive. When a blizzard
strikes the area, separated and not knowing who they can
trust, they must battle not only the monster but also the
elements to survive.

A *Supernatural* novel that reveals a previously unseen
adventure for the Winchester brothers,
from The CW's hit series!

TITANBOOKS.COM

ALSO AVAILABLE FROM TITAN BOOKS

SUPERNATURAL
HEART OF THE DRAGON
BY KEITH R.A. DECANDIDO

When renegade angel Castiel alerts Sam and Dean to a series
of particularly brutal killings in San Francisco's Chinatown,
they realize the Heart of the Dragon is back. Can they
succeed where their parents and grandparents failed?

SUPERNATURAL
THE UNHOLY CAUSE
BY JOE SCHREIBER

1862: Confederate forces charge across a Georgia battle-
ground. Fast-forward to 2009 and Sam and Dean head
down south to investigate a civil war re-enactment that has
become terrifyingly real.

SUPERNATURAL
WAR OF THE SONS
BY REBECCA DESSERTINE & DAVID REED

On the hunt for Lucifer, the boys find themselves in a
small town in South Dakota where they meet Don, an
angel with a proposition, who sends them a very long way
from home.

TITANBOOKS.COM

For more fantastic fiction, author events, exclusive excerpts,
competitions, limited editions and more

VISIT OUR WEBSITE
titanbooks.com

LIKE US ON FACEBOOK
facebook.com/titanbooks

FOLLOW US ON TWITTER
@TitanBooks

EMAIL US
readerfeedback@titanemail.com